THE TEXAS BILLIONAIRE'S BRIDE

Zane had just opened his mouth to ask if Melanie was set to leave when the women parted to reveal the nanny in the midst of them.

The words lodged in his chest, then began pumping like a conflicting heartbeat.

Her blonde hair was swept back into a graceful chignon, which complemented the slim lines of a short jacket and long cigarette skirt worthy of Jackie O. Her makeup was elegant, bringing out the breathtaking blue of her eyes and the lovely heart shape of her face.

She fitted the role of a princess and, for a taboo instant, he envisioned her on his arm at a charity event, shining like the brightest of stars.

Seconds must've passed. Maybe even minutes. And during each escalating heartbeat, he kept himself from saying something he would regret to this new woman, even if, under the makeup and clothing, she was still the same lady who'd hooked his attention that first day.

THE TEXAS
BODYGUARD'S PROPOSAL

Impulsively, she held the apple out to Rafe and asked, "Would you like a bite?"

She expected some joke about Adam and Eve, or a retreat on his part. That's what he usually did if she didn't do it first.

But instead of retreating, he leaned forwards, clasped his hand under hers, and took a bite of the apple. The world stopped and then seemed to move in slow motion as Rafe chewed his bite of the apple, his gaze on hers the whole time. Her stomach somersaulted, and any coherent thought she possessed vanished. A breeze blew between them, awakening everything about the moment.

He reached for the apple, took it, then set it aside on the balcony ledge. "What do you want, Gabby?" he asked as if he really wanted to know.

Boldly she replied, "I want you to kiss me again."

First published in Great Britain 2010
Harlequin Mills & Boon Limited,
Eton House, 18-24 Paradise Road, Richmond, Surrey TW9 1SR

The Texas Billionaire's Bride © Harlequin Books S.A. 2009
The Texas Bodyguard's Proposal © Harlequin Books S.A. 2009

Special thanks and acknowledgment are given to Crystal Green and Karen
Rose Smith for their contributions to The Foleys and the McCords
mini-series.

ISBN: 978 0 263 87994 0

23-0910

Harlequin Mills & Boon policy is to use papers that are natural, renewable
and recyclable products and made from wood grown in sustainable forests.
The logging and manufacturing processes conform to the legal environmental
regulations of the country of origin.

Printed and bound in Spain
by Litografia Rosés S.A., Barcelona

THE TEXAS BILLIONAIRE'S BRIDE

BY
CRYSTAL GREEN

THE TEXAS BODYGUARD'S PROPOSAL

BY
KAREN ROSE SMITH

MILLS & BOON

THE TEXAS BILLIONAIRE'S BRIDE

BY
CRYSTAL GREEN

Crystal Green lives near Las Vegas, Nevada, where she writes for Mills & Boon® Special Edition and Blaze®. She loves to read, overanalyse movies, do yoga and write about her travels and obsessions on her website, www. crystal-green.com. There you can read about her trips on Route 66, as well as visits to Japan and Italy. She loves to hear from her readers by e-mail through the "Contact Crystal" feature.

To Gail Chasan,
who reigns over these stories that have provided all of
us with so much life, love and happiness.
Thank you, Gail!

Chapter One

The toughest tycoon in Texas.

That's how Melanie Grandy's prospective employer had been described, to one extent or another, in nearly every article she'd read on the Internet before her quick trip down here.

Thing was, those articles had also painted Zane Foley as a slightly mysterious man who didn't talk about his personal life to the press, even if he led such a public existence otherwise.

But if anyone understood secrets, it was Melanie.

Sitting at one end of a long mahogany table, she watched the head of Foley Industries saunter over the hardwood living room floor of his luxurious Dallas townhouse while he flipped through her personal portfolio, which showed her creative side.

Lordy, it was hard to keep her eyes off of him, although she knew she should.

Yet…

Well, she couldn't help but notice the details. His dark hair was obviously cut at a pricey salon, but in spite of its neatness, some of the ends flipped up ever so slightly near his nape. It made her suspect that he hadn't caught the deviation, and as soon as he did, those ends would be right back in place.

He was also very tall, with broad shoulders stretching a fine white shirt he probably had made to order. His chest was wide, his torso tapering down to a honed waist, his legs long. She didn't know much about his hobbies, but she could imagine him getting fit while horseback riding, could see him sitting tall in a saddle, just as easily as he no doubt commanded a boardroom.

During his scan of her portfolio—he'd seen it during their initial interview two days ago, so was he only perusing it to make her squirm?—Melanie took the opportunity to read between the lines of his silence.

And, boy, did he ever enjoy his silence.

He'd stopped at the other end of the room in front of a stained-glass window, the subdued early May colors bathing him as he glanced over at her. Dark leather furniture surrounded him with a Gothic stillness, each piece angled just so.

Caught checking him out, Melanie's stomach flip-flopped, but she nonetheless sat straight in her chair, under the intense scan of his hazel eyes.

Probably, it was a bad idea to let her could-be boss know that she'd been assessing him, yet she didn't want him to think she was the type to look away or back down. She was here to get this job, taking care of his six-year-old daughter, Olivia, whom she'd met briefly during the previous interview.

And Melanie was going to win him over, just as his daughter had thoroughly won her at first sight.

Calming her fluttering nerves, she watched as he coolly refocused on her file, as if he'd only glanced her way to take her measure when she'd least expected it.

But was there some satisfaction in his expression?

Had she passed the pop quiz?

"Oklahoma," he said, apropos of nothing. But he'd done it in a low, rich voice that smoothed over her skin just as if he'd bent real close and whispered in her ear.

Melanie made sure her own tone didn't betray that she'd been affected. "I was born and raised just on the outskirts of Tulsa."

They'd covered these basics during their first meeting, and she knew he'd combed through the dossier she'd presented to him, as well. Over these past couple of days, he'd no doubt checked her references, which she knew would speak for themselves. After all, she'd been recommended to him by a business associate he trusted, and that was most likely the only reason she'd gotten her discount-rack shoes in the front door.

Why did she have the feeling that he was going over her information again, just to see if she'd trip up?

Or maybe she was being paranoid. That tended to happen to folks who might have something to hide....

He wasn't saying anything, so she continued talking, supplying more personal details than she had the other day. "It was just me and my mom at first. She put me through day care by keeping the books at a small business, and the minute I was old enough, I dealt with the household after school hours."

Melanie didn't add that those books her mom had kept were located in the back room of the greasy spoon where Leigh Grandy primarily waited on tables between double shifts and numerous dates with the "nice men" she brought home for "sleepovers." In fact, Melanie wasn't even sure which date was her father in the first place; she just knew that he hadn't stuck around.

Now Zane Foley moved toward the long table where Melanie sat, nearing the other end, which seemed a mile away. It lent enough distance for her to risk another lingering glance at him while he closed her portfolio, placed it on the table, then picked up her dossier.

Darn, he's handsome, she thought before forcing herself to get back into interview mode. But the notion wouldn't go away, brushing through her belly and warming her in areas that should have come with "off-limits" signs.

She would be the nanny, he would be the boss. End of story, if she should be so lucky as to be hired.

"Your information," he said, his gaze still on the papers, "indicates that you started a child-care career early. I'd like to know a little more about your brothers and sisters and how they led to your choice of profession."

"Actually, they were my stepbrothers and stepsisters."

"I stand corrected."

She smiled, avoiding any hardball, but still not standing down.

He didn't smile at all, yet she was getting used to that.

"My mom married the man she called her 'true love'

when I was fifteen." It was wonder enough that her mother had finally settled down, but it was even more amazing that her marriage was still intact today. "He had four children. Two of them were much younger than I was—little girls—so I watched over them, in addition to other work. The older two were twin boys, but they weren't around much, because they liked their sports."

Zane Foley cocked a dark eyebrow as he leveled a look at her. "'Were' younger? 'Were' twin boys?"

Melanie tightened her fingers where they were clasped on the table.

He sat in the leather armchair at the other end, perfectly comfortable with being the inquisitor.

Please let me get through this, she thought. She'd spent nearly every last penny in her bank account to get here, traveling to Dallas for these interviews, in the hope that her lucky stars would shine and she'd secure this new job, this new direction.

"You keep using the past tense when you talk about your stepsiblings, Ms. Grandy," Zane Foley said.

"My mistake." She was determined to keep smiling. "We all still keep tabs on each other, even though we're adults." If you counted the odd e-mail as healthy familial relations.

But since she'd left her brood back in Oklahoma, they *were* the past to Melanie. She was the same to them, too, except for her mom, who called quite often for loans.

When her mother remarried, Melanie had ended up in the valley of a no-man's land. Her stepfather had preferred his own kids to her, making no secret about his feelings, either. To him, she was his wife's "bastard issue," and instead of taking out his frustrations about that on Leigh, he'd put it all on Melanie.

Of course, Melanie had approached her mom about this, actually thinking that it would help if Leigh were to address it. Silly her. Her mother had only accused Melanie of trying to sabotage the happiness she'd finally found.

It'd been a stunning moment of betrayal—an instant in which Melanie had realized that her mother would always prefer her guys to her daughter, who'd worked so, so hard to matter more than any of those "nice men."

"When I was a teen," she added, directing the interview back to the more positive aspects of her life, "I took courses at the YMCA for babysitting, and you could say I managed a cottage industry early on. I was booked every weekend, and even during the week, if I could handle it with my studies."

"Evidently, you could, because you aced your classes in school. You graduated with honors, in fact."

"I knew I'd never get anywhere without a good education."

She'd supplied her school records for him, and she was sure someone on his staff had already double-checked those, as well as her employment history.

She only hoped that the one job she'd left off her résumé wouldn't come back to dog her—a gig that had gotten her through college. A paycheck-earner that she preferred to leave behind with the rest of her past.

Her time as a showgirl in what she now considered to be a seedy off-Strip casino in Vegas.

She blew out a breath, continuing, praying she wouldn't give herself away. "Besides babysitting, I took up waiting tables at a burger joint after classes. But I was known as the go-to babysitter of the neighborhood, and that got me more and more jobs. So I gravitated toward that, since I think I was good at it." She laughed a little. "Besides, I could charge more than I made in a restaurant that catered to teens, where the tips were…lacking."

"Industrious," he said, but she couldn't tell if it was just a random comment, or if he was truly impressed.

After all, the Foleys were known far and wide for rolling up their shirtsleeves and working for their fortune. They were self-made men, and Melanie was hoping he would want that in the nanny who was raising his child, too.

"I saved every dollar," she added, "splurging only on my dancing lessons. Lots of them. I couldn't go without."

"We all need an outlet," he said, but he sounded distracted as he looked at the dossier again.

At his next question, she knew they'd entered the most dangerous part of the interview.

"Why did you head toward Vegas right after graduating high school?"

Nerves prickled her skin. "I'd heard the economy was booming at the time, and the opportunity seemed ripe for the taking. The waitress job I got in a local café paid far more in tips than I'd ever made before."

He didn't answer, as if expecting more.

She smiled again, giving as good as she was getting. "Didn't *you* also gravitate there for the same general reason, Mr. Foley? You've developed several projects in the area."

Maybe it was her chutzpah, but a slight grin tilted his mouth.

That was his only answer, and it disappeared before Melanie could be sure she'd even seen it. Then he was right back in boss-man mode, scribbling some notes on the cover of her dossier.

Was he thinking that she was naïve for dropping everything and heading to Vegas, just as thousands of dreamers without his kind of money had done before her? Get rich quick. Double your income with the right gambles.

And gamble she had, just not with money.

She'd been "discovered" one night when she went out dancing with some fellow students from community college. A talent coordinator from The Grand Illusion casino had given her his business card, inviting her to an audition.

At first, she'd denied him, thinking that her waitress job would hold her. Then her mom had started to write her, asking for loans, and in spite of how Melanie had wanted to escape Oklahoma, she couldn't say no to helping out the family.

And that's when she'd decided to audition. The Grand Illusion had a small, fairly cheesy revue that was half bawdy magic and half sexy musical, although nothing distasteful. Heck, no one even took off their sequined tops. She told herself she probably wouldn't make it anyway. Yet, much to her surprise, she'd breezed through the process, with them offering her a modest wage and, more importantly, the promise of open days during which she could keep going to school and wait a few tables.

It was an ideal setup, and it wasn't as if she was doing any exotic dancing. Just as soon as she had her degree, she'd be done with it anyway.

When she had the degree under her belt, she quit dancing, just as she'd promised herself, and she'd signed on for her first nanny job, thanks to a glowing recommendation from her advisor to his personal friend.

Her employer had been an affluent single mom, a prominent business developer who was in dire need of a helper; and it'd been the perfect job for years, until Melanie's boss got married and decided to become a stay-at-home mother.

And that's how Melanie had come to Dallas at the age of twenty-eight—because her first employer had worked with Zane Foley on the development of a Vegas mega apartment-village complex, and when the businesswoman heard that his latest nanny had quit and he needed to hire another one pronto, she'd given him Melanie's name.

He nudged the dossier away from him and, for a heavy moment, Melanie wondered if Zane Foley, a man who seemed to cover every base, had dug deep enough into her life to expose her crowded double-wide-trailer beginnings and dancing days.

Was he going to spring it on her now?

"As you've heard from Andrea Sandoval," he finally said, referring to Melanie's first nanny employer, "I'm eager to get someone in place to care for my daughter. And you almost seem too good to be true, Ms. Grandy, dropping into my lap like this."

She felt heat creeping over her face, mainly because she could just imagine what it might be like to drop into his lap—*Lord have mercy*—yet also because she didn't want to panic at what he might've uncovered.

"No one's perfect, Mr. Foley," she said, hoping he would agree.

He didn't, so she kept talking, seeing if she could maybe use a little flattery as backup.

"Although," she said, "your family seems to come close enough to perfect as it gets."

He remained distant, over on his side of the table. "We're hardly perfect."

"Then you should tell your PR people to stop selling that image," she said lightly. "The media seems to think that the Foleys are the epitome of what's good about our country."

His tone grew taut. "You've been looking into my family, have you?"

How could she deny it? News about the business doings of the Foleys, whose holdings had started from a few oil rigs to an empire based on prime real estate and media interests, was legion. Then there were all their charitable causes, behind-the-scenes political power plays and even the social adventures of Zane's brother, Jason. Hard to ignore, when the media—and the nation—was fascinated with them, even if Zane, himself, tended to avoid the limelight.

"I only did my research," she said, "because I need to make sure you're the right family for me, just as you're making sure I'm right for you."

Her smile returned full force, but not because she was trying to win him over this time. She was remembering the freckled nose and doe eyes of his daughter. There'd only been a short introduction, yet it'd been enough to convince Melanie that she didn't belong anywhere else in this world. Something about Olivia had profoundly tugged at Melanie, maybe because the girl reminded her of herself—a little lost and isolated.

Zane Foley didn't return her smile. In fact, he seemed intent on avoiding it, while the sun from outside shifted enough to slant a patch of red from the stained glass over the strong angles of his face.

Her chest went tight.

"I like your optimism," he said. "You'd need quite a bit of it with Livie, you know. As I pointed out during our first interview, she's gone through five nannies in six years."

"I remember." Her former employer had already cautioned Melanie. After Olivia's mom had passed away, the girl had rejected everyone she perceived to be taking her mom's place.

Melanie had known from the start that this wouldn't be an easy job; but she wanted to make a difference in the girl's life, because she sure wished someone had made a difference earlier in her own.

"My daughter's a handful," he said. "I'll make no bones about that."

"I've got more perseverance than you can imagine."

"Your predecessors thought they had it, too. And on their way out the door, most of them even told me that I ought to think about applying some of that perseverance I show in my own business to my household." He leaned forward in his chair. "Just to give you fair warning, I don't employ nannies to get advice from them."

Melanie kept eye contact, thinking that there was a chink in the steeliness of his gaze—a darkness that showed more than just that notorious arrogance.

"Mr. Foley," she said softly, "I'd never presume to judge *anyone*."

He stared at her a beat longer, then sat back in his chair

again, even though he didn't let up with his gaze. It held her, screwed into her, until a slight thrill traveled her veins.

"The family businesses are important to me," he said. "Among other things, they're Livie's legacy, and I intend to give her a great one. As an only child, she'll take over all of my share one day, the oil holdings, as well as real-estate interests."

He said it as if he planned to never get married or have children again. In some weird way, that got to Melanie.

But...jeez. Like she should even be mulling over his most intimate decisions.

"I'm sure your daughter will be grateful for everything you do," she said.

"You should also know that I spend a lot of time defending our investments, not just building them up. That's what takes up the majority of my schedule, and the work's too important for me to spend as much time in Austin with Livie as most people expect."

"Right," she said, figuring she would show him just how much research she'd done. "I read that you have to defend against people like the McCords."

His mouth tightened once more, this time at the name of the family who'd been taking part in a well-known feud with the Foleys for generations.

Oops. She made a mental note never to mention them again.

Zane Foley seemed eager to be rid of the subject. "The bottom line is this—my commitments require a lot of me, and that's why I need someone to depend on for Livie. Someone who's more or less my proxy, enforcing my rules and raising her the way I need her to be raised."

She chafed at his authoritarian tone. What was his

daughter to him—another project to develop, like the ones he oversaw in his office?

But Olivia—Livie—was a little girl, and—from what Melanie had seen in her eyes, even for the few minutes they'd conversed—she needed more than rules and routines.

Melanie was on the cusp of saying so when she remembered how much she wanted this job.

"I understand, Mr. Foley," she said instead, keeping the peace, even if she didn't really understand him at all.

He gave her one last look from those striking hazel eyes, and she fortified herself against it—almost successfully, too. He only got her tummy to flip one more time.

Then he rose from his chair, leaving her dossier and portfolio on the table.

Melanie held her breath. Was the interview over?

But he only walked away from the table, toward the hushed hallway.

When he saw that she wasn't following, he waited, and she realized that he wanted her to come, too.

Okay then.

As she stood, she grabbed her suit jacket from the back of her chair, then smoothed down the skirt of the only conservative business outfit she owned.

She made her way across the room to him, her heels clopping on the hard floor, echoing way too loudly for her comfort.

He avoided the door and led her down the hall.

Where was he taking her?

"Livie will receive a full education," he said, beginning to fire off his expectations, "even when she's not in school."

"I'm prepared to teach Livie," she said, excitement churning. He was going to make an offer! "With Ms. Sandoval's daughter, Toni, I planned a different learning experience every day, and doing the same here would be wonderful."

"Livie would benefit from your dance background in particular."

Melanie's blood jolted, but then she realized he was probably talking about all the classes, from ballet to jazz to hip-hop, she'd taken. "Livie has taken dance before?"

"No, but she needs to let out her energy in a constructive manner."

"I see."

"Other than that, her schedule is set. Firm. Don't deviate from it, because she responds well to structure. It might be your biggest saving grace."

Based on Zane Foley's well-ordered townhouse, as well as all his comments, Melanie wondered if, when she arrived in Austin, she would find Livie inhabiting something like a high-class jail.

Fuming inwardly, she told herself to stay quiet. *You want this job, you need this job, so keep your opinions to yourself for now.*

They came to what looked to be a study, with more dark, finely etched antique furniture carefully placed about the room: a desk set that held a laptop computer and organized files, a curio cabinet, shelves teeming with leather-bound books that lent the air a thick, musty scent.

There were also large, framed paintings on the walls, the biggest being an old family portrait of the Foleys that featured brothers Jason and Travis, both of whom couldn't have been more than ten years old at the time, even though Travis looked a little younger. They stood next to their dad, Rex, an affable looking man with a charming grin. Then there was Olivia Marie, their deceased mom, who wore her own gentle smile as she hooked her arm through Rex's.

On the fringes of them all was Zane, who even in his early teens seemed to carry himself with a combination of cockiness and seriousness.

When Melanie glanced away from the portrait, she found that Zane was behind her, standing in front of a different painting. Livie's.

A recent depiction of a sweet little girl in a pink dress, her wavy dark hair held back by a lacy headband. She smiled faintly and held a stuffed lamb.

The picture got to Melanie, yet it was the expression on Zane's face that just about melted her altogether.

Naked love and devotion.

But then it turned into something else—destruction—and Melanie wondered what could have possibly turned one emotion into the other so quickly.

As Zane stared at his daughter's portrait, he wasn't seeing Livie so much as someone else entirely. Danielle.

His wife, dead six years now, but still so agonizingly alive in the face of his daughter.

He couldn't stand the questions that always came afterward: would Livie grow up to be just like her mother? Would his daughter break her own husband's heart someday, too?

Would she have the same mood swings—from dark to manic—that had escalated into that awful day when Danielle had taken her own life?

He glanced away, his attention locking on the svelte figure of Melanie Grandy. With sunny blond hair that swept her shoulders and blue eyes that seemed to sparkle even when she wasn't smiling, she was the opposite of Danielle and Livie. But from her heart-shaped face to her ill-fitting blue business suit that he supposed she'd purchased just for these interviews—she'd worn the skirt the other day, too—he got the impression of vulnerability. A leggy wisp of a woman, she might not be so different from Danielle after all.

At his inspection, she raised her chin, a habit he'd become familiar with even during their short acquaintance.

No, this woman had a core to her. She also had an innate dignity that sent a buzz of heat through his veins.

Raw beauty, he thought, flashes of an unpolished diamond lighting his mind's eye.

But the glare of it made him realize that there was no room for any kind of attraction, especially since she seemed to be a perfect fit for Livie. And thank God for Andrea Sandoval's timely reference, because the last nanny had quit, leaving Zane at loose ends. He'd needed a quick hire, and since Ms. Grandy didn't have a criminal record and had come with the highest recommendation from a family friend, he seized the opportunity.

It was just a bonus that his daughter would match well with her new nanny. Livie required someone with spine enough to stand tall and firm, as Ms. Grandy had gracefully done throughout their interviews.

He chanced one last, long second of looking at her, turning the air into a humid fog.

And she seemed to feel it, too. He could've sworn it, because she set her jacket on a nearby end table and folded her hands in front of her while concentrating on the picture, a pink tint to her cheeks.

He got back to business, as well.

Always business. Safer that way.

He moved toward his computer, then woke it out of hibernation mode. He'd brought Ms. Grandy into his study to show her the virtual layout of the Austin estate where Livie resided, but even so, he held off on opening the computer file.

She was still back at Livie's portrait.

"She's a beautiful child," Ms. Grandy said, and he could sense that she was being genuine in the compliment. "I can't wait to start our first day, maybe with some art, where she can express ideas that she might be too shy to say out loud right away."

"The last time a nanny got the paint out she was scrubbing it off Livie for what seemed like hours. It was even supposed to be washable."

He could see a battle playing over Melanie Grandy's face, and it wasn't the first time. She was clearly wondering if she should put in her own two cents about her child-rearing philosophies, instead of listening to his own cynical point of view.

The other nannies had always kept quiet, but when Ms. Grandy spoke, he was pleasantly surprised that she even dared, although it raised his hackles, as well.

"I'm not afraid of some extra cleanup," she said, "if it's the result of something positive for Livie. Maybe she's the type who would benefit from stepping out of that structure she's so used to?"

Now he wasn't even pleasantly surprised with her.

She obviously noticed. "Mr. Foley, I'm not suggesting anything radical. I'm only interested in getting to know Livie."

He didn't tell Ms. Grandy that, aside from that one out-of-control paint day, his daughter generally liked to keep her dresses and hands clean—and it wasn't just at his insistence.

Or was it?

Guilt set in, just as it always did when he thought too hard about how he'd raised—or not raised—his girl. That's why it was better that he'd adopted such a hands-off policy; he was far more adequate at shaping Foley Industries and concentrating on other important matters, like keeping those damned McCords in line.

Plus, he didn't know anything about females at all. That was apparent from what he'd let happen to Danielle.

Melanie was still smiling as she looked at his daughter's portrait, and his heart cracked at how a stranger could so openly display emotion for Livie, when he had such a hard time himself.

He opened the computer file that contained the slides of Tall Oaks.

"Ms. Grandy," he said.

She glanced at him, and he could see the hope in her eyes.

He didn't let that affect him. He and hope had parted company a while ago.

"When can you start?" he asked.

She beamed with one of those warm smiles. "When do you want me, Mr. Foley?"

He couldn't help thinking that, despite the temptation, on a personal level the answer to that would have to be "never."

Chapter Two

After accepting the job and then rushing through a whirlwind of formalities, such as a salary agreement and a computer-aided tour of Zane Foley's Austin estate, Melanie had followed her new employer down the hall and to the foyer, barely able to contain a bubbly grin.

Success!

Melanie Grandy, nanny for the eldest Foley's daughter. She liked the ring of it, and when she found out that she was to be driven in a town car to her motel, where she would pick up her two pitiful suitcases before heading straight to Austin and Livie, she already felt as if she were flying first class.

Okay, maybe *business* class, because it wasn't a limo, but, heck, she'd live.

As they came to a halt near a leather settee under a

gilt-veined mirror, she tried not to be too aware of how their image reflected him towering over her. Tried not to get fanciful about how they stood side-by-side, a tense space the only thing separating them.

She fairly hummed from head to toe, as if charged by his presence, but... No. She'd worked hard to get here, and jeopardizing her new position by stepping out of bounds with her new boss had to be the worst idea in all creation.

She tried not to look in the mirror again: his strapping body, his Texas-noble bearing...

"The drive to Tall Oaks is nearly three and a half hours," he said, thankfully interrupting her weakening will to stop lusting after him. "It should give my staff enough time to put together the final paperwork for your hiring and then fax whatever we need to sign."

"I'll look for those papers when I get there then."

"Mrs. Howe might even have the documents in hand when you arrive. She's got run of the house and has been taking care of Livie since the last nanny left less than a week ago."

"I look forward to meeting everyone at Tall Oaks," she said, extending her hand for a deal-closing shake. "Again, thank you. I was really hoping you'd choose me to be a part of Livie's life."

And there it was again—that flash of anguish in his gaze.

But then he took her hand in his, wrapping his long fingers around hers.

Warm, strong...

For a moment she forgot that she was supposed to be shaking his hand. He must've forgotten also, because the hesitation between them lasted a second too long—one in which her heartbeat fell into a suspended throb.

As she pulled in a breath, his eyes darkened back to the cool, detached gaze that had already become so familiar.

But how could she be used to anything about him when she didn't know him at all? she reminded herself, coming to her senses and finally gripping his hand in a professional shake.

She doubted she would ever really know Zane Foley, and that was for the best.

They disengaged, and he stepped away from her. "I anticipate that you'll be around much longer than the other five."

As he began to walk away, she said, "I sure will."

He paused for a moment, and she thought that maybe he was about to say something else.

But then he moved on, traveling with the ease of a shadow lengthening at sunset, until he blended into the dark of the hallway.

Melanie watched him go, her heartbeat near the surface of her skin.

But she had to get over it; this was her chance to prove that she really was better than the girl who hadn't been expected by her stepdad to do much more than be "bastard issue."

She exhaled, sitting on the leather settee by the door and preparing for the responsibilities ahead of her. Livie—the child who would depend on Melanie to raise her to be all she could be, too.

A stately grandfather clock stood across from her, ticking, tocking, marking the passing seconds as

Melanie waited for the driver. Meanwhile, her excitement leveled off to something like a Champagne buzz.

She wondered what the Austin estate would look like in real life, how different it would be from her and her mom's first ramshackle apartment, then the trailer that had served as home back in the day.

On a sigh, she went to grab her suit jacket and purse, preparing for the moment she would walk out this door and into the car, where she would be driven off and away to find out.

Her purse was there, but not her jacket.

She remembered that she'd brought it into Zane Foley's study, putting it down when she'd been looking at the portrait of Livie.

Duh. She'd been too excited by the job offer to pick it back up again.

Okeydokey then. Her new boss had gone in the direction of the study, so she would just scoot back there, knock on the door, grab her jacket, then be out of his hair.

In and out.

But when she went down the hall, her body started doing the jitterbug about seeing him, heart racing, stomping.

Cool it, she told herself. In and out.

She came to the study, noticing that the door was ajar just enough for her to hear his voice. And, Heaven help her, she couldn't resist standing there a second to bask in the appreciation of how he sounded while talking to someone on the phone.

But the more she listened, the more she felt the bass of his voice scratching down her skin, leaving her hair to rise and the heat to play all over her. She thought of what it might be like to see him smile, just once.

Would it feel like a rolling ball of sun inside her stomach? A burning ache that sizzled and made her go weaker than she was even now?

Then he stopped talking, and the person on the other end of the speakerphone started.

The different voice—still appealing, but not nearly as much as Zane Foley's—was enough to kick her right out of fantasyland.

She rolled her eyes at herself, then prepared to knock just before her boss responded to the other person on the phone.

"I hired another nanny today."

Melanie's fist paused in midair.

So help her, she stood rooted there, waiting for what he might say, curiosity killing the cat.

The voice on the other end of the line laughed. "How long's *this* one going to last, Zane?"

He cut him off. "Not amusing, Jason."

Zane's brother, and, according to everything she'd read, the scamp of the three siblings. But he also had the more solid reputation of being the hardworking chief operating officer of Foley Industries—a man who wasn't above getting dirt underneath his fingernails or on his fine suits.

Zane was still talking. "And this time, don't you dare suggest that we bet on her longevity."

"Damn," Jason said, "because if I bet she wouldn't even last a year, just like most of the others, it'd be a smarter proposition than anything Granddad ever put his money on." There was a pause. "So what's this one like? Can you tell me that much?"

In spite of her better judgment, an all-too-human Melanie leaned closer to the door.

Zane was standing by a window with a showcase view of downtown Dallas, across from the gleaming Trinity River. He wasn't sure how to answer his younger brother's question about what he thought of Melanie Grandy.

Should he be honest?

There was something about the new nanny that made him want to tell Jason about her bright hair and brighter smile, even though he knew he wouldn't.

With any luck, he would never see her much, anyway. Staying away from Tall Oaks was best for Livie *and* him.

"This nanny," he finally answered, "enjoys using art to bring out the creativity in children. She likes dance especially, and I think that'll be good for Livie. Ms. Grandy's got a lot of…spirit."

Jason, as perceptive as he was, called Zane out.

"That's not what I meant, and you know it."

"That's all you're gonna get." Zane turned away from the window and headed toward his desk. It was second in size and comfort only to the one in his downtown Dallas office, where he would be right now if it hadn't been for the interview. "Now, I suspect you didn't call to gab about nannies, Jace. What's on your mind?"

"The McCords."

Zane could almost picture his brother behind his own desk in Houston, as his voice lowered to a more serious tenor. They'd all spent too many years sharing an intense dislike of the other family for Zane not to recognize the signs of a very serious discussion about them coming on.

"Travis gave me a heads up about something I thought you'd want to hear, too," Jason said. "It's about his ranch."

God, the ranch. The property had sparked a feud between the families way back when Grandpa Gavin had put the West Texas land up for grabs during a poker game that a card cheat named Harry McCord had been manipulating. To add insult to injury, the place had produced silver—the foundation for the McCord jewelry store empire, which catered to the rich and famous and was renowned worldwide as the height of luxury—the premier jewelers of the earth.

"What about the ranch?" Zane asked, an edge to his question. "We signed a long-term lease for the land after the mines were played out. The McCords have no reason to be sniffing around it just yet."

Of course, the McCord matriarch, Eleanor, had once been courted by Zane's father, Rex, so that might've had something to do with the olive branch the other family had offered. And one would think that her generosity would've defused the feud, but her husband, Devon, a devil who was surely getting his just desserts now, after his recent death, had still kept the animosity alive with all his talk about how he'd "won" Eleanor and Rex had lost.

"But," Jason said, "they do seem to be sniffing, and if Grandpa Gavin were still alive, he'd be yelling like thunder. We didn't all pitch in and make that ranch what it is, only so he could live his last years there. Dad accepted the lease because he thought you, me and Travis would benefit from what it could yield."

"Damned straight." Zane would sooner brave the

fires of hell, before he saw the McCords relocate Travis, who'd decided to forgo family business in favor of ranching on the property that should've belonged to the Foleys in the first place. "It's just like the McCords to rub salt on a wound. I wouldn't be surprised if they were just trying to remind Travis that they're the ones who still own the property."

"And they've got to know it burns him, with all the blood and sweat he's put into it." Jason's tone grew even angrier. "But I'm not sure it's just about reminding Travis of what's what. The McCord kids are taking after the old man after all."

"Why do you say that?"

"Because, when Devon passed from that heart attack, the clan actually backed off for a while. He was always the one who took the greatest pleasure in the feud. That's what I thought, at least. Now I'm not so sure. Rumor has it that the family lawyers have been taking a real long look at the lease…"

Zane didn't even have to hear the rest.

"…just as if they're trying to find a way to get out of it."

His blood ran hot at the notion of his baby brother losing what meant the most to him.

He wanted to strike out at the McCords, but as his gaze fixed on the portrait of Livie, he pulled his temper back.

Again, he saw Danielle in his daughter.

Living with a bipolar wife had taught Zane that losing his head only made everything worse. Retreating— whether it was into work or into himself—had been the best way to handle her.

She'd also taught him that there was a difference

between his personal life and business. In the latter, he could uncork the frustration that built up at home, striking quickly and lethally during deals, allowing him a sorely needed outlet.

And the McCords were just asking for it.

Dragging his gaze away from Livie's image, he refocused on the old family portrait above the fireplace. There was a measure of serenity at seeing the picture that'd been painted just before his mom, his daughter's namesake, had suffered a fatal fall during a horseback ride. His father had tried his best to raise the three boys on his own, but they'd missed their mom terribly.

And sometimes her death even made Zane wonder if all the women in his life would leave before their time.

At any rate, her absence had bonded all of them, and it had molded Zane into a man early on, as he'd taken up where his father had to leave off in raising Jason and Travis. Even now, at the age of thirty-six, Zane felt as if he was still in charge of so much: their holdings, their tanglings with the McCords.

Jason was speaking again: "At first, I wasn't sure why the McCords would be so interested in the ranch right now. I thought maybe they wanted to sell off the acreage, if those rumors about money trouble in their jewelry business are true. But then, what difference would that relatively small cash influx make? Then I thought about the silver mines on the property."

"Those are abandoned, Jace. Tapped out. That's why the McCords leased the land to us."

"I take it that, during this latest nanny search, your ear hasn't been to the ground."

He stiffened until Jason chuckled, revealing that he'd

only been injecting a little humor where some was sorely needed. But Zane took his duties as oldest brother seriously. Having the McCords get the best of them during his watch was never going to happen.

"One of my assistants," Jason said, "heard that Blake McCord has been buying up as many loose canary diamonds as possible on the world market."

Diamonds?

Zane started to see where his brother might be going with this.

Jason added, "I imagine you're remembering those news reports from several months ago?"

"The Santa Magdalena Diamond," Zane said. He'd filed the information in the back of his mind, way behind Livie and other more urgent matters, but he sure as hell hadn't forgotten.

A flawless, forty-eight-carat canary gem with perfect clarity, the Santa Magdalena Diamond was legendary, said to transcend even the beauty and brilliance of the Hope Diamond itself. Supposedly, the piece had been mined in India, and was cursed, because it had resulted in bad luck for everyone who ever owned it. It was only when the gem rested with its rightful owner that any personal misfortunes would end.

The diamond had been missing for over a century, but fairly recently, divers had uncovered a wrecked ship that was supposed to have been carrying the jewel, in addition to other treasures of murky origins.

Really, the only reason the Foleys were interested in the diamond was because their great-grandfather, Elwin Foley, had been on that ship, which might have also been populated by thieves, although that never had been proven. When the transport went down, a few passengers had survived, including Elwin, and according to family stories, he'd snagged the gem, along with a jewel-encrusted chest of coins. But since no one had found either object since, the tale had passed into legend.

However, the ship's recent discovery had resurrected all the rumors, especially since the diamond and the chest hadn't been located.

"The Santa Magdalena Diamond came to my mind, too," Jason said. "I've been going through a lot of scenarios, but the best I can figure, maybe the McCords believe that Elwin Foley did get away with the gem when he survived the wreck, and he hid the diamond somewhere on the land where Travis's ranch is located now—land that used to belong to Elwin before it passed to Gavin, who lost it in that poker game. And don't you think the Santa Magdalena would pay a few bills for a cash-strapped business?"

"The theory's a stretch," Zane said.

"But the timing's pretty telling. The divers find the shipwreck, rumors recirculate about Elwin taking the diamond, then the McCords express a heightened interest in the property."

"Whatever their intentions, I'm not about to let Travis be hassled by that family."

"Glad you're on board then." His brother sounded as confident as ever.

Zane shot a skeptical glance at the phone. "What exactly did I board, Jace?"

Right about now, his sibling was probably grinning to himself about one of his genius ideas that kept Foley

Industries in the black. "If the McCords want to give us trouble, I say we find out about it ahead of time. Cut them off at the pass."

"Your lawyer friends—the ones who got you that information about the McCords looking into the lease—will only get us so far."

"Exactly. I'll be taking matters into my own hands until we know Travis isn't in for some harassment."

Zane waited for it.

"The McCords have a few soft spots," Jason said, elaborating. "One of them is named Penny."

Penny. Penelope McCord. Zane recalled one of the daughters of the other family—the quiet twin in a set of burnished blond-haired sisters. A jewelry designer who basically kept to herself.

In a contest between her and Jason, the so-called lady killer, she had no chance at all.

"What are you intending, Jace?" Not that Zane had sympathy for any McCord, but…hell, a lady was a lady, and there were limits.

"Nothing fancy. I just discovered we'll be attending the same wedding pretty soon. I've done business with the groom, so he invited me to his big, high-society bash. I figured I might just happen across her table, sit myself down for a rest, offer my own sort of olive branch in polite conversation…"

"…and feel her out for what she might know, without being too obvious about it."

It wasn't a bad idea, and when Jason didn't say anything, Zane knew he was probably in his desk chair, relaxing with his hands behind his head, content with the plan.

"Okay," Zane added. "A wedding sounds like a good place to casually learn if the McCords have discovered the location of the diamond, and to find out just how true these rumors about the McCords's finances are."

"And if that wedding should turn into something afterward…"

Zane raised an eyebrow. "Jace."

"I'm talking about a coffee date—or whatever."

No, his brother was talking about more than that. Zane knew how Jason loved his women, especially ones as lovely as Penny McCord.

Zane was just about to mention it, when he heard something outside the door.

"Wait a sec," he said to his brother, then went over to check on the noise.

But…nothing.

Still, he thought he smelled a hint of sunshine-like perfume that traced the rough edges of his heart until it felt about ready to fall out of him.

Steadying himself, he closed the door to the dim hallway—and to the very idea of sunshine, too.

Melanie was halfway through the drive to Austin when her nerves finally settled.

She'd only managed to calm down by gazing out the black-tinted window at the passing scenery, as well as chattering with Monty, the town car driver, who, as she now very well knew, had four daughters with tempers as quick as their mama's and tastes way beyond his table wine budget.

The conversation almost made her forget that she'd been standing in a hallway and eavesdropping on her boss. And that her boss had only said that she was… "spirited."

She tried not to let that bother her, but it did. Deep inside, she'd been hoping to hear Zane Foley say that she had a great smile. She'd been wishing for a lyrical description that would've belonged in a song, like maybe there was something in the way she moved….

Right. Anyway, after telling herself that she was being eleven kinds of fool, she'd found that she was sitting there still listening to him and Jason talking about the McCords.

And the Santa Magdalena Diamond.

If Melanie hadn't been confused and intrigued by her new boss before, she sure was now. Since she hadn't been living under a rock, she'd heard about the diamond and how it had been connected to the recent shipwreck discovery. Hearing Zane and Jason discuss all of it just piled one more question upon the other questions that had been weighing in her brain about the Foleys.

Monty glanced in the rearview mirror, checking on her during a lull in their talk. On the downhill side of his thirties, he had thick-lashed, dark eyes that tipped up at the corners in perpetual good humor, dusky skin scraped by a five-o'clock shadow, and a long nose that topped a smile.

"You need me to turn the air on higher?" he asked.

She crossed one leg over the other, aiming her body in his direction and away from the window. "No thank you. It's just…"

"Come on, spill it out to me. Long rides go by a lot quicker with a good discussion."

He was too nice to shut out, but she wasn't going to "spill" anything about Zane Foley.

"I remembered that I left my suit jacket back at the house," she said instead. "Excellent start, don't you think? Mr. Foley probably believes I don't have a brain in me."

Laughing, he shrugged. "Listen, once I fill up my stomach with leftovers from Cook's fridge, I'll be turning this baby right back around, to be on standby for Mr. Foley in Dallas. I'll fetch that jacket for you and make sure you get it soon enough."

"Really? I hate to be such a bother."

He made a dismissive gesture, and she thought it was sincere.

She told him where she left the jacket, before adding, "Must be nice for Mr. Foley to have a driver whenever he needs one. He's worked for it, I know, but what perks, huh?"

He rested his hand on top of the steering wheel. "Mr. Foley doesn't take nearly the advantage of his good fortune as I would. Sure, he has a great place in Austin, but he uses it to house Livie more than anything else. He's never around to enjoy it. And he has that nice town home, too. But with his money? It could've been a castle."

"He *never* comes to Tall Oaks?"

"No. He's not there much at all. Birthdays, Christmas, an annual fundraiser for the Dallas Children's Hospital, and that's about it. Mr. Foley's a busy man, but he gives Livie what she needs otherwise."

Yes, nannies.

Yet, as Melanie had told her boss, she wasn't one to judge, and she needed to keep that in mind.

Monty seemed to have shut himself off from saying any more about it, so Melanie decided to pursue another avenue.

Then she would stop. Really.

"Funny how life works. I mean, if Harry McCord hadn't cheated in that card game with Gavin Foley, the Foleys might've been the ones with the jewelry empire that the McCords developed."

"True," Monty said. "There were five abandoned silver mines on that property. *Five.* That's a lot of cannoli they missed out on because their grandfather made a bad bet." He chuckled. "But, depending on who you talk to outside the family, you're going to get a different story about that poker game."

"What do you mean?"

Monty looked over his shoulder, amusement written on his face, then returned his gaze to the front again. "None of this goes out of the car, understand?"

Heck, she didn't want to summon the wrath of her coworkers by betraying them. "Absolutely."

Her pulse got a bit louder in her ears.

"It's sour grapes, that's what I say. Gavin made the bet, and he should've owned up to it. But it must've been tough to see that land pay off in so much silver to the McCords."

"I can't imagine what it must've been like," she said.

"Fortunately," he added, "the Foleys found their own strike of luck in their East Texas oil fields, but Gavin always claimed that the McCord silver should've been theirs, too. The boys grew up on those sorts of tales, especially young Travis. He practically lived at his grandfather's knee, while our Zane ran the roost over at his dad's house." The driver smiled. "Testosterone Lodge. That's what they called their household after their mother passed on."

Melanie remembered the woman in the family

portrait in Zane's study. She'd looked so gentle and caring, traits she'd never really grown up with herself.

"So," she said, feeling an ache in her chest, "Mr. Foley—Zane—was the second man of the house, right after Rex Foley?"

"Yes, ma'am. And the absence of a woman's guiding touch is why you have the competitive, aggressive Zane Foley, who lords it over the real estate and oil businesses. He's the leader of the pack."

Sitting back in the seat, Melanie allowed the image of Zane Foley's hazel eyes to mist over her thoughts. She sighed without even knowing it, then recovered when she saw Monty watching her in the mirror.

"He's a haunted man, too," the driver said, as if he knew just what kind of effect the boss had on her.

Then again, she wouldn't be surprised if he attracted every woman who came within ten feet of him.

"The missus—Danielle—did a real number on him." Monty shook his head. "You're going to hear about this sooner or later, being a part of the family now, so I'll tell you. But it's not to be talked about to anyone else."

"I understand."

He slumped a little in his seat. "Danielle was bipolar, and during a time when she went off her medication, she took her life."

Melanie instinctively covered her heart with her hand. Now Zane Foley's avoidance of discussing his personal life with the press made sense.

But what had the suicide done to Livie?

To Zane?

She recalled his devastated gaze, and she knew.

"I'm so sorry to hear that," she said softly.

"We were all sorry. It's been almost six years now, but she still has an effect on every moment, every inch of space around us."

Melanie stayed quiet. She was going to live in what amounted to a haunted house, wasn't she? She was going to walk on the floors where Danielle had walked, brush her fingers along the same walls….

"He married her right out of high school," Monty continued, "but a short time after that, she started showing extreme highs and lows in her mood. Mr. Foley didn't know how to handle that, yet he did everything he could. The doctors even put her on meds, but when she went off of them…"

Melanie closed her eyes, wanting to hear, but not wanting to.

He added, "Mr. Foley isn't a helpless kind of man. He'd always been so good at everything—school, home life, sports and then business. But he couldn't come up with any way to aid Danielle, beyond getting her all the professional treatment he could. When she overdosed on pills, he blamed himself and buried himself in work."

She opened her eyes. "How about Livie?"

"She was nothing more than a baby when it happened, but every year she grows to look even more like Danielle. You can imagine what that does to Mr. Foley."

Monty didn't say anything more, but Melanie figured out the rest of it.

Did her new boss fear that history would repeat itself? Was that why he rarely visited Livie, because he thought his daughter would be just like the mother, not only in appearance, but in everything else, too?

Most importantly, had Livie gone through five

nannies in six years because she was acting out, missing a dad who found it painful to be around her?

Now the shadows in his gaze made so much sense.

Yet, as the town car purred on toward Austin, all Melanie really knew was that she was on her way to aid a young girl who needed someone to be there, to help her overcome all the anguish.

Even if that someone was a woman who was trying to leave her past behind, too.

Chapter Three

From outside, the Victorian mansion and sweeping lawns of Tall Oaks made it seem as if every single rich-girl fantasy that Melanie had conjured in her life was coming true.

Grand willow and oak trees, majestic wrought iron furniture on the porch under the fine gingerbread woodwork…

But then she stepped foot inside.

As she struggled not to drop either of her suitcases, Mrs. Howe, the estate manager, closed the door behind them, whisking past Melanie on her way to the staircase.

"Ms. Grandy?" the bun-wearing, gray-dressed red-head said, pausing near the faded walnut handrail.

Melanie took a moment to gander at the Spartan foyer, then through the open pocket doors that led to a parlor. The furniture, from a closed rolltop desk set to a loveseat, was what a person would call "bleak." The wooden herringbone floors were bare of warming rugs. And although the ceilings boasted hand-painted images of angels flying in cloudy harmony, the colors were leeched to almost nothing.

Ghostly, Melanie thought again.

Was it too late to quit?

Her gaze fell to a corner of the parlor, where a tall, unpolished gold cage held a lone canary that stirred on its perch, not even singing.

"That's Sassy," Mrs. Howe said. "She's been in the family for a couple of years. Livie likes to try and persuade her to sing sometimes, but that bird doesn't always oblige her. She's a stubborn, quiet little thing."

Melanie wanted to ask how often a canary like Sassy might *want* to warble in a place like this, but instead she blinked herself out of her stupor and followed Mrs. Howe, who was already mounting the steps.

Her suitcases seemed to weigh a ton, made all the heavier by the oppression in here, but she had politely refused Monty's and Mrs. Howe's help outside, and now she was paying for it as she climbed the stairs.

When they arrived at Melanie's bedroom, her expectations were already low. And thank goodness, too, because the bed with its circa 1950 turquoise spread, and the muted lamps resting on the dull chests of drawers, didn't exactly give off any kind of princess vibe.

But she wasn't here to be royalty, she reminded herself.

Still, she recalled what she'd thought back at Zane Foley's townhouse, when she'd wondered if she would find Livie stuck in a high-class jail.

She just hadn't expected to be so right.

Heaving one suitcase, then the other, to the top of the bed, Melanie thanked Mrs. Howe for her welcoming attention.

The manager nodded, continuing the briefing. "Livie's got some playtime at the moment, then it's dinner at six, study time afterward, a bit of relaxing time and bed. She wakes up at seven on the dot for you to prepare her, then drive her to school."

Zane Foley had already gone over all this, even supplying Melanie with directions to the private institution Livie attended for kindergarten.

"Study time?" Melanie asked, still hung up on that one detail. "Livie's six. What does she have to study?"

Mrs. Howe smiled patiently, and Melanie suddenly saw from up close that the older woman couldn't have been more than forty, given her smooth skin and the absence of deep wrinkles around her eyes. It was the bun and lack of cosmetics that had made Melanie think Mrs. Howe was even more mature at first.

But, beyond that, she couldn't read the manager.

"Mr. Foley," the other woman said, "has Livie read picture books and listen to phonics on her own, applying what she's learned at school."

"So much for being a kid," Melanie said lightly, testing Mrs. Howe, to see just how strict *she* was.

The woman widened her eyes a tad, and Melanie realized that she might have surprised Mrs. Howe with her *spiritedness*.

"Sorry," Melanie said. "It's only that I got the impression Mr. Foley is rather…"

Okay, how could she put this?

Mrs. Howe helped her out. "A hard case?"

Now Melanie smiled.

But the other woman merely adopted a tolerant grin. "He makes sure Livie toes the line, and we all respect that, because he's also a good, fair employer."

The insinuation—Mr. Foley's way or the highway—was clear.

And that was all she said, although Melanie kept thinking, *What about Livie? Is she an employee, too?*

Before she could even dare ask, Mrs. Howe's brown gaze moved to the doorway, focusing on something behind Melanie.

She turned around just in time to see the last of a flowered spring dress flare out of sight in the hallway.

"I believe," whispered Mrs. Howe, "you've drawn some interest."

Melanie's heart folded, as if trying to embrace itself. Livie.

She walked to the door, but when she got there, no darling little girl was in sight.

Frowning, she glanced back at Mrs. Howe, who was fussing with the bedspread, correcting the wrinkles Melanie had already made by putting her suitcases on the cloth.

Oh, dear.

The manager straightened, ran her hands down her gray skirt. Then she walked out the door, saying one last thing to Melanie as she passed.

"You might want to continue up the staircase, Ms. Grandy, to Livie's playroom." She smiled once more. "Best of luck to you."

And as she eased down the hall, Melanie could've sworn she heard Mrs. Howe add, "A *lot* of luck."

After wondering if her ears were just playing tricks on her, Melanie went to the staircase again, traveling up to a dead end, where a closed door bled light from around its edges.

Lest she doubt that this was Livie's playroom, she saw a sign written in the tremulous letters of a dark purple crayon.

LIVIE.

Somehow, the name felt like a territorial statement, and Melanie hesitated to knock. After all, with the structure put on Livie, didn't she deserve a private place that allowed her some time alone when it was actually scheduled?

After knocking, she waited a moment, listening for a muffled "Come in" that never came.

She put her ear to the wood. Nothing.

"Livie?" she said. "Remember me from the other day? I'm Ms. Grandy, your new nanny. I'd like to say hello to you."

Still no response.

Was the girl even in there?

Cautiously, Melanie tested the doorknob, finding it unlocked. It wasn't a shock, since she doubted that Zane Foley would stand for being shut out of anything.

She thought of her own room in the quiet of night. Her own door creaking open. Mr. Foley paying a surprise visit....

A quiver ran through her, but she chased it away as she pushed at the door.

At first she only saw an austere attic, clean and ordered, with a couple of low, wood tables and several closed chests amongst shelves of toys.

Then, as she looked down, she found herself blocked by an army of stuffed animals that had been hastily tossed in a semi-circle.

A little voice came from the left.

"They don't want you in here."

Melanie glanced toward the sound, finding Livie sitting in a miniature rocking chair, her hands folded in her lap. She was wearing Mary Jane shoes with ankle socks, and her dark hair was held back by a lacy band, the bridge of her nose lightly freckled, just as the portrait in Zane Foley's study had shown.

All that was missing was the stuffed lamb in her hands, but there was something Melanie saw in Livie that the painting hadn't captured sufficiently at all.

The sadness in the girl's big eyes.

It dug into Melanie's chest.

"I thought the room might be empty." She used her smile in a peacemaking fashion, gesturing toward the animals. "You've got a real collection."

The little girl just kept serenely assessing her new nanny, and Melanie thought of how pretty she was, how pretty her mom must've been, too, although she hadn't come across any published pictures of her to know for sure.

Livie glanced at her stuffed menagerie. "Daddy had them sent for my birthday this year. He couldn't visit me this time."

Owie.

Melanie only wished she had a huge bandage that would cover Livie's heart from the damage done to her. She herself knew what it felt like to have a special time like a birthday fall to the wayside. It had happened every year with her own mom, until Leigh would suddenly remember after the fact and try to make it up to Melanie with day-old cake on sale at the bakery.

"So what are the animals doing right now?" she gently asked Livie, even though she knew they'd been set there to bar Melanie from intruding.

The girl stood up from her chair, and the rocker stirred, creaking, adding an odd level of discomfort. She went to a toy shelf, her back to Melanie. "It's their room, and they want you to know that."

And the gauntlet hits the floor, Melanie thought.

"Excellent," she said. "I'm sure you'll agree that there are other ground rules we'll need to establish besides that, Livie. Why don't we sit down to talk about them? I didn't get much of a chance to do that the other day with you, and I'd really like to."

Even with her back to Melanie, it was obvious that the child was crossing her arms. "My name is Olivia."

"All right." Melanie wasn't going to lose even an iota of patience—not with what this child had gone through with her mother. "Olivia, maybe you'd enjoy lemonade on the back porch with me. How about it?"

"Lemonade has sugar. Sugar makes me hyper. Daddy says so."

Melanie came this close to rolling her eyes, but she refrained. Zane Foley wasn't even here, and he was still being a pain.

"Then if you can't have sugar," Melanie said, "perhaps I can wrangle up some ice tea without sweetener."

Livie sighed, as if exasperated, and went about picking through her toys and ignoring Melanie altogether.

But the new nanny didn't go anywhere. Nope. She

just stood there and memorized the details of the room, the display of toys that would tell her something about Livie, whether or not the child wanted her to know.

Stuffed animals—dogs, sheep, dolphins. All gentle creatures.

Puzzle boxes nearer to the doorway that looked to have never even been opened.

Dolls—especially Barbies.

Melanie grinned to herself, then retreated down the stairs, but only because she had a secret weapon that had also served to disarm her first charge in those initial days with her.

She went to her room, to one of the suitcases, and pulled out a smaller bag that was filled with sewing materials and doll dresses. She'd taken up this hobby early, back in her babysitting days, because she'd found that Barbie clothes were catnip for ninety-nine percent of all little girls.

Then she went back to Livie's domain.

There, she sat within the semicircle of sentinel animals and took out the most exquisite wee bridal dress. She began to fluff the airy sleeves and spread the sheer, belled skirt.

She didn't call attention to herself, but then again, she didn't have to.

Over the course of the next few minutes, Livie gravitated from one shelf to the other, closer to Melanie, although she wasn't obvious about it.

Melanie lay the bride's frock on her knee, smoothed it out, then reached into her bag for a long, splashy pink satin party dress that always made Barbie look like even more of a knock-out.

As she traced a finger over its sleekness, the glitz took her back to neon and jangling slot machines, and she shoved the memory of her old casino life away, just as if it were baggage she would keep in her own attic.

Soon, Livie was near Melanie, although still on the other side of the animals. Melanie glanced up, as if surprised to see her.

She casually offered the wedding dress, and Livie touched it with her fingers, then drew them away.

"It's okay," Melanie said. "Why don't you get one of your dolls and see how she looks in it?"

Without meeting Melanie's gaze, Livie went across the room to her toy shelf, and when she returned with a brunette Barbie, her gaze was fixed on that dress, her eyes shining.

As she put the frock on her doll, Melanie's gaze lit on the bridal dress, too, unable to look away, as thoughts of Zane Foley taunted her with something she knew she would never have with a man like him.

Zane hadn't moved an inch from his desk, ever since getting off the phone with his brother. Jason and he had been cut short by a slew of phone calls from Zane's office, and he was just wrapping up the latest one while he multitasked, paging through a bound hard-copy file for the Santa Magdalena Diamond that he'd pulled from his library.

Magazine articles, news transcripts—everything, he thought, as he scanned a computer printout about Great Grandfather Elwin and his alleged role in making off with the gem. Zane was going through it all, just to see if he could find something he'd missed, a clue that might

let him know where that diamond could've gone—
something to lead him to it before the McCords saw it
first.

Meanwhile, he listened to his assistant, Cindy, as
she talked over the speakerphone.

"Just in case you're wondering," she drawled in her
wry manner, "we've got your Fourth of July Dallas
Children's Hospital charity event about set and ready."

"Two months ahead of time?"

"I aim to please, sir. Expect a crew to be descending
on Tall Oaks within the month, to start whipping the
estate into shape. You've commented yourself that it's
not exactly in showcase form."

Zane was still looking at the diamond file. Sometimes Cindy could be incredibly direct, like a less-
tactful version of—

As he thought of Melanie Grandy, his gaze drifted
from the paperwork. Lively blue eyes, a spark in every
gesture…

He wondered how she was getting on with Livie so
far. Wondered if he would be having to hire another
nanny soon.

Something like disappointment sank within him, but
he ignored it.

"Next item on your list?" he asked.

"I'm working on your other charity commitments,
but there're no updates on those yet. However, we've
got a lot to cover about that state representative seat.
Judge Duarte's been ringing my phone off the hook to
get through to you about running during the next elec-
tion."

"I know." Zane had been avoiding any and all calls

about it. "That man's head is thicker than timber. What's it going to take to get him to understand that I'm not interested in running for anything?"

"You'd be perfect for it, Mr. Foley. Besides, your family isn't exactly the hands-off type when it comes to politics."

True, but Zane preferred to let his fundraising abilities and civic activism do the talking.

"I'll call Duarte tomorrow," he said. "By the way, isn't it about time you headed home? Mike probably has dinner all cooked up for you."

"Carne asada. I love being a newlywed and having a barbecue master for a hubby."

"Then scram before he leaves you."

"Yes, sir."

With that, they ended the call, but it wasn't two minutes later that Zane got another one.

He didn't mind, though. Business kept him going, gave him less time to think about everything else.

He saw his youngest brother Travis's number on the caller ID, so he donned his earpiece, left the study and went to the kitchen, since his stomach felt empty.

"Hey, Trav," Zane said as he walked down the dark hall. He knew every unlit step by heart. "You out on the range?"

"Just got back in from seeing to some fences that needed fixing. I hear Jason told you about the McCords' unwelcome interest in the ranch."

"That's right."

"I already talked to him about the grand plan with Penny McCord. I don't love this sneaking around Jason's going to be doing with her," he said, "but if it clears the air in any way, I'll live with it."

He distrusted the McCords just the same as any of them, yet Travis was a cowboy, a loner, and loathed being distracted by what he thought to be less important matters, such as the other family's "sniffing around."

"Jace and I didn't want to go forward on anything without your knowing it," Zane said, opening the fridge, discovering that it didn't contain much more than a drop of milk in a carton, and several long-neck bottles of beer. He grabbed one of those and headed for a pantry cupboard.

"Jason said the same thing." Travis waited a beat, and Zane could hear the change in his voice as he switched gears. The less time he could dwell on the McCords, the better. "Aside from the drama, I hear you've got yourself a new nanny. Jason thinks you like her."

Zane almost dropped his beer, and it wasn't just because Travis was being a smart-ass.

It was because a bolt of contained need had shot through him, released from somewhere deep down, where he'd repressed the longing, thinking that it was useless.

He recovered in time to say, "For Pete's sake, do you two live in a middle-school locker room?"

Travis laughed softly. "Just bustin' your chops. But he did tell me that Livie's finally going to have some dedicated company again. I have to say I'm glad for that, because I imagine she's lonely over there."

Zane wrapped up all remainders of desire that he'd felt this afternoon, packing it tightly away at the mention of his daughter.

Travis and Jason adored their niece, and occasionally they tried to let Zane know that he could improve his fatherly skills.

But they didn't understand how tough it was. They hadn't lived with Danielle, hadn't tried to keep it all together after her death.

How could they understand Zane's failures and his need to keep it from happening again with Livie?

"Zane," Travis said, clearly knowing that he was treading on thin ice, "I know the anniversary of Danielle's death is coming up, and I'm sorry for broaching this again, but what're you going to do about Livie?"

"Stay out of this, Travis."

Every inch a Foley, his sibling did no such thing.

"You think it's a good idea to keep sweeping every mention of Danielle under the carpet?" his brother asked. "It's not like Livie's ever going to forget she had a mother. Your pretending as if Danielle never existed is only going to do more harm than good."

Zane's temper crept up, squeezing his temples.

But maybe *"temper"* was the wrong word. *"Remorse"* was more like it.

"I don't need to hear this from you," he said.

"Zane—"

Unable to stand any more, he hung up on his brother and leaned against the cupboard in the darkness of his home, wanting to say he was sorry.

And not just to Travis, either.

At ten minutes to six, a bell clanged from downstairs, and Livie jumped up from her spot on the floor in her upstairs playroom, immediately beginning to tidy all the Barbies and stuffed animals she'd brought out.

"Dinnertime," the little girl said, as serious as ever.

Melanie gathered the doll clothes, watching her

charge bustle here and there, as if her life depended upon a spic-and-span performance. Once again, she felt for Livie, who'd actually began removing those stuffed animals bit by bit, until she'd opened a hole for herself to come through and get closer to Melanie.

Of course, she'd done it slyly, as if her new nanny wouldn't notice, and Melanie had played along, trying not to look too happy about even that bit of progress.

Livie was so efficient that she had most of the stuffed toys back in place before Melanie had cleaned her own mess, and before she knew it, the little girl was standing at the side of the door, her back straight as she expectantly folded her hands in front of her.

Melanie wasn't sure what was happening until Livie said, "This is where you're allowed to come in to make sure everything is in its place."

Oh. Right.

But Melanie kept near the doorway, on her side of the invisible semicircle that the girl had created earlier with the stuffed animals. "Do you mind if I come in, Olivia?"

The child gave Melanie a sidelong glance, as if she couldn't believe what she was hearing.

The hint of a smile pulled at the corners of her mouth, revealing darling dimples, and she nodded. And went back to not smiling.

Melanie didn't mind, though; she entered the room, making sure all the dolls they'd played with were lined up on the shelves. She was tempted to mess them up ever so slightly, just because she wondered what Zane Foley would do if he saw the aberration, yet she resisted.

"Top-notch job," she said, turning around just in time to see Livie watching her, then quickly fix her gaze on a spot above Melanie's head. "You're a hard worker, aren't you?"

"Yes, Ms. Grandy."

She walked toward her charge, wishing she could rest her hand on Livie's dark head or touch her shoulder, offering some reassurance.

But sensing that this wouldn't go over well—not just yet—she instead said, "Let's get washed up and see what's on the menu."

Livie spent one more second checking Melanie out, then spun around and dashed down the stairway.

"Careful," Melanie said, and the girl stopped, then slowed down, using the banister.

But, as if realizing that she was being too nice to the nanny she still had to haze, she sped up again, yet not enough to be chastised for it.

Good heavens, Melanie thought, wishing she had a million more Barbie clothes to use as placating lures from this point on.

After cleaning up herself, she went to the dining room, which was just as stark as the rest of the house, with a long table—an item Zane Foley seemed to favor for the distance it established between diners—and plain chairs and a sideboard. The only ornamentation, if you could call it that, was a bland chandelier, with frosted glass cups lending illumination.

Livie took a seat at the long side of the table, and just as Melanie sat down opposite her, Mrs. Howe appeared through a door.

It was only when the manager cleared her throat that Melanie noticed Livie's saucered eyes that stared at her new nanny sitting at the main table.

Oh.

"Ms. Grandy," Mrs. Howe said, "Livie will eat here. Why don't you follow me?"

Livie looked down at her table setting, and Melanie couldn't read her expression.

Without causing a scene, Melanie rose, went through the door with Mrs. Howe, but stopped the manager before they got too far.

"I appreciate that there are certain ways you've done things around here," Melanie said, "but I'd really like to be with Olivia tonight. She's not resisting me as much as she did earlier, and if I could continue that streak…"

Mrs. Howe's face was unreadable. "That would be between Mr. Foley and you, Ms. Grandy. He's the one who wants the help to eat in the kitchen."

Really now?

"Well, I'm willing to answer to him for this," Melanie said evenly, smiling at the manager.

With a curious look, the woman left her alone.

Truly alone, too, because when it would come time to answer to Zane Foley, it'd be all on Melanie.

But, seriously—like she was going to leave poor Livie to eat by herself?

She went back into the dining room, and when the girl looked up, her sad eyes softened a tad.

Then she glanced back at her plate; but it was too late—because she'd already wrapped her tiny fingers around Melanie's heart.

She waited, not trusting herself to speak for a moment.

Finally, when she'd gotten some composure, she said, "I like it better out here. It's nice and quiet."

"Yes." The girl peeked at Melanie.

Melanie gave her a reassuring grin, and from the way Livie held back her own smile, she guessed that the child understood that her nanny had risked a spot of trouble just to eat with her.

The door behind them opened again, and a young blond man with a scraggly beard stepped through with a table setting for Melanie. He was dressed in chef's whites, so she assumed he was the cook.

Without saying anything, he nodded to her, then winked.

Approval. Thank goodness there was *someone* here who wasn't giving her the near-silent treatment.

Then he left, but only to bring out a well-balanced meal of meatloaf with broccoli, fruit cocktail and macaroni and cheese.

Livie dug right in after the cook was gone, then slowed down when she saw Melanie's are-we-at-the-zoo? expression.

She swallowed. "I'm only eating fast because Mrs. Howe said I can play with my new present from Daddy after dinner and study time."

"Oh?"

The girl nodded, a fork full of mac and cheese half-way to her mouth now. "An American Girl doll. Daddy sends one every week if I'm good."

Livie chowed down again, but Melanie didn't touch her food yet. Her stomach roiled a bit at the thought of how Zane Foley couldn't be bothered to visit his daughter, seemingly buying her off with gifts instead.

And when Livie next spoke, she only confirmed Melanie's heartsick suspicions.

"I like the dolls," she said softly, "but they'd be even better if *he'd* bring them to me."

Melanie held back a swell of emotion. This little girl needed the love and attention of the only parent she had left.

Why couldn't he see that?

"I know what you mean, Olivia," Melanie said, thinking of her own mom. "I know exactly what you mean."

The child didn't look up from her plate, but her next words revealed everything, even if her tone was just as subtly guarded as it'd been earlier in the attic.

"My name's Livie."

Melanie swallowed back the tightness in her throat, then picked up her fork so they could eat their meal together.

She only wished that Zane Foley could be here, too—for his daughter, of course.

But when an unwelcome, low burn heated her belly, pooling down and down, Melanie admitted that maybe she also wanted him here for a different reason altogether.

Chapter Four

The days sped by with more dolls being delivered to Livie, more meals that Melanie took at the table with her charge and even more instructional hours for the girl.

But to supplement those regular study sessions, Melanie also brought her love of dance into the playroom, where Livie had been allowing her nanny to slowly but surely spend more time.

Still, out of all of those passing days, Zane Foley hadn't paid a visit to Tall Oaks once, nor sent for Livie to come to Dallas.

Not even one darn time.

Oh, sure, there'd been phone calls to the little girl—about one every few days—but Melanie guessed they were more out of habit than a true need to connect with Livie, because each one left the child looking sadder than ever.

Yet, this only encouraged Melanie to step up her "save Livie" campaign, paying the child as much attention as the girl was open to on any given day. She showed her that someone really did care, even if Livie turned away from Melanie at times, and let those stuffed animals that had protected the playroom on that first day speak for her.

"They want you to leave them alone," Livie would say sometimes. "They don't need anyone to pretend they like them."

Little did she know that Melanie wasn't pretending; so the newest nanny hung in there, doing her best to give Livie her all.

She just wished she knew how to confront the problem of Zane Foley himself. How to talk some sense into him. How to make him see that he wasn't doing Livie any favors by staying away.

Melanie wanted to despise him, but then night would come, when the wind thumped branches against the old house, when the moon shined through her window and lulled her to close her eyes and imagine how it had felt to touch him when she shook his hand.

How the contact had shaken her to the core.

And morning would arrive again, and she'd go right back to thinking about what to do about him and Livie.

Today, as the June sun spilled through the attic window, Livie had decided to celebrate summer—and her leaving kindergarten behind—with an impromptu performance for some of the house staff. Accordingly, the audience of two sat on the quilts spread over the floor in front of a makeshift blanket curtain that Livie and Melanie had constructed.

The little girl was behind it now, while Mrs. Howe and Cook waited.

Cook, who was in his chef's whites, crossed his legs Indian-style and grinned at Melanie, who was just in front of the curtain, ready to open it. His name was Scott, and from that first week forward, he'd encouraged Melanie to call him that.

Meanwhile, Mrs. Howe sat in a ladylike position, her knees to the side, her pale skirt covering her legs. Her name was Sue, but when Melanie had dared use it one time, she'd gotten a raised eyebrow and hadn't tried it since.

"Is it almost showtime?" Melanie asked Livie.

"Five minutes!" the girl said from behind the curtain.

"Okay." Melanie smiled at the audience, then walked toward them, sitting on the edge of the quilt while making sure her sundress skirt was in place. "Last-minute rehearsals behind that curtain, I imagine," she whispered. "Livie's nervous."

Scott shrugged, but he was so mellow that Melanie often suspected life was one big "oh, well" for him, anyway.

"It's her first show," he said. "The squirt can take her time to give us the premiere."

Mrs. Howe sighed at the nickname "squirt." She sighed a lot about Cook's surfer-in-Texas attitude.

Melanie grinned at Scott. "I guess that's the beauty of summer—no school to work a schedule around."

"But," Mrs. Howe said, "a schedule's still important."

During the past weeks, Melanie and the manager had experienced some…philosophical differences… about many things, although Mrs. Howe hadn't tipped off Zane Foley to the new nanny's slight adjustments.

At least, that's what Melanie suspected, because her boss hadn't rung her up yet to give her a talking to or fire her.

"You're right," Melanie said, "schedule's are important, and we still have one. Livie does well with them, so it seemed counterproductive to change her way of life midstream. But there's room for flexibility when it's warranted."

Scott playfully made the sign of the cross, like he was extending Mrs. Howe some help in fighting off Melanie's words.

"Mrs. Howe," he said, "would lose her mind without lists and charts and diagrams. Them's fightin' words, Mel."

The manager made a dismissive gesture at him, as if that would cause him to disappear, but she had an air of barely restrained amusement just the same. Melanie had decided that Scott was like Mrs. Howe's little brother, and their relationship was one long drive in a backseat where they get on each other's nerves.

Nothing romantic, though, Melanie thought. Mrs. Howe had a husband down the hill in their own cottage, and Scott had mentioned something to Melanie once about a serious girlfriend.

Livie's voice came from behind the curtain. "Almost ready!"

"Okay," all the adults answered back.

Scott kept looking toward the performance area, but now there was something pensive about him.

Melanie leaned near so her voice wouldn't have to carry. "What is it?"

He started to talk, then stopped, shrugged and smiled vaguely.

Melanie knew if she waited long enough he would go on.

And he did.

"It's nice to see her like this," he said. "I don't know exactly what you're doing, Mel, but I can't imagine Livie ever wanting to give any kind of performance before you came along."

Melanie blushed, knowing she was no miracle-worker.

Whispering, she said, "Livie's giving her performance in an attic, so it's not as if this is some grand coming out for her."

"Oh," Mrs. Howe said, "but it is."

For the first time, Melanie saw a pleased openness about the other woman, and that took her aback.

Melanie glanced away from the others and their approval; she wasn't willing to accept credit for anything, because there was still such a long way to go. There were even times when Livie would sit quietly staring out the window, and Melanie feared that no one would ever be able to get in. And there were the days when Livie could be so stubborn that it stretched Melanie's supply of patience to the breaking point.

Those were the moments when she could see why the other nannies had walked away. However, Melanie had come to the realization that it hadn't been Livie who'd driven the others away, so much as it'd been the hopelessness of the situation itself. Maybe it even broke their hearts to be so strict with the child.

The difference was that Melanie vowed to never give up.

"At any rate," Scott said, getting her attention again, "you're a real find, Mel. Mrs. H. agrees with me, too."

The manager hmphed. "I wasn't sure at first."

"You came around quick enough from the opinion you used to have." Scott made his voice higher, imitating Mrs. Howe. "'Mr. Foley has no idea how to pick 'em, does he? Set a pretty face in front of him, and he's sold.'"

"Cook," Mrs. Howe admonished.

"That's what you said," Scott added, that little-brother mischief in his eyes.

But Melanie was barely paying mind to that.

Pretty?

Zane Foley had only called her "spirited" on the phone to his brother, but did the employees at Tall Oaks know something else?

And… *Wait.*

Had the *other* nannies caught Zane Foley's eye?

A spear of jealousy stabbed her, and she scolded herself. Ridiculous to even be thinking it. Or to believe he'd hired her because she was slightly above average.

Still, she'd been spending so much time tuning in to any and all clues from the staff about the distant Mr. Foley that she all but vibrated now with this tidbit from Scott. No one but Monty had really talked about their boss—or the subject of Danielle—so she was much too open to any leaked detail.

"Ready!" Livie finally called out.

Melanie stood and went to the boom box by the curtain. She selected the Enya song Livie wanted to dance to and pulled back the material to reveal the little girl, who was dressed in a pink leotard and ballet slippers that Zane Foley had sent the second day of Melanie's tenure.

Mrs. Howe and Scott applauded, but as the synthesized strings began to play, the child just stood there, staring at them.

"Livie?" Melanie stage-whispered.

The child fixed her doe eyes on her nanny, as if forgetting everything Melanie had taught her about any of the dances they'd tried so far. They hadn't even come up with a routine for this performance, because Melanie had just encouraged her to do whatever the song inspired at any given moment, whether it was ballet or contemporary or even a few tap moves.

Maybe that had been a mistake.

Maybe Livie *did* need that firmer structure she was so used to. Maybe she couldn't depend on anything else.

Heart contracting, Melanie took the girl's hands and began to dance with her. Livie reacted immediately, still looking into her nanny's eyes as if nothing else existed, and laughing as she imitated everything Melanie did.

Soon the song was over and the audience clapped again, shouting out their "bravos" as the performers took their curtsies.

Livie's cheeks were flushed while she kept smiling up at Melanie.

The breath caught in Melanie's throat. No one had ever looked at her that way—not even the other children she'd cared for—and without thinking, she bent to wrap her arms around Livie.

The girl hugged her back, resting her head on her nanny's shoulder.

For a moment the world seemed to stop, to clarify

everything about what Melanie wanted: being needed and being able to give as much as she got from just one simple embrace.

Her imagination kicked into motion, picturing another pair of arms around them, hugging them all close together, creating the cocoon of a family that Melanie had never truly had.

Zane Foley's arms.

The sound of hammers against the back of the house knocked Melanie out of the moment. It was the maintenance crew, getting Tall Oaks in shape for the charity event that would take place here on the Fourth of July. Obviously, their break was over.

At least Livie would get to see her father then, Melanie thought, drawing back from the girl and smoothing a dark, wavy strand of hair away from her face.

As if she could read Melanie all too well, Livie got that sad look in her eyes, then hugged her nanny once more before backing away and going to Mrs. Howe and Scott, who congratulated her with their warm gestures.

It was nice while it lasted, Melanie thought. Maybe *she* was just as starved for affection as Livie.

When Mrs. Howe's phone rang with a chirping tone, Livie listened to Scott as he told her about his favorite part of the dance. In the meantime, the woman extracted the device from her pocket, checking the ID screen, and her relaxed demeanor altered as she answered the phone.

"Good afternoon, Mr. Foley," she said.

A burst of adrenaline jolted Melanie from head to toe, warming her—no, *heating* her—through and through.

She shut off the boom box, lending the attic silence as she noticed that Livie had gone bright-eyed and hopeful, watching Mrs. Howe talk to her dad.

Once again, Melanie hurt for her, because she knew that he'd just called Livie yesterday and he wasn't yet scheduled to do so again.

Darn it all, what could she *do* to take care of this situation?

Mrs. Howe kept talking to him, nodding, assuring him that the maintenance crew was making headway with the exterior of the mansion. In the meantime, Livie grabbed the manager's skirt, as if to get her dad's attention through Mrs. Howe.

Unable to stand it anymore, Melanie went to Livie, resting a hand on the girl's head.

"Can I talk to him?" the little girl whispered to Mrs. Howe.

Something like a heartfelt reaction overtook the manager's face. She looked at Melanie almost regretfully, while tacitly asking her to usher Livie out of the room so Zane Foley could conduct business without interruption.

Anger boiled in Melanie, taking over—or maybe even mixing—with the surge of awareness she'd been feeling before.

She got down to Livie's height. "Maybe we should try calling him later," she whispered, "after business hours?"

That sorrow—so familiar, so gut-wrenching—consumed Livie's gaze.

Scott shook his head while wandering out of the room, and Melanie thought that he might've been expecting more of her—the woman who'd taken Livie under her wing.

And shouldn't he?

Mrs. Howe signed off, silent, as if not knowing how to react or what to say to the little girl who'd been all but forgotten here at Tall Oaks.

Forgotten. Melanie knew exactly what that felt like—to live in a place where there were people crowded all around you, but you didn't seem to exist in any significant way.

It was the last straw.

"Know what?" she said, tweaking Livie under the chin, trying to distract her, even though it was so tough, with her throat choking every word.

Livie's mouth formed around a silent "What?" She was trying hard not to cry.

"I'm going to make sure you see your daddy soon," Melanie said, skimming her fingers over the girl's hair.

She heard Mrs. Howe gasp but ignored it, because Livie's eyes had already gotten that gleam of hope in them, and Melanie would move mountains to make her promise come true.

Too late, she wondered if she was crossing a line— if this vow would get her fired. Flying in the face of Zane Foley's wishes might take away all the security she'd won by landing this job.

But no one had been fighting for Livie.

"Really, Ms. Grandy?" the little girl asked, as if she couldn't believe any promises when it came to her dad.

"Really." Melanie stood, facing Mrs. Howe. "Father's Day is just around the corner, isn't it?"

She wasn't so used to celebrating the holiday, but she knew it was sometime near mid-June.

"Ms. Grandy…" the manager began in a warning tone.

Brushing that aside, Melanie took Livie's hand and squeezed it. "We're going to make a present for him. And we're going to be hand-delivering it."

As Mrs. Howe closed her eyes and sighed, Melanie smiled down at her charge, who was already hopping up and down.

"Yay!" Livie danced in front of a cautious Mrs. Howe. "We're going to Dallas!"

Yes, they were going to Dallas.

And somewhere in the back of Melanie's mind, she realized that perhaps the trip was just as much for *her* to see Zane Foley as it was for Livie.

Even if it was a Saturday, it'd been a typically long day at the office for Zane: putting the finishing touches on acquiring an old, junky amusement park near San Antonio, with the intention of polishing it into a environmentally conscious spa complex; having yet another needless discussion with Judge Duarte about that state representative seat; hearing from Jason about how he'd met Penny McCord at that wedding this past weekend.

Zane showered and donned some sweats and a T-shirt. All the while he went over what his brother had told him about pouring the charm on Penny, as he'd tried to subtly coax any information he could about her family's interest in Travis's ranch. She hadn't seemed to know much, and Jason hadn't believed it, so he'd decided to pursue her further, perhaps through another "chance" meeting soon.

Truthfully, it'd all worn Zane out—maybe because, in spite of his support of the plan, it still wasn't sitting well with him.

Then again, this had to do with the McCords, so all was fair.

Since he'd already had dinner at his downtown desk, he grabbed some paperwork about the Santa Magdalena shipwreck from his briefcase, then went to the living room and turned on the TV, thinking he would sit and read for a spell.

But he was interrupted by a knock on the door.

Zane looked at the clock on his DVR unit. 8:00 p.m.

Who the hell was paying a visit?

He set down the papers and went to the foyer, accessing the security video screen console that was hidden in a wall panel.

When he saw a hint of blond hair, his libido instinctively went wild because he'd been imagining that same light shade, plus a slender body and long legs, every night since he'd met Melanie Grandy.

And as his vision focused, allowing him to see the rest of her standing right there, in the flesh, in front of his door, the air deserted his lungs, stirring him up, electrifying him in a way he hadn't felt for years.

He hadn't had time for it, and business took up all his energies. Women had gotten him into too much trouble before, and staying away from them made life easier.

Didn't it?

Angered at all the questions—and even more so at Melanie Grandy's presence—he was about to press the security speaker and demand to know what she was doing here.

Then he spied Livie next to her nanny, holding Melanie Grandy's hand, and paused.

Livie.

Guilt consumed him until he banished it, focusing instead on the anger because it was so much simpler to understand.

He unlocked the door, yanked it open, and the force of the motion made the warm air outside stir Melanie Grandy's hair.

The soft-as-silk strands that he'd been fantasizing about...

"Hello," she said as calmly as you please, with a polite smile to match.

But Livie's grin was much more excited as she said, "Hi, Daddy!" and held up a light blue construction-paper card decorated with feathers and sequins and doodads.

It read "Happy Father's Day!"

The sight almost brought him to his knees, and that made him even angrier.

Still, he gently took the card from Livie, giving her all he could with a half smile that he hoped expressed everything he wasn't able to say out loud, because he knew emotions and investment in them would only backfire someday.

When he didn't say anything else, Livie's smile faltered.

Dammit. Dammit to hell.

But he didn't know how else to handle her.

The helplessness got to him again, and he refocused his frustration on a less vulnerable target.

The nanny.

"I don't remember arranging a trip out here," he said, his teeth clenched because he was trying so hard to rein in his temper.

And his inadequacy as a father.

She didn't back down even an inch. "Father's Day is tomorrow, and we thought we'd wish you a happy one. Livie made you a gift, too."

He could see the nanny squeeze his daughter's hand, urging Livie to present a slim box to him. But the child seemed reluctant to do so after how he'd responded to her card.

He couldn't blame her.

Unable to stand himself, he relented just this once and bent down to Livie, accepting the box, then opening it to find a hand-sewn tie made out of flannel R2-D2 material.

Livie spoke up quietly. "Ms. Grandy helped me."

"It's made out of pajamas she'd grown out of," the nanny said.

God help him. He just stared at the gift, thinking he'd never seen anything so wonderful in his life.

But when he glanced at his daughter, he saw Danielle's smile—the sweet, innocent expression his own wife had worn when they were young.

Back then, it had been so easy to think everything was going to be okay. Yet, then hell had hit, and he'd realized that he should've been so much more careful.

He tried to say something to Livie, failed, then tried again, even though the words scraped on the way out.

"Thank you, sweetheart," he finally managed, touching her cheek.

"You're welcome."

He could see in her eyes that she wanted more than just a thank you, so he awkwardly held open his arms.

She hesitated, but Melanie Grandy helped out by guiding Livie forward.

When his daughter fell against him, he closed his eyes, squeezing her tight. Probably too tight, because she backed away and went back to holding her nanny's hand.

His own daughter, preferring a near stranger.

But that's what *he* was, wasn't he?

If thoughts could make a person bleed, he'd be dying.

"Why don't you go inside, Livie?" he said, his tone measured. "The TV's on."

"TV?" she asked, clearly intrigued about an activity she rarely got to indulge in.

He gestured for her to enter, and after she did, he tried to contain himself in front of his guest.

But there was too much to bottle up: the frustration, the shock of his unwelcome attraction to her, the barely quelled rage of both combined.

He dragged his gaze over to meet hers, and the flash of her blue eyes twisted into him.

His words were low and tight. "You've been making ties and cards instead of concentrating on schoolwork?"

She furrowed her brow. "Mr. Foley, Livie's out of school for the summer."

Mortified by not realizing that, he found a million other reasons to still be put out with the nanny.

"And what did you expect to accomplish by bringing her?"

She smiled oh-so innocuously. "Aside from the fact that you have a new tie, she wanted to wish you a Happy Father's Day. In person. Coming here was a gift to her, too."

Was this woman brazen enough to be pointing out his shortcomings to his face?

No one had dared before—not until *after* they were out of his employment.

Before he could erupt, she added, "We got a late start on driving, mostly because when I called your number, an assistant answered and said you wouldn't be home until after seven."

"Then you'd best get back to Austin, since it's a long ride."

She crossed her arms over her chest, and her agenda hit him square in the middle of the forehead.

"You set this up so I'd feel compelled to have you both overnight," he said. "Is that it?"

"I didn't think it'd be such an imposition. She's your daughter, not a nuisance."

He shook his head, ready to terminate her employment. But…

Dammit all, he didn't have time to go through another nanny search. He'd felt terrible enough after his daughter lost yet another caretaker. Besides, switching nannies so often did nothing for her structure, and Livie seemed to really be getting on well with this one.

But in the back of his thoughts, he wondered if there was another reason he was hesitating to let Melanie Grandy go….

Hell no.

Not even remotely.

Still, as much as he didn't want to admit it, the nanny was right. It was the eve of Father's Day, and what kind of dad would he be to turn out his daughter?

Holding up a finger, he said, "One night, and I'm only agreeing to it because I don't want you driving Livie home in the dark all that way."

"Fair enough."

Maybe he should add more for good measure. "I'm extremely busy, and I don't want either of you underfoot."

Hollow, he thought. It all sounded as hollow as he felt.

"I understand," she said, her smile strained.

Then she turned around to retrieve two suitcases—one scuffed, one pristine.

Melanie Grandy's and Livie's baggage, he thought. But he wasn't about to let it become his own.

After entering, the nanny set the suitcases by the circular staircase, then immediately went to Livie. He took up the luggage, intending to get it out of the way and into the upstairs guest rooms, where he wouldn't have to look at it. His own bedroom was on the ground floor, so it would keep him removed, just the way he wanted it.

Yet, when he came back downstairs to hear his daughter and her nanny laughing about something or another on TV, he found himself walking toward them.

But then he changed direction, moving toward the sanctuary of his study.

But he could still hear them.

And weirdly enough, he kind of liked the sound.

Chapter Five

That night, Melanie couldn't sleep. Not with Zane Foley in the same townhouse.

She lay in the guest bedroom with the sheets tangled around her legs, trying to find a position that worked.

But she was restless, unable to stop thinking about him. And when she paired the stimulation of just being in the same pheromonal range as Zane Foley with the fact that she hadn't been intimate with a man for a long time, this resulted in one wide-awake woman.

For a while, she'd dated a Vegas bartender who nursed ambitions to open his own place, and the relationship had gotten serious enough, so that she'd developed what she'd believed could become serious feelings—at least until he dumped her. Otherwise, over the years, she spent her emotions wisely, knowing that sex didn't feel right unless there were fireworks during kisses, and dreams of being with that man for the rest of her life.

But thoughts of intimacy with a certain nearby boss weren't the only thing keeping her eyes wide-open tonight: it was also hard to wait until morning, when Father's Day would really arrive.

Boy, she hated having to plot and scheme like this, but she'd seen Zane Foley's eyes go gentle when Livie had given him that tie, and it had justified the chance Melanie had taken of losing her job altogether. However, if there'd been any sign of his closing himself entirely to Livie, Melanie would've cut the plan short and taken the little girl back home.

Yet, that hadn't been the case.

It was clear that Zane Foley loved his daughter and he didn't know how to show it. But Melanie wasn't so simple as to think that the situation could be changed in the course of one holiday, because Danielle's death had left too many scars.

As the grandfather clock downstairs struck twelve, Melanie sat up in bed. No use trying to sleep at all. Her mind and emotions were all over the place.

Maybe she could dig through his cupboard to see if he had any soothing tea?

Yeah. Right. Like he'd have tea. Yet, maybe he'd have some milk. Soothing, good old milk worked every time.

Melanie crawled out of her guest bed, then adjusted her above-the-knee, rose-sprigged linen nightgown and headed for the door.

The clock stopped chiming as she crept down the hall past Livie's room, where Melanie peeked in to find the girl sprawled over the mattress, all relaxed knees and elbows.

Sleeping like a rock, as always, Melanie thought.

Warmth lodging in her upper chest, she shut the door and continued on her way. Down the circular stairs, quietly, slowly. Toward the kitchen.

But before she got there, she heard something in the living room. A wall blocked her view, but that didn't stop her from wondering if it was Zane.

Her heart butted against her chest.

Was he up, too?

She peered around the wall, but she must've already made some noise, because she saw him under the light of a dim Tiffany lamp, shoving some object into a small chest, his shoulders hunched.

Heart in her throat, she pulled back around the corner. Maybe she should go back to her bedroom and leave him alone.

Yet that was the last thing she really wanted—her body was very clear about that, too, as it began a sultry melt—hot, liquid, weak.

"Livie?" she heard him ask gruffly from the other room.

Shoot! No escaping now.

"No." Melanie realized she was wearing a nightgown. Conservative by most standards, but…a nightgown. Her breasts pressed against the linen, her nipples hardening at the sound of his voice alone.

But she couldn't hide here like a kid playing games.

Exhaling, she pulled her gown away from her chest, hoping that would do as she walked around the corner.

"It's me," she said. "I was going to the kitchen for something to drink, and I…"

He was staring at her, and it ratcheted her pulse up

to high speed, enough so that she could feel the tiny, propulsive rhythm of it in her neck veins.

Just the two of us, she thought—*after midnight.*

While she'd been behind the wall, he'd clearly placed the wooden chest on a shelf to the side of his massive TV, but her mind wasn't so much on that, or even what might be inside of it.

One hundred percent of her was concentrated on *him.*

As he put his hands on his hips, making the muscles in his arms that much more obvious, making him seem like that noble, Western everyman, she corrected herself.

She was paying one hundred and ten percent attention to him now.

Those shoulders under his T-shirt, she thought. *And that broad chest...*

She bet that he had corrugated abs under his shirt, and she could just about feel them under her fingertips right now—ridges, muscle, flesh.

Hot and smooth...

"Sorry I bothered you," he said in a low voice that shook her, even over the quiet hum of everything else.

"No bother." What to say now? *Hi, yes, I'm sporting a nightgown, but you must admit it's prettier than that business suit you saw me wearing at our interviews.*

"You want me to...?" He motioned toward the kitchen, as if asking if he should fetch her something to drink.

My, how polite they suddenly were with each other.

"No, no, I've got it." She started to leave, thinking she would skip the beverage and just scram.

"Wait."

It was as if he had a pull on her, and she didn't go anywhere.

"Yes?" she said.

During his pause, she looked at him again, to find him running a slow gaze over her. When he saw that she noticed, he crossed his arms over his chest.

She was tingling all over. How could just a look do that?

"About earlier tonight…" he said, business as usual.

Great—did they have to talk about this now? "If you're going to fire me, could you do it tomorrow? I'd like to at least say goodbye to Livie—"

"I'm not going to fire you."

She stared at him as he leveled a firm gaze at her.

"Not yet, anyway," he added.

This man. Dear God, she couldn't make heads or tails of him. Was he angry because she'd brought Livie here, or not? After all, he'd retreated to his study right after they'd settled in; then they'd gone to bed after saying good-night. No more mention of anything. But she figured she would have to pay the piper when the timing was more convenient for him—like in the morning.

Yet, now she couldn't predict him at all.

He was as mysterious as whatever he'd put back in that chest by the TV.

"Then I'm glad you're not going to kick me out of the job," she said, gathering her guts, standing up for herself *and* for Livie. "I think I'm good for your daughter."

"I see that. She looks…happy." The corners of his mouth seemed to rise for a fleeting moment, then stopped as if his mouth was so unused to the expression that it rejected any change.

"She's happi*er*," Melanie said.

She waited for him to react, but he only got that shadowed look in his eyes again, the one she'd seen so many times during her interviews.

What could she do to get rid of it?

"You know what she'd really like?" Melanie asked.

"What?" The shadows were still there.

"If you'd do something with her tomorrow. Even just lunch. Or, if you could spare any more time, she talks about trying some horseback riding. Maybe that'd be an activity you'd both like."

As if he'd been waiting for something to reject, he said, "Livie's grandma died from a riding accident. I'd prefer we didn't go that route."

Talk about stepping on a mine in a field full of them.

"I'm sorry. I didn't know."

She hadn't come across any family history articles that went so deep beyond rumor and innuendo, and that family feud with the McCords.

"I try to keep most things private, if I can manage," he said. "Even from the press."

She thought of Danielle but didn't say anything. She didn't have to, when it looked as if those shadows were about to wrap around him and drag him into the walls.

"Instead of riding," she said, "how about an hour in the neighborhood park with us? I saw one about a block away."

He hesitated, and Melanie stabilized herself.

For Livie.

"She's missed you," she added. "This would mean the world to her."

When he glanced at that chest on the shelf, the tightening of his jaw made her think he was going to refuse the invitation. But then he started to walk away from the object, toward that hallway, as if leaving whatever was in the chest behind.

Or at least putting distance between him and it.

"One o'clock," he said as he continued toward the hallway, but she wasn't even sure she'd heard him right. "I have to go into Dallas before that, but I'll work the rest of the day from here."

"Did you say—?"

He paused, staring at the ground. "One o'clock."

Melanie could've shot through the roof. "Perfect. I'll pack a lunch, so don't worry about eating."

"You'll find the cupboards pretty empty around here," he said, meandering away again, barely looking at her. "Maybe I should leave money, if you don't mind stopping at the market."

"I don't mind. I don't mind at all."

She was smiling to beat the band, and he lifted his head, his gaze coming to rest on her mouth.

Then his eyes met hers again, thrashing her with a slam of that awareness she'd been trying so hard to dodge.

But dodge she did, nodding at him and then leaving before he could, walking past the kitchen and back to her bedroom, where she intended to shut the door nice and tight behind her until tomorrow.

He'd meant to get to the park for their Father's Day date.

He really had.

But Zane had found some accounting errors while reviewing a monthly report he was catching up on, and by the time he'd finished smoothing out the near damage, he'd looked at his watch to see that it was past three o'clock.

Three o'damned clock.

How had that happened?

He wanted to blame anyone but himself: why hadn't Melanie Grandy called him when he hadn't shown up at the park?

Yet, he figured the nanny had probably given up on him and hadn't bothered to even pick up the phone, because he had only confirmed that he was the worst dad in existence.

As his hand fell to his side, he wondered how Livie had taken his absence, but the answer wasn't hard to come by. She'd had plenty of practice at dealing with disappointment in him before, and he imagined that her opinion hadn't changed today.

And there it was—the exact reason he'd excused himself from bringing her up in the first place.

He called Monty to pick him up. When Monty arrived he didn't make any comments. Then again, unlike Melanie Grandy, the driver knew it wasn't his place to do so.

No, his employee only handed him a box after Zane had settled in the town car's backseat.

"What's this?" he asked Monty.

The driver pulled the vehicle away from the valet station in the office building's parking structure. "Ms. Grandy sent it for you. She said she figured you might need it."

Steam fogged over him, an equal mix of disliking the position the nanny had put him in and…

God. He remembered last night, when she'd been standing there in her nightie. Even though the sleepwear had been modest, it had shown more leg than he'd ever seen of her.

Long, lean leg. And he'd wanted to go to Melanie Grandy, bend down to curl his fingers around her ankle, then start from there on up, skimming over her toned calf, the soft, damp back of her knee, higher....

But he'd barred himself from doing any of it, mostly because of what he'd stowed in the chest just before he'd heard her moving around while going to the kitchen.

Danielle's ashes in an urn.

He supposed that the approaching anniversary of his first wife's suicide had urged him to take out her remains. But then again, he often contemplated her—the memories of what he could've done. The penance for not being able to stop her...

In any case, he'd been in a brooding mood, and the nanny had broken it open for a short time before he'd told himself to get out of the room, to resist a situation he just couldn't handle.

Now he looked at the box she had sent for him to open, and like that chest, he wished he could just keep it closed.

But since he had a feeling about what was inside, he took off the lid.

The R2-D2 tie.

He tossed the box lid to the seat. *Damn that woman.* She'd probably found it where he'd placed it on the kitchen counter last night.

Legs or not, she was making his life hell.

Zane caught Monty's gaze in the rearview mirror just before the driver looked away.

The rest of the ride was like a session in a torture chamber, with the world's most invisible, cutting, self-inflicted weapons. Zane went back and forth between cursing himself for blowing it with Livie today and thinking that he should just send her back home, until Monty pulled up to his townhouse, with its luxurious, sleek façade that didn't offer even a hint of the darkness inside.

They would be waiting in there for him: Livie, with those eyes that slayed Zane every time he saw them. And Melanie Grandy—who had quite a way of killing him softly, too.

Dammit.

He took off his Armani tie and put on the R2-D2 one, feeling like an ass, but not just because he was wearing a cartoon character on his chest.

Then Zane got out of the car, held up a hand to thank Monty and watched his driver pull away in a stream of red taillights.

He ran a hand through his hair, took a deep breath and entered his home, thinking that he'd never been so cautious about coming into his own doggone place before the nanny had arrived.

Standing in the foyer, he set down his briefcase, listening for any signs of life. No TV. No clanging around in the kitchen.

He went back outside to check the stand-alone garage, to see if Melanie's designated Tall Oaks Volvo was still there where he'd parked it for her, last night before retiring.

Present and accounted for.

When he wandered back inside, ready to capitulate

and call her cell phone, he heard something floating down from the stairway.

Laughter.

The roof terrace, he thought, his veins going taut as he took in the sound. It rang through him, and for a forbidden moment, he allowed it to settle.

What would it be like to have a house that sounded like this all the time?

Then reality returned. He had to go up to the roof, and the minute they saw him the laughter would stop.

Okay, you're a man, he told himself. *Face the consequences.*

He straightened the R2-D2 tie and climbed the stairs, following the laughter—actually drawn to it, as he'd been last night, when it had filled this house.

When it had even filled something else that he wasn't sure he could define.

Arriving at the roof, he found them sitting in lounge chairs that faced the Dallas skyline. The river sparkled in the late afternoon sunshine. They'd turned on the small rock waterfall near the hot tub, and the splash of it mingled with Melanie's voice as she told Livie some story about a time she'd gone waterskiing.

"I never drank so much water as I did that day on the lake," she said at the end of her tale. "I had a stomachache for hours afterward."

Livie was giggling and sipping from a straw in a glass that looked to be full of milk. Her gaze was fixed on her nanny, as if she were the most incredible thing to drop from the sky since stardust.

As Zane watched them, *his* stomach ached with something sharp and empty stabbing it.

When was the last time Livie had looked at him that way?

Last night, he thought. And he hadn't returned the affection.

Worst father ever, he thought again, taking no pride in this accomplishment.

He felt like such a nothing, all he wanted to do was change the perception—even if it were just for the final hours of Father's Day.

He cleared his throat and both females looked back, Livie watching him, her gaze wounded.

And Melanie?

She was watching him, too, but she looked about ready to throttle him. Yet, how could he be offended when she was angry for the sake of his daughter?

"I apologize," he said, "for missing our date. I lost track of time."

The excuse didn't hold any water at all. In fact, with the way the nanny was visually shooting bullets at him, his words seemed punctured.

He continued. "Livie, I know how much you wanted me there."

Her gaze had come to rest on his tie. That darn R2-D2-riddled tie.

And lo and behold, she smiled. An injured smile, to be sure, but at least he'd done something right today.

Thanks to Melanie, he reluctantly admitted to himself.

The nanny saw the tie, too, but that didn't change her expression. "We understand. Work's important."

Yes, it is, he wanted to say, but he didn't. It didn't seem so true right now.

They were both still sitting in their lounge chairs,

their bodies slanted toward the skyline, as if they knew better than to commit to turning all the way toward him.

"We had fun, Daddy," Livie said. "Ms. Grandy made peanut butter and jelly starfish sandwiches. And we shared oranges with Sheree and Tammy."

Zane almost flinched. Even after what he'd done, his daughter was still talking to him as if he hadn't screwed up?

"Sheree and Tammy are neighbor girls," the nanny said, grinning at Livie. "Their mom told me that they're six and seven years old, almost twins with Livie."

"And they have American Girl dolls, too!" his daughter added.

They laughed again, and Zane wished he could join in.

But he could—couldn't he?

Even though he wondered, he knew that he would have to make it up to Livie somehow, because having her go back to Austin just after he'd pulled the rug out from under her was unthinkable.

Distance was fine, he told himself. It was subtle. But this afternoon he'd done something cruel—and he even wondered if he'd done it subconsciously, because he knew that going to the park would lead to daytrips and that would lead to week-long trips, and...

He stopped himself, vowing to give them a great night instead. Afterward, they could all go back to where they belonged, feeling the better for it.

"We're going to do something else right now," he said. "So why don't you get yourselves up so we can go?"

Now Livie swung her legs to the side of her chair, and Zane smiled.

"Where're we going, Daddy?"

"To a place that'll make you real happy. Trust me on that."

As his daughter clapped her hands, he couldn't help but notice that Melanie wasn't applauding at all.

Melanie had always told herself that she couldn't be bought off, but as she stood in front of the mirror of the personal shopper's boutique in Westenra's, a high-class department store in the swanky Garden Faire Mall, she wasn't so sure.

"Gorgeous," said the sales associate as she adjusted the skirt of the sea-blue cocktail dress that Melanie was trying on. "It compliments your eyes, hair and skin tone. You look like a movie star!"

In back of Melanie, Livie glanced up from her picture book from where she was sitting on the leather sofa. Zane had already bought her a bunch of stuff at a bookstore.

"Oh, Ms. Grandy," Livie said. "You're bea-u-ti-ful."

Melanie smiled at her while avoiding looking at Zane, who was sitting right next to his daughter.

"We'll take this last dress, too," he said.

Ecstatic at the commission she'd rung up, the personal shopper scooped up the six other outfits her client had tried on and flitted off, leaving Melanie alone in the mirror.

She tried not to give in to the lure of all this, but at the sight of herself she went a little dreamy. She looked like she'd found a glass slipper, but like Cinderella at the stroke of midnight, she knew this was only transient.

Still…

Zane Foley seemed to catch her doubt. "That dress is all yours, if you want, just like the other outfits you've tried on."

Yes, she wanted. And…*darn him, he knew*. She could tell from the contented way he was sitting there, taking it all in, as if this made up for his ditching Livie this afternoon.

Melanie ran her hand over the silk of the dress's haltered neckline. It wasn't that she didn't believe he'd lost track of time at the office. Oh, yes, she *truly* had faith in that. And that was the problem.

He would always lose track at the expense of Livie unless something was done about it.

Turning around, she faced him, and once again she was thrown off by his mere presence. The dark hair that seemed slightly ruffled from a long day. The hazel eyes that were even now stroking over her and making her get butterflies in her tummy.

And the R2-D2 tie.

He was still wearing it, and she couldn't help but appreciate that, even if she'd pushed it on him.

"Mr. Foley, I don't think—"

"Stop with the polite refusals," he said. "As Livie's nanny, you need to look the part."

"You already told me that."

She shot him a glance that said the rest: *and this has no connection to how you win over people? With how you buy Livie all those dolls instead of showing up to be with her every once in a while?*

She couldn't say it out loud. Not with Livie here, even if the child had gone back to reading her books.

"Besides," Melanie continued, "I'm guessing that Livie and I probably won't be attending many cocktail parties together."

He leaned forward, and as those butterflies painted the lining of her belly with flutters, she almost touched her stomach, calming them.

Chasing them away.

"Okay, maybe I'm aiming for more than appearances," he said quietly.

He left it at that.

But what did he mean? Was he using these dresses as a means to thank her for what she'd done for Father's Day?

She searched his gaze for more of a hint, and when she didn't find any, she looked further for a shade of dishonesty.

None of that either, but she had to turn back to the mirror, because he made her feel like a hypocrite.

Talk about dishonesty.

She ran a hand down the dress. Classy—so unlike the former showgirl or lower-class daughter whose family skimmed the poverty line.

But even in this dress, the old days still seemed to cling to Melanie, refusing to let go, no matter how hard she was trying.

The secret of her past levered down on her as, in the mirror, she saw Zane Foley come to a stand. He whispered something to Livie, and the girl sprang to her feet, clutching her books.

"We'll be back soon," he said as he began walking away with his daughter.

Melanie gave him a quizzical look in the mirror.

He smiled, and it ripped through her, upending every cell in its wake.

"We're headed for the pièce de résistance," he said, glancing down at Livie, who gazed back at him adoringly. "There's a massive Toys 'R' Us store that rivals the one in Times Square, and I thought Livie might have some fun there."

"But…" Melanie began.

By now, his daughter was tugging him away, and he actually seemed amused by that.

"Don't worry," he said. "You'll be busy here."

As Livie pulled him out of the boutique, the personal shopper returned, seeming so chipper that it almost scared Melanie.

"Are you ready?" the woman asked.

Melanie wasn't sure if she liked this or not. "For what?"

The other woman laughed, almost sounding like one of those twittering birds who'd created Cinderella's dress in the Disney movie.

"You've got a makeover waiting for you, ma'am."

Melanie's pulse leaped before she tamed it.

A…makeover?

She glanced in the mirror again, and instead of seeing the present, she thought back to a girl who used to wear drab dresses, the young woman who'd worked hard to get where she was today.

A makeover.

How could she refuse?

Chapter Six

When Melanie called Zane's cell to tell him that her makeover appointment was done, he made sure Monty had all the toys Livie had purchased in hand.

Then, since Livie begged to go with Monty to the parked car where she could begin to tear into her new toys, Zane let her escape the tedium of the department store and headed there alone so he could settle the bill while their packages were carried to the valet station.

Hopefully, he thought after rapidly taking care of money matters and boarding the Up escalator, *this shopping trip and makeover would improve Melanie's mood.* If so, he would look forward to getting back to the townhouse with a more chipper nanny, then prepare to say goodbye to her and his daughter in the morning.

A niggle got to him, but he didn't pay any mind to it.

Yup, they'd be gone tomorrow, and life would go back to normal.

He came to the personal shopper's boutique, where Melanie had evidently gone to put on one of her new outfits with the sales associate's encouragement. When he got there, a few women were in front of the mirror, flittering about and doing what women often did over new clothes.

Zane had just opened his mouth to ask if his employee was set to leave when the women parted to reveal the nanny in the midst of them.

The words lodged in his chest, then began pumping like a conflicting heartbeat.

Melanie?

Her blond hair was swept back into a graceful chignon, which complemented the slim lines of a short jacket and long cigarette skirt worthy of Jackie O. Her makeup was elegant, bringing out the breathtaking blue of her eyes and the lovely heart shape of her face.

She fit the role of a princess, not a nanny, and for a taboo instant, he envisioned her on his arm at a charity event, shining like the brightest of stars.

Seconds must've passed. Maybe even minutes. And during each escalating heartbeat, he kept himself from saying something he would regret to this new woman, even if, under the makeup and clothing, she was still the same lady who'd hooked his attention that first day.

She just had an extra sparkle in her eyes, and that was what took his breath away.

She was staring right back at him with something that resembled hope as she folded her hands in front of her—a nervous gesture he was just starting to recognize.

Melanie, he thought. Not "the nanny."

Not now.

"You…" He trailed off.

Surely he could find a comment somewhere in his brain. Any comment. Zane Foley was the last man on earth who should've been searching for words.

A couple of the sales associates laughed softly, and heat crept up Zane's neck.

He pushed his hands into his suit pockets as he addressed his employee. "Looks as if you're ready."

His back-to-business tone seemed to bring Melanie—no, it *had* to remain "the nanny"—back to reality, too. But as she nodded at him, then thanked the women around her, he could tell that she'd lost the glimmer that had made her more beautiful than ever, and he hated that he'd done this to her.

But what was new?

He turned to leave, getting the hell out of there, and she caught up just as they were crossing the marble floors and coming to the baby grand piano near the escalators. The musician was playing that song from *Casablanca*.

He hoped she didn't notice.

"But," she said, "I didn't tip them yet."

"It's taken care of."

Without looking at her, he motioned for her to climb aboard the Down escalator before him.

Cold, he thought. Didn't he have it within himself to be more than that?

She got on the conveyance, turning around to face him while holding the moving handrail. "But shouldn't I—?"

"It was my treat. Besides, I know the owners and my credit's good with them."

"Oh." She patted the side of her hairdo, as if not knowing what else to do. "Of course you know them. You probably know every top tax-bracket entrepreneur in the country."

"I know them because I helped develop this center, among others that Westenra's also uses."

At the news, she went silent, as if he'd intentionally reminded her of his station in life and hers—and the chasm between them.

But he hadn't meant to.

Even so, the sudden space between them bothered Zane. God knew why, because it wasn't as if they would ever be close.

They got off the escalator and moved through the men's shoe department toward the exit where Monty would be waiting. Zane couldn't help noticing that the suit-and-tie salesmen were watching Melanie Grandy, and he wanted to take her arm and link it through his in a show of…

He stopped himself before he used the word *"possession."*

Not him. Not for her.

Nevertheless, he didn't appreciate the staring, so he shot the men subtle *back-off* looks, while approaching the doors to the valet and pickup area.

When they got out there, Monty hadn't yet arrived, and Zane guessed it was because Livie was probably going through her new purchases and making it nearly impossible for the softhearted driver to get the packages in the trunk.

He would give them three more minutes before calling.

As they waited, a couple of valets were giving Melanie the eye, just as the guys inside had been doing. With one extra long look at them, Zane persuaded the boys to go back to being valets instead of slobbering dogs.

Melanie didn't seem to notice any of it. She stood there, face forward, the silence deafening.

Luckily, she broke it.

"And how did Toys 'R' Us go with Livie?" she asked.

In spite of himself, a smile captured his mouth, and when it stayed, it surprised him a little. "She was really excited. They had a Ferris wheel in the middle of the store. We went on that thing three times."

"Good." A smile broke out over her face, too.

My, wasn't she content about her schemes to get father and daughter together?

Her happiness would end soon enough when she realized that tonight wasn't going anywhere beyond this.

He shifted under the weight of the thought—and under the heft of the tension that remained between them.

But she still seemed to be in a positive mood. She even laughed a bit, yet it sounded more self-aware than anything.

"What is it?" he asked.

She gestured to her dress, her face and hair. "This whole night. Me getting made over at your pleasure."

He almost coughed.

She caught herself. "That's not exactly what I meant." Sighing, she shook her head. "I don't know. Maybe it has something to do with… Well, I heard that you make sure all the Foley nannies have looked good to one extent or another."

What was this about? "Meaning…?" he asked.

"Rumor has it that in the past most nannies were easy on the eye."

That heat began its slow crawl up his skin again, from his neck to his face. "And who told you this?"

"You're not confirming or denying my comment."

He knew she wouldn't give up her source, and even though that got to him, he also had to respect her loyalty. It was a decent quality for anyone to have. Besides, if he really cared about the mild gossip that much, he could narrow it down to one of a few other employees with whom she had regular contact.

"Pretty has nothing to do with it," he muttered. "It's never been a job requirement."

And that was the truth. Even now, he couldn't say if the other nannies had been good looking or not. All he knew was that Melanie Grandy affected him like none of the others had, and it didn't sit well.

"If appearances don't matter," she said, "then why give me a makeover, even as a thank you?"

She'd turned to him in her direct manner. He faced her, too, and out of habit, he actually thought he might be able to make her look away if he stayed quiet long enough.

Yet she stood her ground, and he was the one at the disadvantage, overtaken by the depth and color of her eyes. There was a vivid strength in her gaze, like the undertow of the sea, and he'd noticed it even prior to the makeup bringing it out.

Before he knew what he was doing, he raised his hand and rested it on her cheek, where there had always been a natural blush, even without the aid of all these cosmetics.

Then, realizing what had just happened, he rubbed his thumb over the makeup as if to take some of it off.

"You don't need all this," he said.

And it was true. Achingly true.

Her eyes had gone wide. He'd shocked her, he knew, and he wondered if it was because of his brash move or because she could feel the same current that sizzled when his skin met hers.

He could see her throat working as she swallowed, and his breathing picked up.

What if he moved his fingertips down over her jaw, to her neck, where he could brush over the delicate, smooth lines? What would she do then?

What would *he* do after that?

Nothing around them stirred, the air seeming to hover in place, locking everything in to this one moment, this one touch. Locking them into each other's gazes, where he could see a different world, a livelier one, hued with the laughter he'd heard on the roof of his townhouse a few hours ago.

But then he remembered how he'd put an end to the gaiety, just because he was Zane Foley—bad husband, bad father.

He'd promised he wouldn't add any more "bad"s to his list.

Slowly, he removed his hand from her face and turned away, going for his cell phone to see where in tarnation Monty was.

As he accessed speed dial, he could feel Melanie beside him, awkward in the aftermath. And he hated himself for doing that to her—putting this otherwise self-assured woman in a place where she had no firm footing.

That's right, he thought, *once again Zane Foley's made a mess of things.*

But he was going to make sure it didn't happen again.

Ever.

Melanie arose early the next morning, getting out of bed at the crack of dawn.

Since sleep hadn't come easy—*once again*—she thought she might as well make the most of her last morning here. So she showered and threw on a sundress before going down to the kitchen, where she'd stored all the food she'd purchased from the market yesterday, including the makings of a meal that had been a hit with kids in the past—fluffy biscuit sandwiches teeming with egg, bacon and cheese. Hearty and filling.

As the biscuits baked in the oven, she began whisking the eggs, milk, garlic salt and pepper together, but all the while she kept looking toward the hallway that led to Zane's study and bedroom.

Couldn't she stop thinking of how he'd touched her last night? How her heart had nearly exploded at the feel of his hand on her cheek?

She stopped taking her frustration out on the eggs and fanned a hand in front of her face. *Whoo.* Maybe it was the heat of the oven, combined with the vulnerability of her skin after last night's makeover facial.

Or maybe it was because Zane Foley had a power over her that no man had ever come close to.

Either way, he'd pulled away from her in the end, sending her belly sinking. Because…seriously?

She and Zane Foley—the *billionaire?*

Chuffing, she told herself that he'd just been wiping makeup off her face, and that was that. He was a control freak, and that obviously extended to making sure his nannies were just the way he wanted to see them, if anyone should ever get a gander.

But…

She closed her eyes. How about the desire she'd seen in his gaze? At least, that's what she thought it'd been when it'd just about buckled her knees.

She opened her eyes again, wishing she could figure him all the way out.

Her gaze wandered to the living room, where he'd been looking at something in that chest the other night.

What if she took a peek, just in case it offered an answer?

Any answer.

Glancing around at the still house, with its blur of stained glass muting the morning, she put down the egg bowl before second guessing herself, then went to the living room, heading straight for the TV and the chest sitting on the shelves right beside it.

All while, she chided herself. *Mel, think about what you're doing.*

But if this helped her to understand him, it couldn't hurt, right?

She unlatched the chest—there was no lock, thank goodness—then eased it open to get a glimpse.

What she found made her close it and put it back the way she'd found it, her heartbeat strangled.

An urn.

Danielle's ashes?

Feeling as if she'd intruded into someone's most private secrets, Melanie retreated back to the kitchen to finish making breakfast.

She should've known that was what Zane had been hunched over the other night. If they *were* Danielle's ashes—and Melanie would bet on the truth of that—he kept his deceased wife close. Physically close, not just mentally or emotionally. Six years, and he hadn't let her go for even a few yards.

No wonder he had that darkness in his eyes: because the shadow still resided in his house.

She stared at the mess on the counter, the bowls and ingredients fuzzing before her. If she'd entertained any thoughts of Zane's interest in her before, they were beaten down now. After all, how could she compete with a woman who would always be here?

And just who had this woman been, to have such a hold on him?

She heard a door opening upstairs, then footsteps treading down the steps. When Livie came around the corner, her hair tousled from sleep, Melanie motioned her over for a good-morning hug.

No one should have to compete with a ghost, Melanie thought as the little girl smiled and rubbed her eyes, coming to her nanny. Not Livie and not…

Well, not anyone else.

She heard another person enter the kitchen from the opposite direction, and her pulse kicked.

Then his voice.

"I thought I smelled something good," he said as Melanie and Livie parted.

His daughter got that shy grin on her face, as if she were wondering whether or not to go to her daddy. But out of the corner of Melanie's eye, she saw him bend down—an invitation for the child to come on over.

It was an improvement, she thought, taking the biscuits out of the oven.

The embrace between father and daughter was tentative, but it was a start. And as he finished hugging her, keeping a light hold on her pajamas as she drew away, Melanie became acutely aware that he was in a pair of sweats and a T-shirt, just like the other night.

All that was missing was her nightgown and the tick of a clock while they looked at each other from across the living room.

"Morning," he said.

"Morning." She sent a quick glance of acknowledgement over her shoulder, intending to get right to work again.

But when Livie came back over to Melanie and leaned her sleepy head against her leg, Nanny Workhorse lost direction.

And it only got worse when Zane's gaze fell on her and Livie, a look of such longing about him that, for a brief moment, it made her want to cry.

Such a strong, solid man, she thought, and to see a crack in his defenses made her want to reach out.

Made her want to make him happy.

"Hey, Livie," she said, resting a hand on the child's head. "Breakfast is coming right up. Maybe you and Daddy can sit at the table and start drinking your orange juice together. He'll have to get to work soon."

Zane's eyes met hers, and along with the zing of electricity that always came with it, she also noticed a bared gratefulness.

She grinned and nodded toward a cabinet that she knew contained the glasses. He understood, going to it, getting three out.

Three, not just two.

But the plan was to get *them* together, and the last thing Melanie wanted to do was act as the go-between she'd been for the last couple of days. They should relate to each other without her around, just as they had at the toy store last night.

"Mr. Foley," she said, "I need to eat on the fly while I pack up for Livie and myself."

She could feel Livie grip her leg, but Melanie stroked the girl's hair, soothing her. They would have to leave sooner or later.

"I see," he said. Then he set the glasses on the counter.

Livie spoke up. "We can't stay another day? Not even so we can listen to the band in the park tonight in the hot tub?"

Livie and Melanie had found fliers advertising a family group playing in the nearby park that night during a farmer's market. And since Zane's townhouse was so close, they would probably be able to hear its amplified sound from his roof, where the little girl had been begging Melanie to try the spa.

He'd braced his hands on the counter, and Melanie could tell he was fighting with himself.

Help him, she thought.

"We don't have any pressing engagements in Austin," she said, giving him an opening. "And the maintenance crew can do work inside the house while we're not around."

Finally, he slid her one of those looks—pulled apart by two different, warring sides.

The dad versus the haunted man.

Melanie silently tried to lend him encouragement. *Please,* she thought. *Do it for Livie.*

He opened the fridge, took out the juice, then began to pour. "All right. You can stay another night then. But I've got work."

Success!

"Yes, you do," Melanie said as Livie hugged her nanny's leg.

Melanie squeezed the little girl's shoulder, smiling down at her. Because after tonight, when they went back to Austin, smiles would probably come few and far between.

Melanie had spent the day seeing that Livie kept to her schedule while her dad was at the office.

After a morning full of dance and drawing, they'd picnicked in the park again, watching tonight's event being set up. Then they'd gone to a nearby café, where Livie had enjoyed the "adult experience" of drinking tea, then climbing on one of the rented computers to play some phonics games that Melanie had read about in a child-care magazine.

As her charge was doing her thing, Melanie went on her own computer, making sure Livie didn't see the subject of her Internet search.

Danielle Foley.

However, about an hour later, Melanie didn't know a whole lot more than she'd started with. It seemed that Danielle had shunned the press, just as her husband did. But Melanie *had* been able to uncover a few links to high school reunion sites, and there she'd been able to get a few more tidbits about the woman who still seemed to be such a presence in the Foley lives.

Although any hints about Danielle's death had been vague, Melanie had seen a few pictures of someone who resembled Livie so much that it was eerie: the same dark eyes and hair, the same gentle expressions of disappointment floating over every feature.

Melanie had also pulled up some articles about bipolar disorder, and by the time she was done, Livie was ready to go.

Doing her best to act as if the research hadn't bothered her, Melanie asked Livie to help her put together a dinner of beef tostadas and fruit salad.

But it was hard to keep her mind off Danielle, especially with Livie—her miniature double—right here. Melanie could see how the resemblance to her mom might affect Zane, could see that he must've been crushed by Danielle's passing to still keep her so close.

Again, she thought that his grief must be so strong that he chose to avoid his daughter.

A dull throb beat through her chest, but she ignored it until Zane came home, joining them on the roof terrace while the band kicked into gear at the nearby park, lending the warm air graceful notes.

As the group played "Waltzing Matilda," Melanie laid out Zane's and Livie's meals, then started back to the kitchen to eat hers while the other two did more bonding. She would go up there again soon, so Zane could retreat to his study and she could supervise Livie in the hot tub.

"Hey," Zane said from his seat at the glass-topped table, as she made her way through the sliding doors. "Where're you going?"

She smiled. "You two enjoy the music. I've got things to—"

Now Livie turned her big eyes on her nanny.

Both of them were watching Melanie. They seemed so forlorn, even with their meals sitting there in front of them. Despite that food on the table, the scene somehow looked empty.

Zane stood, pulling out a chair. "We'd enjoy your company."

As he waited, she could see herself with them, a part of the family, and she only wished it could be real.

"Ms. Grandy?" Zane asked, his voice softly raking over her skin, destroying every "but" she could think of.

"All right," she said, grinning at Livie. "Just let me get my plate."

She left, catching father and daughter as they traded smiles.

Had they talked about how she had been missing during breakfast? *Nah,* she thought, gathering her stuff and climbing the stairs again. Although maybe their nanny was the only subject they had in common right now.

The very idea made her sad, so after she joined them, she made a real effort to introduce subjects that would help them to connect: Livie's uncles, her schoolwork, her favorite things about both Austin and Dallas.

Zane listened intently to all of it, even smiling sometimes at the cuteness that was Livie. And the little girl ate that right up.

By the end of the meal, Melanie thought it was time well spent—a great springboard for their relationship.

But then it happened.

"I love Mexican food," Livie said, nearing the last of her tostada. "You make it yummy, Ms. Grandy."

"Thank you."

She could feel Zane's gaze on her again, and goose bumps shivered over her. Actually, she'd felt his attention throughout dinner, but she couldn't stop from picturing how he'd probably once looked at Danielle, too, back when they had first fallen in love.

Yet Melanie kept telling herself that the way he felt about his wife was none of a nanny's business, even if she found herself wishing that it were.

Livie was still talking. "Cook says that Mommy liked this kind of food." She paused. "Didn't she, Daddy?"

It was as if a cold wind had come off the river and frozen Zane in his seat. After a second that lasted way too long, he wiped his mouth with his napkin. The gesture was controlled, so very careful.

Then he said, "Yes, she did, Livie."

But he changed the subject back to his daughter's schooling so quickly that Melanie almost got whiplash. Then, after finishing the rest of his food, he excused himself, heading for the sliding-glass door.

Just as Melanie was about to despair, he seemed to reconsider, coming over to touch Livie's shoulder, her cheek.

Then, averting his gaze, he left.

Melanie gauged Livie's reaction, but the child was quietly finishing her tostada without as much as a second glance to where her father had deserted her yet again.

Without thinking, Melanie wrapped an arm around her and kissed her forehead.

Livie just kept eating, not even acknowledging her nanny.

Yet Melanie still hugged the girl, unwilling to let go.

One step forward, two steps back, she thought.

And, at this moment, she couldn't imagine how it would ever be any different with Zane Foley.

Chapter Seven

The sunlight descended through the windows of Zane's study, casting stained-glass reflections as he sat in his desk chair.

He told himself to go back to the roof, to tell Livie not only that her mom had loved Mexican food, but that she had collected porcelain figurines that she'd talked about giving their daughter someday. He wanted to relate how her mother had also loved a nice, old-fashioned scary movie, like those you would've gone to at a drive-in. He wanted to let Livie know that, on some afternoons, Danielle had ridden her bike around the Dallas estate they used to live on before Zane had sold the place to move here, by himself.

And on the days that the sun would shine over the Texas landscape, as well as within Danielle, she'd driven that bike to a park—her favorite—where she would sit on a tiny bridge while a stream burbled just underneath her dangling feet.

But those had been on her good days.

Sometimes Zane couldn't separate the positive stories from the negative, because, looking back, it all seemed to fade together—good days into bad—like a blurred canvas of memory.

He leaned forward in his chair, digging his fingers through his hair. *Damn you, Danielle,* he thought. *Damn you for leaving her...me...alone to live this way.*

Glancing up, he saw the portrait of Livie.

His daughter was just upstairs, and so was Melanie— a woman whose smiles came so easily, without any threat of a cost to them later.

Or that's how it seemed, anyway.

So it was tempting, very damned tempting, to go back up there, because there were times when Melanie almost made him forget. Maybe not entirely, but she did cause him to think that he could learn to live beyond the past.

At least that much had been true for the last couple of days, when he'd caught himself thinking that there might be a little light ahead.

Yet, he also knew other things were ahead of him, too—namely the anniversary of Danielle's death.

Just over one week away.

The thought pinned him to his chair, and he didn't go back upstairs. Instead, he awakened his computer and sought work, a refuge.

His eternal saving grace.

Since Zane had retired to that study of his, Melanie didn't expect to see him for the rest of the night. So after dinner, she and Livie got into the bathing suits they'd purchased in a superstore during their market run yesterday, then eased into the hot tub.

As always, Livie seemed to leave her father behind and, bit by bit, get into the moment. Melanie made it easier for her by initiating a skirmish with bottled bubbles they'd also purchased, blowing the balls of soap at each other through the wands. It got Livie to giggling, until they both settled down to listen to the last of the music from the band in the park, the tunes floating away into the night.

Deciding they'd had enough for the time being, Melanie got Livvie out of the tub and ready for bed, tucking the girl in before reading her a story about The Three Little Pigs.

Halfway through, she heard Livie's breathing even out, and Melanie closed the book, glancing beside her to where the child lay, her eyes closed, her lashes long and angelic.

Dreamland, she thought, grateful that Livie's tendency to sleep deeply provided her a haven of sorts. The hot tub had probably even relaxed her further.

Melanie rested her hand on her charge's arm, closing her eyes, too, smiling. She was so lucky to be here.

Best job in the world.

She must've floated off, because after she opened her eyes, kissed Livie's cheek, shut off the light, then went to her own room, Melanie's travel clock read about an hour later than when she'd put Livie to bed.

Still, it was pretty early yet, and she thought it might be nice to stay up, maybe watch some TV downstairs, then crawl into bed.

But was Zane in his study? Would she run into him down there?

Thinking of her boss brought the end of dinner rushing back. Livie had only asked a simple question about Danielle, and Zane had withdrawn into himself yet again. Although he'd made progress with his daughter recently, he'd sure hit a wall tonight. And when Melanie thought of how Livie had gotten quiet right after he left, frustration burned deep inside again.

This had to end, Melanie thought, and if there was a chance that she could get Zane Foley to come around even a little more before they left for Austin tomorrow, she should take it.

Dedicated to what she would do now instead of watching TV, she decided that she would make *sure* she ran into him downstairs.

She was wearing one of her modest nightgowns, but among the new outfits Zane had purchased for her she'd found a robe that she hadn't tried on at the department store. He must've requested one from the personal shopper on the sly. Melanie wondered if he'd done so because he took offense to her scampering around in her nightgown.

But she could've sworn that offense was not what she had seen on his face that night when he had lavished a hot, long look over her body, making her tremble.

She slipped into the white silk, tying the sash around her waist, pausing at the elegant feel of the material.

So tasteful, she thought. This wasn't the type of robe girls like Melanie Grandy wore. Sure, she'd fit well enough with those sequins and feathers on that Vegas stage, but this was the real thing, not an act.

Then it struck her that, by keeping her past from

everyone, her whole life was an act, and she pulled the robe closer around her, heading for her boss's study to complete her mission as Livie's advocate.

She would talk to him and get out of his hair. In and out.

When she saw that his light was on behind the door, she ventured a knock.

After a moment, she heard him.

"Yes?"

"It's me. May I come in?"

A hesitation.

Heck, she could almost imagine him cursing at having to deal with her, because he had to know what this was about.

"Door's unlocked," he finally said.

Heart thudding—it always did that Pavlovian trick when she heard Zane Foley—she opened the door to find him facing toward her at his desk, his computer on, the screen tilted toward the doorway enough to show a picture of the Santa Magdalena Diamond. He kept his eyes on it.

What do you know, she thought, *he's working.*

She shut the door behind her and he looked up, sitting straight, his jaw tensing.

The nightgown, she thought. *The robe.*

She pulled the silk robe even tighter around her, but the whisper of it against her skin only made her realize that the hairs on her arms were standing at attention.

"I'm sorry for bothering you," she said, "but I thought we might have a word, since Livie's down for the count."

He tore his gaze away from her, and she actually reveled in the effort it seemed to take.

But she shouldn't be reveling with him.

"I can guess what this is about," he said, pressing a button on his keyboard, shutting down the machine.

"Then it's no surprise I'm here."

"Ms. Grandy," he said, finally glancing at her again, but this time he was all coolness. "I'm never surprised when you approach me on Livie's behalf. But you don't seem to remember something I told you during our second interview."

"I remember. You told me advice wasn't appreciated."

"So why do I have the feeling you're about to give me some anyway?"

She forgot about the robe and approached his desk. "Do you realize what it's like to sit by and watch her suffer? If I *didn't* say anything, I'd never forgive myself. I'm only too glad to overstep my bounds."

He rose from his chair, and she couldn't help but think of a pillar of fire. His eyes certainly had a flare to them.

She pressed on. "Is it *that* painful for you to give Livie even some indication of what her mother was like? She has no idea, and more than anything, she wants to know. A child needs a mom, whether or not she's actually there."

"That'll be enough."

"No, this isn't *nearly* enough." Her emotions were spilling out of her; she'd held on to them so tightly that she couldn't stop them now that she'd uncorked herself. "Livie's got a heart of gold, but she's buried it so deep that I wonder how long it'll be before she can't find it altogether. People have a tendency to shove their feelings away when they're rejected over and over again, and one day, you're going to find that's what happened to your daughter." She took a deep breath, exhaled. "If you're around to see it."

"I will be ar—" He cut himself off, and she wasn't sure if it was because he didn't deign to have this conversation or if he didn't know how to respond.

He hid whatever it was well, but then again, he always did.

She started to talk again, but he drilled her with a glare while beginning to come around the desk with such a deliberate pace that her adrenaline raced through her, prodding her to back away, to run.

But she stayed, even if she was getting pummeled by her heartbeat.

"I've seen how much you love Livie," she said, her voice sounding tangled. She tried to recover. "So I just can't understand why you constantly push her back. Why you push—"

Pressing her lips together, she saved herself just before she said "—*everyone back.*"

He'd rounded the desk by now, coming to stand only a foot away. Tall, overbearing.

She raised her face to meet his intense gaze, and anything else she might've added to her impassioned diatribe only disappeared, taken over by the brutal pounding of her blood in her veins.

"If you have more for me," he said, low and contained over a fierceness she knew he was keeping in check, "put it on the table."

She wanted to. Lord knows she did. But since this discussion had seemed to go beyond his daughter now, how could she keep lecturing him on shortcomings when she had so many herself?

He was so close that she could smell the soap on his skin—fresh and manly, like he'd lathered himself after a hard day of work. She could imagine him under the pelting force of a shower, his skin bare....

Her mind got fuzzy, her judgment was gone.

And when he leaned even nearer, daring her again to keep on talking, she reached for the desk, knowing it was the only thing that could hold her up.

Yet, like her, he seemed to have lost his train of thought.

He was so close she could feel his breath on her face.

So close that all she would have to do was—

It was as if something had pushed her forward, and she canted toward him, pressing her lips to his, knowing it was wrong but unable to stop herself.

At the feel of him, a sparkling bouquet of color popped through her, showers of heat jerking through her limbs, all coming together in the center of her to explode in one spray of bliss.

Fireworks, she thought, her brain scrambling in a whirl of sensation.

At first he seemed surprised at what she'd done, and as her common sense returned, she started to pull back from him, keeping her eyes closed so she might hold on to the kiss.

But then she *kept* them closed in dread of what she would see on his face.

My God, had she just surrendered the job she loved for a kiss?

Granted, it'd been a real kiss, yet still...

Bracing herself, she opened her eyes to see the helpless desire returned in his own gaze.

"I'm…" she began to say.

Yet, before she could finish, he slid his hands under her jaw and crushed his mouth to hers, sending jags of white light through her head and blanking out all other thoughts.

There was just him, his lips sucking at hers, devouring as he dug his fingers into her hair.

With something near to a sob, she grasped at his business shirt, wanting more.

As Melanie returned his kiss with a fervor that matched his own, Zane realized at this moment that he needed her more than he had ever needed anything.

Nothing else existed—not the pictures around him, not the walls of the room that seemed to be tumbling down with every passing draw of their lips.

Not the world outside of those walls.

She helped him to escape it all, and for better or worse, that was all he wanted right now. Her borrowed serenity. *Her.*

He would think about the consequences later.

"Melanie," he murmured against her lips, saying her name by itself for the first time out loud.

She moaned, sending a shot of lust through him—a feeling he hadn't enjoyed for years.

Not since…

No, he couldn't think about anyone else, not even his ex-wife, as the passion he'd built up all this time threatened to crash.

All he wanted was to tear off that robe he'd bought Melanie the other night, push her back onto the desk and release all the pressure straining to burst within him.

But he forced himself to slow down, to absorb the summer scent of her hair and skin, then let the reality catch up with the fantasies he'd harbored ever since first seeing her.

He tilted her back in his arms, running his lips along her neck, nipping at her warm skin, taking her ear into his mouth and hearing her groan this time.

Her little sounds overwhelmed him, sending him beyond the realms of control he clung to so fiercely, and he yanked at the sash of the robe he'd given to her.

That sense of possession rocked Zane again. She belonged to him—his to take and his to let go when the time came.

But he wasn't going to think about letting go right now....

He slid the silk off to reveal her bare shoulders, then ran his hands over her skin. He'd known how soft it would be, but now he shuddered at the feel of such smoothness under his fingertips.

His libido took over, and he found himself whispering, "I've wanted you so badly."

"Me, too."

His mouth brushed against hers, yet they hesitated in kissing. Instead, they stayed like this, panting, her breath entering him in a profoundly intimate moment, one he'd never thought to experience again.

Swept away by that, he touched her neck, just as he'd wanted to do last night after shopping, then lightly dragged his fingers downward, over her chest, between her small, firm breasts.

She hauled in a sharp breath, and the blood rushed to his groin, getting him ready for her. And he stayed ready as the tips of her breasts hardened under her nightie.

He traced the outline of one, bringing it to a more stimulated peak. Then he bent to her, touching his tongue to the nub as she lifted one of those gorgeous, long legs and wrapped it around him, urging him even closer.

Close enough so that he was against the center of her, pressing, letting her feel how much he wanted her.

He moved his hips, barely grinding, and she let her head angle back, exposing her throat.

Guiding her backward, he used one arm to clear a spot on his desk, papers and file holders falling to the ground before he laid her on it.

There, where he spent so many of his hours in the blank numbness of business, her hair spread like rays.

Like sunshine, he thought, bending to her breast again and catching her scent, taking more of her into his mouth, dampening the cotton of her nightie while he sucked and worked her with his tongue and teeth.

Now both of her legs were around him, clamping, bringing him to her, where he nudged against her undies.

"Zane," she said, and the sound of his name made him even harder.

He slipped a hand under her nightie, feeling for her panties.

Her hand stopped him, pushing his questing fingers away.

"The door," she said unevenly, "not…locked."

His mind raced around that, but he was too far gone to stop.

Too far gone to even think of what it would be like between him and Melanie after they…

Scooping her into his arms, he walked purposefully to the door, but instead of locking it, he opened it, peering around the hall to see that they were alone, then continuing to his bedroom.

Nothing could stop him. Not even common sense.

His door was already ajar, and he kicked it open the rest of the way, crossing the threshold and then leaning back against the door to shut everything out.

He locked it behind them.

Then he went to the bed, barely realizing that Melanie was gripping his shirt, her face buried against his neck.

As he laid her out on the mattress, she said his name again.

"Zane?"

It was a question, dizzy, uncertain, almost slurred with what he knew she had to be wanting, too.

Yet his name had also been steeped in…feeling. Emotion.

For a torn second, he wondered if they should be doing this—what the price would be for getting it on with the nanny. But then, from somewhere deep inside, a roll of warmth swamped him.

He knew that this woman had been more than just a nanny. She *was* more, and his body had just realized it before any other part of him had.

And it was his body that was in command now. Thankfully, it shut down his brain, and his feelings. It blocked the possibility of emotion from entering this equation—if he even had more to give than the temporary warmth he'd just experienced.

Even so, just looking at her made him want to

please her, and he found himself stroking the hair back from her face.

Just one time, he thought. *Just for a moment.*

She closed her eyes, giving into his caress. Then, easing his hands lower, down her chest, her stomach, her hips, he came to her legs.

Her amazing, endless legs that had been driving him wild.

As he'd dreamed about before, he skimmed a thumb over one slim ankle, then upward, exploring every contour until he got to her knee.

She shifted under his touch, asking for more without even a word.

"Dancer's legs," he said, a strange hint of wonder and appreciation in his tone.

A flush settled over her face, and there was something in her eyes…

Before he could decide what it was, the look disappeared, and he couldn't help embracing a sense of relief.

And…disappointment?

No. He couldn't afford disappointment.

"Once you start dancing," she said softly, a quiver to her tone, "it's hard to stop."

No kidding, he thought. He'd been dancing away from a lot of things for years.

He pushed up her nightie, and she squirmed under his hands as he touched places she'd probably never expected him to explore.

Damn, her waist was tiny, her stomach flat, delineated. He ran his thumbs lower, over her hip bones, then down into her panties.

Melanie pressed a hand to her face as he came back

up to rub her belly, up and down, making her shift her hips with his every motion.

He was pulsing, eager for her, and he wasn't going to last much longer, but he couldn't stop watching her face—how she bit her lip, how she arched her neck.

Hell, was he really enough to elicit such emotion from her?

Something deep and low within him responded to the matter of whether feeling truly *wasn't* a part of his life anymore.

As he blanked out that question—he was tired of fighting it, ramming against it—he coaxed Melanie's undies down her legs, then off. He helped her to a sitting position, taking her nightie by the hem and whisking it off her body.

She sat before him, naked and so beautiful that it made his belly tighten.

Steam driving his every move, he started to unbutton his shirt, but he didn't do it fast enough.

Not for her.

She helped him, fumbling with his buttons.

Her insistence got to him, and while she worked on his shirt, he took care of his trousers and the rest of his clothes, until he was as bare as she was.

Now she was looking at him with such yearning, with such—he had no idea what else was in her gaze, or maybe he just didn't *want* to know—that her attention stoked him to a new level of need.

He had a few condoms in a nightstand, just as he kept one in his wallet—an option, he'd always thought, even though he'd never pursued it. But the expiration date on one in the nightstand was still good. He ripped open a packet and sheathed himself.

She backed toward his headboard, reached behind her for a pillow and reclined against it.

He moved at the same time, kneeling between her legs, resting himself there.

"Oh," she said as his tip smoothed over her folds. "Inside. Come inside."

He wanted to be there, too, and an inner pressure pounded at him, persuading him to hurry it up.

Taking her by the hips, he slid into her, wallowing in the sensation of her around him, clenching, slick.

And tight, too.

When was the last time she'd been with a man?

His thought process crashed as he thrust inside her again; she took him, grasping his hips, urging him on as they found a rhythm, their own dance.

But this time, instead of dancing away, he moved toward something—a brightness, a lightness, a feeling that he was floating and leaving the rest of it behind for as long as he could.

They churned, their rhythm quickening as he pushed into her again, again…

"Zane," she said once more, as if his name had turned itself inside out to become something different. Something that only she could see.

She arched under him, rocking, riding the cadence of his thrusts as he disappeared into that light he'd seen.

Blinding, lifting, heating and burning…

It singed him with a blaze of fire, eating at his skin and roaring through him in an explosion that blasted him apart.

She held him through all of it, even as she came soon afterward. Their skin glistened with sweat, their bodies sticking together as if not wanting to separate.

But he *had* separated, he knew as their breath battled, chest to chest.

He'd come undone.

And much to his shock, it hadn't done him in after all.

Chapter Eight

Afterward, they ended up resting next to each other in his bed, and Melanie had no idea what to say or do, except to just lie there and…

And just breathe, she guessed.

She'd never participated in anything close to a one-night stand before, but as the all-encompassing sensual fog dissipated, she wondered if this might be the first instance, because she didn't see how anything could ever develop between her and Zane.

To think, it'd seemed like such a wonderful idea when he had first kissed her. It'd seemed…right. Perfect. As if life had been a rehearsal for everything that had led up to his lips touching hers and making her lose all sense of reason. She'd never felt that way about any man.

Her pulse seemed to stop now.

But just how *did* she feel about Zane Foley?

Did it even matter now that they'd stopped kissing and embracing and...

Her temperature rose during the replay of it, sending her heartbeat back into motion while she pushed her damp hair back from her forehead, then tugged the disheveled covers up and over her body. For some reason, she was suddenly shier than before.

"Well," he said from his side of the bed, where he'd also pulled up the covers, but only to his chest. Just as she'd expected, it was muscled and defined, making her want to put her hands back on it.

"Well," she echoed.

Maybe he would go ahead and fire her, if things would be *this* unimaginably awkward from now on.

It wasn't just that he was the boss, either. Sex wouldn't erase the issues he still had with his first wife. Plus, getting in deeper with him would mean that Melanie would have to come clean about her past, and she couldn't imagine *that* ever going over well.

Just imagine if the press got a hold of that one.

For a man like Zane, who shielded his private life from public scrutiny the best he could, it would be a complication he couldn't afford.

Melanie drew the covers up even more. She didn't intend to tell anyone about where she'd come from or who she'd been. She'd left all that behind, and having to keep her secrets from a lover wouldn't be fair to him at all.

"I sure wasn't planning on this," she said lightly, hoping to introduce the subject, to let him know that she'd lost her head this one time.

As she waited for his response, she thought that this was one of the hardest conversations she'd ever made herself take part in.

He laughed softly. Was it her imagination, or did he seem relieved at how she was laying all the cards out there?

"I wasn't planning on this, either," he said. "Even though I was thinking about it quite a bit."

She tested him with a glance. He'd curled an arm over his head while fixing his eyes on the ceiling. He'd hardly gone back to the cold man she was afraid would return. No, he actually seemed relaxed, with a slight smile on his mouth.

The best man she would ever get, she realized, and she would have to give him up.

Why hadn't she thought this through way back in the study, when they'd still been kissing?

Her libido answered: *because you were swept away, missy.*

"I never believed it would be a smart plan to get this close to my boss," she said. "Any boss."

"Generally, it's not a good idea. Believe it when I tell you that I've never overstepped like this before, either."

"I do believe you." And it made what she had to say all the tougher. "Zane, this has to be just a one-time event. I wouldn't call it a mistake—not remotely—but the last thing Livie needs is a more complex home life to deal with."

She wanted to take it back; then again, she knew she wouldn't, even if she had to do it all over again.

There was no future at all, she reminded herself. Not if she wanted to outrun what she'd left behind.

"You're right," he said, still watching the ceiling. "One time will have to keep us."

When she rolled to the side to see him better, her heartbeat stumbled. His expression had become almost…vulnerable. More open than she'd ever seen it, even though he was watching the ceiling and not her.

Then something flashed over his expression, altering it enough to make her wary of what had no doubt just gone through his mind.

After another moment, he sat up, the sheet bunched around his hips as he reached toward a nightstand, then opened the drawer to bring out a small box.

When he turned to her again, he'd gone all the way back to normal—the closed-off man she was so used to.

She missed the other guy already, she thought, running a wistful gaze over him. But she had been the one who'd chased him off.

Again, she got after herself for not thinking about the consequences from the very first. Too impulsive. Too taken in by how he owned her when he was near.

But she wouldn't fool herself into thinking that she'd rocked his world so hard that he'd forgotten all about Danielle.

The wounding thought gave her pause.

Was it possible that, by cutting off a relationship before it had really even started with him, she was also protecting herself from the heartbreak she knew would be in store?

Turning that over in her mind, Melanie sat up, too, pressing the covers against her chest. He was holding a black jewelry box etched with fancy lettering.

"I bought it the other night—and you can bet it

wasn't from the McCord franchise." He was so serious. So Zane Foley. "It was a whim, really, along with the wardrobe and the makeover. I was going to put it in your room before you left."

Jewelry…?

Why was he giving this to her right now? she wondered, not taking the box.

A heaviness descended within her as she remembered Livie's dolls. A guilt gift?

Was he pushing her away, too, but in his own manner?

As he cracked open the lid, her hand whipped out to shut it. She wasn't going to take any expensive presents from him, especially after they'd just been together.

"Zane, I can't accept this," she said.

"Melanie…"

Then he seemed to realize the more tawdry aspects of what she might be thinking.

"Oh, damn," he said. "You know, I'm not paying you off or…"

He shook his head and, cursing, got out of bed, as if he needed that distance.

She told herself to avert her eyes as he sought his trousers, then stepped into them, zipping them up. She didn't want to get revved up again, losing her common sense just as she'd done earlier.

But she could still see him in her peripheral vision. Actually, she couldn't bear to *not* see him.

He set the box on the mattress and went for his shirt, putting it on and buttoning it, clearly burying himself in the clothing. "I was waiting out the first fifteen minutes of your personal shopping when I saw what's in that box. It made me think of you. So I bought it before I came to sit with you and Livie in the boutique." His voice got huskier than ever. "It'd look just right on you, Melanie. Just right."

What could she say? In spite of her refusal, he was still offering her this gift, but she wasn't sure exactly why.

Confusion wound through any of the responses she should be making, tangling them so badly that she couldn't pick anything out.

Taking care of his last shirt button, he moved toward the door, but when he got there, he rested his hand on the knob before opening it.

"By the way," he said, "maybe you and Livie can just go ahead and stay a few days more. But it's not because of what…just happened…of course."

"Of course not," she said, finding her voice.

"Because there can't be a second time."

"Right."

He nodded, then left the room, stranding her with whatever was in the box.

Had he been distancing himself in a very Zane Foley way, while brushing her off?

Or maybe, just maybe, had his gift meant more, and he just had no idea how to give it?

With a trembling hand, she pushed the lid up, and the sparkle of a diamond bracelet hit her full force.

Disbelief overcame her first.

Then breathlessness at receiving such a present.

How many times had she dreamed of a better life? Not necessarily *this* much better, but for a girl whose biggest encounter with decadence came in the form of rhinestones, this was flabbergasting.

But didn't he realize that he'd already made her feel on top of the world without any gifts? That just being with him gave her a glow that no diamond could compete with?

She wished he were still in here so she could thank him, yet reiterate that she couldn't accept such a present from him or anyone else.

But if this really was a heartfelt offering, wouldn't it be bad form to give it back?

Would it be like a refusal of *him?*

Since it was likely that the only way Zane even knew how to express himself was through dolls and shopping sprees and jewelry, she wasn't sure what to do.

But he'd asked her and Livie to stay longer, and maybe she could figure it out with the extra time.

Yet, even if she did accept the jewelry, or the cosmetics and spiffy clothes she'd been given at the makeover, she knew nothing could change who she'd been.

It wouldn't make her suitable for Zane Foley, even if in her heart, she knew there couldn't be any other man who fit her so perfectly.

Days passed, and Zane found that it was easier than usual to spend time with Livie after his hours at the office. As a matter of fact, his daughter had ended up lingering for more than just a few days; one had stretched into another, and it'd gotten to the point where Zane didn't even mention their staying longer anymore. It just happened on its own.

He'd even started to think that, when it finally came time for them to go, it wouldn't be easy.

Then again, neither was being around Melanie.

She hadn't been wearing the bracelet he gave her, and she told him once, when they were alone, that she appreciated the bracelet, but that donning it right now wasn't appropriate.

He wasn't sure what that meant, but then again, they hadn't been alone long enough for her to explain. In fact, they'd only been together that one night, yet he couldn't forget how he had gone from pure happiness at making love to her, to something else entirely.

And that was why he'd given her the bracelet, he thought a few days later, as he, Melanie and Livie took a stroll through the neighborhood while the sun dipped its way to dusk. He wanted to thank her for giving him even an hour of forgetfulness and then letting him off the hook as far as a commitment went because, honestly, he hadn't wanted one.

Yes, he had flashes of wondering what it might be like as he'd joined with her, moved within her, but when he'd come back to earth, he knew it couldn't last. He wasn't very good at relating such matters with words, although he had meant the gift with all of his soul. He'd wanted to see her eyes shine, wanted to show her that she was worth diamonds and jewelry.

Unfortunately, she had misinterpreted his gesture at first, but now he wouldn't be surprised if she'd had it all figured out: a diamond bracelet had been the best he could do in a world where he couldn't allow his heart to be touched by anyone, ever again.

Now, as Livie wandered ahead with Melanie to a walking trail that wound through pine trees, he took what he could from the time he would have left with his daughter and her nanny.

It would have to be enough.

Livie scampered up ahead to investigate some stones, leaving Melanie between her and Zane; he slowed down, hanging back, just watching, not getting too close.

Maybe that was because of the anniversary, though, he thought. Danielle's death.

Only two days away.

He leaned against an oak tree, but the bark felt rough against his business shirt. With every hour that counted down to Danielle's day, he felt that much more abraded.

"Ms. Grandy?" his daughter said as she used her long summer shirt to hold a few stones.

"Yes, Livie?" Melanie peered over the girl's shoulder, seeing what she was doing.

"Don't look, okay?" His daughter smiled, her eyes lively as she hid the stones from her nanny. "I want to make a castle for you."

Zane's heart swelled at Livie's apparent joy. They had Melanie to thank for bringing them so far along.

Yet he knew that there were still miles and miles to go.

Playfully, Melanie walked away from Livie, her hands up as if in surrender. And as she came near him, he thought how there were also miles and miles that stayed between him and so many things.

He tried to strengthen himself against the temptation of her, concentrating instead on how the trees smelled in the warm air, how a breeze rustled the pine needles. But nature was hardly enough to keep him from thinking about her body, naked and lean, perfectly formed and so alive under his hands as he'd slid them along her.

Quivers vibrated in his belly, inviting the blood to rush downward.

He resisted, though, still musing about those trees.

Not that it did any good.

She smiled almost shyly at him as she approached, and Zane did the same. But when she got about five feet away, she stayed there, just as if there was a bubble of tension between them, and it was filled with every memory of a caress, of what they'd said to each other, of how she'd touched him....

"Thanks for coming with us," she said, clearly opting for a neutral topic that wouldn't shatter the bubble.

"Livie seemed excited about the prospect."

"She insisted on waiting until you got home."

This was prattle, and it unnerved Zane.

He looked too long at Melanie's inquiring gaze, and he could tell that there was something else she wanted to talk about.

Should he ask?

Dammit, there was no way he could tolerate himself if he continued to practice avoidance, as he had before Melanie had come along. Before his relationship with Livie had started to improve.

"What's on your mind?" he asked.

She gave him a "nothing big" glance, and he motioned for her to come out with it.

"You're not going to want to hear," she said.

"I'm sure I'll hear it anyway at some point."

He laughed a little, and she did, too. Maybe sleeping together had done something for their working relationship.

As well as for *him*.

Trying not to put too much stock in that, he said, "Why don't you just go ahead and tell me, then I'll decide if I should've heard it or not."

"Okay then. It's about…" She folded her hands in front of her, nervous tell. "Livie's mom."

Zane felt punched, but he didn't want to show it.

He wouldn't be able to duck any questions from Livie, either, because it was only natural for his daughter to be asking more of them, now that she was getting comfortable around him.

Melanie continued, keeping those few feet away from him, and he thought that it might be because of the subject, not just him.

"Livie was asking again about things Danielle enjoyed," she said. "I think she wants to imagine what it might've been like to have a fun day with her mom."

He might as well give up a tidbit, so they would be satisfied for the time being. "Danielle was a homebody most of the time. She would've liked teaching Livie to make cookies or play the piano. But when she went out, she might've taken her to a park over near White Rock Lake, where there was this little place called the Wishing Bridge. She would've brought a picnic, just like you do with Livie."

He hadn't meant to compare Melanie and Danielle; it'd just come out, and the aftermath was like recovering from another slam from an invisible fist.

She must've felt it, too, because her face reddened.

He wished he could brush the embarrassment away, make her feel better. He even wished he could tell her that, out of everyone in this world, she was the closest Livie had ever come to a mom.

But he didn't. Neither Livie nor he could survive another Danielle.

"Six years ago Saturday," he said instead, creating more distance, "Danielle died."

Melanie blinked, as if taken off balance.

Why had he said it? Because he needed to keep that bubble intact between them?

She kept her hands folded in front of her. "Livie doesn't know about this anniversary," she said.

"No. I never wanted to put that on her."

"Zane…" Cutting herself off, she glanced at Livie, who was choosing more rocks to put into the scoop of her shirt. Then she snagged his gaze. "Zane."

Her voice was softer, with a hint of emotion he wished he could connect to again, yet, with Danielle's name filling that bubble with so much, there was no chance.

Melanie seemed to realize that as she went on. The sadness in her usually sparkling eyes told him so.

"Don't you think," she said, "that Livie might be getting old enough to take a day when she can remember her mom? Maybe not this anniversary—not yet— but even on Danielle's birthday, which I know you don't acknowledge, either?"

"Stop it, Melanie." His voice was harsh, guarded.

"Zane, please, I'd like to take her to that park on Saturday, to that bridge, where she can be with her mom, and if she doesn't know why, that's okay. Can't you see how badly she wants to be with Danielle, even if it's only in a place her mom *used* to love?"

Rage—not at Melanie, necessarily, but at everything else—blinded him.

"Can't *you* see that she's better off without Danielle?" he asked in a crushed whisper.

She got that fighting look about her again—that chin-up, David-against-Goliath strength.

"No one is better off without their family," she said quietly. "Take it from me. You're doing her no favors by never talking about her mother at all."

Zane's anger filtered out everything but the "take it from me" part.

It occurred to him that Melanie didn't talk about her family much at all. Sure, she had done so during her second interview when he'd pressed the issue, but even back then he'd noticed a cautiousness that came along with her answers.

She seemed to realize it, too, veering back to the subject at hand.

"Please, Zane," she said.

He was still simmering, but underneath it all, he had to admit she was right.

He hadn't merely been withholding *himself* from his daughter, he'd been keeping her mom away from her, too.

But what would it do to Livie when she found out just how bad off Danielle had been? What would she do when she realized that her mom's worst days had come after childbirth, which had seemed to drive her into a dark place—for which she'd taken stronger mood stabilizers—a place that had consumed her when she'd become too confident about her "wellness" and secretly gone off the meds that had been prescribed when she'd gotten worse?

The more you keep from Livie, he thought, *the more she's going to want to know.*

Yet, his daughter didn't have to know everything, did she? Not even when she was older. But for now, maybe it really would benefit her to get acquainted with the woman Zane had loved.

He warmed slightly to the idea—as much as he could.

This trip to the bridge didn't even have to include *him*. In fact, it wouldn't, because he would have no part of a day that marked the discovery of his wife in the bathroom, lethal pills spilled over the tile next to her slumped body.

He made himself forget.

"I won't go with you," he said, "but you can take Livie to that bridge Saturday."

Melanie nodded, as if knowing he didn't have it in him to change all that much.

"Thank you," she said. "And if you decide that you want to come, too, we'll be there."

We'll be there.

He didn't answer, but then again, he didn't have to, as Livie called to Melanie to come see the stone castle she'd built. A structure that would probably crumble all too soon.

Melanie didn't prepare for Danielle's anniversary until that Saturday morning, when the sun didn't shine as brightly as usual.

It was only after she'd garbed Livie in a pretty sundress, combed out her wavy hair for a pair of pigtails and driven her to Crane Park, that she told the child just where they were going—but not why.

Yet, even then, she hardly trusted her voice to hold

itself together as they walked over the grass toward a quaint wooden bridge etched with dove carvings.

There were plenty of things Melanie wouldn't be telling Livie: that her father had refused to be here with them on this important day; that she suspected he would never move forward, never mend himself so he could…

Melanie swallowed and clutched Livie's hand.

She'd been having wasted dreams that maybe he would mend enough that they *could* have a future together, no matter what she'd determined on the night they had been intimate. But it was only wishful thinking, because even then, that wouldn't get rid of her own reasons for staying away from him.

Yet, if she wanted to stay away, why had she let out a piece of her past the other day, when she mentioned how everyone needed family? She'd never meant for him to know how she felt about the people she'd left behind in Oklahoma, but when she had that slip of the tongue, she'd hoped that she'd given Zane enough room to share his burdens with her, too.

Apparently, he hadn't wanted to, so here she was, with his daughter, taking up where he'd left off.

Livie was watching Melanie with those big eyes, just as if she knew something was different about today, and Melanie squeezed her hand as they came to the foot of the bridge. Around them, only a few other people meandered through the park, and the birds only gave little chirps, as if they were just as subdued as Melanie was feeling. Even the stream seemed to lack some burble.

"You like this bridge?" Melanie asked, her throat acting as if it was closing in on itself.

Livie nodded. "It looks like Snow White."

Yes, Melanie could see some Seven Dwarves in the structure, just as she could see Danielle in Livie.

She brought the little girl onto the planking, then to the center, where they sat just above the water.

"I heard," she said, "that this was one of your mom's favorite places."

Livie's eyes lit up. "My mom?"

"Yes."

The little girl smiled so wide that Melanie's gaze blurred, hot and watery. Years from now, she would finally understand why Melanie had brought her to the park today, and hopefully it would, among other things, show Livie how much her nanny had loved her.

The child placed her hand on the carved rail above them, where a wooden flower bloomed. "I was a baby, but I think I remember her."

A tear wiggled down Melanie's cheek, but she subtly dried it with a finger. "Really?"

"She sang me songs. Monty told me, and he sang one when he had to drive me to the doctor for..."

"A checkup?" Melanie touched Livie's back. So small, so frail right now. So in need of someone. "Which song?"

Livie looked into the water, as if trying to recall. Then she began to hum a sad tune. A lullaby that stopped after a few notes.

"That's all I know," the child said, softer now.

Another tear ran down Melanie's face as she hugged Livie to her. She wished Zane was here to tell his daughter which song it had been, maybe even to hum the rest of it for her.

"She smelled like oranges, too," the child said, leaning against Melanie now. "Monty said that, but I don't really remember."

"Oranges…" Melanie could barely get the words out, so she cleared her throat, waited a moment, then tried again, even though she succeeded in only whispering. "That was no doubt her perfume. Orange blossom."

Livie turned her face up to Melanie, still smiling, and she knew that she'd done good in bringing her here.

Done real good, even for a woman who'd grown up on the wrong side of the tracks.

Then Livie's gaze settled on something behind Melanie.

Her blood expanded in her veins when a voice followed.

"Orange blossom," Zane Foley said, his tone that of a man who was living a certain hell by just being here. "I remember that perfume, Livie."

His daughter sprang up to greet her dad as Melanie turned around, tears destroying her vision until she wiped them away, allowing her to see him desperately embracing Livie, his eyes closed tightly. He was holding Danielle's urn in one hand, his little girl in the other.

He came, Melanie thought.

And when he and Livie paused to look at each other, Melanie could see how red his eyes were, how quietly devastated he'd been all these years, while trying to keep it from everyone else.

She stood, thinking she should leave him and Livie alone.

But then he spoke.

"Melanie?" he asked, his voice ragged, and she could see that he was asking her to join them.

Without hesitation, she went to them, the tears coming freely as they both drew her into their circle.

Melanie held on to them. Lord help her, she hadn't just fallen for Livie.

She'd fallen for all of them.

Chapter Nine

The morning had ended up being a catharsis for Zane.

Ever since Melanie had asked to take Livie to the bridge, he'd wrestled with his conscience—and his emotions. By the time Saturday had arrived, he'd been mentally beating himself up with such frequency that he was exhausted.

While he sat in his study, listening to the stirrings of Melanie and Livie departing for Crane Park, the house had seemed to suck in on him, making it hard to breathe.

It only got worse after they were gone, with the clock in the foyer ticking away, providing the only sound.

Buried alive, he kept thinking, and each *thunk* of the clock's hand was like another shovel full of dirt against him.

This would be the rest of his life. In so many ways, he was just as absent as Danielle was.

But as the chime marked the hour, he realized that he'd felt a hell of a lot more present since Melanie and Livie had come around.

So why was he now accepting this never-ending descent into nothing?

Why was he forcing himself to live like this?

Before he could change his mind, he'd taken Danielle's ashes out of that chest, unburying the urn for all intents and purposes, then went to the park, at first hanging back from Melanie and Livie, then approaching them step by slow step.

After they'd welcomed him, he felt free for the first time in years, as if he'd escaped the fate he'd sentenced himself to. And as the trio of them had embraced upon that bridge, the truth became so very clear.

He didn't want Livie and Melanie to go anywhere.

Zane wasn't sure what he should do about that, or even if he could manage to never let them down again, but he wanted to keep them near.

Afterward, they'd spent another hour at the park, spreading Danielle's ashes at both entrances to the bridge. It had seemed so symbolic. A bridge, spanning from one side to another. A crossing.

Then, while Melanie left them alone so he could walk with Livie, he'd told his daughter about Danielle's good days, although he took care to hint that her mother hadn't been perfect. But she'd loved her daughter in her own way, even if she had died long before her time.

He would tell Livie more as the years went by, he thought, but for now, she seemed content to have her father finally talking.

When they arrived back at the townhouse, Melanie

left father and daughter alone again, and they went through boxed pictures of Danielle that Zane had pushed to the back of the garage. He chalked up their nanny's absence to her ongoing respect of what he and Livie needed to clear with each other; but once, when Melanie had looked in on them to ask if they were hungry, he saw a cloudiness in her gaze, and that had tweaked something within Zane.

After she'd left the room, he thought about just how to thank her for all her guidance and softhearted patience. For everything she'd done for him and his family.

So he'd gone about it in the only way he could manage.

Which brought him to the present, and his newest gift, which was steered into the driveway by Monty. Zane thought that Melanie couldn't possibly refuse *this* gesture. Surely she would see, this time, that he wasn't thanking her with a bracelet for needing him or trying to win her over with a night in a posh department store.

Monty opened the door of the new silver Mercedes S Class and stretched out his long legs.

"Drives like butter!" he said, as happy as any man behind the wheel of a dream machine.

Early this morning, after telling Zane that he wanted to give this baby a spin before it fell out of his hands, Monty had been picked up by a sales representative. And, now, as Livie darted out of the front door and into the driveway, Zane fully recognized the lure of this shiny present.

It was the very best he could offer.

"Mr. Monty!" the little girl said, running to the driver, who ruffled her hair in greeting. "I like your car. Can I drive it?"

"Sure, but I should let you know this belongs to Ms. Grandy, not me."

"Oh, she's *lucky*."

Monty grinned at Zane, entirely skipping over the need to explain the subtleties of Melanie's new car. Hell, Zane hadn't bothered to tell the driver anything except that Melanie was receiving a bonus for a job well done, and it was a believable story, since Zane often doled out high-priced rewards to other employees.

"Hop right in," Monty said to Livie, as he held open the driver's door for her.

She climbed inside, and Zane knew his daughter wouldn't be burning rubber out of the driveway; Monty occasionally allowed her to play in the cars while he watched to see that she didn't cause any mischief.

As a shiver waved over his skin, Zane turned to find Melanie coming out of the townhouse, too. Even while she remained at the top of the driveway, the impact of her presence scrambled him to the point of jagged confusion.

Gratefulness. Tenderness.

Guilt?

He wasn't sure exactly what he felt, but whatever the emotion, he seemed to exude it, because he could've sworn that she had momentarily held her breath at the sight of him, just as affected as he was by merely being in the same area.

He swept his hand toward the car. "Your coach awaits."

"*My* coach?"

With a doubtful expression, she folded her hands in front of her in that anxious gesture, and he had the feeling that she was beginning to understand what he was up to.

If only he knew, too.

"It's yours," he said.

From the side of the car, where Monty was watching over Livie, the driver added, "A bonus! We all get 'em, Ms. Grandy, so don't look like the rug's going to be pulled out from under you."

As Melanie took that in, Zane could see her shoulders slump a bit. Why? Did she *want* to be *more* than only an employee?

Yet, he already knew that she was much more than someone he gave a paycheck to, or even someone who'd eased his pain yesterday, as well as on that one, earth-moving night they'd been together.

She was so much more.

He just didn't know what, exactly.

Zane stepped toward the car. "What do you say we take this on the road?"

"Mr. Foley…" she said, using his formal name around the others.

He stopped her before she could tell him that she wouldn't accept this, just as she had done with the brace-let.

"'No' isn't an option," he said.

Monty was already ushering Livie out of the front seat.

"I *love* your car," the girl said to her nanny as the driver shepherded Livie toward the house.

Melanie only smiled as Monty indicated he would look after the child while Melanie enjoyed a test drive. Then he got Livie through the front door.

Zane started to go around to the passenger's side. "Let's go."

"Where? Back to the dealership?"

"Come on, Melanie." Zane opened the door and leaned on the top of it. "Indulge me?"

She sighed and he took that as a good sign, getting in and closing his door.

When she slid in, too, she didn't start the engine. "You know what I'm going to say, right? Thank you but—"

"It's the same thing you said about the bracelet. And, as I recall, you never did give that back to me, so I assume it's accepted."

She kept looking at him as if she were about to hand him a much more detailed answer that he probably wouldn't want to hear.

A refusal, he realized, and it chipped away at him, revealing a raw side that he thought he'd gotten control of after getting home from Danielle's bridge yesterday. It was a part of him that would come out next anniversary, then the next, and that was all he could allow.

Then again, Melanie hadn't run away at any point. Hadn't she seen the worst of him already?

What was he afraid of, then?

"Do you know just how much you've meant to me and Livie?" he asked quietly, taking a chance, breaking his own rules and hoping she wouldn't get out of this car and leave him.

She touched the steering wheel, longing written all over her face. Yet somehow, he got the feeling that she wasn't craving a car.

"I know how much you two appreciate me," she said. "So you don't have to give me things to prove it."

"I only want to—"

She faced him. "Did you love her so much that you can't bring yourself to dig all the way out of it, Zane?"

Melanie was referring to Danielle, and for a deci-mated heartbeat, he didn't know how to answer.

"I'm sorry," she said, raising her hands from the wheel. "I can't believe I just asked. I shouldn't have."

He gently grabbed her wrist before she could go anywhere, and she stayed, watching him with those eyes—that clear gaze hazed with gathering clouds.

"I did love her," he found himself saying, even though there was still a part of him that warned against it. "I loved her so much that, when she died, it killed most of me, too."

Zane let go of her wrist. He was numb again, hardly believing the words that had come out of his mouth.

Just shut up, he told himself. *Stop now.*

But he didn't, because he was sick of holding it in, and yesterday, when some of it had been released, he'd actually felt like a new man.

Thing was, he didn't know who that man was or where he was going—or even how to get there.

The image of that bridge entered his mind, but it faded all too quickly.

"I'm not even sure," he heard himself saying, "that I'll ever really be there for anyone else. But you've come the closest to showing me the way, Melanie. You…" He almost didn't say it, but it came out nonetheless. "You were the first woman I've been with since Danielle."

God, he sounded like a monk—but hadn't he shut himself away just as thoroughly?

Gaze softening, Melanie opened her mouth to re-spond, but he got there first.

"I know, I know—withdrawn in the extreme. But I wouldn't have been good for anyone. You could prob-ably testify to that. And I only wanted to give you back a little of what you gave to me, whether it was with a car or a bracelet…."

"I understand."

She came into vivid focus now—Melanie, a constant that was so much warmer than the work that had sustained him before.

But she was also more volatile. Work would always be there for him, no matter how he treated it; yet, she would take so much more care, and there was no guarantee that she would stay.

She laid her hand on his arm, and those shivers of desire returned to thrust at him deep inside.

"I just wish I could take all that pain from you, Zane," she said.

When he looked into her eyes, he saw that she truly would if she could.

He shook his head. "You don't want to know everything."

"Why? Because I might break under all of it?"

Melanie rubbed her thumb back and forth over his arm, not in a seductive way, but in a manner that reminded him of a soft breeze blowing over cushioning grass.

She continued. "I did some research into bipolar disorder, just to try and understand that, too. I didn't get past a lot of the technical information, though."

Right. The definitions of BP—*abnormal alterations in moods, energy and the ability to function*—were easy to learn.

The rest wasn't easy.

But she'd tried, Zane thought, and the proof of it touched him.

"All along," he said, "Danielle would have episodes,

both manic and depressive. She had blamed me and her family before for her troubles. She even had to be hospitalized a couple of times before the pregnancy. But after Livie was born, she just…" He blew out a breath. "She started saying that she was a burden—that she'd brought me too much trouble, even though I did everything I could to show her that I loved her and Livie. That's when she went on stronger mood stabilizers, and they seemed to work."

"Until she went off of those?" Melanie added.

Zane nodded, not wanting to talk about the suicide itself. Not yet. Maybe not ever, because it cut too close, even after a six-year anniversary.

"And Livie?" Melanie asked, sounding anxious. "I heard that children of parents with the illness are more likely to have the disorder."

"She's visited doctors, and they believe she's normal."

Yet his daughter had been through so much that Zane wasn't sure what normal really was.

He added, "But she'll keep seeing them. I want to be sure."

"Right." Melanie slid her hand down his arm. "You did everything you could do, and you're doing the same thing now, Zane. So stop hounding yourself."

Melanie was holding his arm, as if trying to transfer strength, and oddly enough, he actually felt it.

Or did he just want it so badly that he was imagining it?

"You don't have to tell me that you're afraid Livie's going to be like Danielle," she said. "You've set yourself back from her, just in case it ever does happen again.

But, good heavens, Zane, there's no guarantee there'll be a next time. You can't live in anticipation of it."

"I wish I could believe that."

As if making him want to believe, Melanie brought her fingers to his temple, where she brushed the hair away from his face.

He allowed the wash of comfort to ease through him. She was the only one who could make him think that there were wonderful possibilities ahead, and he wished he could accept everything she had to offer.

But what else was he going to do? Keep going backward instead of moving on?

When he didn't react right away, Melanie stopped touching him, starting up the car instead and then backing it out of the driveway for the spin he wanted her to take.

And although her acceptance of this latest present gratified him, it was the afterburn of her fingers on his skin that kept him going.

Move on, he thought as he gave himself over to the idea.

Because if he was ever going to do it, the time was now.

Throughout the drive around the neighborhood, Melanie finally accepted that this car was hers, and she acknowledged the magnitude of this bonus that Zane had given her.

But she was even more overwhelmed by his other gift: the truth about Danielle.

"I loved her so much that, when she died, it killed most of me, too," he'd said, and the confession still seared her, like a brand that would always be there.

She hadn't expected him to forget about Danielle anytime soon, but when he said that...?

The words still lingered, becoming darker with the reality of how difficult it would be to love a man with such ghosts.

Then again, she was used to difficult, wasn't she? Couldn't she be up to the challenge of telling him that she loved him enough to work with his demons?

As she aimed the car back into the driveway of his townhouse, she knew she would never even get the chance, because that would mean coming clean about her own truths.

But, dammit, she was doing so well as this new person—a *decent* person—who'd helped Zane and Livie. Couldn't she continue as Melanie the nanny?

Couldn't she avoid beating him back down again by slamming him with the truth of her own past?

She'd gotten in too deep; yet, she wanted to be here with all her heart and soul. The new Melanie was good for him and his daughter.

He used a remote to open the door of the stand-alone garage, and she parked next to his personal ride—a black Jaguar that he didn't drive much. Since he'd already done away with the vehicle she'd been driving before, that left room for her.

For Melanie Grandy, the woman who would do almost anything for him.

Almost.

While she got out, he shut the garage behind them, and she began to walk toward the regular door, which stood opposite the townhouse.

But then he slid his arm around her waist, turning her to face him and keeping her from going anywhere.

The contact made her circuits go haywire.

"Zane, what are you—"

He stopped her with a soft kiss, and she held on to his arms, leaning into him, helpless.

Every nerve ending seemed to short out, sparking her skin as he kept his mouth against hers while she talked.

"What are you doing?" she murmured.

"Kissing you."

Oh, not a good idea, she thought as she went pliant under another kiss—soft, tender. She was going to be a pool of nothing in another second.

When he came up from her, he smiled, and there was something like hope in his eyes.

And that hope kept her in his arms, because she hadn't seen such a thing in him before; she knew that she helped to put it there.

"There's no need to remind me that we said we wouldn't have anything more to do with each other." He pressed his mouth against her ear. "But dammit, Melanie."

No, dammit, *Zane.*

Their discussion in the car had been an opportunity to relieve himself of feelings he'd been containing for a long time. And when Melanie had touched him, comforting him, he'd probably seen that as...

Well, she wasn't sure. She hadn't meant to escalate anything, only to make him feel better.

But now, as he ran his lips around her ear, heating it with his tight breaths, she thought that his body was taking the place of the other gifts. He was expressing his thanks in a much more physical way that she wasn't able to resist.

Yet she had to.

"We should stop," she said, knowing where their kiss had ended up the last time.

Hardly stopping, he pressed his lips against her jaw, her cheek, working his way back toward her mouth.

As she nearly swayed under the flow of feeling, she recalled when he'd told her about being with no other women since Danielle. She'd been shocked, but it also made such sense. Zane had been closed; but now, with her, he could release everything he'd kept back.

She'd been the one who brought that out in him. The new Melanie Grandy.

Didn't that count for anything at all? Shouldn't that allow her to enjoy his kisses, his…

His *everything?*

Guilt still reared up and made her draw away, even if her body hated her for it.

But he kept a hold on her hands. "I keep thinking about the first time with us. I can't forget."

"Same here, but…"

Lord, there were too many "but"s to bring up.

"Hey. You just got shyer on me. You do that sometimes." He tipped a finger under her chin. "What're you all about, Melanie Grandy?"

A flush shot through her, from neck to chest. He wanted her to talk about herself, didn't he?

Oh, no.

"You're the one who interviewed me," she said. "You've already got the answers."

"Hardly."

As much as she wanted to stay away from the subject altogether, she knew that Zane wouldn't be happy until she offered him a little bit of her.

Yet, what would she do when he wanted more?

She couldn't think about that right now. "I've always been a tad shy, even though you might not know it."

"No, your bashful streak is there, all right."

He skimmed his fingers over her cheek, and she almost lost it.

"I was just never the dating-around type, I suppose." She shrugged, willing to tell him this much, but intending to skip over the section of her past where she went on a few innocent dates, all right, but she'd done it mainly to avoid going home to that double-wide trailer. "There're only a couple guys of note. One in high school—puppy love."

"Was he your first?" Zane asked, looking amused.

She was glad to see that this conversation at least cheered him, taking him far away from the memory of Danielle.

"Yes," she said. "I thought he was *it* for me. But it didn't turn out that way after he went off to college."

"I was with a few girls in high school before Danielle came along. Then…"

The shadows started coming back, and she fought to fend them off.

"My second 'big thing' was a guy in Vegas," she offered.

And…yes: success.

The shadows fell away from his gaze and she smiled, encouraging a growing light in his eyes again; it caused that love she'd named only yesterday to swell up through her chest, making her feel elevated.

He tucked a strand of her hair behind her ear. "What about that guy in Vegas?"

"He wasn't the one."

The words just hung there, as filmy and sticky as a web to avoid.

But he seemed to get caught in it, maybe even translating her message as it was meant to be: *Zane* was the one—a man like no other. Yet there was no way she could say it out loud.

With a passion that made her pull in a breath, he held her against him, reaching over to lock the garage door at the same time.

Oh, no.

Oh, yes.

She wanted this more than anything, and once again she was starting to forget all the reasons they'd stayed apart.

"You know about the Fourth of July charity event at Tall Oaks?" he asked, as he inched her shirt out of the shorts she was wearing.

She nodded, unable to do anything else.

"I'd be happy if you'd be by my side to help me see to the details," he said, running his thumbs up and down her stomach.

Although she could hardly think at all, she thought he might be asking her to be a hostess.

Was he?

Did he want her to be out on the lawn at Tall Oaks with him and all his friends and family?

Half of her panicked, but the other half was encompassed and embraced in a way she'd never felt before.

"Be there with me," he said, moving in back of her, one hand staying on her belly. "And be with me *here,* Melanie. I'm ready for it. I swear."

But was *she* ready?

As his hands traveled up to cup her breasts she gasped, leaning back against him.

Such a bad idea, she kept thinking, but only because she was still hiding so much of herself from him. Yet, if he only knew who she'd been, he would drop her.

And from this height, she wouldn't be able to stand the fall.

He kissed her neck, sending lightning bolts of heat through her, and soon he had her clothes off, exploring every inch of her body.

His, she thought. She was all his.

She turned around, helping him with his clothing, too, as he backed her toward the backseat of her new car.

Suddenly, she felt like a teenager—giddy and fresh and a little afraid of what was going to come next.

But it was that newness that made her think that this *could* work—that they were both starting out together in a different direction. That they were going to try their damnedest to turn everything around and be the family they'd both been lacking.

As he eased her down to the backseat—the upholstery leather soft, smooth and creamy—he used his fingers to prepare her, even though it didn't take long, because she was already there.

And after he got a condom out of his wallet, slid it on and then slipped into Melanie, she cried out, softly, joyfully.

Whole. This is what it's like to have every missing part come together.

All those parts swirled, whirling up and blasting

through everything in their path, as the two of them moved together, blazing, zooming, driving…

Delivering her with a crash to that new place she'd been hoping for.

Chapter Ten

As the Fourth of July approached, Melanie, Zane and Livie returned to Tall Oaks to see to the last of the party details for the annual Dallas Children's Hospital charity event.

Although Melanie claimed the guest room again, she didn't stay there at night.

Rather, she spent every hour possible with Zane, just as they'd been doing ever since that day when they'd decided they couldn't stand to be apart.

Everything else had fallen into place after their reunion: Livie continued to grow closer to her nanny, and there were even times when Melanie felt more like a mother to her than a caretaker. And unlike her "previous life," Melanie now felt financially secure—or actually, she felt *secure,* plain and simple.

It all had to do with the fact that she was in love with Zane, though neither of them had said it yet.

But she felt it, and that was a good enough start.

On the afternoon of the charity event, Melanie flitted around anxiously, checking with Mrs. Howe regarding how they would handle people who wished to tour the Victorian mansion, and putting her head together with Scott, the cook, about catering arrangements, then going over logistics one more time with Zane's assistant, Cindy.

Initially, Melanie had approached the situation with an acute awareness that nannies didn't usually take over like this. But if the others thought it odd, no one said anything, maybe because they saw that Melanie only wanted to be as helpful as she could.

With everything in place now, she calmed herself by giving one last inspection to the house and, finally, the sitting room: the pastoral oil landscape on the wall, the organ in the corner, the bars of Sassy, the canary's, cage.

Maybe the bird had picked up on the change in the household, because it was singing at the moment, tweeting away and making Melanie laugh.

She glanced around the new and improved interior of Tall Oaks. There hadn't been enough time to restore the paintings on the ceilings, but the rest of the place gleamed more than it had before.

Danielle would've been proud, Melanie thought, feeling a connection with the woman, although Zane had told her that his first wife had only used Tall Oaks on some weekends. He'd sold their main house following her death.

The notion smoothed out Melanie's smile until Livie bounded into the room.

The little girl was already set to celebrate, and she was so cute, with that light dusting of freckles over the bridge of her nose and the dimples she'd started to show more and more, that she could've melted the polar ice cap. She wore a prim pink sundress, her dark, wavy hair in a low, understated ponytail. Her outfit matched the occasion—a fancy Texas cocktail party, complete with steaks and all the trimmings.

"I smell like sunscreen," Livie said.

"You'll need it out there." Melanie wiped at a streak of white on Livie's cheek. "Even if we're going to be in those big tents most of the time, I want to make sure you're covered."

"And when are you getting ready? I can't wait to see you. You'll be the prettiest lady there."

Although Melanie thanked Livie, she highly doubted it. The cream of the social crop would be present today, and her stomach kept turning at the thought of mingling with them and having them realize that, truthfully, she didn't really belong.

Had she only been fooling herself with Zane, while they'd stayed pretty much to themselves in Dallas? Would any of these new, genuinely elegant people see an area of her own personality that hadn't been polished enough?

Would they know where she'd really come from?

But when Livie took her nanny's hand, leading her toward the stairs and her room to get ready, Melanie thought that where she'd been didn't matter as much as where she was now.

When they came to the upstairs guest room, Melanie said, "Did you put sunscreen on your arms, Livie?"

The child wrinkled her nose and marched off toward the bathroom where the lotion was kept. "Aw, Ms. Grandy."

"Aw, Livie. Please do it. I'll be checking."

She grinned at the girl, then closed her door just after Livie returned the smile and marched down the hallway.

That left Melanie alone with the blue cocktail dress that hung from a hook inside the closet door. It was one of the pieces Zane had purchased for her during the makeover, and there'd been no occasion to wear it since.

Yet, now Melanie sloughed off her regular-girl shirt and shorts, going to the dress, slipping into it. Then she fixed her hair as the stylist had taught her during the makeover, applying cosmetics just as carefully, too.

As she stood in front of a full-length mirror, going over herself as she'd gone over the final arrangements for the party itself, she heard her door open, then close.

Zane eased up behind her, holding her to him, and her body went crazy with heat.

"I'm not going to be able to take my eyes off you," he whispered into her ear.

The sight of him snuggling with her in the mirror made her weak in the knees. "You'd best try, Zane. Among the other guests, you've got a hoard of business associates who paid a thousand dollars per ticket."

"Forget business."

He kissed her in the sensitive place between her ear and neck, and although she trembled, she knew he wouldn't forget business. He'd taken some unprecedented days away from the Dallas office, but he still brought contracts and other stacks of paper with him.

It was almost as if work was the one thing he couldn't leave behind at all.

Yet, he would come out of that, she thought, optimistic until the end. She was going to make sure he saw that his workaholic nature was to blame for his hiding away from Livie, and that he would never go back there again.

It was still something to work on, but they would succeed, just as she'd always tried so hard to do herself.

He was watching her in the mirror, and she reached back to brush her fingertips over his cheek.

"I wish we had more time before we have to go down to the party," she said.

"Same here." He kissed her jaw. "You're perfect, so perfect, Melanie, but I can't help thinking that there's just one thing missing." He smiled against her neck. "Where's that bracelet?"

She'd accepted all his gifts by now, and she went to fetch this one from a drawer, taking it out of the box and bringing it back to him so he could help her with the clasp.

In front of the mirror, he took the bracelet, coaxed the diamonds around her wrist and, oh, dear Lord, the lovely weight of them shimmered, just like the future she'd always aimed for.

"And…" he said, taking another small box out of his suit pocket.

He lifted the lid to reveal a pair of diamond earrings.

She should have been over the moon for them, and she smiled as if she were, but she couldn't stop thinking about how he was still offering these gifts, when all she wanted was to hear a simple "I love you" instead.

Melanie held back a sigh. She wouldn't push it, because when that day came, she would come face-to-face with having to tell him about her past. She didn't see how any kind of life-long relationship could survive without that happening.

She would have to make a choice—one she was struggling with even now—because the last thing she wanted was to lose him.

Which, thanks to her, might happen either way.

As fear clutched at Melanie, Zane turned her toward the mirror, clipping the earrings on her lobes, then resting his hands on her shoulders.

"How did I get so lucky?" he asked.

"I'm the lucky one." Meaning that with a profundity that shook her, she leaned her head against his.

They stayed like that for a moment, before he guided her away from the mirror and toward the door.

"My family's in the dining room," he said. "They're looking forward to meeting you."

Melanie wound her arm through his, trying not to be nervous. She wondered exactly what he'd told his dad and brothers about her, because she and Zane hadn't broached the subject yet. There'd been a lot of last-second prep for this event, a lot of time spent with Livie.

At any rate, it would be obvious to the Foleys that Melanie was more than just a nanny, and she had no idea how they might react to Zane's interest in an employee.

But when he opened the door to the dining area for her and their arms unlinked from each other, Melanie asked herself if he even *was* planning to tell them about their relationship.

What if she'd overestimated what she had with Zane?

She lifted her chin a notch and walked into the room.

The Foley men turned toward her: suave yet earthy, dignified in a way *she* only hoped to be.

Clasping her hands together in front of her, Melanie tried not to shrink into herself, even though she felt like the girl from Oklahoma again.

Had a makeover been enough?

"Melanie," Zane said, still standing close, but feeling too far, "this is my family." He gestured to his dad, a handsome man with salt-and-pepper hair and a charismatic glint in his eyes. "My father, Rex."

The patriarch came forward, extending a hand as he drawled, "Ms. Grandy, I want to thank you for all the fine work you've done. Zane tells us how Livie's come around under your care."

"Please call me Melanie. And thank you so much, Mr. Foley."

"Please, it's Rex."

As she shook hands with him, she thought about how much she liked the man's mellow tone. He had a way about him that made her feel as if she'd known him for years.

Then Zane gestured to a brother who wore a sidelong grin, and if she hadn't already been so enamored of Zane, she would've given this tall, dark charmer of a man a second glance.

"This is Jason," Zane said.

Ah, the voice on the phone, Melanie thought, recalling the day she'd overheard Zane talking about the McCords and the Santa Magdalena Diamond.

When Jason greeted her, he acted as if he were about to kiss Melanie's hand, before mischievously peering at Zane and making everyone laugh.

"Be good, you old Casanova," their father said to Jason.

Melanie laughed right along with them.

Then Zane introduced the youngest brother, who cut a lean figure dressed in the cowboy version of a suit, with a bolo tie and fancy Stetson. With his soulful eyes, Travis seemed to be the quietest of the bunch.

And as the group fell into small talk, Melanie indeed saw that he was a man of few words. Yet, he seemed the most observant, she thought, noticing that Travis had been the only one who'd really assessed her.

But—no. There was no way in the world that he could've pegged her for the imposter she felt like.

Trying harder than ever to be the new Melanie, she joined the conversation, which had turned into sibling-flavored jests about how long the brothers could last out in the heat with their full suits, and if the cooling system in the main tent would keep them from wilting.

When Livie came into the room, she was warmly greeted by her granddad and uncles, yet she gravitated to Melanie, as Zane stood close enough again for his arm to brush hers.

That was when everything brightened up.

I'm theirs, Melanie thought.

And that's all the identity she needed.

With the event in full swing, the Foleys greeted guests left and right, while the aroma of wood smoke filtered the late-afternoon air, riding the breeze that stirred the oak and willow leaves.

Interspersed among the trees, tents covered the lawn, some of them boasting games that had been set up to raise money for the hospital, some holding wine and food tastings, one bursting at the seams with a country-and-western band that had filled a temporary dance floor.

But most folks were mingling in the huge main tent, where a podium had been set up for the scheduled auction and presentations, one of which Zane would be giving. Around the floor, linen-covered tables had been set up for the coming dinner.

Currently, Zane was watching Melanie from across that tent as she and Livie chatted with a young socialite who was cradling her infant son. His daughter was clearly love-struck, and Melanie and the other woman were laughing over Livie cooing at the baby.

It felt as if half of Zane was right there with them. His family.

He found himself smiling just as they were, but little by little, it faltered. And the reason was obvious, because it'd been gnawing away at him for a while now.

He just wished he could bring himself to say those three magic words to Melanie: I. Love. You.

But every time he almost did, a creeping panic would quiet him down. "I love you" was a commitment—one he'd made to a woman before, and look how that had turned out….

"Yup," said a voice he recognized all too well as Jason's as he joined Zane, "he's a goner."

Zane glanced over, discovering that his brother was standing next to Travis and their dad—and they were all giving Zane curious, amused looks.

Travis merely drank his beer while their father reached over to grasp Zane's shoulder and give him an energetic paternal shake.

"She's a beaut, that nanny of yours," their dad said. "I'd be staring at her, too."

"When did you two start…?" Jason said, using a hand to insinuate the rest.

"That'd be none of your business." Zane took a gulp of his single-malt scotch on the rocks. He'd known this grilling would come someday, when his family saw how nuts he was about Melanie. He'd just been hoping to put it off a little longer.

But how could he, when his craving to be with her was so apparent that it practically shouted itself to all of Texas?

"Well, now," his father said. "I'm sure I speak for each of us when I say that it's just good to see you happy, Zane, whether or not you want us to know it yet."

"Damn good," Jason echoed.

Travis nodded slightly, still quiet, but Zane thought that might be because of this whole ranch mess with the McCords, which was probably weighing on his mind.

Uncomfortable with a spotlight on him, Zane made an attempt to step out of it. "Thanks, but I feel compelled to point out that I'm not the person who's grinning the most around here."

He gestured to Jason, and his brother lifted his eyebrows.

"Yeah," Zane said, relieved that he'd succeeded in getting the attention off him. "I'm talking about you."

Jason acted casual. "And why would I be grinning all that much?"

Like they didn't know.

Jason had been updating them on his plan with Penny McCord, and in private, Zane, Travis and their dad agreed that it seemed as if the guy was invested in the scheme way more than for the sake of gaining information about Travis's ranch. Forget that "the plan" hadn't yielded much of anything so far; Jason had "run into her" at a coffee house recently, and was talking about arranging yet another so-called casual encounter.

"I'd suggest," Zane said, "that there be no more wedding run-ins or random coffee dates before this thing goes too far."

"It won't," Jason said in his confident manner. "In fact—"

Without saying a word, Travis held up his hand, silencing everyone, his gaze on a trio of well-heeled people who'd just entered the tent.

"Well, I'll be damned," their father muttered when he saw them, too.

There, near the cocktail bar, were the last folks Zane had been hoping would show up.

"McCords," Jason said.

The eldest brother, Blake, walked just ahead of the rest, and when Zane spied him, he couldn't believe that there were people around the state who had the guts to compare Zane and the McCord golden child. Certainly, both were "arrogant," both were leaders of their siblings. But it was idle talk, all the same.

Behind Blake came Tate, a doctor who'd just returned from Baghdad, where he'd worked with the International Medical Corps. Although he didn't seem as easygoing as he'd once been—where was his infamous grin and the upright way he used to carry himself?—he was still escorting his girlfriend, Katerina Whitcomb-Salgar, a stunning heiress with dark hair and eyes, who filled out her dress like a movie star.

Not that Zane noticed her so much—he was zeroed in on Blake in particular.

There was a growl to Travis's voice. "What're they doing here?"

Zane answered. "Blake and Katie are both on the hospital board of directors, and naturally Tate would come along with his girlfriend."

Across the tent, the trio stopped at the bar, where Tate seemed to distance himself from the others, staring at nothing in particular, while Blake remained at Katie's side, ordering for her, then making sure she got her drink first.

Zane's dad spoke. "Looks like Tate better pay more attention to Katie than he's doing right now. His brother seems more interested in her than *he* is."

It wasn't long before Tate's wandering gaze found the Foleys on their side of the tent.

None of them acknowledged each other, as Tate returned to Katie and Blake, where he and his brother began to talk.

Blake glanced at the Foleys, and this time Zane made a mocking toast.

The other man did the same before his group moved a few feet from the bar, Blake turning his back on the Foleys to face Tate. When Katie left them to greet some other members of the board who were already seated at the dining tables, it wasn't Tate who tracked her with his gaze.

It was Blake.

Zane filed that away.

Soon, other partygoers blocked the McCords from view, and it was tough to see them from that point on.

"Hard to believe," Jason said, "that someone as decent as Eleanor McCord gave birth to that bunch."

As the brothers agreed, Zane noticed that his dad didn't say anything.

Actually, Zane thought that maybe there was something…odd…about the brief expression that had colored his father's gaze.

Was he remembering the young love he'd held for Eleanor before Devon McCord ruined it?

His dad caught Zane watching him, and the older man rested a hand on Jason's arm and began guiding him out of the Foley circle.

"I believe we'll make the rounds," Rex said. "Besides, I'd like to freshen my drink."

"Have at it," Zane said, watching as his dad and Jason entered the crowd of cocktail dresses and suit jackets, the latter of which were gradually coming off as the party went on.

That left Zane and Travis alone, and his younger brother visually swept the room, not addressing Zane head-on.

"Melanie seems to be a natural with Livie," he said.

It was a real change of subject, and Zane assumed that his sibling was only bringing it up because he'd had enough of the McCords for now.

He tried to find her and Livie amongst the throng, yet failed. Maybe she'd taken his daughter outside to play some of the charity games.

"During her final interview," Zane said, "I told her she appeared too good to be true, but her records are clean—and I'd have been a fool to ignore her reference from a personal friend. And that reference was right about Melanie. She really is an outstanding…" he tripped over the word "…nanny."

Travis sent Zane a long, hard look.

"What?" Zane asked.

"Nothing." Travis shook his head and drank his beer.

Then he excused himself, saying that he saw an old friend and wanted to say hello.

As Travis left, Zane kept an eye on his brother, wondering what the hell his comments had been about. Travis's reticence even burned him a little, because this was Melanie—the best woman Zane had ever…

Loved?

God, why did that notion rattle him every time?

But he knew: Danielle. History repeating.

He should've been over it, but he wasn't.

Zane finished his drink, and was just about to leave his spot, when Livie jumped in front of him, all smiles and snow-cone blue around her mouth.

No matter what kind of mood he might've been in, he laughed, and Melanie showed up with a facial wipe, as if she'd been chasing Livie around with it.

"Come here, you," she said to the girl.

Exasperated, Livie closed her eyes and raised her face so Melanie could clean her up. Meanwhile, in diamonds and silk, Melanie grinned at Zane.

Her love for Livie—and for him?—shone through, and he wanted to kiss her, right here, right now. Wanted to thread his fingers through her blond hair and bring her close, tasting her, consuming her.

"This party is going off well," she said when she was done with Livie.

The girl spotted another child her age close by and

shyly wandered over while both he and Melanie began to follow, their steps slow, unhurried.

"Thanks to you and the staff, the event's going to haul in more than ever," he said, meaning it as a compliment.

But when her cheeks went pink, he realized that she'd paid more attention to being lumped together with the other employees than in what he'd actually been saying.

"Hey, now." He halted them both near Livie at the side of the tent, where she'd sat down on the grass near the other girl, who introduced herself to Livie by showing her a doll she was playing with.

Zane touched Melanie's arm, fingertips on skin, sending voltage through her. "You know what I meant."

"Yes," she said, smiling, even though he could tell it was forced. "I know."

All the voices around them seemed to drop off into nothing as Zane looked into her eyes, the blue capturing him.

His future. His Melanie.

Not caring who saw, he slipped his hand to the small of her back, where her dress dipped.

Her flesh, silky warmth.

"You're tempting me to take you right out of here," he said softly.

Her smile went dreamy, and it perked up his heartbeat.

They kept walking until they heard a familiar chuckle, and Zane almost took his hand away from her.

But he didn't.

Instead, he kept it right where it was, claiming Melanie, for anyone to see.

Jason was still laughing as Zane and Melanie halted near his brother and his father. The other two seemed to be sharing some kind of private joke.

When their dad saw Zane, he assumed a "you're not going to believe this" glance, including them in the conversation. "Odd what you hear during a party when people think their conversation's being covered by all the chatter around them."

Zane got a bad feeling about this.

"If you're thinking," Jason said to Zane, "that we sidled right up to the bar, unseen by Blake and Tate, you'd be right."

Their father had the grace to look sheepish. "We only overheard them for a short while, and not on purpose…at first."

"I hope they didn't see you," Zane said.

"No. The McCord boys went off to join Katie before they even looked our way."

Clearly, Jason had only been continuing his information-culling "plan," and with the possibility of some progress in that area, Zane's fingers tightened on Melanie's back.

It made him talk before he really thought about what he was saying.

"If you don't mind," he whispered, leaning toward her so only she would hear, "this is business. I'll find you in a bit."

Her spine straightened, and he caught a pained cloud in her gaze as she murmured something about Livie, then left before he realized what had just truly happened.

Business. He'd dismissed her because of it, and she knew it.

Was she wondering if she came in second to office hours and the McCords?

Surely she realized how he truly felt about her—even if he hadn't told her in so many words....

Jason continued, totally unaware of Zane's muddled emotions.

"If we had any doubts about money troubles in the McCord camp," his brother said, "we shouldn't anymore."

"Blake McCord didn't say anything outright," their father added. "He's damned proud, and he seemed reluctant to even be talking about it to Tate."

Zane watched from afar as Melanie stood next to Livie while his daughter played with the other little girl.

He wanted to be there.

But he had to see to the McCords, too. Business was...more important than anything?

"Zane?" Jason asked.

He glanced back at his brother and dad, who were gauging him as if he'd dropped his brain somewhere on the floor and hadn't ever picked it back up.

"I'm listening," he said, but he sounded as distracted as he felt.

As his father kept measuring up Zane, Jason went ahead.

"We couldn't hear very well, only a phrase here and there, but Blake and Tate mentioned the Santa Magdalena Diamond, all right. Something about how it relates to Travis's ranch and the land deed that Grandpa Gavin lost to Harry McCord in that poker game. So, as you can tell, Zane, my instincts were right. Never doubt a man with a plan."

Zane didn't even have time to chuff before his dad added, "It sounds like there're some clues on that deed that lead to one of the property's abandoned mines."

"The Eagle," Jason said, referring to the name given to just one of the five mines. "But, again, that's all we could hear, so I don't know how they got from point A to B and so on." He grinned that lady-killer grin. "I'll find out, though."

With Penny McCord, Zane thought.

Jason was, by now, scanning the crowd in his charming, cocky way, as if it was time to move on, meet some women, go from there. "Blake mentioned their sister Paige's name along with the words *'diamond'* and *'mine'*, and I figure, since she and Penny are twins, they've got to be close. Penny's going to know something about whatever scheme Paige is cooking up along with her brothers."

"Good, Jace," Zane said. "That sounds reasonable."

But once again he was looking away from the conversation, just like his brother, and it had nothing to do with anyone but Melanie. Yet, she and Livie weren't in the same place anymore.

They were gone.

A pang got to him, but it wasn't just because he already missed her.

When he caught up to her, how was he going to explain his attachment to business at her and Livie's expense?

As he tried to figure it all out, the party went on around him, even though, without her nearby, it was so much less festive.

Chapter Eleven

The party was over, and as the crews deconstructed the tents and tidied up, Zane knew he needed to do a bit of the same with Melanie.

Take apart the hurt he'd seen after he'd dismissed her. Clean up the mess he'd left.

He didn't find her again until he got back to the house. She was putting Livie to bed, and he joined in what had become a nightly ritual, with his daughter asking him to read from one of those vividly illustrated Golden Books. Then, in turn, he and Melanie kissed Livie good-night.

They would seem like a real family to anyone who casually looked in on them, Zane thought. But he sure hadn't treated Melanie like a true part of his life tonight.

She told him that she was going to get ready for bed in her room, then come to his, as she'd been doing for a while now, in order to keep from flaunting their sleeping arrangements. So he went to his own quarters, took a shower and put on his sweatpants and T-shirt. Then he waited for her, tempted by a pile of contracts near the bed, but denying the call of work.

Because that had been the issue, he thought. Work. The McCords.

And right now, neither of them appealed.

When Melanie took a longer time in coming than he'd anticipated, he couldn't wait any longer, so he headed for her room and knocked on the door.

"Come in," she said, sounding far away.

But he was here to make sure she would always be close.

The realization washed through him. He needed to let her know, once and for all, exactly how much he'd come to love her, how much she added to his and Livie's lives.

And he was ready, by God. So ready to lay himself out there because, out of everyone in this world, he could trust Melanie. She had already accepted everything about him, and it was up to Zane to let her know that he was going to do the same with her.

Nerves humming, he found her dressed in a white peignoir, taking off her makeup. The outfit was one he'd recently bought, lacy, silken, as refined as she was becoming more and more each day. Her hair was down around her shoulders, combed out, soft.

Zane loved to see the changes in her, but he would always value the image of the woman in the knockoff-quality business suit, too.

Leaning against the bathroom door frame, he said, "Long time, no see."

She gestured toward her half-removed makeup; she'd worn more than usual for the party. "I've got a lot more to deal with tonight."

He took a deep breath, ready to apologize for how he'd treated her. "Tell me about it."

At first, he wasn't sure why her shoulders slumped a little. But then he realized she had taken his own comment to mean that he'd been forced to deal with the extra burden of the McCords during the party.

Was she reliving that moment he told her that he needed to take care of business? That thoughtless instant when he'd basically let her know that she was secondary to his other pursuits?

Well, he was going to put that worry to rest. He was a new man because of her, and second by second, everything that used to consume him became more irrelevant.

She finished taking off her makeup.

"Melanie," he said, allowing her name to carry all the affection and adoration he felt.

She turned away from the mirror, and he noticed how beautiful she still was, with or without those cosmetics.

"Tonight," he said, "I made the mistake of putting you off because of business. It was wrong, and I want you to know that I'm never going to do it again."

She smiled softly, but there was a tinge of sadness to the gesture, too, and he wondered if there was a lot more to tonight than he was realizing.

Even so, he was going to finish the apology. Then they could move on.

"I don't want there to be any secrets between us," he added. "I want to be able to come home at night at a decent hour, be with you and Livie, then talk to you about anything, whether it's about what I'm doing at the office or it's about the McCords." He grasped one of her hands. "I want to be as open with you as you've been with me."

She lowered her gaze, but he thought he saw the blue of her eyes go cloudy with something he couldn't begin to fathom.

So he touched on everything she should know as the woman he wanted to spend the rest of his life with: a brief version of history between the Foleys and McCords, the Santa Magdalena Diamond, this whole issue with Jason's plan and how it affected the way Zane had acted with her at the event today.

She listened, seeming to grow more uncomfortable with every passing minute, until, at the end, he said, "You look like you don't want to hear any of this."

It was as if she was trying to make some kind of heavy decision, and she held his hand to her chest, cradling it.

Then she sighed, releasing him before she walked out of the bathroom.

"I do want to hear all of it," she finally said as she sat on a chair near the bed, her hands folded in her lap, her knuckles going white with the pressure she was putting on them. "I...I *did* hear, Zane."

What the hell did she mean?

She continued, watching him as if she meant to test him with what she was about to say. "During our second interview, I forgot my suit jacket in your study, and I went back to get it. But you were on the phone with Jason. I loitered in the hallway and heard what you two were talking about, so I already knew about the diamond and Jason's plans with Penny McCord."

"You were eavesdropping on me?"

She nodded, still measuring him with that cautious gaze. Again, he thought there might be more to this than the obvious.

"I started listening in," she said, "because Jason asked you about me, and I was curious, because even early on I was smitten with you."

Zane didn't know whether to be angry or touched. Both emotions warred with each other, and much to his surprise, touched was winning.

"So," he said, "this whole time you knew about that piece of business."

"I was embarrassed to tell you."

He hated that she felt this way, hated that she looked so sad. And even though he wished she'd told him about this earlier, she didn't need to be punished any further.

But it was funny, he thought, because, only weeks ago he would've been quick to strike out with a lot more defensive ire.

"What else haven't you told me yet?" he asked, almost in jest.

Yet, she must have misconstrued his tone, because her face paled.

A tiny niggle—a guarded habit he thought he had overcome—lashed at him.

What's she hiding? How's this woman going to hurt you, and are you just going to stand there letting her do it?

But he was overreacting. And he didn't want to disappoint her like that. God, he wanted to make her the happiest woman on earth, and if she had believed that she couldn't confide in him, he bore that responsibility.

He took a seat on the bed. "What do you say we come

clean with each other right now. About anything and everything."

She closed her eyes, biting her lip so hard that he thought it might start bleeding.

In spite of not understanding what this was about, he saw her slipping away from him with every moment that she couldn't meet his gaze.

And he couldn't take it.

He couldn't lose Melanie.

"I'll start," he told her. "I made a big mistake today. A couple of them, actually. The first one was in not making it crystal clear to everyone at that party that you and I are together. I should have, even though all they had to do was look at me to see that I'm yours."

She shook her head. "Zane, that's not—"

But he couldn't be stopped. *She* was what he wanted. *She* was what he was stepping up and claiming right damned now.

"My second mistake," he said, "was excluding you from a part of my life that I haven't been able to let go of. Maybe I thought that my job—my old existence—was going to be my safety net, just in case you and I didn't work out. But I'm not going to do that anymore."

Her eyes were getting a sheen to them, but it didn't look like the start of happy crying. It looked like frustration.

"If you say it won't happen again," she said, her voice wobbling, "it won't. But it's been a long day. Maybe we should sleep on this, and…"

He leaned forward to cup her jaw with one hand. "Melanie, I've been so afraid of failing as a husband. As a father. But by protecting myself, I've been setting us up for failure all along."

"No…" She stared at her lap, where her hands were still clenched. Then, as a single tear spilled down her cheek, she fended off a sob. "It hasn't just been you, Zane. I've done things to set us up, too."

Right. Zane almost laughed, because the opposite was true.

He stroked her hair back from her face, wishing that she would look at him again, that he could see the steadiness in her gaze that he'd come to treasure.

He loved this woman, and by not telling her before tonight, he had been giving her up slowly but surely.

So he got to his knee at the foot of her chair, holding her hand in the two of his.

"I love you, Melanie."

A tiny sound came from her throat—another sob?

But why?

He kept on. "I want you with me, now and always, and I can't imagine a future without you in it." He rested his forehead against their hands, feverish, carried away. "Marry me. Be with me. Spend the rest of your life with me."

Pressing his lips to her fingers, he waited for her answer.

Yet, tears seemed to be her only response.

Even as joy welled within Melanie, it was blocked by the unrestrained fear of the look she would see in Zane's eyes when she told him who she was and where she'd come from.

He would be disgusted, she thought. And although he hadn't reacted as badly as she'd believed he would when she tested him with her minisecret about eavesdropping on him and Jason, she was sure that wouldn't hold true with her bigger bombshell.

Nevertheless, she'd come close to revealing her history when Zane had said that he didn't want there to be anything between them.

So close.

Yet, then she'd come to her senses, because how could one of the world's biggest tycoons have any kind of positive reaction to her mortifying past?

How could a man who hadn't been big on trust in the first place ever forgive her?

She actually wasn't afraid of him getting angry, either; in fact, she would welcome it because it would be well deserved. It was his disappointment that would get her.

He would be disappointed that, even after they'd made love and grown closer every day, she'd backed away from being truthful with him. And he would be disappointed that she wasn't the woman he'd fallen for.

As the seconds dragged by, Zane raised his gaze, still clasping her hand while retaining the fervid glow that had come along with his proposal.

She held to him tighter, not wanting to let go.

But the longer she didn't give him an answer, the more the shadows began to crawl back into his eyes.

And those shadows were encroaching because of *her,* not Danielle.

He released her hand, and she realized that he'd already taken her hesitation for a refusal.

Tears rolled down her face now, and she felt as if a fist had a grip inside her chest.

"For some reason," he said, staying on his knee, "I

thought a proposal would turn out differently. I pictured you crying from happiness, not…this."

Melanie opened her mouth to say something to make him feel better, but the words balled in her throat, and she feared she would choke on them.

She just wanted to tell him that she hadn't refused him in the least. That he was the best thing that had ever happened to her and all she wanted to do was make sure they stayed in love.

But how could they do that when the only way to appease him was to be truthful? She wouldn't pile more lies on top of the ones she'd already committed.

He got to his feet. "I guess I just bring out the tears in women."

She shook her head, but it was like the sky was crashing down on her, and she knew that she couldn't let this continue any longer.

"Zane," she said, barreling ahead. "I'm crying because—"

He held up a hand, halting every word she didn't want to say.

The proud man she'd met during those first interviews was back, his posture stiff, his tone stern, his gaze dark and guarded. But underneath it all, she could see that he was crushed, and she had done that to Zane.

Her—the woman who'd had such good intentions with Livie, with him….

He headed for the door. "I'm leaving. You just stay here with Livie."

She bolted to her feet, her heart ripping out of her chest, but as he opened the door, his gaze was so full of wounded rage that it stopped Melanie in her tracks.

"Don't come after me, understand?" he said. "I…"

His voice caught and he went out the door, shutting it softly behind him, leaving her frozen in guilt and devastation.

Her crying was the only sound she heard. She'd been so afraid of seeing disgust, but there was no way his reaction to her past could've been any worse than this. No way she could have done any more damage to him and, by extension, Livie.

At the idea of his daughter returning to the shadow she'd also been, Melanie forced herself to move, to open the door, then go toward his room. She had to tell him everything so that he would know she'd wanted to say yes.

Yes and yes, a million times over.

But when she got to his room it was empty.

And after she went to his window to see if she could catch sight of any taillights streaking away from the main house, she went back to her room for her cell phone and tried Zane's number.

As his voice mail intercepted her call, she began to understand just what "empty" really meant.

Zane only made it to the massive on-property garage, where he was about to take off in one of the cars—he barely even knew which one—before he asked himself just where he was going.

To Dallas, so he could fade into his townhouse?

To the office, so he could go back to a place that didn't hold as much attraction for him now?

He had no idea where he should go, but he did know that he'd put his heart on the line and Melanie hadn't taken it.

Anguish made him lean against a car door. All those feelings he'd suppressed for years were clawing him apart.

No wonder he'd banished them.

But Melanie—God, he couldn't even think of her name without another claw swiping at him… She had to be just as in love with him as he was with her. He'd been sure of it. And he knew she would walk through fire for Livie, too.

So what had gone wrong?

He replayed everything in his mind: their talk, her reactions…

And he realized now that she'd been close to crying even before he'd gotten to the proposal.

"It hasn't just been you, Zane," she had said. "I've done things to set us up, too."

And in his eagerness to make up for all he'd done wrong today, he'd completely ignored whatever she'd been working up to telling him.

What *had* she been attempting to say before he'd rushed into the proposal?

And what if everything hinged on the answer?

But even as he wondered, he left the car and made his way out of the garage, still not sure where he was off to. Still not sure if he had the courage to let himself feel again, to get back what he'd given up after Danielle's death.

As he walked, getting his head together, he stayed within view of the mansion, where Melanie might still be waiting for him if he found it within himself to go back inside.

Unfeeling, Melanie had gone from Zane's room back to her own.

Although she held the attacking emotions at bay,

they still raced around in a swirl of despair and confusion: should she go to the garage to see if Zane had taken a car out? And how would she even know if he had?

Instead, she walked through the house, hoping to find him in a sitting or dining room. Yet he wasn't anywhere around, and the questions increased in volume, nearly deafening her.

When Melanie arrived back at her room, the buzz of her mind came to a screeching halt as she found Livie at her door.

She was wearing a pair of new summer pajamas Zane had purchased for her, and they were decorated with R2-D2s, replacing the old pajamas Livie had used to make that Father's Day tie.

At the reminder of better times, Melanie got to her knees and pulled Livie into an embrace, burying her face in the girl's hair and holding back the threat of more tears.

Livie hugged her, too, patting her nanny's back. She was sleepy, and right now Melanie could get away with a short hug before the girl caught on that something was wrong.

Get it together, Melanie thought. *Don't let Livie see how upset you are. Don't pile this on her.*

So she held back her sorrow, attempting to dry her tears before Livie saw them.

She put on the perfect nanny smile for the child, trying to fool both of them. "I thought you'd be sleeping straight through the night."

Melanie's voice was thick, and she told herself to try harder.

Livie rubbed her eyes. "I thought I heard daddy in the halls and I couldn't sleep again. Why isn't he in his room?"

"He's somewhere around," Melanie said. "But I'm sure he's going to be back in his room soon."

If anything, Melanie would go after Zane herself, returning him here for Livie's sake. She would understand if he didn't want anything more to do with *her,* but she would still keep battling for this little girl.

And as Melanie put her hands on the child's arms, she realized that she'd come so close to having Livie be *her* little girl, too. Yet she'd allowed ugly pride to get in the way.

Pride and self-preservation, she thought. She'd been practicing it just as much as Zane had.

"Ms. Grandy?" Livie asked, tilting her head.

"What is it, sweetheart?"

The child's eyes were as serious as they'd been the day they met, and Melanie couldn't bear to see her return to the shadows, just like her father.

"Someday," the girl said, "are *you* going to not be in your room?"

Melanie tried not to jerk away from the question. She had seen it in Livie's eyes often, and she'd only been waiting for the child to ask it, so Melanie had merely done her best to always let the girl know that her nanny would be around, no matter what.

And this was the "no matter what," wasn't it?

Yet, what if Zane did fire her? How could she reassure Livie without giving her false promises?

"I'll always be a part of your life, Livie," she said.

And she meant it, even if she had to call or write long, long letters or...

"Oh," the little girl said, revealing that Melanie's answer wasn't the one she wanted.

But Melanie couldn't lie, not above what she'd already done to Zane.

As the child lowered her head, Melanie picked her up, cradling her small body, and started off for the girl's room.

"I'll be wherever you need me," she whispered to the child, who wrapped her arms around Melanie. "And I mean that. Never forget it, Livie."

As she lay her charge down to sleep again, shutting out the lights after Livie finally blanked out, Melanie went back to her room, preparing herself for a long, lonely night. She was going to stay here in case Livie woke up again, but come morning, she would hunt Zane down if she had to.

Hours passed, the dark outlines of the trees outside shifting over the walls. But, near dawn, just when Melanie was half asleep, her burning eyes no longer able to stay open, she thought she heard footsteps creaking up the stairway.

She sat up in bed, hoping.

Praying it was Zane.

Chapter Twelve

Zane took the stairs, his gaze fixed at the very top of them.

For most of the night he'd sorted things out on the lawn, which had become empty, once the tents were taken down and the laughter from less than a day ago had died.

Melanie's laughter, Melanie's smiles.

He'd sat on that lawn, debating with himself until he ultimately decided that he wasn't going to accept things as they'd ended tonight.

He was going to go back into that mansion and put himself out there again, no matter how much of a wreck it might make him in the end. He owed Livie that much.

And he owed himself.

When he reached the top of the steps and came to Melanie's door, he didn't even knock. He just opened it, his blood jerking as the predawn room revealed her sitting up in bed, as if she'd heard him coming up the stairs.

As the air went still around them, chopped into sections by his heartbeat, they sat there, watching each other. His body rhythms went off the charts, merely because he was near her—the woman he couldn't stop loving, even if she hadn't accepted his offer of marriage.

He could hear her breathing, see her chest moving underneath the nightdress he'd so carefully chosen for her, knowing how she'd look in…and out…of it.

"I…" She put a hand to her heart, as if to stop it from punching its way out of her. "I thought you might have left Tall Oaks for good."

Did she think he was still the man who continually distanced himself from life?

It stung to believe that she thought he hadn't changed at all.

"I was on the property the entire time," he said. "I wasn't about to go anywhere without hearing why you turned me down."

"I never said no, Zane—"

"Melanie, I know damned well when you refuse something, whether it's a gift or a proposal."

Her hand fell away from her chest in response to the whiplash tone he'd used; but he was hurt, too. He wouldn't admit it: his ego, his intentions…his very soul. Bruised and aching.

When she spoke her voice shook, and he took a step toward her before halting, fisting his hands with the effort. He couldn't lay himself bare to her again—not without a sign from her.

"I never wanted you to know," she said, lowering her head, her blond hair covering most of her face so he couldn't see it, not even by the faint light in the room. "But I realized that I'd have to tell you someday, even though I kept procrastinating...*hoping* I could somehow outrun myself. And, tonight, *I* was the only thing holding myself back. All I wanted to do was jump up and accept your proposal, Zane. I would've said yes in a heartbeat, if I could have."

She was coming around to what she meant when she said that she was "setting them up," and he just wanted her to get there.

"And why can't you say yes?" he asked. "What's going on, Melanie?"

She brought her knees up, wrapping her arms around them. It was a shelter he recognized all too well, because he'd felt like that inside for a long time.

"I'm ashamed to tell you," she whispered raggedly. "I always have been."

A tug of war pulled him toward her and away from her at the same time.

Yet, all he could do was wait for her, because he wasn't going to leave this room without the truth.

"Ashamed of what?" he prompted.

"Ashamed of...me." She bit her lip, as if trying to keep herself from crying again, but her voice went shaky and thick anyway. "Of who I really am."

Of who she...?

His mind blanked for a minute, but then it started to piece together what was what.

"Today's party..." he began. "It was the first time you were in my world, and you felt out of place as the family nanny. That's why you think I didn't want to claim you in front of God and country—because you believe we were all thinking that a girl like you didn't belong."

She started to glance up, and he took a step closer to the bed.

"You're wrong, Melanie," he added. "Maybe I'm slow to announce a relationship after what happened with my first marriage, but that has nothing to do with you."

Her next words froze him.

"That's not it at all, Zane. I've been lying to you."

And there it was—stark and simple, enough to make him take a step back. His vision swirled as his mind struggled to catch up.

Had he made the day's biggest mistake in coming up here again?

"Lying...how?" he asked.

"There're some details," she said quietly, the shame weighing on her tone, "that I left off my resume."

The oxygen deserted him, but he still managed to ask, "Then who *are* you?"

She paused, then looked him straight in the eyes. He could tell it was taking every bit of strength she had to do it.

"I'm a girl who was raised dirt-poor. A woman who took up dancing in a Vegas casino to make ends meet for her family back in Oklahoma. A person you would've never hired if you'd known."

His first urge was to be angry with her for lying to him—right now he couldn't give less of a crap about her being poor or dancing. But Danielle had hidden things from him, and he'd promised that it would never happen again. Yet here he was, and...

And his heart was breaking as Melanie lowered her

head again, shaking it in such obvious self-hatred that he couldn't take it.

He saw what he'd been like only weeks ago, before she'd come along. He would have fired her after this revelation. Banished her from his life.

But, calling on what she had taught him about loving and patience, he came to sit on the bed near her, resting a hand on her sheet-covered ankle. That seemed to steady her a bit.

She angrily wiped the tears from her eyes. "Why aren't you throwing me out yet?"

Zane kept holding on. "Just explain this to me."

Melanie didn't speak for a moment. But then, tentatively, she told him everything; as she went along, her words came faster and faster, and she was relieved to be rid of them.

She talked of her mother's tendency to date the wrong men, how Melanie didn't even know the identity of her own father, how her mom had a constant need for loans and how that had led to dancing in the Grand Illusion casino.

Then she told him of her decision to wipe that part of her life off the map and head for greener pastures.

Every confession was a slice to Melanie's hopes, as she watched his expression, which hadn't changed since he'd sat on the bed.

But she'd known it would turn out this way. And she wouldn't love Zane any less for cutting her loose when she was done speaking.

"I only hoped to become the person I always believed I could be," she finally said, struggling to keep from breaking apart. "And I know I might not have gone about it in the best ways possible, but I think I did some good for me, and for others. At least, I wanted to."

"You did a lot of good."

Melanie's spirits rose, but then crashed again as she searched his face for any meaning beyond what he'd just said. Yet, he was still inscrutable, and she feared he'd go back to being halfway across the world from her, even though he was sitting right there.

That's what hurt the most about this, she realized. The fact that she'd put him in a position where he was disappointed in someone once more.

He took his hand off her ankle, and it felt as if she were alone—just as utterly and truly alone as she had known her life's story would make her if anyone discovered it.

"I wish you would've just told me," Zane said.

"When? I wanted the nanny job. I adored Livie from the first time I met her, and I knew that you'd never hire a downtrodden ex-showgirl to raise your child."

He started to protest but didn't make it all the way through.

"I didn't know you then," he said instead. "So you're right—no matter how quickly I needed to hire someone, I probably wouldn't have chosen you."

"And if you hadn't hired me," she added, "we would've never..."

She couldn't say it. It seemed like such an impossibility right now—something that had slipped right through her fingers.

But he finished for her. "We would've never fallen in love."

Just the sound of it drilled into her, and she forced herself not to lose her emotional hold again.

"I wouldn't blame you if you never forgave me," she said. "I'd deserve that, because by not telling you about myself, I kept buying stolen time. I had a beautiful daughter in Livie. I had a family I would've done anything for." She swallowed, and it felt as if a rock was being wedged down her throat. "And I had you. So I don't regret what I did, Zane, even if it's only because it gave me all of that, until I couldn't have it anymore."

He stood, and panic flared through her.

He's really leaving this time, she thought. *And I can't do anything about it.*

She bolted to her knees anyway, willing to do anything for him, just as she'd said.

But then he paused, robbing her of speech as she sucked in a hopeful breath.

"I've spent a lot of time unable to forgive," he said, his words mangled.

Forgive?

She wondered if he would have it within himself to forgive her, and the hope grew until it pierced her chest from the inside out.

"There were years," he continued, "where I blamed fate for bringing the worst down on me with Danielle. And those years were such a damned waste." He leaned toward her. "Back then, I would've been angrier than hell with you, Melanie. But…"

Before she knew what was happening, he scooped her against him, crushing his mouth to hers in a kiss so raw that she crumbled beneath him.

He hadn't left.

He wasn't going anywhere.

As his mouth ravished hers, she took his head between her palms, keeping a hold of him, taking everything he was offering, because *he* was all she needed.

No diamonds, no cars—he was the greatest gift of all.

He swept his tongue into her mouth, and she met it with her own, the kiss wet and greedy, wild with the passion she would never lose for him.

A forever love, she thought. She'd never hoped to find one, but here it was, with Zane.

He suspended the kiss while easing her backward into the crook of his arm.

"I can't be angry with you," he said. "I found you, and I'm not letting you go that easily."

Pure bliss shot through her, sizzling every cell and making her laugh on a sob—but now it was one of joy, not sadness, and he seemed to realize that.

"Is that a yes?" he asked, his tone rough, like a man on the edge.

This time she answered right away.

"Yes," she said. "Yes, yes, yes."

And she kept saying it, even while his mouth descended on hers again and he lowered her to the bed. He kept kissing her to within an inch of consciousness, as her world reeled, creating something out of what she thought to have been nothing.

As he lifted his head from hers just to look into her eyes, the morning came through the window and turned over in one instant of awakening sunlight.

"Yes," he repeated, as if rolling the word over them both.

It felt as if she were on a mountaintop, the wind

whipping around her, the air thin in her lungs. "What will we tell your family?"

"That we're getting married as soon as possible."

Nerves mingled with her light-headedness, and he noticed her anxiety about how the Foleys—and everyone else—might react to him marrying his nanny.

"Don't worry," he said, tracing his fingertips over her collarbone. "They like you. Believe me, they won't be thinking I've married someone who…"

He trailed off.

"Is so different from you?" she finished, saving him from having to finish.

His eyes took on a warrior's glint—the brash, arrogant gleam that had defined him in business. But now she was what he clearly intended to fight for.

"If you don't want to tell them about your personal details," he said, "you don't have to. It's none of anyone's business but our own."

"And the press?"

"I know how to manage the press. But if it comes down to it, I'll talk for days about the woman who pulled herself up by the bootstraps and made herself into the force who changed my life."

Melanie touched his face. "You would do that?"

"Hey, didn't Cinderella come from the ashes before she started wearing ball gowns?"

Oh, he knew just how to put it.

"Besides," he continued, "I fell in love with a woman who doesn't even need ball gowns to shine."

Melting. She couldn't stop melting.

But he must've seen the remaining fear that mingled with her excitement.

"Maybe," he said, "we could take it a little slower then? Would it help if we eased you into my lifestyle?"

"Zane, you wouldn't mind?"

"No, Melanie."

She could tell that he wasn't taking this as another hesitation on her part, but just to emphasize how much she loved him, she pulled him down to her, tenderly fitting her lips to his.

And when she had kissed him, she said, "So, I assume we'll be keeping our engagement quiet for the time being, except with Livie? I can't imagine not telling her."

Melanie would bet her life that his—no *their*—daughter wouldn't say a word. She had all the trust in existence for Livie.

"Then we'll tell her." Zane ran a hand through Melanie's hair as a changing light filtered through his gaze.

He smiled. "So…a dancing girl, huh?"

She nodded, ready for the shame to cover her again, but when she saw Zane's heart in his eyes, too, the mortification never came.

"I guess," he added, "during our long engagement, I'll just have to make sure you see yourself as I do, then you'll be calling every newspaper in the nation with the announcement."

She had no doubt that in no time at all she would. His love had that much power.

"I love you, Zane."

"And I love you. I just wish the whole world could know about it sooner. But I'd do anything for you, Melanie." He pressed his lips to hers. "Anything."

* * *

As she responded to him with a desire that matched his own, Zane reveled in the knowledge that every bit of Melanie was his: her future, her present and now even her past, which she'd finally released, just as he'd let go of his, too.

And in giving it up, he'd found something he'd never expected—a heart.

Melanie had been the one to help him rediscover it, he knew, and that mattered more to him than any of her history.

Still kissing her, he dragged her lacy nightie off her shoulders, then down the rest of her body, exposing every inch of her to the emerging blush of sunrise. When she was naked, he went back on his haunches, just to get his fill of her.

Then again, he knew he'd never be able to, and that was because she was about more than just a slender, streamlined body. More than long legs and perfect breasts. She was his soul, regenerating him moment by moment.

Blood pounded through him, heating him up, making him feel more alive than ever, as he parted her legs and bent to her.

He touched his mouth to the soft area between her thighs, and she moaned, encouraging him. Then he ran his tongue through her folds, up, then up again, until she was arching away from the mattress and fisting his hair.

"A long, very slow engagement," she said on a laugh that sounded so cleansed that he couldn't help but to feel the same way.

"And more," he said before separating her and loving

her thoroughly, making her churn her hips, rocking against him as he kept kissing, kept bringing her to the brink…

…and beyond.

After she climaxed, he stripped off his shirt, then the sweatpants he was straining against.

He fit himself over her body, feeling her sleek muscles against his own, as his erection nudged her.

"Do we…?" she began to ask on a breath.

He knew she was asking about a condom.

"I don't want anything to come between us," he said, repeating what he'd told her earlier.

Melanie cupped his face, her expression glowing with the love she'd confessed, along with everything else.

"Me, either," she said. "I want it *all* with you, Zane."

Then, so slowly that it slayed him, she skimmed her fingers down his chest, his stomach, resting them on his length, which was pulsing in anticipation of being inside her.

She made his wish come true, guiding him into her and then rising up to take him all the way in.

At first, his vision went blank at the feel of her, but it returned in blazing color as he slid out, then in, again and again, as she kept time with him.

Wanting to go deeper, wanting everything he could get from her, he lifted one of her legs, and she answered by bending it to the side.

Her flexibility pumped him, and he drove into her once more…twice more…another time….

Pressure curled inside of him, melting inward, then arching. Arching some more.

And his passion kept arching, escalating, expanding into something like a bridge stretching from him to her, connecting them, its apex climbing and climbing until…

The arch shattered, but the link remained, as he kept hold of Melanie, his future wife, the woman he would forgive just about anything.

Because love had allowed it, he thought. Love made anything possible.

He stayed inside her as they leisurely kissed, his arm curled over her head, one of her legs wrapped around him.

It wasn't until long afterward, when the sun had risen all the way and they'd showered together, that they got ready to tell Livie the toughest secret she would ever have to keep.

At least until Zane could show Melanie that the world didn't matter when it came to them.

"Do you think Livie will be…happy?" Melanie asked while donning a sundress.

"I can't believe you'd think otherwise." He took her into his arms. "My daughter loves you beyond comprehension, just like I do."

Her smile was filled with wonder, as if she couldn't believe love was this simple. He could hardly believe it either, but they were going to make it so.

He'd forgiven her, and it'd been easy.

Still, a stray notion chewed at the back of his mind.

Forgiveness. If Melanie had taught him so much that he could forgive *her,* shouldn't he let it branch out to other parts of his life?

The image of the Santa Magdalena Diamond floated through his consciousness, but he blanked it out.

He wasn't going to think of the McCords now.

He wasn't going to think about them for a good, long while.

Taking Melanie's hand, he led her out of the room and to Livie's. And when they awakened her, she smiled up at them, as if unsurprised to see them together, greeting her first thing in the morning.

Zane squeezed Melanie's hand, then asked his daughter, "Can you keep a secret?"

Livie blinked, nodding eagerly as she made her way to a sitting position.

Melanie beamed. "When I told you I'm never going anywhere, I meant it."

As the child's eyes grew wider, Zane and Melanie explained the rest, and when they were done, she bounded into their arms, hugging them with a fierceness that told him she'd been hoping for this moment.

And when they broke apart to laugh with each other, as the girl started firing off when, where, why and how questions, Zane didn't see his past in his daughter anymore.

He just saw Livie—a happy little girl who wanted to move forward, too.

Soon, they were all embracing again, the family they were meant to be.

* * * * *

THE TEXAS
BODYGUARD'S
PROPOSAL

BY
KAREN ROSE SMITH

Award-winning and bestselling author **Karen Rose Smith** has seen more than sixty-five novels published since 1991. Her first taste of Texas was a barbecue at a Dallas ranch. She had great fun revisiting the city in this book. Karen lives in Pennsylvania with her husband – who was her college sweetheart – and their two cats. She has been writing full time since the start of her career. Readers can receive updates on Karen's latest releases at www.karenrosesmith.com.

For my husband – happy anniversary!
Love, Karen

Chapter One

The door to the library at the McCord family mansion suddenly opened and an absolutely stunning woman with long, wavy, honey-blond hair rushed in—Gabriella McCord. Her face and figure had been on every fashion magazine cover in the free world…and in a few tabloids.

Rafael Balthazar's breath hitched, though he'd never admit it. He did not want to protect a socialite model who'd grown up with every luxury at her fingertips! But as security consultant for McCord Jewelers he had no choice, not when Blake McCord had asked him for this favor.

In a peacock-blue, figure-fitting dress, matching high heels and swingy gold earrings, Gabriella could take any man's breath away. Just not his. He didn't go for divas.

"I'm sorry I'm late," she began with a smile that added punch to her beauty.

Their gazes locked and, for a few moments, Rafe actually felt a shift in his universe.

No way.

"My…plane was delayed," she explained, her gaze still on his. "I just checked in and rushed over—" She stopped when she realized he wasn't smiling or crossing the room to greet her.

If she expected him to fall at her feet, she was going to be disappointed. "Miss McCord, I'm your bodyguard. My duties will begin tonight when you return to the Sky Towers. Blake assures me a driver will chauffeur you back to the hotel after his mother's birthday dinner. I'll meet you there and we'll go over your itinerary for the upcoming week."

Gabriella's small, well-defined chin came up and her back straightened. "It's so good to meet *you,* too, Mr. Balthazar. I just want you to know I don't feel I *need* a bodyguard. This is Blake's idea, not mine."

Nope, Rafe wasn't moving toward her. He had to establish an impenetrable boundary now. In a low, controlled voice, he responded, "You don't need a bodyguard? I understand there was a scene at the airport when you arrived." Blake had filled him in on *that* disaster. Rafe hadn't been available sooner. He'd been handling a security problem in Houston and had just returned in time to meet Gabriella before Eleanor McCord's birthday dinner.

Gabriella's cheeks flushed a bit. "Paparazzi somehow found out when I was arriving. I managed to slip away."

"More than paparazzi found out. There was a crowd waiting for you and it blocked the limo from leaving. Two things you'll learn while I'm guarding you. One, you have to be honest with me. Two, you must not put yourself at risk unnecessarily. Understood?"

Gabriella's golden-brown eyes sparkled with defiance. "Understood? I understand that you were once a Secret

Service agent, and a very good one. That's super. I commend your service. But I will *not* let you dictate where I go and what I do. Do *you* understand?"

He had to admit she was one beautiful, feisty package. Something he had to ignore…yet manage. "My job is to keep you safe."

"So you'll just have to do your job. As spokeswoman for McCord Jewelers, I'm going to do whatever Blake has planned for me and that will probably involve crowds. I also have a few engagements of my own and I can never predict what will happen."

"Like a stalker accosting you?" Rafe knew that had happened last year.

Gabriella's face drained of color, then she recovered her composure and gave him a new smile. "I haven't had any stalkers recently, so no worry there. And you only have to cover me for a few weeks. I'll be returning to Italy for a short time at the end of August. When I return to the States, Blake will have screened someone else and you can go back to your job concentrating on the security of the stores."

"In the meantime, we have to work together."

"No, Mr. Balthazar. You just have to make sure fans don't tear me apart."

Unbidden, an image took form in front of Rafe's eyes, a photo of Gabriella that had appeared in a tabloid last month. The paparazzi had snapped a picture of her dancing in a London club. It was a money shot because the clasp on her designer dress had malfunctioned. Just as the top of the dress had fallen—

Had the episode been an accident? Or had the whole situation been planned for publicity's sake?

This time Gabriella's face rapidly gained color, and he knew she was recalling the same image. Abruptly she turned away from him.

"Miss McCord…"

"We'll talk later," she murmured. "I don't want to keep my aunt waiting on her birthday."

And Gabriella McCord was gone.

"That went well," Rafe muttered and raked his hand through his short-cropped, black hair.

Gabriella McCord would be even more trouble than he'd expected, but he could deal with her. He'd protected the president of the United States. He wouldn't let one pretty model throw him off his game.

Not now. Not ever.

An hour later, Gabriella sat at the huge mahogany table in the mansion's dining room, still feeling shaken to her core. Why had she reacted so strongly to Rafael Balthazar? It had only been a month since she'd finished an emotional entanglement with Mikolaus Kutras that had turned out to be the worst relationship in her life. She certainly wasn't ready for another.

And she wasn't the only one who wasn't herself tonight. This was supposed to be a celebration of Eleanor McCord's birthday. A widow for about a year, Eleanor had asked all of her children to be with her tonight, and had included Gabby. Gabby and her aunt Eleanor had always been fond of each other. When she was in the U.S. and her own mother was back in Italy or finishing a film somewhere, Gabby knew she could count on her aunt.

Eleanor usually wore a smile, but tonight it was a thin replica of itself. The rest of the family wasn't much better. Blake, CEO of the McCord jewelry store empire, wore a sober expression. Tate, who had been engaged and easygoing before working in Baghdad as a surgeon with the International Medical Corps, had returned a changed man. Instead of happy-go-lucky, now he was brooding and disillusioned. And

Gabby could see that everyone around the table saw the changes in him.

Beside Tate sat Paige, who every once in a while gave her brother Blake a quick look. Gabby wondered what common knowledge they shared. Paige had always been a tomboy. A gemologist now, as well as a geologist, she took trips to Africa and South America to unearth the beauties underground. Penny, Paige's twin, was quiet and refined. She designed jewelry for the McCord stores and had sold pieces to European royalty, movie stars and jet-setters.

Charlie, the youngest McCord sibling, sat to Gabby's right. He was twenty-one, and would be returning to Southern Methodist University in a couple of weeks. Charlie was very social, but tonight he'd hardly said two words. He and his mother hadn't looked at each other once. The undercurrents of tension at the table were like rippling atmospheric tremors. Gabby didn't think she was the only one who could sense them because conversation lagged, there were awkward lulls and this family who usually had so much to say was much quieter than it had ever been.

Still trying to change that, Gabby took a bite of her tiramisu and said to Eleanor, "The dessert tastes wonderful."

"Yes, dessert is wonderful," Blake agreed with Gabby. "I want to wish you all the best, Mother, for your birthday."

Gabby felt relieved Blake was finally making conversation.

But then Blake's voice took on the hard edge of stony determination. "I've postponed telling all of you as long as possible what you probably already know. McCord Jewelers is losing revenue. With the economic downturn, even our rich consumers are holding back. They're postponing purchases, eliminating others. And the general public... We've got more lookers than buyers."

"Just the U.S. stores?" Eleanor asked.

"The stores Joseph oversees in Italy are holding their own for now, but I want to make sure that continues."

Gabby was proud of her father though he hadn't been around much when she was growing up. These days, they had a great father-daughter rapport and she still loved wandering around the stores he ran in Florence, Rome and Milan, admiring all of the beautiful pieces.

"With the competition in the marketplace today," Blake went on, "our brand isn't as important or prestigious as it used to be. We need to do something about that *now*."

Eleanor looked stricken. "My goodness, Blake, how bad are things?"

His handsome face became grim, and Gabby knew her cousin didn't like his judgment to be questioned.

"Bad enough. That's why I'm telling you tonight. After Dad died and I took over, I found out McCord's wasn't as solvent as we thought it was. I had audits done in all the stores and the pattern is the same. If this continues, we might have to close Atlanta and Houston, maybe even Los Angeles. Our flagship store here in Dallas needs a lift, too, so we're going to give McCord Jewelers a PR boost to generate excitement around our brand."

His gaze met Paige's for a moment and then took in everyone else again. Gabby wondered if Blake had already discussed all of this with his sister.

"I've developed a multifaceted campaign," he went on, "based on the discovery of the Santa Magdalena diamond."

"The Santa Magdalena diamond has been lost since the 1800s!" Penny offered.

"Yes, it has been," Blake agreed.

"Treasure hunters found the ship it supposedly went down on about six months ago," Penny explained further. "I followed the news reports in case there was any jewelry found."

Gabby knew Penny was always on the lookout for stimuli for jewelry design ideas.

"Since the diamond wasn't found," Blake said quietly, "rumors that it was stolen by the crew surfaced again."

"Wasn't one of those crewmen Gavin Foley's father?" Tate asked.

Gabby expected to hear a unanimous gasp from everyone at the table. The name Foley was never spoken in this house, never spoken when the McCords gathered, never spoken if anyone could help it.

Responding to Tate, Paige answered his question. "Yes. The rumor was that Elwin Foley made off with the diamond. We're assuming that that rumor is true for a very good reason."

Gabby had learned the story of the feud between the Foleys and McCords long ago. It had begun when Blake's grandfather, Harry McCord, had won property with abandoned silver mines in a poker game from Gavin Foley. From what Gabby understood, Gavin had been a gambler rather than a laborer. The five mines his father had opened had never produced any silver, and his father had gotten killed trying to find it. Gavin had decided he wouldn't be that unlucky. He'd also never intended to be so unlucky that he'd lose the property in a poker game. Booze and adrenaline had caused him to put it up and Harry McCord, Blake's grandfather, had taken advantage of him. Afterward, Gavin had sworn that Harry had cheated.

The feud had begun.

At that time, everyone thought the mines were worthless, but Harry McCord dug deeper in those mines and he'd found silver. He'd become rich. The Foleys, including all of the descendants, hated the McCords.

"Our family tried to end the feud," Eleanor interjected. "Devon gave Rex a lease to the property."

Through keeping her ears opened on her visits to the

mansion when she was small, Gabby had overheard conversations and learned that her aunt had been part of the feud, too. Supposedly both Rex Foley and Devon McCord had courted her at the same time. Devon, Blake's father, had won. That love triangle had created more tension between the families.

"Your father tried to appease the Foleys," Eleanor insisted to everyone gathered at the table.

"I'm sure that Travis Foley, who's living there now," Tate remarked sarcastically, "faces the sunrise each day cursing the McCords because the land under his feet doesn't belong to him."

"Maybe so," Blake admitted coldly, "but the McCords still own those mineral rights and I have reason to believe the Santa Magdalena diamond is hidden in one of the mines."

"You're kidding!" Penny blurted out. "Why would you think that?"

"I think that because I went through Dad's personal papers again trying to find ideas to reestablish our brand. I found the deed to the property. After studying it, I realized it held the clue to the Santa Magdalena diamond's whereabouts."

"And nobody saw it all these years?" Tate asked skeptically.

"There's a border on the deed," Blake explained. "Apparently no one has paid any attention to it. Incorporated into that border are replications of petroglyph symbols. One of them is an eagle with a diamond shape in its claws. The border is faded so I sent the deed to an expert. After analysis, he agreed the symbols were drawn on the deed *after* the border. When I was a teenager, I explored the mines to see what they were all about, and I think the eagle mine is the key to finding the diamond."

Paige explained further, "Each of the mines has a petroglyph etched on a rock outside the mine—a turtle, a lizard, a tree, a bow and an eagle. We believe Gavin's father hid the diamond in the eagle mine. Since he stole the diamond, he couldn't easily sell it. After all, it's supposedly the largest canary diamond in the world. Everyone would have known. So what could he do but hide it somewhere until he could figure out how to make a fortune with it? He also knew mining was dangerous work so he drew the clues on the deed so his wife or son could discover it after he was gone."

Blake's shoulders squared as he assured everyone, "I know this is a long shot, but it's a long shot that could have a giant payoff. I'm buying as many loose canary diamonds as I can. I think they'll make a huge leap in value once the Santa Magdalena diamond is found. Just the publicity from its discovery will be huge. We'll have our stores ready to roll out a line of canary diamond products. Penny can work on that aspect. In the meantime, I'd like to initiate a new campaign for all the stores."

He glanced at Gabby. "Gabby has agreed to be the spokesperson for this campaign and we're so lucky to have her. She's as well-known as Paris Hilton, but since she spends much of her time in Europe, the U.S. press is dying to get hold of her. She'll go a long way to promoting this campaign. We're going to start with in-store appearances, beefing up our customer service, letting select clients e-mail Gabby for suggestions and advice, giving some of them appointments with her. In the meantime, Penny can work on designs for the canary diamonds and Gabby can build a wardrobe around that jewelry. We want a lavender box in a lavender bag in every customer's hand who leaves our store, not through high-pressured sales tactics, but through making them feel so special they're eager to buy. I'm considering initiating breakfast at McCord's, croissants and espresso, as well as champagne and hors d'oeuvres some evenings. This is an all-out effort to save our legacy."

Gabby considered the ideas Blake had suggested. She liked all of them and some even sounded like fun. Although much of her wardrobe came from European designers, she had a few favorites here in the States, too. In fact, one of them lived in Houston. She'd call Tara Grantley tonight and find out when they could get together.

Would Rafe accompany her to Houston where Grantley lived? A tingle shot up Gabby's back at the thought.

Blake had pushed his chair back and was about to rise to his feet when his mother stood instead. "Stay where you are, Blake. Now I have something to tell the family."

At Gabby's side, Charlie rearranged his tall, thin frame in his chair, pushed his dessert dish away and began tapping his foot. So there was something happening between Charlie and his mother. What?

"I won't keep you much longer," Eleanor assured them. "But there's something important I need to say. My bout with breast cancer last year made me rethink many aspects of my life. I do have regrets. With your father gone now, I feel I can reveal a secret that has been a burden to me for so many years. I thought about who this secret might heal and who the secret might hurt. But I just can't keep it inside any longer. I've already spoken with Charlie because this concerns him most of all. There is no easy way to say this, so I'll just say it. Twenty-two years ago, during a particularly unhappy time in my marriage, I had an affair with Rex Foley. Charlie is the result of that affair. Your brother is not a McCord. He is a Foley."

Gabby saw the shock and then the pain on all of their faces. Charlie's head was down as if he expected his brothers and sisters to reject him. Penny, Paige and Tate looked perplexed as if they couldn't imagine how one of their own could be a Foley. And Blake. Blake just stared at his mother, looking angrier than Gabby had ever seen him. The emotions in this house could explode tonight and she wasn't comfortable being part of that. She was not one of Eleanor's children. She could not help them sort this out, not yet anyway. Maybe after they'd reacted to the news with each other.

Gabby reached over to Charlie and clasped his hand. "Everything's going to be all right." She knew words wouldn't help him, but she said them anyway.

He raised his head and looked at her. "Nothing's ever going to be all right again."

Gabby stood then and laid her hand on Charlie's arm. She did the same to Penny then Paige and Tate, but she stopped when she reached Blake. He was rigid in his chair.

Gabby dropped her arm around his shoulders, leaned down to him and simply said, "Call me."

He'd have to call her about their next step. Maybe then he'd talk about what had just happened. But she doubted it. Blake was a world unto himself.

When she went to Eleanor, there were tears in her aunt's eyes. As Gabby stopped to hug her, Eleanor whispered, "I wanted you to know, too."

"Thank you for including me, but I really think this should be a private time for all of you. I'm going to go back to the hotel."

When Gabby left the dining room, silence still reigned there. She wondered who would break it first. She wondered if any of them would see that maybe this was the way to end the feud forever.

Whether it was or wasn't, Gabby needed to escape to a quiet hotel suite and forget about the tension not only from tonight, but from the past few months. No one here knew the real story behind what had happened in that London club a month ago. No one here knew the real story about her relationship with Miko Kutras. She just wished she had awakened to the truth sooner.

She just wished the truth had been kinder.

* * *

As soon as Gabby stepped inside the luxurious lobby of the Sky Towers, a security guard approached her. "Miss McCord? I'm supposed to escort you to your suite."

Gabby scanned the lobby, looking for Rafe Balthazar. He said he'd meet her here, but apparently he hadn't arrived yet. Or else he'd arrived, gotten tired of waiting and left. Still, taking a stab at doing what she was supposed to do, Gabby checked the guard's ID tag. His name was Joe.

"Have you seen a tall man with black hair in a military haircut? He's got really broad shoulders and dark brown eyes. I'm supposed to meet him here."

"Oh, I met him tonight. He's the one who asked me to escort you to your suite."

Apparently Rafael Balthazar had someplace more important to go. That was fine with her. She wouldn't have to deal with him until at least tomorrow. All she wanted to do now was sink into a bubble bath and ease the tension in her neck. It had been building all day, from her delayed flight to the scene at the airport, to the dramatic conclusion of the dinner with her aunt. Poor Charlie. She could hardly even imagine how he felt, his whole history being kicked out from under him and everyone else. She felt so sad for all of them.

That bubble bath was becoming more and more inviting. She'd called the hotel's maid service on the way over and asked if the bath could be drawn before she got there. All she had to do was add more hot water and she'd be in heaven. At least, her version of it.

The elevator whooshed her and Joe up to her suite. He didn't try to make conversation and she was glad of that. She was too tired to try to make small talk.

However, outside her door he asked, "May I have your autograph? It's for my teenage daughter. She thinks you're right up there with Jessica Simpson."

Gabby always said yes to autographs. If it weren't for the people who thought she was something special, she wouldn't be.

Joe produced an index card and a pen. Gabby asked his daughter's name and wrote a little note to her wishing her success and happiness. Joe just beamed and couldn't thank her enough. She inserted the key card into the lock and assured him again she was pleased she could make his daughter happy. Then she slipped inside.

The silence was a gift she needed right now.

Set on the uppermost floor of the main tower, the suite was large. There was an immense living room with a baby grand piano, French doors leading to a balcony and attractive, superbly fashioned sofa and chairs in cream with green accents. The dining room with its mahogany table and exquisite chairs could seat eight.

But she didn't head for the living room or dining room. She went straight to her bedroom and her bathroom beyond, dropping her clothes as she went. Her dress landed on the bed, her bra and panties on the bedroom chair. Her shoes she left cockeyed right inside the bathroom door. Although the night was warm, as August in Dallas always is, Blake's revelations as well as Eleanor's had given Gabby a chill. Goose bumps rose on her skin as the air-conditioning wrapped around her. She hurried to the huge tub with its wonderful bubbles, climbed the two marble steps and slipped into it, letting the bubbles rise to her chin as she switched on the hot water tap to give her even more warmth. She didn't care that her hair was getting wet as she closed her eyes and sank deeper.

She thought she was mistaken when she heard her name called. She thought maybe she had fallen asleep and was dreaming. But then she heard it again.

"Miss McCord." It was louder this time as if he was afraid she hadn't heard him.

He? She recognized that voice. Rafe Balthazar! What was he doing in her bathroom?

Slowly she opened her eyes, hoping she was dreaming. But nope, there he was. He'd rolled up the sleeves of his white shirt. His tie was gone and he looked more than a little perturbed. *She* was perturbed, too.

"Why are you in my bathroom?" She quickly turned off the hot water, not wanting any of her bubbles to disappear. After all, they were the only cover she had.

He must have realized the same thing as he backed away a few steps.

"We had a meeting, remember?"

"Oh, I remember. I looked around the lobby for you and you were nowhere to be found. Just how did you get in here?"

"I've *been* in here. Blake cleared me to have a key. When I arrived, you weren't in the lobby and I had work to do."

"What work?" She couldn't believe she was having a conversation with a fully-clothed bodyguard while she was naked. Bubbles kept popping in the air and she knew she had to finish this conversation quickly.

"I had to sweep the suite for listening devices and cameras. I didn't think you'd want to be caught—" he motioned toward the tub "—in a situation like this with a video camera running."

"Did you find anything?" she asked.

"No."

"Blake told me I won't have anything to worry about here."

"There's always something to worry about with a celebrity." She wasn't sure she liked the way he said the word.

She sighed. "Can't this meeting of ours wait until morning?"

"I don't think so. The first item on our discussion list is the fact that the adjoining room to this suite is booked for the next few nights. That means I'm going to have to bunk on the couch."

That made her sit up straighter, only she was very careful

she didn't sit up too far. "I don't understand. Why would you bunk on my couch?"

"Because I'm your bodyguard."

Their gazes locked and she realized she didn't feel embarrassed. She felt hot. And her heart was beating mighty fast.

"Right. My bodyguard. You're going to drive me to my events and make sure I'm safe."

"No, Miss McCord. I'm *not* going to be your chauffeur. I'm your personal bodyguard. Blake wants me inside this suite."

"I don't think so!"

Rafe patiently crossed his arms over his chest. "I do think so. And if you have any questions about it, call your cousin."

"I'll do just that," she said, starting to rise from the bubbles, then quickly sinking down again. "Will you please leave so I can get this settled?"

"I've already left," he responded tersely. "I'll be waiting in the living room." He turned away and glanced back over his shoulder. "Watch your footing on that marble. It could be slippery."

Then he was gone.

Gabby fumed. She stood and let the bubbles slip from her body. How dare he walk in here like that? How dare he think he was going to sleep on her sofa?

When she stepped out of the tub onto the marble floor, she picked up one of the towels by the edge of the tub and wrapped it around her. She wouldn't slip, and she'd get this settled right now.

Crossing to the phone on the wall, she dialed Blake's cell phone. What if Blake *did* want Balthazar to stay?

He couldn't. This was a mistake. Fifteen minutes from now, she'd be in bed, in her bedroom, and Rafael Balthazar would be gone.

Chapter Two

Gabby knew this was an awful time to call Blake after he'd just found out Charlie was only his half brother…after he'd just discovered his mother had had an affair. Both revelations would shake any man. But she couldn't stay in this hotel room with Rafael Balthazar, not when all her senses went on high alert because he was within ten feet of her, not when she was still in so much turmoil about what had happened with Miko. She'd believed he was every woman's fantasy and look what had happened with that!

Blake answered before his phone went to voice mail. "McCord," he answered tersely.

"Blake, I'm sorry to bother you. It's Gabby."

He took a few seconds to compute that. "Gabby, I really can't talk—"

"I'm sorry to intrude right now. I know you might be feeling torn apart. But…your Secret Service agent was in my suite when I got back. You didn't really mean for him to stay with me all the time, did you?"

Blake was a confident man, and the quality sometimes bordered on arrogance. Ever since they were kids, he'd taken the role of big brother to her, not that they ever had that much contact. But he'd never cut her off or made her feel as if she didn't matter.

He seemed to be pulling patience from deep down inside of him when he responded. "Trust Rafe, Gabby. I chose him because he took a bullet for a former senator and believed it was his duty. I wouldn't have chosen just anyone to guard you. I wanted someone who wouldn't try to take advantage of you. Rafe won't. His job and reputation are everything to him."

"The adjoining room was booked and he wants to stay on the sleep-out sofa in the suite."

"And you have a separate bedroom."

"Yes, but—"

"Gabby, you've had two stalkers in the last three years. One of them came after you. If anyone recognizes you when you walk down the street, you're lucky to get away with your skin, never mind the paparazzi who will push cameras into your face. I don't want anything to happen to you while you're under my watch. It won't if you let Rafe do his job."

She swallowed hard. "You really think this is necessary."

"I do, or I wouldn't have arranged it. If he crowds you in any way, tell him to stand back. He will."

"The truth is, Blake, I don't want to be around any man right now."

"He was a Secret Service agent. Ignore him. He'll feel right at home."

That made her smile. She wished she could make Blake smile. She wished she could help his whole family. "I'm sorry about what happened tonight. If there's anything I can do—"

Blake's voice turned almost icy. "There's nothing any of us can do. But I do know, none of us will ever look at our mother in the same way again."

Gabby could hear the resentment in Blake's voice and she hoped what he said wasn't true. Eleanor would be devastated if all of her children turned away from her.

"I've got to go, Gabby. Paige is waiting for me. I might need you at the drop of a hat. Will that be a problem?"

"I don't have that many commitments while I'm here, so I should be available whenever you need me."

"Trust Rafe," he said again, then wished her good-night and clicked off.

Trust Rafe.

Because Blake said she should? Maybe she should have had him give her advice on Miko. But would she have listened? Miko had seemed to adore her. At the beginning, he'd filled that empty hole that had been in her heart ever since she was a child. But then, he'd changed.

Or had *she* changed?

No, she'd done nothing to deserve his contempt. She'd loved him, or at least that's what she'd thought. How could she have fallen for a man she didn't really know?

Gabby headed into the bedroom to get dressed. The maid had unpacked her suitcases. She quickly scanned the clothes in the closet finding a long caftan in swirling pink and purple. Plucking it from its hanger, she dropped it over her head, straightened the fabric and decided to forget shoes.

She emerged from the bedroom and went into the living room where Rafe was sitting in an easy chair, examining a painting on the wall. He looked calm and serene, tough and dangerous, all at the same time. Although he'd been staring at the landscape on the wall, his gaze targeted her before she'd come within ten feet of him. She knew she hadn't made a sound.

He rose to his feet. "You got hold of Blake?"

She didn't want to see the satisfaction on his face that he had won. "I did. He said that I need you. He doesn't want to be responsible for anything happening on his watch."

The self-satisfied smile she expected on her bodyguard's face didn't come. Instead he suggested, "So Blake feels you should listen to me."

"No, he didn't say that. He just said you were good and you were necessary."

"And he convinced you?"

"No, he didn't. I don't like to be watched or told what to do. I'll warn you about that right now."

"Like I didn't expect that in someone like you."

Now he *was* getting under her skin. Although she knew she shouldn't, although she knew it was dangerous because the hairs on the back of her neck were prickling, she crossed a few more feet toward him. "Someone like me? Do you want to explain that?"

"I shouldn't have said anything," he mumbled.

"You did."

"I usually keep my mouth shut." The fact that he hadn't seemed to surprise him.

"You know nothing about me."

"I know you're the daughter of Joseph McCord and an Italian actress who is descended from royalty. I know you began modeling at seventeen and rocketed straight to the top magazine covers. I've been told women copy what you wear, how you walk and how you do your hair. I also know crowds have practically torn you apart and paparazzi think they have the right to follow you wherever you go, listen to whatever you say and photograph whatever you do. Because of all that, I imagine you're treated as a star…as a princess. That's what I meant by someone like you."

His assessment of who she was made tears burn in the back of her eyes. She would not let him know how his words had affected her. Unfortunately, she remembered every word from Miko that had affected her that night a month ago…words that had hurt terribly.

Rafael Balthazar was studying her now. She didn't let him see anything. "Mr. Balthazar—" she began.

He cut in. "It's Rafe. After all, if I'm going to hang around for a few weeks, you might as well call me what everyone else does. What would you prefer I call you? Miss McCord?"

Standing here, just a few feet from him, she could see the character lines on his face and figured him to be in his late thirties. She could also see the astuteness and intelligence in his dark brown eyes. Most of all, she could feel the strength and male power that emanated from him. It was tantalizing and quickened her heartbeat. How could that be when she was so disappointed in Miko? How could that be when she didn't know if she could trust her own judgment? How could that be when Miko had cheated on her because he'd felt that was his right as a man?

"Miss McCord is fine," she answered, trying to distance herself from any attraction she might feel toward this bodyguard.

Then she turned away from him. "I'll get a blanket and pillow from my closet. If you're going to sleep on the couch, you'll need them."

Rafe yanked on the pullout bed with much more force than was necessary. He hadn't heard Gabriella McCord's conversation with her cousin, but he knew how persuasive Blake could be. He also knew Gabriella had gotten off the phone without getting her way. She wanted him to leave. He was staying.

Because he was staying, he had to stop looking at her as a woman. He'd guarded mostly men since he'd gone out on his own—billionaires who didn't want to be kidnapped, tycoons in a foreign country, a few movie stars attending high-profile events. There had been that woman CEO he'd protected who'd been testifying in a fraud trial. She'd been beautiful, but he'd merely considered her an assignment. There had been a congresswoman who'd also been a looker. She'd simply been another assignment.

But Gabriella? He had to convince himself she was just an assignment, too. Yet every time he looked into those expressive eyes, he had questions. Why had she become a model? What was the real story behind her relationship with the Greek tycoon? Had they really broken up as the tabloids shouted? If so, why had he been standing over her shoulder as the photographer took a shot of her half-dressed?

Rafe told himself he didn't care about the answers. He told himself he had no right even to ask the questions. He told himself he still loved Connie and the unborn child they'd lost. Although the grief and sadness had diminished, the missing was still there after five long years.

Gabriella suddenly appeared again, dropping the pillow and blanket onto the bed. His gut tightened as the caftan molded to her whenever she moved, as her partially wet hair brushed her shoulders, as her beautiful face finally showed signs of fatigue.

"I won't need the blanket," he said. "I usually sleep without covers."

Her cheeks pinkened a little and he wondered if she was imagining him without clothes. Maybe Blake could find someone else to take his place.

"Do you have any commitments tomorrow?" he asked in a businesslike tone. "We didn't go over your schedule."

"I only have a speaking engagement tomorrow evening unless something else comes up with Blake."

"All right. Then in the morning we'll sit down and you can lay out your routine, parties you'll be attending while you're here, anything else on your schedule."

Her chin came up and Rafe was beginning to recognize that sign. When her temper flared, she got that look in her eye.

"I won't be attending any parties while I'm here," she told him. "As I said before, you don't know me so don't try to predict what you think I'm going to do. I'll see you in the morning, Mr. Balthazar. Good night."

She whirled around and left the living room. The sway of her hair across her back led Rafe to rub his hand up and down the back of his neck. He wished to hell he wasn't sleeping in the living room. He wished to hell he was sleeping in the next county.

Gabby heard the light rap on the door the following morning. Then she heard Rafael Balthazar's commanding voice, low now, asking, "Miss McCord. Are you awake?"

To her surprise, he didn't wait for her to answer. The door opened.

Making sure the covers were pulled up to her chin, she yanked off her sleep mask and blinked fuzzily at the tall, fit man who had half entered her room.

After she glanced at the clock on her bedside table, she saw it was only 7:30 a.m. Pulling the sheet up over her face, she mumbled, "Go away. No one sees me like this in the morning."

"I can't go away," he responded.

When he didn't say more, she pulled the sheet from her face and peered up at him over it.

He hadn't moved into the room but was standing just inside the door.

Her hair had fallen into her eyes and now she brushed it away. "I know you're under orders from Blake to watch over me, but not this early in the morning."

"Blake called. He wants you at the Dallas store at 11:00 a.m. He's notified the press and he wants to reveal the first step in his new PR campaign, something about a once-in-a-lifetime experience."

"Already?"

"Blake doesn't let grass grow under his feet," her bodyguard acknowledged.

He was certainly right about that. Blake did what he said he was going to do and made sure everybody else did, too.

"He wants customers to e-mail me about their jewelry and wardrobe selections, even make appointments, and do it personally. I'll have to fit that in with the ad shoots, speaking engagements and everything else I have going on." She was more or less thinking out loud, figuring out what she could adjust in her schedule and what she couldn't.

Rafe's eyebrows arched. "Maybe no one will want an appointment." After that succinct assessment, he turned and tossed over his shoulder, "I'll put the coffee on," and was gone.

Gabby didn't know why he annoyed her so. He just did. She made a face at his back.

Maybe he wanted to get fired.

No maybe about it. Rafe wanted to go back to being an independent security consultant, contracted to safeguard the McCord stores, not McCord's model and spokesperson.

He hadn't slept last night and he could blame his disgruntled attitude on that. Granted, he hadn't heard Gabriella moving about, turning over in bed, switching a light on and off but he'd been well aware she was there. Too well aware.

He filled the coffee filter and started the coffee. Rummaging through the cupboards, he found stocked shelves. Pancake mix was among the offerings. When he went to the refrigerator, he discovered eggs, milk, juice, yogurt, cottage cheese, fresh fruit and the makings for salad. He secured a griddle from a bottom cupboard and decided to start breakfast. Gabriella could either eat or not eat, call room service or not. It was all the same to him.

He'd just finished stirring the pancake batter when he got a wisp of a womanly scent—flowers and spices—the same scent he'd smelled on Gabriella last night…a scent that affected him as much as everything else about her. To his surprise, she was dressed in a knit lounging outfit. She was fresh-faced with her hair wet as though she'd just stepped out of the shower. Maybe he expected her to be primping for the next three hours before they left. He'd never expected her to look this…vulnerable.

He pointed to the stack of mail on the table that security had brought up. "Someone brought this stack over from the jewelry store. Apparently the public at large knew you were going to arrive in town this week."

"Last weekend there was an article in the Style section about me. It mentioned I was coming to town."

She went to the counter, found a mug and poured herself a cup of coffee. Rafe couldn't keep from watching her. She was slim, but not too slim, rounded in all the right places. Her golden-blond hair was darker wet. Unstyled, without makeup, she looked like the girl next door. Yet he knew better than that.

She crossed to the refrigerator, took out the milk and poured some into her coffee.

He motioned to the letters on the table. "Do you answer any of them?"

Gabby tasted her coffee and then peered at him over her mug. "I try to."

She couldn't seem to look away from him and he was having trouble finding another topic of conversation. Why wasn't his brain working this morning?

Then he remembered what he had been about to do. "I'm making pancakes. Would you like some?"

"Maybe one."

"One? You *are* kidding. No one eats one pancake."

"I do, and if I put butter and syrup on it, that means lunch is going to be sparse." She glanced at the batter. "But it might be worth it."

She was a model, a model who made her living being photographed. He studied her more carefully. "You *are* serious, aren't you?"

She took her coffee to the table, pulled out a chair and sat. "Very serious. And I have to have some protein with the pancake or I'll crash in the middle of the morning."

"I can fry a few eggs."

She laughed. "You're determined to raise my cholesterol. No, I think I saw some low-fat cottage cheese in there. I'll have a spoonful of that. But don't worry about me. I can make my own."

"I'll make your one to my four. Sunny-side-up eggs do sound good with that."

She just shook her head at him and pulled a few letters in front of her.

The aroma of pancakes and fried eggs filled the kitchen as Rafe flipped the last pancake onto a plate and took it to Gabby. She was deeply engrossed in a letter and to his astonishment, he saw she had tears in her eyes! He set his own plate of pancakes and eggs on the table and rounded the corner to peer over her shoulder.

He read:

> *Dear Miss McCord—I read in the newspaper that you were coming to town and I just had to write to you. I'm eleven. My mom died last year and since then I've*

been so unhappy. My dad really tries but he doesn't
understand me or what I need. My nose is too long and
so are my legs. I don't know how to dress. The other kids
make fun of me. I'm spending days at a summer camp
until school starts and I hate it. But Dad won't let me
stay alone.

Can you write back and tell me what I should do?
I was thinking maybe I should get a nose job, but I
don't know if my dad will let me, so I might have to
wait until I'm eighteen. How can I make the other kids
like me? How can I figure out how to dress right?
What would you do?

Libby Dalton

As Gabby realized Rafe was reading the letter too, she murmured, "This just breaks my heart."

He wondered why. Certainly she didn't identify with this girl, did she? How could she? Gabby was beautiful, accomplished and still had both parents.

"Are you going to write back to her?"

"I'm going to do something. I just have to consider what."

"Right now you'd better eat or your pancake will get cold."

"Thanks," she said, with a small smile, her eyes still shimmering.

Rafe quickly moved away from her to the other end of the table, sat and began his breakfast. He didn't have to worry about small talk, though. Gabby was quiet as she went to the refrigerator, found the cottage cheese and put a spoonful on her plate.

He had just taken a few bites, after which he was going to discuss their schedule for the day, when his cell phone rang. He excused himself. "It's one of the store managers. I have to take this."

She nodded as if she were preoccupied, and soon he was

deeply involved in the conversation. When he looked up again, she'd finished the breakfast on her plate and disappeared from the kitchen. A few minutes later, he heard the sound of the hair dryer.

A half hour later, Rafe was stacking the dishes in the sink when Gabby entered the kitchen. She was wearing a red-and-white plaid halter top, white jeans and sandals. She'd styled her hair in the fluffy, wavy, trademark tumbled mass that encouraged a man to think about running his fingers through it. Although she wasn't wearing much makeup, what she had on was effective. In fact, the red on her lips—

He felt drawn toward her and shouldn't be. He felt irritated by her and shouldn't be. He felt a combination of awe at her beauty and denial that it affected him.

"There's someplace I want to go before we attend the Dallas store's PR campaign opening," Gabby told him.

She really wasn't dressed for an appearance at McCord's, more like she was attending a picnic.

"Where do you want to go?"

"To Libby Dalton's day camp."

He was about to laugh, and then saw she was deadly serious. His mind clicked into gear. "I'll have to make arrangements, go in and find her, clear an area where you can meet her."

"No. I don't want it done that way."

"I'm your bodyguard, Miss McCord. It has to be done that way. I want to make sure you're safe."

"This is a day camp, Mr. Balthazar."

"It's Rafe," he snapped, tired of formality.

She eyed him for a moment. "Okay, Rafe. I want to make an impression, but not that kind of impression. I want to help Libby, not hurt her. I'd like this to be a surprise to the people at the camp and to her and her friends."

"That's not wise, Miss McCord."

"Gabby," she said softly. So softly, he took a few steps toward her.

"I want to do this incognito until we get there," she explained. "I don't want press. I don't want any outside influences affecting the visit. Blake asked you to protect me for a reason. Can you make this happen?"

He had a feeling the next few weeks were not going to be ordinary in any sense of the word. Gabby McCord was not going to be an acquiescent client. He supposed he might as well get used to it.

He might as well just make this work.

She came a few steps closer to him now. The scent of flowers and spice was stronger. The wavy tendrils of her hair were within reach. If he lifted his hand and touched her face—

"Rafe, I want to do this for a lonely eleven-year-old who doesn't seem to have any friends. Can you please make it happen?"

Was she flirting with him? Did she know the power of her golden-brown eyes, the hint of her perfume, the sensual look of her body? Was she using it all to convince him to do what she wanted him to do? Or was she just making a plea, one person to another?

Was he being played?

He thought about what she was asking, the logistics involved, what he'd have to do to get them there without being followed.

"Are you going to the store like that?" he asked.

"No. I have to come back here to change."

"It's going to be tight."

"I'm a fast changer."

Now he *did* want to touch her. More than that, he wanted to taste her.

But he was her bodyguard. He had her reputation to protect, as well as his. Most of all, he had his own self-respect to deal with when he woke up each morning.

He took a step back. "I can make it happen, but you can't stay long."

"I only need fifteen or twenty minutes."

If they could get in and out of there before anybody knew they were there…

"All right, twenty minutes tops. Then I drag you out of there whether you're ready or not."

"Deal," she replied with a small smile that sealed his fate.

He was going to regret this. He just knew it.

Chapter Three

Gabby waited in a darkened corner near a back exit to the hotel. Rafe had warned her to stay put. The expression in his eyes and the tone of his voice had warned her she'd better do it or he wouldn't be doing her any favors again.

Favors from Rafe Balthazar? Did she want them?

Then she remembered those moments he'd stepped closer to her and she'd stepped closer to him. Something other than hard neutrality had glimmered in his eyes. Their deep brown depths had flickered with…desire? Had he wanted to touch her? Wanted to kiss her?

If she were honest with herself—and she usually was—she had wanted him to do both. How silly was that? How insane was that? He was her bodyguard. What did she think? That she was in some kind of movie? No good could come of getting involved with him.

Yet an inner voice was telling her he was not like Miko.

Some inner voice. Where had it been when she was infatuated with Miko? She should know better than to listen to it again.

She adjusted the sheer white scarf over her head and tossed it over her shoulder. Her hair was going to be smashed to bits. She'd just have to fluff it out again. Adjusting the dark glasses that covered half her face, she was sure she wouldn't be recognized. Hotel security was good. Leaving by a back exit this hour of the morning, no one should be within camera shot. At least she hoped not.

The door suddenly opened and Rafe beckoned to her. "Come on. This way. The coast is clear for the moment."

"Where's your car?" she asked as she tried to keep up with him in the platform sandals.

He took her elbow as if he was afraid she couldn't see in those sunglasses. Her body went on alert. There were calluses on his fingers. From hard work? A tremor rippled through her and she realized how much she liked his touch…how much he made her feel safe as he guided her along.

Abruptly he stopped in the service driveway in front of a small green hybrid vehicle.

"This is it? Did you rent it?"

"This is mine. No one would be expecting you to be riding in a car like this. They expect a black sedan or a limo."

"Yours? Really? Do you live in Dallas?"

"We can have this conversation now, but someone might see us if we do. Hop in. Let's get going. We can talk as we drive."

He was right, of course. If someone caught them out here in the open, they could get cornered or surrounded. Still, she was sad that she couldn't have a conversation like anyone else. She'd been living like this for a long time now. When she'd been with Miko, he had kept her separated from family and from regular people doing regular things. It had taken her a while to catch on. She wished she could just do what normal people did, drive herself around, have a house, a garden, a dog. That inner voice was gnawing at her again and a longing tugged at her with it. Someday she wanted children.

She turned off the inner voice. At least in a few weeks she might find a house. She was determined to buy one in Tuscany near her parents' villa. Just a small cottage, maybe a little bungalow, just so she could feel normal.

Once Gabby had climbed into the car and fastened her seat belt, Rafe took off. He quickly drove away from the hotel, filed onto the interstate and headed toward Libby Dalton's day camp. He kept glancing in the rearview mirror. He changed lanes again, zipped around two cars and changed lanes once more.

Satisfied, he seemed to relax just a little. "I don't see anyone following us and my instincts aren't clicking in."

She loosened her scarf and let it fall to her shoulders. Removing her sunglasses, she turned to him. "You rely on them?"

He cut her a sideways glance then focused on the traffic in front of them. "Don't you?" he asked, not exactly answering her question.

"Sometimes my instincts are dulled by the crowds around me and the noise, even by my own expectations."

"How do you stand it?"

She laughed. "It's the way I earn my living. This is growing into something much bigger than I ever imagined. All I ever wanted to be was as fashion perfect as my mother and someday be on a magazine cover."

"What cover *haven't* you been on?"

She stopped to think about it. "I've never been in or on *National Geographic*," she joked.

"*Rolling Stone, TV Guide,* women's magazines on the newsstand. You've hit them all."

"I've had a lot of years to hit them. I've been doing this since I was seventeen."

"How old are you?"

"Twenty-eight. How about you?"

"Thirty-seven."

Thirty-seven. Certainly he'd known love. Certainly he'd had serious relationships, hadn't he? She couldn't ask. She really couldn't. She didn't know him well enough yet.

Yet? She shouldn't *want* to get to know him. They were from two different worlds. And speaking of…

"I thought Blake told me your home base was New York."

"I have family in Dallas. That's why I keep a car here."

"How much family?" It wouldn't hurt just to ask a few questions. Maybe they'd get along better.

"My mom and a sister."

"Are you going to spend time with them while you're here?"

"If I get the chance."

She knew what that meant. It all depended on her schedule and whatever else she required of him.

The navigational system in his car gave out a series of directions. Their conversation stopped and Gabby took the opportunity to study him more carefully. Unfortunately, she liked what she saw. Not just on the outside. A picture of the inside man was forming. Yes, he annoyed her, but she was beginning to like the way he acted and what he did and what he said.

"Looking for something?" he asked, catching her studying him.

"You're supposed to have your eyes on the road."

"My sixth sense is working. I trust it even more than I trust the other five."

She kept quiet. She wasn't going to tell him why she was watching him. She wasn't going to tell him that she found him an enigma, different from most men in a lot of ways. He wasn't trying to charm her or flatter her. Actually, the opposite. She caught herself trying to earn his respect and that was odd. She usually just tried to be herself.

"Tell me about your mom and dad," he suggested.

She didn't know if he was asking because the silence between them bothered him or because he really wanted to know. "You know who my dad is. He oversees all of the Italian stores."

"Besides being a well-known actress, I heard your mother was descended from royalty. Is that true?"

"Somewhere, way back," Gabby said dismissively.

"I also heard she's still in the top twenty of the most-photographed women in Europe."

Gabby didn't know what to say to that. Her mother had stopped making films a few years ago.

"I can't believe I made a comment you don't have an instant comeback for." His voice held a tinge of amusement.

"Are you trying to dissect me?"

"No, just trying to figure out what makes you tick. That helps in the protection profession. I can learn to predict what you might say or do, then I know how to cover you."

Cover her.

All of a sudden she had the image of the two of them in bed, his body covering hers. What was wrong with her?

To sidetrack her thoughts, she responded to his comment. "My mother's involved in a lot of charity work and she travels with my dad whenever she can. They're still very much in love."

"How long have they been married?"

"They'll be married twenty-nine years this winter."

"Love stories that last are hard to find these days."

"I know. My dad was thirty and my mom was twenty when they met. They fell in love instantly. He was already the manager of the Rome store."

"Did he have to fight for your mom's hand?"

"Do you mean, did her parents approve? Dad managed stores and came from a good family, although they were newly rich."

Rafe laughed. "There's a difference?"

"You've protected billionaires. You know there is. There's a snobbery among rich folk sometimes. But my mom's parents—they just wanted a good man for her to love."

"You have a tiny touch of an Italian accent. Was it spoken in your house when you grew up?"

She didn't want to get into growing up. Not because there was anything to hide, but because she always felt guilty about how lonely she'd been even though she'd had advantages that other children didn't have. Her nanny had spoken Italian. Her parents spoke both languages.

"My mom and dad usually spoke English." That was all she was going to say on the subject.

The voice on the navigational system told them what exit to take. They did and five minutes later, they were driving down the road to the camp.

Automatically, Gabby took a mirror from her purse, checked her makeup and ran her hands through her hair, fluffing it to counteract any damage the scarf had done. When she was finished, she found Rafe watching her.

"You look...fine." He finished as if he'd been about to say something else and substituted that word.

"I have to look more than fine. I want to wow Libby Dalton's friends."

"You will. I'm just worried someone will get on the phone and call the press before we can make an exit. So let's try to do this in the shortest amount of time possible."

"I understand, Rafe, really I do, but I came here to help Libby and that's what I intend to do." Then she picked up her clutch bag and opened the car door.

* * *

Moments later Rafe stood outside a rustic-style cabin. He let Gabby precede him inside. As she slipped by, her hair brushed his jaw. He didn't breathe so he wouldn't inhale the scent. He'd had enough of that in the car. Enough of that and her. What was this chemistry? With Connie, sex had been easy and enjoyable and tender. This heat he felt when Gabriella McCord was anywhere near him frustrated him and taught him about the control he didn't have.

Gabby turned to look at him. He saw the heat he felt come alive in her eyes. But then she broke eye contact and headed for the woman dressed in jeans and a T-shirt seated at a desk.

"Mrs. McLaren?" Gabby inquired.

Rafe had found out that Sandra McLaren was the one in charge.

The gray-haired woman glanced at Gabby and did a double take. Her mouth dropped open and her glasses practically fell from her nose. She pushed them back up and jumped to her feet. "You're Gabriella McCord! It can't be you. Is it you?"

Gabby smiled kindly, "Yes, it is," and extended her hand. Sandra McLaren shook it. "I'm here to see one of your campers—Libby Dalton. Would that be all right? I can't stay very long."

"You want to see Libby? Sure." Mrs. McLaren glanced at her watch. "This is her age group's arts and crafts hour. They'll be under the trees at the tables in the picnic area. Come on, I'll show you where. You're sure you want to see Libby?"

Mrs. McLaren glanced at Rafe.

"I'm sure. This is Mr. Balthazar. He's here to make certain I'm safe. We didn't want the press to get wind of my visit. That's why I didn't call ahead."

"I understand completely."

They followed Mrs. McLaren out of the cabin down the

footpath that led between other cabins similar to the first. It took them past a much larger facility. "That's the dining hall," Mrs. McLaren pointed out.

Rafe glimpsed a pool on the other side of the dining hall and guessed that's where the campers spent their afternoons. He was amazed at how easily Gabby chatted with the counselor about the facilities and the campers, the scholarships for students who couldn't afford to attend yet had no one at home in the summer to watch them. The counselor explained the seven-, eight- and nine-year-olds were at the playground while the ten-, eleven- and twelve-year-olds completed craft projects. They weren't far from the tree line when they heard children's voices.

After they entered the tree-shaded picnic area, Mrs. McLaren pointed to the second table on their right. She gestured to Libby who was studiously using a paintbrush on a ceramic figurine. The kids were engrossed in their work and didn't pay any attention to Gabby until she stopped beside Libby's bench.

"Libby Dalton?"

The eleven-year-old, tall and coltish, with brown eyes and medium-brown hair, wore a T-shirt, cutoff jeans and sneakers like most of the other kids.

When Libby saw Gabby, her mouth widened in surprise, her eyes grew big and then a grin spread across her face. "Miss McCord! You got my letter."

At the sound of Gabby's name, everyone took notice. The group of four at her table started coming forward to see if it was really her.

Gabby put her hand on Libby's shoulder. "I certainly did get your letter and I was going to write a reply, but I thought it was better if I visited you in person."

"I can't believe you're here!" Libby said in awe.

As the kids came closer, Rafe stood by Gabby's side and watched them carefully.

Gabby bent close to Libby so only the eleven-year-old could hear. "Your letter said you were considering a nose job. You look perfect the way you are. You'll grow into your own beauty, so wait and see what happens."

"But my nose is so long and straight," Libby whispered back.

"I think as you grow, your face will fill out more and your nose may not seem so long. Really, Libby, it's so much more important that you like who you are and become comfortable with who you are. Then you can be confident."

Now her voice wasn't confidential and was for everyone to hear. "I made a call to the owner of Jeans & More. You and a friend can set up an appointment with Mrs. Valaquez." Gabby gave Libby a business card with the name written on it. "She's the manager of the store and she'll help you select a fall wardrobe for school, absolutely free. How does that sound?"

Rafe watched the almost-teenager as she tried to find words but couldn't. Her eyes were tearing and she threw her arms around Gabby. "Thank you! Thank you so much. You don't know what this means."

Gabby didn't hesitate to hug her back. "Oh, I think I do."

Rafe studied Gabby as she stood there hugging the eleven-year-old, her beautiful hair blowing in the wind. Her sandals were covered with dirt from the path, but she didn't seem to mind. Was all of this a show for her own benefit? Did she plan a press release that she'd befriended an eleven-year-old? She seemed genuine, she really did. But *this* Gabby didn't seem to jibe with the Gabriella McCord pictured in the tabloids…the Gabriella McCord rumored to be having an affair with a Greek tycoon…the Gabriella McCord who jet-setted to a different location every week, leaving broken hearts in her wake.

While she couldn't break his—the death of his wife along

with his child had done that—he would not start something with her that would ruin his career.

When Libby stepped away from Gabby, she asked, "Can I show you what I'm doing?"

He leaned close to Gabby. "We should go."

"A few minutes more," she said. "This is important."

He checked his watch. They were nearing twenty minutes since they'd arrived. He knew too well what could happen in the next five. In fact, he'd seen one of the boys taking a picture of Gabby with his cell phone. She might get press coverage if she wanted it or not, if he called or sent the picture to someone.

But Gabby had already seated herself next to Libby and was examining the horse figurine.

"I want one someday," Libby confided, "but I don't know if I'll ever be able to afford a horse. Daddy says they cost lots of money."

"If you can't buy one, you could take care of one," Gabby assured her. "But don't you ever let go of your dream of owning one. If you want it bad enough, you can make it happen."

"Are you doing what you always dreamed you'd be doing? You're so famous. Everybody knows who you are. Isn't that wonderful?"

"Sometimes it is. Sometimes it isn't. I guess I'm doing what I always dreamed of, but I have other dreams, too."

Another girl about Libby's age poked her head between Gabby and Libby. "Does she really know you?"

Gabby was about to turn to answer when another group of kids approached Gabby from the other side of the table. They all held out scraps of paper. "Can you give us your autograph?"

Rafe said warningly, "Gabby…"

"Three more minutes," she pleaded.

Those beautiful eyes. They could make a man believe in almost anything.

"If I say no?"

"I'll stay anyway," she returned with one of those glowing smiles that he shouldn't let disarm him.

He shrugged. "I think you want the press to catch you here."

Since he couldn't keep the note of accusation from his voice, she glanced back at him, eyebrows raised. "Think what you want." Then she took a pen from her purse and signed about twenty slips of paper.

After saying goodbye to everyone and giving Libby another hug, telling her to send pictures of herself in her new clothes, Gabby nodded to Rafe. "I'm ready."

He took her by her arm and hurried her down the path. When they'd almost reached the dining hall, he hooked his fingers around her elbow and ordered, "This way."

"But your car—"

Then she heard the sound of voices, too, and realized he was leading her to an escape route.

He grabbed Gabby's hand and ran. To his surprise, she kept up with him. They cut through cabins and came out at the parking lot where a news van was parked. He didn't have to tell her to hurry. They scrambled into his car, he fired up the engine and they left, a cloud of dust settling over the gravel behind them.

Rafe glanced into the rearview mirror before he veered onto the interstate. "You were lucky," he muttered.

"And you were helpful. You've got good hearing. You heard them before I did."

He scowled as he peered into the rearview mirror again. "You're not taking this seriously."

"Rafe, sometimes I have to take a few chances or I'd have to stay locked up in a hotel room all the time. That's not living."

All the way back to the hotel, he thought about what she'd said. He'd been born to be cautious and ever since Connie had been gunned down by a drive-by shooter, he was even more so. Maybe that's why his clients hired him. They knew he'd be cautious even if they weren't.

Still, he wondered if all that caution had kept him from living a full life.

Rafe took a circuitous route back to the hotel. Gabby looked lost in thought and he didn't interrupt her musings. They were better off if they didn't talk. He didn't need to learn any more about her. She didn't need to learn any more about him. He was her bodyguard. She was his client.

He kept telling himself that as they parked at the rear of the hotel, as he snuck her in the back entrance, as they made their way up to her suite. Her suite. Did he wish *he* had one to take her to?

He made enough money, but his needs were simple. What would she think of his apartment in New York that was more of a landing field than a home?

Once inside the suite, Gabby went to her bedroom. Rafe checked the hotel phone for messages. One was from Penny McCord. Another was from a publication who wanted an interview with Gabby. A third was from her mother. The voice was as sweet as Gabby's with a heavier accent.

He'd never meant to be Gabriella McCord's secretary. He should have let her retrieve her own messages, but he had to screen her calls. He took the message sheets with him to her room. After he rapped, he walked in, all three messages still on his mind. But her mother's most of all.

"We can't wait until you come home. Your dad and I both miss you. You should see what we did to the stables. We think you'll like it. Call me back when you have some time. Ciao, bambina."

Rafe heard Gabby's gasp before it registered. Then he realized she'd unbuttoned her blouse. Her bra was a lacy white concoction that fired up all his fantasies.

The truth was, he didn't know what to say so he tried to keep it light and said the first thing that came into his head. "You're wearing more now than you were in that tabloid photo."

Gabby's complexion went white. She looked as if she wanted to disappear into the floor.

He was instantly sorry he'd teased her. Apparently her skin wasn't as thick as he'd imagined.

Stepping close to her, he kept his eyes on hers, rather than on the creamy skin showing above her bra. "What was the real story behind that photo?" he asked.

She studied his face as if she was trying to figure out why he was asking. He wasn't entirely sure himself.

"I don't want to talk about it," she said, her voice small, not at all defiant as she rebuttoned her blouse. She looked like a young woman who'd gotten caught up in something beyond her ken. Was that what had happened? He didn't know. What he did know was that he had to leave. Now. Before he took her into his arms and kissed her.

Instead of kissing her, he handed her the message slips. "You might want to listen to the one from your mother. She sounds as if she really does miss you."

To his surprise and dismay, Gabby's eyes filled with tears. But she blinked hard and fast and held her emotions in check. Did she do that often? Did she pretend she was feeling something other than what she was?

He couldn't take her into his arms. He couldn't. But he *could* touch her. Knowing he was tempting fate, he reached out and gently passed his knuckles down her cheek.

Lightning without the storm.

Maybe he was wrong and this storm was inside of him. He had instinctively known her skin would be soft. This close he spotted the light spray of freckles she usually covered with makeup.

"You ought to let the freckles show all the time," he said softly.

Then before he ran his fingers through her hair, before he pulled her onto the bed, before he kissed her until they both felt what passion was all about, he turned and left her bedroom.

Right now he was sorry he was leaving, but he wouldn't be sorry about it later. He'd done the right thing.

He always did the right thing.

Chapter Four

An hour later, Rafe sat on the passenger side of the limo beside the chauffeur and glanced into the rearview mirror at Gabby. He could still feel the softness of her skin on his fingertips.

That was ridiculous! Of course he couldn't.

He rubbed his forefinger against the tips of his other fingers anyway as if to skim the sensation away.

When the limo drew up in front of McCord's jewelry store, Rafe thought the columns out front showed that this was indeed a special place. The lavender velvet displays in the windows, the silver sculptures surrounded by diamonds and rubies, emeralds and tanzanite reminded Rafe of the caliber of clientele who usually shopped here.

He opened Gabby's door and tried not to be affected by her when she climbed out, her dress skimming up her thigh. He shot a comprehensive look at the door to the store and back at her. She'd changed into a white dress with crisscross straps across the back and the front. Although the style was almost demure, there was nothing demure about the material. It hung in loose folds from her breasts and molded to her when she walked. And with those spike heels—

He came up beside her and leaned near to her, her long pearl earring brushing his jaw. "Stay close. Move quickly. Let's get inside before a crowd forms."

When she didn't argue with him, he found himself placing his hand at the small of her back to guide her forward so she didn't dawdle. His fingers skimmed bare skin. She looked up at him and almost tripped.

Damn, but he wished this assignment was over.

Just then the front door of the store opened and Blake motioned them inside. To Rafe he said, "Everyone here has been personally invited so there's no need to worry about security inside."

"I always worry about security."

Blake sent him a quick rueful smile. "Just stay close to her. Don't let her out of your sight. I don't want anyone backing her into a corner or…getting too friendly. She's been through a rough spot and I want that to be over for her."

Rafe was Gabriella McCord's bodyguard. He didn't need to know the details of her life. But he did wonder if that rough spot was all about her relationship with the Greek tycoon. Just how rough had it been? Had the relationship itself been rough…or the breakup?

The floor in the entrance level of the store was gray marble. A lavender-and-silver theme was obvious in the cases lining the walls on either side. Up ahead marble steps gave way to lavender-and-gray plush carpeting, mirrored cases with gray leather club chairs and stools at the engagement diamond case. Black trim edged the ceiling and the floor.

Automatically he checked the security mirrors that accompanied the cameras. There were at least twenty to twenty-five clients on the first level and about that many on the second. Some of them carried cups of coffee from an urn at the side of the room. Others nibbled on delicate pastries. Gabby had already sped off to speak to a group in front of a case with an assortment of necklaces and bracelets.

When Rafe moved up behind her, he heard one of the men say to her, "I should let *you* pick out a necklace for my wife."

Gabby gave him a slow smile. "Now, T.J. After twenty-five years, I'm sure you know what your wife wants much better than I do."

"What if I pick out a couple of things and you give me the pros and cons of each?"

The man was twenty years Gabby's senior and married or not, he was definitely flirting, Rafe decided.

"I'd be glad to give you the pros and cons, but I have to warn you, I have this knack for picking the most expensive piece."

He let out a mock groan. "I should have known. But your choice will be well worth it if she really likes it."

Gabby escorted T.J. to the counter where one of the many clerks stood ready to help him.

Gabby lightly touched the man's arm. "I'll be circulating. Just flag me when you want me."

"Will do. It's good to see you again, Gabby. You should spend more time in Dallas."

"There's never enough time," she replied and crossed to another group of people.

"He was interested in you," Rafe said into her ear.

Gabby swivelled around suddenly, looking surprised. "He's married! And besides that, I've known him for years, ever since I was a kid. When I'd come to Dallas, he and Eleanor would take me riding on his ranch. He doesn't have any hidden agenda, Rafe, so don't look for trouble where there isn't any."

Rafe almost made a comment but didn't. *Her life is none of your business*, he reminded himself again. But he wasn't going to let her get into a situation today that she couldn't handle.

A woman in a conservative gray suit with her hair done up in a sleek chignon, onyx and diamond earrings at her ears, walked down the steps toward Gabby and gave her a hug. "It's so good to see you."

"You, too, Marjorie." Gabby turned to Rafe. "Do you know Marjorie Dunham?" At his nod, she remarked, "She's a friend, as well as the manager. She does a wonderful job. Marjorie, Rafe is my bodyguard, so if you see him following me around, it's because Blake has hired him to do that."

"It's a very good idea." Marjorie pointed outside the front door where a crowd was gathering. "Word has gotten out that you're in here."

"Word was supposed to get out. This is a publicity event."

"Blake sprung this on both of us rather quickly. Did you manage to sleep after your trip from London?"

"Oh, I didn't come straight from London. I flew to New York first and spent some time there."

The older woman looked at Gabby sympathetically. "Are you finished with what happened in London?"

Gabby went very still and a painful look came into her eyes. From where Rafe stood, she seemed to be transported to somewhere else, somewhere far away.

But then she answered Marjorie's question. "Yes, I am. At least, I hope I am." She hesitated a moment then went on, "I came to Dallas to get away from all of that. So why don't you show me the newest pieces of jewelry that you might want me to model."

"I have the perfect necklace for you to wear with that dress. You can show it off while you're working the crowd."

Then Gabby was off, up the stairs with Marjorie, Rafe on her heels.

Gabby sat on one of the stools while Marjorie showed her a necklace. Necklace didn't seem to be the right name for something so spectacular. There were four strings of diamonds alternating with rubies. When Marjorie clasped it around Gabby's neck, Rafe wished he was doing that. Not because it was his duty. But because it would be his pleasure.

When she turned around and asked him, "What do you think?" the jewels seemed to add brightness to Gabby's eyes, a broader tilt to her smile. If a diamond-and-ruby necklace could do that for a woman, every woman should have one. It lay at the perfect spot, just above the V made by the crisscrossing straps. His gaze automatically went there, went to that V, but then he realized he'd rather look at her face.

There was color in Gabby's cheeks and he didn't think it was all from the makeup brushes he'd seen on the vanity in her bathroom. The eye shadow and the mascara added depth to her eyes, but it was their shot-with-gold-brown color that brought his eyes to hers every time.

"I think you should be able to sell a bunch to this clientele. If you just walk around, everyone's going to ask you about it."

"That's exactly what we want."

Marjorie came around the desk to Gabby again. "Blake is working on the canary collection. I think he'd like you and Penny to get together. If you see what she's come up with, you can plan a wardrobe around her pieces."

"That sounds like a good idea. I'll have to give her a call."

"Now let me introduce you to some of the clients you don't know. I pointed out to Blake that instead of just arranging these get-togethers with his wealthy clients, he ought to think about his more average clients, too, treating them the same way he treats these folks. If each one of them believes they're buying here for a once-in-a-lifetime experience, they'll come back for the next big occasion. That's how we need to grow the business again. We need to remember names and faces and truly know our customers once more, the way it used to be."

"Is there anything I can do to help with that?" Gabby asked.

"There sure is. The people here today are being given an e-mail address we set up for you. They know they can ask your opinion on jewels with wardrobes, the best quality of gem for the money, the artistry of some of the pieces. Just let us know if the e-mails become overwhelming. We can answer them for you. But the more clients you connect with, the better it is for the store."

"Are you going to do this with the other stores?"

"After your trip to Italy, you'll stop in here again, then fly out to the West Coast stores, and try it with them. By then we should have some idea if our strategy is working."

A worried expression came over Gabby's face.

"What's wrong?" Marjorie asked.

"After this six-month campaign, and I *am* dedicated to doing this for Blake, I'll be spending more time in Italy. I want to buy a house there."

"You're tired of jet-setting?"

"Jet-setting isn't all it's cracked up to be." She stepped up to Rafe. "I heard Blake tell you everyone in the room is cleared for security purposes. I'm going to be mingling pretty steadily. It might be easier for both of us if you just stand at the side of the room. If I need you for something, I'll look your way. Otherwise, I'm fine."

"Blake wants me to stick with you."

"I won't be out of your sight. I just want the freedom to move from one group to another quickly, from one person to the next. If I decide to go into one of the back rooms with someone, I'll let you know and you can accompany us."

He knew he still didn't look convinced, because she gave him one of those superbright smiles. "Let's just try this for a little while, okay? If it doesn't work, you can go back to being glued to me."

Glued to her. Now there was an image that would turn him on if he gave it too much thought.

"The store's getting more crowded. We'll try it for fifteen minutes," he decided. "If I lose sight of you, I move in."

For that moment, they focused on each other and the crowd vanished. They were two people attracted to each other, knowing they shouldn't be.

A month ago another man had been looking over her shoulder, maybe looking after her. A month ago. How could she be looking at her bodyguard like this so soon? After five years, Connie's voice still echoed in his heart. What did Gabby do, flit from one man to another every month?

He stepped back, stepping away from temptation.

Gabby looked perplexed, as if wondering what she had done wrong.

A female voice shouted Gabby's name. The woman was dripping with jewelry and looked as if she wanted to buy more.

"Deedee," Gabby said lightly and turned away from him, obviously eager to help any way she could.

Rafe thought she was such a contradiction. One minute she seemed like a social butterfly. The next she was doing her part to help her family, and it wasn't even her immediate family. How close was she to the McCord cousins…her aunt?

It didn't matter.

Still, as the event wore on, he not only protected the socialite heiress, he watched her—watched for a fake smile, watched for a flutter of flirting lashes, watched for inattention when she was supposed to be listening. He couldn't fault her. She didn't seem to be playacting but genuinely attentive to each person she spoke to.

That hadn't been his experience with famous people. Billionaire businessmen had no time for underlings. Stars could be impatient with fans. Politicians listened, but only to achieve their own agendas.

What was Gabby's agenda? Why had she made that visit to Libby Dalton?

Rafe couldn't figure her out…couldn't figure out if she was feeding her own ego or if she had a heart of gold. Connie's heart had been golden. His marriage to her had taught him that.

Gabby migrated around the store for a good hour, taking business cards, giving hers. She asked clerks to take jewelry from the case, held necklaces and earrings up to women's faces in mirrors, motioned to their wardrobe or suggested color schemes, laughed and entertained and never ignored anyone.

After a while, the crowd of invited guests began thinning. Blake appeared at Rafe's elbow. "I'm going to open the doors soon to everyday shoppers. I suggest you whisk Gabby out of here."

"You don't want her to consult with them?"

"No. They're here to see her, not to buy jewelry. Gabby insists I should treat every shopper the same. I'm willing to try whatever will work. But for now, I suggest you leave by the back door."

"I'll round her up. But what if she wants to stay?"

"I'll talk to her."

Gabby *did* want to stay. He overheard her say to Blake, "Let ten shoppers in at a time. Let's spread the word they can talk to me. More fans will come into the store. That will be to your benefit."

Blake agreed and Rafe kept close to her.

After another hour of that, Rafe ordered the limo to the

back entrance. Once in the car, Gabby laid her head against the back of the seat and closed her eyes.

Rafe had climbed in beside her this time in case she wanted to talk. He pressed the button to raise the window between them and the chauffeur.

Stooping to the cooler, he took out a bottle of cold water and handed it to her. "Here, hydrate."

She opened her eyes and gave him a wry smile. "So now you're a nutritionist?"

"If I was a nutritionist, I would have given you granola instead of that pancake."

She laughed, and she was even more beautiful when she laughed. "I guess as a security consultant, you wear many hats."

"Meaning?" He arched a brow.

"Meaning protection doesn't always just involve safety." She uncapped the water and took a few swallows. Her lipstick was still intact, though some of it edged the rim of the bottle now.

"Shouldn't *you* hydrate?" she asked teasingly.

Her expression was too friendly, her lips were too inviting. The desire that rose up in him made him angry. "You know, Gabby, there's no reason to flirt with me. I'll keep you safe whether you do or you don't. Don't look at me as relief from some kind of stress."

She looked shocked at his words and hurt came into her eyes. She was speechless for a moment and that surprised him. He'd expected a quick comeback. She didn't seem to have one.

Instead she peered out the window for a few moments and then she turned back to him. "I was just trying to be friendly, Rafe. I thought if we could have a conversation, it would be easier to be together. Obviously men don't think the same way as women. I really should have remembered that." Then she concentrated on sipping her water and didn't talk to him again the whole way back to the hotel.

He was messing up this assignment big-time. Thank goodness in a few weeks, Gabriella McCord would be someone else's headache.

Had she been flirting with Rafe?

After changing into shorts and a T-shirt, Gabby sat at the kitchen table, reading fan letters. Rafe had settled on the sofa with his laptop. He obviously did a lot of IT work in addition to handling the jewelry stores' physical security systems. She supposed now it was all interconnected. She sighed. The tension between them was much thicker than the syrup she'd used on her pancake that morning.

She hadn't been flirting with Rafe in the car, she told herself now. She'd just been trying to establish some kind of connection between them, even if it was a light joking one. But obviously her attraction to him had shown.

Apparently he wasn't attracted to *her*. His disdain was obvious. He thought she was a shallow model who hopped from one bed to another. If only he knew. As odd as it seemed, Miko had been her first lover. She'd been saving herself for that perfect romance...the perfect man.

But there wasn't a perfect man, just as there were no perfect women. Her idealistic, romantic fantasies had gotten in the way of reality. Rafe was definitely reality and she just wished he respected her.

Rubbing her temples, she realized she had a headache. After setting the letters aside, she wandered over to the baby grand and glanced at Rafe. He looked up and she guessed he was aware of her every move. That didn't help the claustrophobic feeling that was beginning to surround her.

"Do you mind if I play?" she asked. "Will it bother you?"

"It won't bother me," he assured her in a polite tone that was meant to keep distance between them.

If he wanted distance, that was fine. She would just close him out.

Sitting down at the piano, she ran up and down a few scales. The instrument was perfectly tuned. In her mind, she shifted through all the pieces she'd learned to play over the years and settled on one of her mother's favorites—"Moonlight Sonata." She got lost in it, engrossed in it. She disappeared into the music, forgetting about Rafe and the hotel suite and Blake and his family's turmoil.

When she was finished, she sat there with her eyes closed, feeling tears well in back of her eyelids, yet determined not to let them fall. She couldn't get up from that bench. She couldn't face the outside world again. She couldn't face Rafe. So she began another arrangement, a classical piece that was haunting enough to chase any thoughts away.

When the music ended, Rafe asked, "What did that mean?" He sounded as if he really wanted to know.

Rising from the bench, she went to one of the windows and peered out onto the golf course. How honest should she be? Did it even matter? Really, her bodyguard was a stranger. She could say anything.

So she told him the truth. "It meant that sometimes I feel trapped."

She felt trapped when she couldn't walk the streets like a normal person. She felt trapped when someone wanted to get to know her because of what she did, not who she was. She felt trapped when she thought of Miko and how blind she'd been. She was twenty-eight and she'd acted like a nineteen-year-old. She longed to go back to Italy and walk in the olive grove, to sit on the villa's patio and watch the sunset, to go to town to the *trattoria* and not be treated any differently from anyone else.

She was grateful, so very grateful for everything her parents had given her…for everything she had. But sometimes she was still so lonely deep down inside. Over the years, she'd found that loneliness diminished when she concentrated on someone else. Now wasn't so different. If she concentrated on Rafe, she'd just be very careful not to let her attraction to him show.

Crossing to the sofa, she sat, leaving a bit of space between them. "Why did you go to work for the Secret Service?"

He pressed a button on the laptop keyboard and his screen went blank. Lowering the lid, he seemed to debate with himself for a few moments. Then he gave a shrug as if the decision to tell her would cause no harm. "My dad was a cop."

"Where did you grow up?"

"Here in Dallas."

"Did you want to become a cop?"

"I did until I was twelve. The president came to Dallas for a speaking engagement when he was trying to get reelected. My father was on the local detail. He also managed to get me a ticket to hear him speak. I did and although I didn't understand the implications of most of it, I knew this was an important event and my father was part of it. That night we were watching it play on the local news and I grinned at him and said, 'I was there.'"

He pointed to the men near the president and told me, "Those men have the most important job in the world."

Gabby could imagine a twelve-year-old who idolized his father, taking his words to heart. She kept silent, waiting to see if Rafe would say more.

"Whenever anyone asked me what I wanted to be when I grew up, I always said a cop like my dad, or maybe a detective. But Dad's voice constantly played in my mind. After my father died—he was killed in the line of duty—I was in college taking criminal justice courses. The day we buried him, I decided to make him proud and go for the most important job in the world."

Gabby knew Secret Service agents filled more than one role. "How long did you protect the president?"

"For two years. Then I was transferred to a field office where I worked on access device fraud investigations."

"Blake told me you took a bullet for a senator."

Rafe corrected her. "Ex-senator. That was after I started up my own consulting firm."

Rafe had turned toward her and she was angled toward him. They seemed to be closer than when she first sat down. She wanted to say something, but she didn't want him to take it the wrong way.

Obviously as good at reading people as he was at protecting them, Rafe suggested, "Say what's on your mind."

"I don't want you to take this the wrong way. I don't want you to think I'm flirting."

His voice was gruff as his gaze stayed on her face. "I shouldn't have said what I did."

Silence fell between them until she knew she had to break it. No matter what he thought, she had to tell him what she was thinking. "I admire men like you."

"What kind of man am I?" he returned, his expression unreadable.

She didn't hesitate to answer his question. "You're a man who would die for what you believe in. I always wished I had that kind of courage."

"You have to have courage to do what you do, mingling with strangers, walking down a runway, posing for a photograph and having everyone study you almost microscopically. And most of all, keeping your temper and not lashing out at reporters."

"You're being kind." That was a quality she'd felt from Rafe almost from the beginning in spite of his stoicism.

He leaned closer. "Why do you believe what you do doesn't count?"

She so wanted to lace her fingers in his short, thick hair. She wanted to ease the worry lines around his eyes. She wanted to touch him the way he'd touched her. "What I do is so superficial. Sometimes I wonder if there's any meaning in it."

"I heard you helped raise money for SIDS research." His eyes were questioning as if he wondered why she'd chosen that cause.

"I did. I still do. My aunt—my mom's sister—lost a child to SIDS."

"I see. And you want to help."

When she didn't respond, he said her name softly. "Gabby. As impossible as it seems to me, maybe you don't know your own worth."

Maybe she didn't. Maybe that's why she'd let Miko trample her heart.

Rafe tipped her chin up and looked directly into her eyes. "You helped Libby Dalton today. That was very important."

She heard respect in his voice and she couldn't speak. All she could do was gaze into those brown eyes of his. All she could do was wish she and Rafe were even closer than they were.

As if Rafe knew exactly what she was thinking, his lips came closer to hers. Their breath mingled. Then his lips were on hers…warm…firm…moving…passionate. She knew neither of them was thinking. They were both just feeling. When he groaned, she knew he'd given in to the desire. She also knew the attraction she felt wasn't one-sided. That realization made her feel happy, light, even joy filled.

His tongue edged along the seam of her lips. She didn't hesitate to open to him, to fully experience his kiss that had seemed destined from the moment they'd met. As his tongue explored, she responded to the growing desire in her body. The word *destined* tumbled around in her head again. Hadn't she felt destined when she and Miko had met? Hadn't she felt destined when they'd flown to Monte Carlo, to the Swiss Alps? She'd been so wrong about him. Could she be just as wrong about Rafe?

She seemed to pull away the same moment he did. The fire in her body was still burning and she felt stunned by the emotions Rafe had incited in her.

He looked absolutely…stony. "I shouldn't have done that."

He moved away from her, far enough away she couldn't have reached out if she'd wanted to.

"That was a mistake for countless reasons," he added. "It won't happen again. In fact, I should call Blake and ask if he can get someone else to guard you."

"Is that what you want?" she asked, her voice shaky.

"This doesn't have to do with what I want, Gabby. You have to feel safe."

"I do feel safe," she admitted.

Rafe looked torn…between right and wrong, between should and shouldn't.

Knowing he was right, yet hurt because he'd been so blunt about it, Gabby stood. "I don't want another bodyguard, Rafe. But if you don't want to be here, then you should call Blake."

She returned to the kitchen, her body still singing from his kiss, her heart confused because she was falling for Rafael Balthazar and didn't know if she should be.

The doorbell to the suite chimed and Rafe went to answer it. Gabby had been holed up in the kitchen, working on her laptop. She hadn't said a word to him since the kiss.

The kiss.

However, as he crossed to the door, she broke her silence and called in to him. "It's my masseuse. Do you have to clear her?"

He called back. "Yes, I do."

He suspected he'd see the roll of Gabby's eyes, the little sigh that said it was all so unnecessary. Maybe most of it was, but there was always that one chance and that one time it wouldn't be.

Apparently, the tension had gotten to Gabby and she saw the massage therapist as a way to relax. He knew *exactly* what would relax him.

He blew out a breath and studied Helena Bancroft's ID.

Five minutes later, she was set up in Gabby's bedroom, the massage table at the foot of the bed, Gabby waiting for him to leave the room.

"Enjoy yourself," he said as he crossed to the door. "But don't close the door. Leave it open a couple of inches. I'll be standing right outside."

"That's not necessary," Gabby protested. He could tell she was trying not to lose her temper.

"It *is* necessary. Think of me as a statue."

She gave him a look that almost made him laugh. Almost. Then he stepped outside the door, leaving it open just a crack, and stood there like a sentinel.

Rafe had had practice standing still for hours, staring straight ahead, but watching everything around him. During these long stretches, he went over security patterns in his head, improved, hacker-proof systems, better ways to ensure McCord's jewelry stores were impenetrable.

After an hour, he heard movement inside the room—a rustle and the zipper of a duffel bag. Helena exited the room.

She said, "I'll leave the table for now. I can pick it up in the morning. Miss McCord is almost asleep and I hate to disturb her."

"When Gabby's finished with it, I'll have it brought down to the spa."

Helena nodded and then let herself out of the suite.

After Rafe checked that the door was secure, he peeked

into Gabby's room just to make sure she was all right. She lay on the table on her stomach, covered only by a large towel. He certainly wasn't getting any closer.

Backing out of the room, he retreated to the sofa, switched on his laptop and intended to concentrate on work.

However, another half hour went by and he didn't hear any noise from Gabby's bedroom. Returning there, he found her sound asleep on the table, her head cocked on her arms in an odd position. He knew she was going to get a crick in her neck if she stayed that way.

What to do.

He never had to ask himself what to do. He always just knew. But Gabby McCord had seemed to change all his reference points.

Approaching the table slowly, he hoped she'd awaken on her own. She didn't. Gingerly, he laid one hand on her shoulder, "Gabby, you need to move to the bed if you want a nap."

Sleepily, she opened her eyes and saw him crouched down beside her. "Rafe, why are you here?"

Wasn't that the sixty-million-dollar question?

"Your massage therapist finished a long time ago. I'm afraid you're going to undo everything she helped you with if you stay in that position. Why don't you move over to the bed?"

Her gaze shifted to that piece of furniture and came back to rest on him. She pushed herself up to a sitting position, holding the towel around her breasts.

He should leave now. He shouldn't even *try* to have a conversation.

But the current between them was potent and seductive. She didn't move an inch and neither did he. The more he thought about their kiss, the more he wanted another one.

Completely awake now, Gabby kept her eyes on his. "Do you really think that kiss was a mistake?"

He had two ways to go with his answer. One would be a lie. The other would be the truth.

For the first time in his life, he didn't know which road to take.

Chapter Five

A breath away.

Rafe was only a breath away.

Gabby was fully awake now. She'd been half dozing. She gripped the towel in front of her, aware of cool air at her back. But she was even more aware of Rafe—the scent of his cologne, the beard shadow on his jaw and the hungry look in his eyes. She guessed he was weighing should and shouldn't again.

So was she.

The desire in his eyes caused a pressing need in her body. She wanted his kiss and his touch. She wanted to be wanted and needed. She didn't know Rafe well, but instinctively suspected that he wasn't the type of man who kissed one woman one night and another the next.

As if his thoughts followed the same track, he shook his head slightly. "I'm not attracted to my clients. I don't do this."

She kept silent. Although she hungered for his kiss, she

wouldn't make the first move. Miko's infidelity had filled her with self-doubt. She didn't want to merely be desirable. She wanted a man to desire *only* her. And the *real* her, not the magazine-cover version.

Before Rafe had entered the room, she'd been so relaxed. Now her pulse was racing fast, so fast she opened her lips and took in a shallow breath.

"Gabby," he said on the edge of a groan. Then he bent his head and kissed her again.

If Rafe's first kiss had been stunning, this second one was awesome. His fingers delved into her hair as his lips moved over hers. There was nothing easy or coaxing about the kiss. It was all bold passion, a passion that she shared. She needed to touch him, too, and if she had to let go of her towel, so be it. She pulled his polo shirt from his khakis, and slipped her fingers underneath. Her palms met hot, taut skin.

When they did, he pushed past her lips and eagerly explored her with his tongue. She responded as if she'd never been kissed before. She responded from the fire he was fueling deep in the center of her being. From the moment they'd met, they'd seemed to be at odds. Yet underneath that pool of tension had been something much more potent…something that had led to this.

When he came up for air, he saw that she'd let go of her towel. He ran his hands over her shoulders down to her breasts. He cupped them and she gave a soft moan. As he teased his thumbs over her nipples, they became hard buds. She was so aroused and wasn't sure how to express it. His hands moved lower and she reached for him, wanting to get closer.

"We can use the massage table or move to the bed. Unless you have another suggestion," he added with a teasing smile.

Suddenly she went on alert. There was something in his voice—he thought she was experienced! He thought this was matter-of-fact for her. He thought she hopped from one bed to another without thinking twice.

What if she told him Miko had been her first? What if she told him she thought she and Rafe had more than a physical connection?

She grabbed for her towel, slung it around her and held it together at her breasts.

"Gabby?" He looked puzzled.

"Do you think I do this every time I have a massage? Do you think I do this for recreation?"

He cocked his head, measuring her questions. "Are you saying you don't?"

"I think we both miscalculated."

Stepping away from her, he agreed, "I guess I read the signals wrong."

She couldn't let him believe that. "You read the signals right, until I realized you believe I'm that woman on the magazine covers. More important, you believe the tabloids. I'm *not* that kind of woman." Her voice wobbled over the last words and she knew she had to get him out of her room. "I need to be alone for a while. I have to make a few calls and then I have to go over my notes for tonight's speech."

He looked uncomfortable and pushed his hands into his pockets. "Do you want me to order room service?"

"I'm not hungry."

"You have to eat."

"Not before a speaking engagement. I'll get something afterward."

He looked as if he wanted to change her mind, but instead he just gave a quick nod. "I'll be in the living room if you need anything."

As he left the room, she was determined she wouldn't need anything—not from him.

* * *

Rafe felt like a jerk.

He knotted his tie that evening, picked up his suit jacket and slipped into it. Something had gone wrong in Gabby's bedroom and he wasn't sure what it was. It probably had to do with expectations. Gabby had expected one thing and he had expected another.

Just what had she expected?

The crucial question was what had *he* expected? Had his mind-set told him this was the same as going to a party and taking a date home for a one-night stand?

Maybe it had.

He knew now something didn't jibe with Gabby. That little awkward episode in her bedroom had proven to him she wasn't the jet-setting heartbreaker tabloids portrayed. There was something vulnerable about her. Had all the hoopla about her made him miss that?

He made sure his tie was straight, then went to her bedroom to find out if she was ready. He didn't know how to breach the distance that had cropped up between them.

As if she heard him coming, she opened her door. Then he realized he was *seeing* another facet of Gabriella McCord.

She was dressed in a black suit with a simple gold necklace. Carrying a briefcase, she could have been any woman working in the financial district.

But she wasn't any woman. And she wasn't working in the financial district.

"Ready to go?" he asked in a brisk tone.

He didn't know how she was going to react to him, if she might demand he stay at least five feet away. That would probably be a good idea. He inhaled her perfume and felt his body tighten.

She didn't demand anything. In fact, there was a look in

her eyes that made him stay exactly where he was rather than back away.

"What's wrong?" he asked, knowing they'd better get any problem out in the open before they left.

She blew out a long breath. "I'm speaking to a group of women tonight who own their own businesses. This speaking engagement was set up before…before the tabloid layout. I'm concerned they won't take me seriously. They might even laugh at what I have to say. What can I tell CEOs when I can't even keep a dress on at a disco?"

He was surprised she'd alluded to the dreaded event again. He knew whatever he said now was important. "If anyone asks, I guess you could say, *Accidents happen.*"

After a moment of surprised shock, Gabby laughed, a genuine, heartfelt laugh. He felt supremely successful. This was what they'd needed to break the tension between them.

After the laughter died away, she agreed, "Maybe humor is the way to go."

"When the unmentionable happens, mention it, and keep it light."

"Do you know you give good advice?"

The way she was looking at him made him feel ten feet tall. When had a woman last done that for him? When had a woman ever captured his attention the way Gabby had? Because of that, he had to know some details.

"Was there an accident at the disco?"

That vulnerable look came back into her eyes when she replied, "Not exactly."

Sometimes she could be so open with him, and other times she just shut down. This was a shut-down time. Her lack of willingness to confide in him bothered him. But then why should she confide in him? He was only her bodyguard.

A bodyguard who had kissed her.

An hour and a half later, Rafe was acutely aware that Gabby couldn't be compartmentalized and definitely couldn't be given a simple label. She'd spoken to the businesswomen at an Expo Center attached to a complex of corporate offices. Instead of ignoring the recent tabloid layouts, she'd plunged right in making the comment that if she'd been in a business suit, she wouldn't have gotten into trouble.

The women had laughed with her, not at her, and she'd gone on to brief them on how she had to manage her celebrity as a business. Now she was mingling, enjoying the camaraderie while he tried to stay as unobtrusive as he could. Being the only man in the room made that difficult.

Two women in little black dresses with volumes of cuff bracelets and necklaces to weigh them down watched Gabby as if they were noting her every move.

Rafe wanted to guide Gabby away from them, sensing trouble. But before he could try, the two women approached and Gabby turned to greet them.

"Amelia Northrop," the redhead said, extending her hand to Gabby.

The second did the same. "Gail Winslow."

"It's nice to meet you," Gabby replied. "I hope you enjoyed my speech."

"Oh, we did," Gail answered for both of them. "But now we want to get to the nitty-gritty."

"The nitty-gritty?" Gabby didn't seem flustered in the least, as Rafe wondered what was coming.

"When are you going to start making money off your brand?" Amelia asked impertinently.

"I'm not sure what you mean," Gabby returned politely.

"Oh, you know, bring out a fragrance line to keep you going. Your days as a model are soon over, but you have enough celebrity to carry any perfume."

Gabby's face was a study in tact as she answered, "I'll keep that in mind. Since you seem to know all about it, what do *you* do?"

"Oh, we started a business last year. We sell gift baskets." She gave Gabby a business card. "We'd love to carry an exclusive item if you develop one." She made a gesture to Rafe. "Is tall, dark and handsome on your payroll permanently, or is he here just tonight to protect you from all them?" She motioned to the photographers who were standing in a clump outside the door waiting for Gabby to finish.

"He's helping out while I'm here in the States," Gabby replied easily. Before the two women could ask another question or make another comment, she graciously added, "It's been great to meet you. I wish you lots of success with your business."

Gabby moved on to another group of women and Rafe wondered how she handled the constant invasion of privacy. It would drive him crazy!

Finally, most of the women dispersed and he and Gabby were left to face the photographers.

She clasped his arm. "I'm going to stand still for them for about three minutes and then I want to make a run for it, okay?"

"You don't have to leave that way. We can use the back exit."

"No, I don't want to make the press angry. I'm not going to talk to them, just stand still for a couple of shots, then I'll move."

Rafe had to admit Gabby was good at this. As she'd said, she'd been dealing with the press since she was seventeen.

Rafe radioed to the limo driver, then protected her the best he could as they stepped into the swarm. Gabby handled it by first turning one way and then the other, smiling all the while as photographers—or paparazzi, if you wanted to call them that—tossed questions at her that she didn't answer.

Questions like, "Have you seen Mikolaus Kutras since that

episode in the London club? Is it true you split up? Is it true you're still together? When will you be returning to Italy? What does McCord's have in mind for you? A new line of jewelry?"

Gabby ignored the questions and the flashes and the video cameras, and after five minutes, which seemed more like an hour to Rafe, she nodded to him.

He cleared a path for her, his arm around her shoulders. They were at the exit, a police officer on either side of the door, when a photographer appeared out of nowhere. "How about a shot with your bodyguard?"

Rafe blocked the man's path, ignoring the angry thrust of the photographer's chin because he couldn't get a clear shot. After Rafe guided Gabby into the limo, he climbed in beside her.

"Where's *your* car?" she asked.

"I thought getting you out would be more difficult than getting you in. I'm having someone pick it up and take it back to the hotel."

"I guess that's where we're going now," she said with a sigh.

"Would you like to get something to eat?"

"Not really. That would just raise another ruckus."

"But you don't want to go back to the hotel?"

"What choice do we have?" she asked with a small smile.

"We have a choice. Let me check on something." He took out his phone and made a call. When his mother answered, he asked, "Would you like some company?"

"You? Anytime. I don't see you nearly enough. Are you hungry?"

His mother was always concerned whether he was eating enough and sleeping enough. "Actually, this time I am. Is it all right if I bring a friend along?"

His mother paused, but didn't ask questions. "Of course. Bring along anyone you like."

"I'll see you in about half an hour."

He closed his phone. Turning to Gabby, he asked, "Do you trust me?"

She took a few very long moments to answer, but then she replied, "Yes, I do."

"Good. We'll go back to the hotel for my car, then I'll drive you somewhere where you can relax."

"New Zealand?" she joked.

He didn't laugh because he was beginning to realize how difficult it was for her to get away, be herself and live her life.

"Close," he said with a smile, and wondered just what his mother would think of Gabriella McCord.

Gabby trusted Rafe. She did. But she couldn't imagine where he was taking her.

She was losing her bearings, even in a city she almost knew. He wound in and out of streets until he pulled down an alley and into the backyard of a row house. She peered into the dark, spotting privacy fences and the dots of porch lights glowing in backyards. The next thing she knew, he was opening her door. She swung her legs out and the slit of her skirt separated.

"Try not to let that happen inside," he advised in a neutral tone.

Surprised, she looked up at him and saw he was serious. "Do you want me to stay in the car?"

He grinned. "No, that would defeat the purpose. Come on."

She followed him to the back door of a screened porch with flowered patio furniture. When he opened the interior door and let her precede him inside, Gabby instantly saw a small, dark-haired woman standing by the refrigerator.

"Gabby, this is my mother, Lena Balthazar. Mom, this is Gabriella McCord."

Instead of looking impressed, or even surprised, Rafe's mother examined her as if she were a rare butterfly pinned to a board. Gabby thought she saw disapproval in the woman's eyes. She didn't need that now.

Rafe hugged his mom—a big, giant bear hug—and she hugged him back.

When his mother extricated herself from his long arms, she asked, "You're connected to that Greek man, aren't you?"

Apparently trying to keep the atmosphere light, Rafe asked, "You read the tabloids?"

His mother shrugged. "Once in a while. Who can ignore them at the checkout counter?" After another long look at Gabby, she motioned to the kitchen table. There was a platter of sliced roast beef and ham, three salads, a pie and a cake.

"There's enough food here to feed three families," Gabby commented.

"Have you ever seen my son eat?" Lena asked.

They'd ordered room service for lunch and taken their plates to separate rooms. She had no idea what Rafe liked or didn't like.

"He did manage to eat a number of pancakes this morning," she joked.

Lena's brows arched. "You had breakfast together?" The question was inquiring about more than breakfast.

"Mom, I'm her bodyguard. I'm sleeping on her sofa until the room next door is available."

"I see," Lena responded, but Gabby knew she didn't see at all.

An awkwardness settled around the table as Rafe pulled meat from a platter then offered a salad to Gabby. She took it and put a spoonful onto her dish. Taking a deep breath, she decided to plunge in with Lena. This could be a long meal if they couldn't find common ground.

"Rafe told me his dad was a police officer."

Lena took the salad from Gabby with a nod of thanks.

"Yes, he was. A fine one, too. But being on the force is dangerous work. I didn't really want Rafe to follow in his dad's footsteps."

"I can understand that," Gabby sympathized. "I imagine you worried every day, always afraid of getting a phone call."

Lena tilted her head and stared straight into Gabby's eyes. "Exactly. You *do* understand."

"I know it's not the same thing at all, but my father was on the road a lot when I was small. When he was gone, I was always afraid something would happen to him and he wouldn't come home."

Lena nodded, taking another long look at Gabby before she began eating. Rafe had discarded his suit jacket and tie before he'd taken a seat. Now his mother motioned to them lying across the counter. "Where were you tonight? Or shouldn't I ask?" Then she said to Gabby, "When he was in the Secret Service, I couldn't ask any questions."

"You could ask them," Rafe returned. "I just couldn't answer them."

Gabby smiled and said, "I had a speaking engagement tonight. Lots of women who own their own businesses were there. None of them walked out, so I guess I did okay."

Rafe's gaze was on her. "You did fine. I was surprised at how much you know about owning a business."

"Whatever I learned, I learned by experience."

Rafe's mother watched their interchange, then commented, "It's a good thing for women to know about business. When my husband died, I was lost. He took care of paying the bills, our insurance, everything. But my daughter Julie helped me get it all straight and now I handle everything myself."

She looked at her son. "Does she know I'm a seamstress for a dry cleaner?"

Rafe shook his head. "I didn't tell her anything about you.

I just brought her here to get some good food." He winked at his mother.

The conversation flowed more smoothly after that. At least it flowed unless Rafe bumped Gabby's arm or their legs inadvertently touched under the table. At those times, she stared into his brown eyes, wondering what secrets he kept, what heartaches were in his past, what joys he could share with her. Whenever she was with him, a longing squeezed her heart and she didn't even know what it meant. She'd never felt this way before—like she wanted to know a man inside and out, like she wanted to talk to him for hours and snuggle in his arms. It wasn't just sexual attraction between her and Rafe. She was sure of it. Yet maybe he hadn't looked past that attraction. Maybe he still hadn't looked past her outside persona.

After dessert, Rafe cleared the table and took out the garbage. Gabby knew she was smiling.

Lena smiled, too. "His father taught him to be a *real* man."

Both women laughed. "Seriously," Lena added, "my husband was a good role model."

Gabby murmured, "Rafe's a good man."

After Lena stowed leftovers in the refrigerator, she turned to Gabby once more. "Has he told you about Connie?"

"No, he hasn't." Gabby wondered who Connie was. His first love? The love of his life? A wife?

"I thought if he told you about his father, he might have told you about Connie. Maybe in time."

But Gabby knew she and Rafe didn't have much time, only a few weeks.

Gabby noticed a beautiful crocheted afghan in progress heaped onto a side table near the hall. She gestured toward it. "The colors are gorgeous. It looks like a sunset."

Lena beamed. "That's exactly what I intended. A sunset."

She crossed to the table, lifted the afghan—careful with the unfinished end—and stretched it for Gabby to see the full effect.

"That ripple pattern enhances the colors."

"I'm making this one for a customer at the dry cleaning shop. I have a few orders. I work on them in the evenings and weekends while I watch TV. Rafe has one in his apartment he's had since college. I have one put away for him when he settles down. Would you like to see it?"

"I would."

Lena gestured to the hall. "Come to my sewing room."

Gabby followed Rafe's mother past a staircase and living room to a smaller room where hanks of yarn overflowed onto a large table and a sewing machine stood in a corner. Lena opened a closet, reached on tiptoe and removed the afghan encased in a plastic bag. The cover was multicolored and designed in a diamond pattern.

"This one is beautiful, too." Gabby wasn't just flattering Lena. It was lovely. "It could be used with any color scheme."

"That's what I thought," Lena agreed.

"Do you visit Rafe in New York?" Gabby asked.

"Julie and I make a trip there every spring and fall if Rafe is there. We see a show with him and he takes us someplace fancy for dinner."

It was obvious Lena enjoyed the trips and Gabby guessed Rafe really enjoyed escorting his mother and sister around the city.

They talked about New York and Dallas and spending time with family until Rafe joined them—he'd made himself scarce for the past hour. "I hate to break up the party," he said with a grin, "but Gabby should probably be getting back to the hotel."

When Gabby checked her watch to her surprise she saw that it was almost midnight. "Oh, my gosh. I have a shoot tomorrow."

"A shoot?" Lena asked.

"Modeling," Gabby explained, not knowing how that would go over. "I'm going to be representing McCord Jewelers and they're doing a few ads."

"That's nice you're helping out your family."

Gabby supposed that was one way of looking at it, and she guessed family was everything to Lena Balthazar.

As the three of them went into the hall, Lena said, "I'll walk you out. I'm so glad you came over tonight. With Julie out of town, I'm a little lonely."

Lena had told Gabby that her daughter was on vacation with her husband and their year-old baby daughter. They'd gone away for a few days to see her husband's family in Houston.

"It's nice having Rafe back in Dallas," Lena commented. "After he returns to New York, who knows when he'll be in town again."

"You make it sound as if I never get home," he grumbled. "I do."

"As long as I know you *think* about coming home, that's enough," his mother said.

At the door, she gave her son a hug, and then she opened her arms to Gabby, too. "You're not what I expected." She didn't say more and as Gabby and Rafe left, Gabby didn't know if she had exceeded his mother's expectations or had fallen short of them.

Outside in the backyard, the hush of night wrapped around Rafe and Gabby. They descended the porch steps and Gabby looked up at the moon. "I called my mother earlier. She misses me like your mother misses you."

Gazing up at the white crescent with her, his suit coat and tie tossed over his arm, Rafe admitted, "I like coming home. It grounds me. The memories help me remember where I came from…where my parents came from. After my dad died, I told Mom I'd take care of her like he always did. At first, I think she wanted to hear that. But as the weeks and months passed, she eventually told me she wanted to take care of herself."

"It's obvious, she likes her life…likes taking care of you and your sister and her family when she can. Do you and your sister get along well?"

"For the most part. We both have strong opinions and we can agree to disagree."

"You're fortunate. I always wanted brothers or sisters." She knew there was a wistfulness in her voice that she couldn't eliminate.

"Julie was a nuisance when we were little, always bothering me and my friends, wanting to do what we did. But you know, when she hit her teens and started to wear makeup, she found her own group of friends and I missed her."

"Isn't that the way it usually is? We don't know what we have until it's gone?"

His voice turned huskier as his arm brushed hers and he asked, "What have *you* lost?"

"Sometimes I feel as if I've lost my roots—when I have to be in one city this week and another city next week. I have friends, but obviously they're all long distance, and I only see them sporadically. Maybe that's why I want to buy a house in Tuscany. I would have a place that's my own."

"You still live with your parents?" he asked, as if he were astonished by the notion.

"Why are you so surprised every time I disclose something about my private life?"

"I don't know," he drawled. "Maybe because of the press releases your publicist puts out to get you media attention?"

"There's a difference, Rafe, between the press releases my publicist sends out to reputable newspapers and magazines and the bold-faced lies some tabloids print. But apparently you don't read the reputable magazines." She headed for his car, the quiet moments of bonding in the backyard lost.

He didn't go to the driver's door as she expected. He followed her to her door, cupped her elbow and nudged her toward him. "Gabby, I don't know who you are. You put up a front and put on a mask for the press and the paparazzi. Your press releases—and I *do* read reputable magazines—talk about vacations on the French Riviera, growing up in a villa large enough to have a stable, as well as servants, and your taste in award-winning wines. So if I'm a little surprised that you don't live in a penthouse in Rome, or miss your mother, or would rather dress in sweats instead of designer gowns, that's not my fault. You've created an image for the world and that's the image everyone has in their minds. Yet somehow, in a little over twenty-four hours, you expect me to be able to guess who you really are."

"You have a persona," she accused. "You were a Secret Service agent and everyone has an image of them. I'm sure you don't tell your clients details about how you live your life. Yet I've learned to know *you* in twenty-four hours."

"You don't know me."

"Maybe more than you think I do. I know you're a man of integrity. I know you admired your father and wanted to be like him. I know you have respect for your sister and you love your mother. Isn't that who you are?"

He looked uncomfortable under the light of the moon as if maybe she'd seen too much. But that's what close proximity did. She knew he wasn't blind. She knew his sixth sense somewhat guided him. Still, maybe he hadn't chosen to use it with her.

"Why did you bring me to meet your mother?" she asked quietly.

He was slow in answering. Finally, he responded, "You

needed to relax and to eat a good meal. I knew you wouldn't do either at the hotel."

"And just how did you know that?" she asked. But she didn't need an answer.

Turning away from him, she opened the car door and slipped inside. Some communication didn't have to be verbal. That was something Rafe already knew. He just didn't want to admit it. He didn't want to admit that maybe he could like someone like her.

So be it. They'd coexist for the next few weeks. She'd keep her distance and neither of them would get hurt.

Chapter Six

"Let me check the suite."

Gabby knew Rafe's statement was an order rather than a request.

Moments later he called, "Coast is clear."

She walked inside as if this were any normal situation. But it wasn't. The tension between her and Rafe had gotten worse instead of better on the drive home from his mother's. They hadn't spoken. Now they'd have to. After all, they were, in essence, living together.

She should be asleep on her feet, but instead, she was wired. "I'm going to check my e-mail before I turn in." Then she remembered he was sleeping on the couch. "Unless you want to go to sleep right away."

"You go ahead. I'll get my bed ready."

His bed. In the middle of the living room. She was hoping

the room next door would be available tomorrow. That would give them a little breathing space.

"If you want to use the shower in my bathroom, feel free. I know this has got to be tough, not having a room of your own." She almost gave herself a pat on the back at the relatively normal conversation.

"That sounds like a great idea. It will only take me five minutes." As opposed to her thirty, she guessed he was probably thinking.

Before she sat down at the kitchen table, she went to the refrigerator and found a bottle of water. Taking it to the table, she sat in front of the computer for a few seconds, not opening it. Did she really want to do e-mail?

No. She'd ignored it on her phone since she'd arrived Sunday. But she had a full schedule tomorrow and something important might have come in.

Before she clicked on the icon to open her personal e-mail program, she Googled afghans just for the heck of it. Gabby had very much liked the warm homey comfort Lena's afghans projected. She studied the patterns and site offerings until she heard Rafe in the living room, the squeak of the sofa as he opened it into a bed. She closed the search engine and clicked on her e-mail program.

As messages popped up in her in-box, Gabby took a look at them and froze. Miko had sent one. She just stared at the unopened message for a while. Then knowing she was being a coward, she clicked on it and read.

Gabby—I still have some of your belongings. We're not finished yet. MK

"I hung my towel on the back of the door. If it's in your way—"

Rafe stopped across the table from Gabby. "What's wrong? You look like you're going to pass out."

Now that he mentioned it, she did feel a little light-headed. From the long day? From thinking the past was in the past? From believing she wouldn't hear from Miko again and now she had?

Rafe hurried to the table and stood at her shoulder. "Gabby?"

If she told him about Miko, he'd think she was a fool. He'd think she was as naive as a teenager. If she told Rafe what had happened, she'd have to reveal that she'd thought she'd been in love with Miko. She knew now those feelings had been anything but love. The feelings she was starting to have toward Rafe were totally different and they scared her almost as much as the e-mail from Miko.

Rafe didn't wait for an explanation. He peered over her shoulder, read the message and swore. "What does that mean?"

"Rafe, this really isn't any of your business."

"The hell it's not. That sounds threatening to me."

Was it threatening? Or was it just Miko's way of trying to take control? She couldn't let him succeed. For the moment she was going to ignore it. "That's just the way Miko is."

"Is?" Rafe questioned soberly.

"I mean," she explained patiently, "that's Miko's character. He's intense. He does still have some of my things. I left in a hurry. But they're not anything I need back."

"Are you going to answer him?"

"No."

"Do you think that's wise?"

"Right now I'm not thinking much at all." She closed down the program and then shut off the computer. With a snap, she lowered the lid.

"Do you believe that's going to go away because you turn it off?"

Rafe was dressed in a T-shirt and jogging shorts, and looked about as virile as a man could look. But she wasn't going to let him bully her any more than she'd let Miko ever do it again. "I'm tired. I just want to go to bed. I'll set my alarm so you don't have to worry about getting me up. I'll be ready to leave by nine. I have to be at the shoot at ten."

He looked as if he wanted to take her by the shoulders and shake her.

Before anything at all could happen between them, she said, "I'll see you in the morning," and went to her bedroom.

When she closed her door, she knew she probably wouldn't fall asleep anytime soon. Not because of Miko, but because of Rafe. She wanted to be held in his arms again, kissed by him, touched by him.

Instead, she was going to keep her distance and hope the next couple of weeks went by quickly.

"They're gorgeous," Gabby exclaimed as she examined the canary diamonds on Wednesday afternoon.

She and Penny McCord stood in one of the back rooms of McCord Jewelers, both entranced by the yellow gemstones resting on a square of black velvet.

Usually quiet and reserved, Penny was anything but as she used the tweezers to lift one of the gemstones. "Blake is buying them up all over the world market. If he finds the Santa Magdalena diamond, canary diamonds will be even more in vogue than they are now. This is a wonderful idea Blake has."

Although Gabby's focus was on the diamonds, as well as on Penny, she was quite aware that Rafe was sitting in a corner, reading a magazine. They'd stayed out of each other's way since Monday night. The adjoining room to her suite had become available and that had helped.

"Do you know how you're going to set them?" Gabby asked her cousin, focusing on the diamonds once more.

"I'm thinking yellow gold, some contemporary, some in an old Spanish design. I'd like to find several the same size to do a spectacular necklace, just making them the focal point. What I'm wondering is, can you build a wardrobe around the contemporary and the Spanish designs?"

"I can build a wardrobe around anything," Gabby said with a laugh.

Penny laughed with her. "I was thinking about setting a few in chocolate gold."

"That would be fabulous with a brown silk jersey dress, brown shoes. I've contacted a designer I use in Houston. I'll be meeting with her soon. So if you have anything in particular in mind, just let me know."

Penny shook her head. "I'll concentrate on the jewelry. You can take care of the wardrobe."

Gabby lifted one of the diamonds on the velvet tray and set it in the palm of her hand. "That has to be at least four carats. The clarity is wonderful and so is the color. If I had my pick…"

Her voice trailed off and she knew she was adding to Rafe's opinion of her that she was all about fashion and jewelry. Oh, well. There was nothing she could do about that. She loved gems and gold, color and texture and fabric. If she hadn't been a model, she probably would have gone into design, like Penny.

"I have a few questions for Blake about the quantity of stones he's buying," Penny said. "I'll go find him. Do you want me to put these away, or do you want to drool some more?"

"I'm going to take a few more minutes to drool."

Penny gave her cousin an understanding smile and left the room. On another square of velvet, she had laid out a necklace, a bracelet and a pair of earrings already set with the yellow stones. She wanted Gabby to wear them when she was choosing styles and dresses. She believed that was the best way to coordinate and get the full effect.

Gabby lifted the bracelet, admiring it. When she heard

Rafe rise from his seat, she knew he was coming over to her. She felt her body warming at the thought.

"You know a lot about jewelry," he remarked.

She and Penny had been talking for at least forty-five minutes about it. Sometimes she did forget Rafe was there, but not for very long.

"When I was little, my mother would take me to Florence or Rome and let me wander around the store. I'd shadow Dad and he never got impatient with me, just answered all my questions."

"So if you hadn't been a model?"

"I might have been a jewelry designer like Penny or a geologist like Paige. I know it might seem frivolous, but I love sparkle and color. When I was little, I remember sitting at my mother's vanity. She would take her jewelry from the safe and I'd try on her necklaces. She'd encourage me to tell her what I liked and what I didn't."

"That's not frivolous, especially not for a child. I bet your mom remembers those times, too."

As Gabby gazed up at him, she saw the hunger hadn't gone away. That pleased her, excited her and worried her.

"So you're actually going to have dresses designed around the jewelry?" he asked.

"Penny's going to give me a few sketches to work with. It's going to be fun, even better than shopping."

He laughed, a rich, deep laugh, but she realized he wasn't making fun of her. He was laughing with her.

Gabby slipped the velvet envelope covering over the tray of diamonds and then slid the ring onto her finger. The three-carat canary diamond was surrounded by four point stones, all mounted in a heavy gold setting. Lifting the bracelet once more, she let it lie across her wrist while she fumbled with the clasp.

"Let me."

Turning toward Rafe, she stood before him. His fingers were a man's fingers, a little fumbling, somewhat callused. They were hot on her wrist as he tried to convince the lobster-claw clasp to catch. Finally, he did and then fastened the safety chain. She let the bracelet slip up and down as far as it would go.

"It looks like a perfect fit," he noticed.

"It is beautiful, isn't it? The design is a classic." It was difficult to make conversation when she was trembling inside from Rafe's touch. Glad for something to do, she picked up the necklace, designed in a journey style. The rope chain was almost delicate in her fingers. It slipped away twice.

Rafe caught it the second time and offered, "I can do it."

When he brushed her hair to the side, she went hot all over. Thinking she was helping, she tried to gather her hair to lift it from her neck. Her fingers tangled with Rafe's.

"Sorry," she said quickly.

"Sorry," he mumbled at the same time.

She felt his large, warm hands at the back of her neck. He was standing close, so close that if she leaned back just a little, she'd be smack up against his chest…smack up against him. When they'd kissed, she'd felt his arousal and it had fueled her own. If she simply did lean back against him—

His hands were at her nape. His fingers manipulated the clasp. She held her breath.

She felt the clasp catch, but he didn't move his fingers right away. When he did, he leaned closer and murmured in her ear, "It's beautiful on you."

This close, his cheek practically pressed against hers, she couldn't speak. After she took a deep breath, she whispered, "Thank you."

She wasn't exactly sure what she was thanking him for. Reassuring her she was desirable? Awakening her to feelings she'd never had before? Protecting her against the paparazzi? Making her feel safe?

When he leaned back again, she didn't want him to move away. Yet she wondered if his opinion of her had changed. She wondered what he really believed about her. She couldn't give in to her desire when she didn't know where his was coming from.

Her fingers trembled as she felt for the center of the necklace and held on to it as if it were some kind of lifeline. Turning to face him, she saw the glimpse of a kiss-in-the-making in his eyes. But she also saw his determination not to let anything more happen.

"I know this wasn't on our itinerary, but I'd like to go down the street to buy a pair of shoes. I don't want to take the car. Can we just mix with the crowd and disappear and pretend we're normal for just a few minutes?"

He eyed her sophisticated pink sheath and the canary diamonds. "I don't think disappearing into the crowd will be an option. Someone will recognize you."

"Not if I change. That's why I always carry the duffel bag I put in the car. I can look ordinary, really I can."

"I wouldn't place any bets on that," he muttered with a sigh. "Go ahead and change and we'll try it."

She liked the fact Rafe was flexible, that he was giving her some leeway. She liked way too many things about him.

They were so engrossed in each other, neither of them heard the footsteps until Penny was standing at the doorway. Stepping inside, she glanced from one of them to the other. "Am I interrupting something?"

"No," they were both quick to say, which only told Penny that she was.

Her eyebrows arched, but then she smiled. "The diamonds look terrific on you. Are you going to wear them?"

"I don't think so. There's a little shoe shop down the street and I want to stop in there. I'm going to change into a summer tourist outfit so no one recognizes me. Can we just leave them here and we'll pick them up when we stop back here for the car?"

"Sure."

Gabby removed the ring and then the bracelet. Her fingers moved to the back of the necklace. She vividly remembered everything about Rafe's clasping it for her. The expression on his face was neutral, but she imagined he was remembering, too.

She was sure of it when he said tersely, "I'll get your duffel bag," and exited the room.

Penny gave her an inquiring look, but Gabby didn't pour out her thoughts or doubts or questions. She was too confused about what was happening with Rafe. She had to sort it out for herself before she could confide in anyone, even her cousin.

"After I meet with Tara Grantley, I'll let you know how her designs enhance yours. I'll probably do some shopping while I'm there, too, and I'll let you know what I find."

Penny's knowing smile said more than words that she understood Gabby's reluctance to talk about Rafe. Being the tactful, nonintrusive person that she was, she wouldn't ask probing questions.

"I think the collection will be spectacular, and I know you wearing the designs will give my reputation a boost, as well as the store's. Thanks for doing this, Gabby. I know Blake appreciates it, too."

"I'm pleased you're giving me a part to play that helps the stores. It lets me really feel like one of the family."

"You *are* one of the family." Penny gave her a hug. "I can't wait to see your transformation from model to tourist."

Gabby hoped she could pull it off.

* * *

Rafe walked beside Gabby, wanting to hurry her along, yet knowing he couldn't. In her oversize dark glasses, tank top, shorts, ponytail and sneakers, she was *almost* unrecognizable.

She wore a smile as she window-shopped. He had to admit, without makeup and dressed as she was, he was mightily attracted to her the same as he'd been yesterday at the photo shoot for McCord Jewelers. As he'd watched Gabby play in front of the camera—and that's exactly what she'd done as she smiled and turned and tossed her hair—he'd had to drink a couple of bottles of water just to keep his temperature down. She'd looked hot in every outfit. And not only hot, but classy, and sophisticated and over-the-top beautiful.

She bumped his arm with her elbow. "Stop worrying. I've done this before."

"That doesn't mean you're not tempting fate."

"Honestly, Rafe, if you don't stop worrying, you're going to have permanent lines on your forehead."

Reflexively, he smoothed his hand over his forehead and she laughed. He liked her laugh and he wondered why he didn't mind her laughing at him.

Suddenly she stopped in front of a gift shop window that displayed statues, ornaments and little painted boxes that looked very expensive.

However, Gabby seemed interested only in one object—a small crystal cage housing a tiny bird. It had a golden door that opened on the side.

"That's so delicate, yet so symbolic," she murmured.

"Symbolic of what?"

"Of the way I feel sometimes. I'm surrounded by comfortable furniture and pretty things, but I feel trapped by all that."

"The cage has a door," Rafe pointed out.

She studied him for a few moments rather than the cage, their eyes meeting, locking, holding. "Yes, it does," she agreed. "But sometimes I forget that. Sometimes I'm afraid to open the door."

A heat began in his body that had nothing to do with the warm sun on their heads. He wanted to bring Gabby into his arms, let her body melt against his. He wanted to show her freedom and teach her about passion that could take both of them away.

Teach her? She'd been around the globe! Maybe there was nothing he could teach her.

"Do you want to go in?" he asked gruffly.

She pulled her gaze from his and took one last look at the little cage. "No, not now. Maybe someday after I have my house and have a permanent place to put things."

"But you still want to shop for shoes."

"I have to shop for shoes. I left London so quickly that I—" She abruptly stopped.

"That's what your e-mail was about, your clothes?"

A group of teenage boys jogged down the sidewalk. Rafe protectively threw his arm around Gabby's shoulders and turned her to face the window again. Their reflections stared back at them, two very different people, looking at life from their own experience. He understood Gabby was reluctant to tell him about her affair. He couldn't push her, but he wished she'd confide in him—not only for security's sake, but because he truly wanted to know what had happened between her and Kutras.

It would have been so easy to kiss her then, to wrap his arm just a little tighter, to turn her toward him. Easy and stupid.

Instead of kissing her, he asked another question that would take him deeper into her background. "Before you became famous, did you roam the streets? Did you go window-shopping?"

"Even in the village, someone always went with me. When I began modeling, if my mother wasn't along, I had a chaperone."

"A chaperone?"

"She'd been my nanny when I was growing up. She went along with me on shoots when my mother couldn't."

"Didn't you rebel?"

"Against what? My parents loving me? Life on a beautiful estate with horses, tennis courts, anything I could possibly want?"

Gabriella McCord wasn't like any woman he'd ever met and maybe that's why she got to him. Maybe that's why this was the first time since his wife had died that he was feeling more than desire, more than a passion that pushed him to have a physical need fulfilled.

He dropped his arm from around her. "Let's go buy those shoes."

He thought he saw Gabby straighten her spine and square her shoulders. Had she taken his sudden withdrawal as rejection? Just why would that rejection bother her so much? They were still basically strangers, weren't they? Born on different sides of the tracks, let alone oceans. They'd grown up in very different surroundings.

The storefronts displayed many offerings, but Gabby didn't seem as interested in window-shopping now. She was more like a woman on a mission and that was good. They'd get this over with and he'd take her back to the safety of her suite.

Only to *her* the suite didn't represent safety. It represented that crystal cage.

The Shoe House was a small shop wedged between a dress boutique and a leather goods store. Gabby studied the window for a few moments. Her gaze seemed to linger on a pair of sandals. Then she moved quickly, opening the door and stepping inside.

He glanced around swiftly, then took a longer, more particular look. No one else was in the store. A clerk stood at the counter where the cash register was located, but she was on the phone. She called, "I'll be with you shortly," and he could tell she hadn't recognized Gabby. They could easily get lost in the tall shelves and the stacks of shoes. That would make *his* life easier.

Gabby seemed to know exactly what she was looking for. She headed for a shelf that displayed a high-heeled shoe with spikes at least three inches, a sexy strap, the toes pointy. It was displayed in turquoise, red and white.

Gabby smiled, picked up a turquoise shoe and nodded. "That's it."

Her gaze assessed the line of boxes and she pulled out a size six.

Rafe knew nothing about women's shoes.

A small wooden bench sat in front of the shelves. Gabby dropped her purse onto it and sank down, lowering the box to the floor beside her. Bumping the lid aside, she removed one of the shoes. She slipped it on, then bent over to adjust the strap into its clasp. Her fingers fumbled and she couldn't seem to fasten it. He just wanted this whole ordeal over with.

He sank down to his knee in front of her and said, "Let me help."

She was about to protest, but then she gave a shrug. "I should have fastened it first."

"But then it might have been too tight," he warned with a small smile.

"Or too loose," she suggested, maybe just to contradict him. He'd noticed before she didn't like him to get the upper hand.

His fingers fought the leather at first—the clasp was very

small—but then he adjusted the metal buckle properly and the leather strip slipped into place.

He held her foot in his hand and couldn't help but glance up at her. She'd removed her sunglasses and she was staring at him as if he were…a substitute for Prince Charming?

Not him.

"A perfect fit," he admitted.

She looked a little lost in thought for a moment, but then she gestured to the box. "Let's try the other one."

In her shorts and bare feet, he didn't think a woman ever looked more sexy. But he wasn't about to comment.

Two pairs of shoes later, they stood at the counter. Gabby took out her wallet and to his surprise, she paid in cash.

"Name on the credit card," she murmured to him, as the clerk, still on the phone, bent for a bag on the other side of the counter.

"Good thinking."

Gabby was beautiful, intelligent and not as carefree as she looked. She apparently knew how to take care of herself and that made his job a little easier.

Finally the clerk finished her call, rang up the shoes and bagged the purchases. She took a few glances at Gabby. "You look familiar."

Gabby didn't get nervous or back away. She simply smiled sweetly. "A lot of people tell me that." She swiped the bags from the counter and headed for the door.

Rafe followed her with a smile. She knew when she had to make a getaway.

Outside the shop, Gabby quickly headed back toward the jewelry store.

Rafe took the bags from her. "I can carry those." When their fingers met, the shock was electric.

Gabby stepped back and so did he. Before she could see

the hunger in his eyes, he pointed to a side street. "Let's circle around that way. I never take the same route twice."

To his surprise, she stopped and asked, "In your personal life, as well as your professional life?"

"I've always liked to leave the past behind," he explained.

"You can try to take a new path, but that doesn't mean the past isn't always shadowing you."

He thought of his fieldwork as a Secret Service agent, Connie's death when he wasn't there to protect her, the aftermath of all of it.

He thought he'd put it all behind him. But meeting Gabby had seemed to unearth it. A couple more weeks and she'd be in Italy. A couple more weeks and he'd be back in New York.

That would be best for both of them.

Chapter Seven

"Gabby, what's wrong? Your restlessness is driving me crazy!" Spending the evening alone with her in the suite, Rafe was so aware of her that every move she made tensed his body even more.

She'd sat down at the piano and started one piece then stopped. She'd started another, then stopped again. Before that, she'd picked at a dinner they'd eaten almost in silence, checked her e-mail and tried on a few clothes in her bedroom.

Still on the piano bench, she glanced at him over her shoulder, one hand still on the piano keys. "You have your own room now. You can go in there and shut the door."

Yes, he did have his own room, but he didn't feel as if he was doing his job if he holed up in it. "I can't pretend I'm a hermit when I have to keep my eye on you."

"I'm not going anywhere," she said in frustration, standing up from the piano bench. "That's the whole problem."

"Where would you like to go?" he asked, proud of himself for the patience in his voice.

"It isn't that I want to go somewhere specific. It's that I don't have the freedom to go. Do you know what I mean?"

"You're not locked and chained in here."

"All right. I'll say it," she erupted suddenly. "I'm feeling like that caged bird because you're with me every minute of the day. No matter what I do, you know what I'm doing. It's like having a camera on me."

Setting his laptop aside, he stood and crossed to her. "Maybe you've had a camera on you too often and you don't know what it's like to sit in companionable silence with someone."

"And you're feeling completely peaceful, sitting in companionable silence?"

No, because he wanted to kiss her senseless every minute he was with her. But he couldn't say *that.* "I get restless sometimes," he admitted. "But I learned control when I was in the Secret Service. I learned to focus and stay calm."

"I don't want to control the restlessness. I want to just be…free."

"Why don't you ask Eleanor McCord if you can stay at the mansion with her? Would that help?"

"I can't do that, especially not now."

"Not now?"

"The whole family is in turmoil. They're dealing with family…secrets."

"More than the business problems?" Rafe asked, familiar with those because of his work with the jewelry stores.

"This doesn't have anything to do with the business." She sighed. "Besides, I don't know how much that would help. I guess part of what I'm feeling is that I don't have a place to belong. That's why I want to buy my own house. I can go to the market and the shops in town without raising a fuss."

"No paparazzi?"

"That's my dream. Maybe I can find a place with a stone wall rather than a moat."

"That still sounds like a cage to me."

"Maybe after this campaign of Blake's, I'll drop out and stop modeling. There's an Italian designer interested in starting a purse line with me. If I did that, I'd be pretty much out of the public eye."

All of this surprised Rafe. Didn't Gabby need to feed her ego?

"What?" she asked.

"Nothing."

"Tell me what you were thinking."

"I was thinking that most people in your line of work do it for the public acclaim. They like being celebrities. Wouldn't you miss that?"

"I was pressed into this when I hardly knew how to make good choices. I mean, don't get me wrong. I wanted to model. My mother made sure of that before I did it. But it's taken on a life of its own…something I can never get free from."

There was that word again—free. She wanted to feel free. He had to keep his eye on her, but maybe he could help her out. Before they'd returned to the hotel, she'd been dressed to the nines again for an appointment with a cosmetics representative. But now she was wearing a tank top and shorts, her hair pulled back into a ponytail and he had to admit this was the way he liked her.

His gaze went to her bare feet. "I'm going to make a call. You put on some sandals. Maybe I can help you feel 'free' for a little while."

Her gaze was uncomprehending, but he just smiled and took out his phone.

* * *

A half hour later, Rafe led Gabby through the back exit of the hotel. This time, however, the car wasn't waiting for them.

She stopped short when she saw a golf cart. "What's this?"

"Your chariot to freedom. Come on, climb in. I'm a great driver. I've never had an accident in one of these."

She laughed and hopped in beside him, her arm close to his and her leg beside his. She hadn't just been restless because she was with him practically twenty-four hours a day, but because of the tension between them, the fire that erupted whenever they touched, the undercurrent when they spoke, the electricity from being in the same room together. But now the warm night air blew around her. She lifted her face, took the band from her ponytail and let her hair blow free.

"Where are we going?" she asked as Rafe turned off the service road and onto the golf course.

"I want you to close your eyes," he said as the golf cart picked up speed. "Pretend you're on horseback, riding wild and free, no walls, no chains, no paparazzi."

She hadn't used her imagination in this way for a long time. Now she did as he asked. She let tabloid stories, flashing cameras, shouted questions, even what happened with Miko fall from her shoulders as the wind blew around her, as the headlights cut into the darkness, as Rafe plunged her into freedom. After a while, she didn't know if they'd ridden five minutes or twenty.

When he slowed a bit, she turned toward him, placing her hand on his arm. "Thank you."

"No thanks necessary. I was afraid you were going to run screaming out of the hotel and be captured by ardent fans."

She laughed. "I wasn't really that bad, was I?"

He cut her a glance. "I understand, though. Restriction is tough."

Restriction. Control. How much control was Rafe exerting whenever he was around her? Maybe none at all. Maybe this was just his job and attraction was easy for him to corral.

"Do you wish you could spend more time with your family?" she asked.

"You mean if I didn't have to work?"

She could tell he seemed amused.

"Something like that."

He thought about it while keeping a steady foot on the gas. "I'd like to spend more time with my family. My mother, well, let's face it, she's getting older. She has her friends, work, Julie, but when I come home I see that sparkle in her eyes. I know she misses me. I know she wants to feed me." He chuckled. "That's the way she shows love. She likes to have me sitting at that table talking with her. It brings back memories for her of when my dad was still alive. It brings back memories of when Julie and I were growing up. She thinks I don't know it, but I do."

Gabby was impressed by Rafe's insight. But then he had more experience and wisdom than she did, since he was nine years older. Just how much did age matter in a relationship? There was ten years difference between her mother and father.

What was she thinking? A relationship?

But so much about Rafe seemed solid and true. Since when had she been with a man who gave her that feeling?

Not ever.

"What about you and your family? If you live in Tuscany, you'll see your mother, but how much will you see your dad?" he asked.

"Can you keep a secret?"

"You don't know how many secrets I've kept," he returned wryly.

"My dad's thinking about retiring. When I talked with him

last night, he said of course he wouldn't do it until McCord's financial problems are settled, or at least on the right track. But it's in his plans and that would be wonderful."

"You'd really give up your public life altogether?"

"I would for the right reasons."

"And what would those reasons be?"

"To start a business that would see me into my future."

"You probably have enough money that you'd never have to worry about working again."

"That's true, but I'd have to do some kind of work. I need to feel productive. But I do have to admit, if I had children, I would concentrate mostly on them."

He was silent.

"Don't you want children someday?" she asked, curious.

"That's a subject I don't get into."

His voice had changed and become different. There was sadness in it. He'd gone back into Secret-Service-agent mode and Gabby didn't know why. The subject of children?

She didn't want to spoil this wonderful adventure. She didn't want to spoil the feeling of freedom Rafe had given her. So she didn't ask any more questions. She just faced the wind and breathed in freedom.

Gabby chose an apple from the fruit bowl in the kitchen. She tossed it up in the air and then caught it again, smiling. Her ride with Rafe had left her exhilarated, excited and even more attracted to him than she'd been before. He'd gone to his room when they'd returned and she'd wondered if they'd gotten a little bit too close while they were talking in the golf cart.

She strolled into the living room, glanced at the piano, but instead went to the French doors that led to the small balcony. Out there, she took a bite from the apple, realizing each minute, each hour, each day she spent with Rafe, she felt even closer to him. She'd had bodyguards before. She'd had chauffeurs and handlers. But that had been so different from what she was experiencing now.

She'd left the door open so that Rafe would know where she'd gone. He stepped outside now and joined her at the railing. He'd changed into jeans and a T-shirt and looked less formal than any other time she'd seen him. His black polo shirt and khaki cargo pants were like a uniform. Now she took a long look at him, liking every bit of what she saw, even the dark shadow of beard on his jawline.

"You look relaxed," she said, meaning it.

"That's what a good golf cart ride will do," he joked.

"Thank you for thinking of it, for taking me out on the golf course. The ride really did help. I don't feel like I'm going to burst out of my skin anymore."

"Good. We wouldn't want that."

Rafe was always so restrained around her. She almost felt like every response was measured. She wanted to force a spontaneous response from him.

Impulsively, she held the apple out to him and asked, "Would you like a bite?"

She expected some joke about Adam and Eve, or a retreat on his part. That's what he usually did if she didn't do it first.

But instead of retreating, he leaned forward, clasped her hand under his and took a bite of the apple. The world stopped and then seemed to move in slow motion as Rafe chewed his bite of the apple, his gaze on hers the whole time. Her stomach somersaulted and any coherent thought she possessed vanished. A breeze blew between them, awakening everything about the moment.

She could inhale the scent of the soap he used when he'd showered. She could practically feel the memory of their last kiss. The recessed lamp above them gave off enough light for her to see the hunger grow in his eyes as he swallowed his bite of the apple and didn't move an inch. She almost felt as if she were tumbling off a precipice, engaged in a free fall, ready to take off on an exciting new adventure. Rafe's hand was still over hers, the heat from it increasing.

He reached for the apple, took it, then set it aside on the balcony ledge. "What do you want, Gabby?" he asked earnestly.

Boldly she replied, "I want you to kiss me again."

"We decided involvement was a mistake."

"We didn't know each other then."

"And you think we know each other now?" His tone was a combination of surprise and amusement.

"I've been living with you, driving with you, sneaking out with you the past three days. That's like three months in real time."

Now he did laugh, but his laugh was husky and low. "Women's logic never ceases to amaze me."

"Then maybe you should try it and be amazed all the time."

He shook his head and slid his hands under her hair. "This is trouble, Gabby, and you and I both know it."

"I know what trouble is, Rafe, and this, whatever this is between you and I, feels different."

She thought he might question her about that trouble. She thought he might still back away. But there was color high on his cheeks now and his body was taut. She knew the signs and signals. Not that she was experienced by any means, but she was beginning to know Rafe's every reaction and this was one she'd learned the last two times he'd kissed her.

When he was close enough and his lips practically touched hers, he whispered, "What kind of kiss do you like, Gabby? Fast...slow...deep...wet?"

"I like your kisses, Rafe, however you want to give or take them."

His fingers threaded through her hair. "I like a woman who makes some choices."

She didn't know what he was trying to do, what he was trying to find out. But if he wanted her to choose, fine. "Let's start with slow and see where it goes from there." Her voice had a coy quality to it and she hoped it would entice him.

"You don't know exactly how beautiful you are, do you?" He held her head so she couldn't move...so she had to look directly into his eyes. "You are the most desirable woman that I have ever met."

To his credit he did start the kiss slow.

Gabby accepted the gentle nibbling at her lips, the brief kisses on the corners. But that wasn't nearly enough. And that's what she'd meant when she said they could *start* slow.

Her arms slid around his back. She let her hands wander, feeling solid muscle under his shirt. Her touch seemed to push the kiss forward. His lips pressed hard against hers and then opened. She felt the slide of his tongue on her bottom lip and her insides melted until she didn't know if she could stand. Once he was inside her mouth, she reacted without thinking. She stroked against him, gave a response to every swipe of his tongue and found more freedom than she knew what to do with. It sent her soaring with no boundaries and no timetable for return.

Her hands were restless on his back as they reached high and low. Her fingers found the edge of his T-shirt and passed under it until she felt his skin.

Everything about the kiss escalated. He went deeper and wetter. She dragged her nails down his back. Passion broke the barriers of controlled desire, at least on her part. Rafe kept his hands in her hair, on her face, while his mouth told her in a hundred ways how much he wanted her.

The beeping seemed very far away and didn't register until he broke away. When he reached his hand into his pocket, she realized he was going for his cell phone.

She'd thought they were alone...on their own. But they weren't.

He slid open the phone, saw the number and then checked his watch. "It's my mother. She never calls this late. I have to take it."

Still reeling from their kiss, still dizzy and off balance, she pulled herself together enough to nod and say, "I understand."

She would have slipped inside, but he caught her wrist. "We have to talk."

What was there to say about a kiss like that? Thanks, but no thanks? Maybe we can take it to bed later? This is wrong and we shouldn't even be thinking about the next level?

She had no idea what Rafe was thinking as he put the phone to his ear. "Hi, Mom. What's up?"

As he listened, lines cut deep into his forehead. "You want me to bring crutches tomorrow? What are you going to do about tonight? You are *not* trying to climb those stairs. All you need to do is break something else in the process. How do you know your ankle isn't broken?"

Figuring out what had happened from the conversation, Gabby tugged on Rafe's elbow.

He scowled, "Just a minute, Mom."

"How badly is your mother hurt?"

"She fell down the back steps when she was taking the garbage out. It happened about an hour ago and the ankle is swollen now."

"It *might* be broken."

"She doesn't want to think so. She wants me to get her a

pair of crutches and take them over tomorrow. She says she can manage for tonight."

"That's ridiculous! She needs help *now,* not tomorrow."

He went back to the phone. "Mom, I'm going to take you to the emergency room."

Gabby could hear the loud "No!" without Rafe taking the phone from his ear.

She tugged on his elbow again. "Listen, I know an orthopedic doctor in the area. One my aunt sees. I saw him, too, when I tripped and fell during a fashion show last year. Let me call him. We can go to his complex and get your mom's ankle x-rayed."

"Are you absolutely crazy? What doctor is going to want to open up his office at eleven o'clock at night?"

"He'll do it, Rafe, as a favor to the McCord family. Just explain it to your mom. Tell her we'll pick her up."

"We?"

"Yes, *we.* I'm coming along incognito. Knowing you, you won't want to leave me here alone and you can't leave your mother all alone, either."

She saw something flicker in Rafe's eyes, something that caused him pain. But she didn't know what it was and now wasn't the time to ask. She persisted, "If you can make sure we're not tailed from here, we should be fine. Doctor Christopher's office is discreet."

Rafe relayed everything Gabby had said to his mother. She was still protesting when he told her they'd be there in a half hour to forty-five minutes to pick her up.

"If you can't get hold of the doctor, Mom will understand. I'll take her to the emergency room."

"Let me get my phone and I'll call." She hurried away, leaving Rafe on the balcony with the apple…leaving temptation behind.

They'd both been tempted out of themselves and into each other's arms, she thought. That had been nice. It had plunged her into a dream, an old one that after her escapade with Miko, she'd decided could never come true.

Reality always overrode dreams.

When she picked up her cell phone in the bedroom, she went to the address book, found Doctor Christopher's number and pressed Send. She liked the idea of doing something for someone else. She liked it a lot.

And she and Rafe?

Eventually they'd either continue where they'd left off, or they'd ignore the earthmoving kiss.

The problem was, when the earth moved, the world was never the same again.

"This is the best thing for you to do," Gabby assured Lena Balthazar as she stood on one side of the older woman and Rafe stood on the other outside her back door.

"Make sure the door is locked," Lena ordered her son, and Gabby had to smile. She was sure no one else could order him around.

"It's locked, Mom. I made sure."

"This is such a bother," Lena protested again. "Whoever heard of a doctor coming to his office this time of night."

"Honestly, Mrs. Balthazar. It's not a problem. Dr. Christopher patched up all of the McCord kids when they were growing up. He's a family friend."

"You were paying him though, weren't you? I won't let you do that. I pay my own bills."

"We'll make sure he bills your insurance, Mom," Rafe assured her.

After they helped her down the last two steps to the backyard, she saw the car. "This isn't yours," she said to Rafe.

"No, it's not. It's the car I'm using for Gabby while she's in Dallas. Come on, let's get you inside."

Once Rafe's mother was tucked into the backseat of the sedan, Gabby leaned down to her. "Would you like me to ride in the back with you, Mrs. Balthazar?"

"Call me Lena. We're getting to know each other better by the minute. I don't know anyone who would do something like this for me."

"I don't always get a chance to do something nice for someone."

"You make money for all those charities. I see your picture in the paper when you do."

"That's not quite the same thing." Gabby went around the other side of the car and slipped inside, next to Lena. Rafe's mom winced every once in a while and Gabby knew the ankle must hurt her.

"Tell me again when Julie will be back," she said to distract Rafe's mother.

"Not until the day after tomorrow. Friday. I couldn't call her back from her vacation early. Not when they waited so long to take it. If the doctor would just tape up my ankle for me, I know I could get around on it."

Rafe peered at Gabby through the rearview mirror and she knew what he was thinking. His mother might have to stay off that foot altogether.

Since Rafe made sure no one followed them, Lena gave Gabby an odd look once or twice about his method of driving. A short while later, they pulled into the medical complex and went around to the back door, per the instructions the doctor had given Gabby. He was already waiting for them. He was an older gentleman with white hair, a ready smile and twinkling blue eyes.

He put Lena at ease immediately. "Let's go back to my office and I'll examine you. Gabby, why don't you come along."

Fifteen minutes later, after the physician had examined Lena, he sent her to another room where a tech waited. Soon after, Rafe, Gabby and Lena sat in Dr. Christopher's office with him. He explained, "Fortunately, you didn't break anything, but you do have a bad sprain. I'll tape it to keep the swelling down. I want you to ice it for fifteen minutes every hour. But most of all, I want you to stay off it."

"But I can't. I'm alone in my house. I have a job—"

Gabby interrupted with quiet understanding, "You want to get better as soon as you can, don't you?"

"Well, yes, but—"

"Rafe can stay with you tonight. I'll be fine in my suite alone."

"No," was Rafe's unqualified reply to that.

Gabby could see she wasn't going to get anywhere arguing with him, so she quickly came up with another solution. She laid her hand on Lena's arm. "Rafe is using the adjoining room to my suite. You can take his room and he can sleep on the sofa like he did the first few nights."

"But this hotel you're staying at must cost a terrible amount!" Lena protested.

"The room is already paid for. We'll just be rearranging how we're staying in it. I can call room service in the morning to order any kind of breakfast you want. And maybe, maybe we can get a manicure while you're there."

Lena's eyes brightened. "A manicure? I haven't had one of those in years. Julie got me one for my birthday one year."

"Well, now's your chance."

"You really can't go back to the house yet, Mom," Rafe offered, obviously seeing the merits of what Gabby had proposed. "Your shower's upstairs. Your bedroom's upstairs.

If you sleep on the couch, your arthritis will be worse. Please consider this."

Gabby encouraged, "Let me help you. And let me have a little fun while you're there. Rafe can tell you, sometimes I get a caged-in feeling that makes me want to explode. If I can share some of the hotel's niceties with you, that will help."

Lena sighed, looked down at her lap and then raised her head. "I can see this is three against one. I'm outnumbered. I suppose we could try it for one night."

"Off your foot, Mrs. Balthazar, for at least two to three days," the doctor reminded her.

"Julie will be back by then. For now, I'll stay with you, Gabby. I don't have any of my things, though." She appraised Gabby with a smile. "I don't think I could fit into one of your nightgowns." Rafe's mother was pleasantly rounded.

Gabby smiled. "We'll stop at your place again and you can tell me what you need. I'll run in and get it. Or would you rather Rafe did that?"

"You'd be able to tell exactly what I want."

"Thanks, Mom," he said wryly. "Don't you think I take direction well?"

"Sometimes I think you're color blind. Gabby will be able to find what I need."

And Gabby did.

She also called ahead to the hotel and when they arrived, Joe had a wheelchair waiting.

Lena held her small suitcase on her lap as Rafe pushed his mom's chair through the lobby, Gabby walking beside him. A few people in the lobby noticed them because of the wheelchair, but did not recognize Gabby. If they did, they didn't approach her. With her ponytail, tank top and shorts, she looked like any summer guest might. Security here always did a grand job of keeping out anyone who didn't belong.

Upstairs, Lena seemed more comfortable with having Gabby help her get ready in her room. She marveled at the decor. "I feel as if I'm a queen."

"Just enjoy it."

"I'm going to have to repay you."

Gabby considered that, knowing Lena wouldn't feel comfortable unless she did. "I told you I'm thinking about buying a house near my parents in Italy. When I go home, I'm going to seriously look. I'd love to have one of your afghans to cuddle up with in front of a fireplace. Would you consider making me one for repayment?"

"Of course I would! You'll have to tell me your favorite color."

"Blue—any shade of blue."

Lena held out her hand. "It's a deal."

Gabby could see Lena took this kind of deal very seriously and Gabby guessed her son would, too. Rafe hadn't said much after she'd made the offer and she realized she really didn't know exactly how he felt about his mother sharing the suite.

We could have all gone to Lena's house, Gabby supposed. But this could be such a treat for his mother. However, maybe he'd had a different idea.

There was only one way to find out. She had to ask him.

Chapter Eight

A deepening turmoil swirled inside Rafe as he opened the couch again. He thought about his first night on it and how his opinion of Gabby had shifted and changed. The attraction he'd felt when he'd first laid eyes on her had been difficult to shut down. But he *had* shut it down.

Until he'd gotten to know her.

Now each minute with her was a struggle to be professional…to be her bodyguard. With that last kiss, he'd definitely crossed the boundary. He'd let chemistry take over without the thought of consequences. Yet from the moment his mother had called and Gabby had offered her assistance, he'd known any involvement between them had to end.

They were worlds apart.

He knew Gabby had something on her mind when she stepped into the living room. The tilt of her head, the set of her shoulders, the uncertainty in her eyes told him she had something to say or ask that was going to be uncomfortable.

He braced himself as she crossed to him and said, "I should have asked you first."

He was trying not to catch the scent of her perfume, not to remember their kiss, not to remember how needing her had seemed more important than anything else in his life.

When he didn't respond, she explained further. "I should have asked you if you wanted me to invite your mother to the suite."

He shrugged. "If you had asked me, I would have said it's between you and my mother."

"It's not that simple."

He knew the uncomfortable part was coming. But he tried to prevent Gabby from leaping in. "My mother's grateful to you, Gabby. Let's just leave it there."

His mother's gratitude was the problem. He knew he couldn't repay Gabby in a monetary way. She would never accept that. He knew it would be hard to repay her in any other way, either. She could buy whatever she wanted and he could, too, to a certain extent. But tonight had lifted a mirror to the differences between them. He'd come from a blue-collar background, a row house with a cop for a dad and a mom who stayed home to take care of her kids. That was very different from the way Gabby had grown up.

Blue collar versus royalty.

But Gabby wasn't content to take his advice and drop the conversational thread. "If I acted impulsively, I'm sorry. I thought your mom coming here would be best for her. But maybe we should have all gone to stay at *her* house."

That made him forget the sheet he'd been unfolding onto the bed. "You wouldn't have had room service at our house."

Now she eyed him as if he were a stranger. "Do you think I *care* about room service?"

"Can you cook?" he asked reasonably.

Her eyes filled with a shiny luminescence he would rather turn away from. But he couldn't.

"I guess you doubt whether I could have taken care of your mom at her house," she said, lowering her voice. "Did you ever think I might have surprised you?" When he didn't respond, she went on, "I simply saw this as the easiest road to taking care of her and solving our problem."

He knew he should end this conversation. But he asked anyway, "What problem is that?"

"That you wouldn't leave me here alone to go home with your mom."

Gabby was right. He wouldn't have left her here alone. Both women were his responsibility.

After a long moment, Gabby came a step closer to him, searched his face and then his eyes. "Did that kiss on the balcony tonight mean anything to you?"

No matter what he answered, he'd be in trouble. So he decided no answer was the best reply of all.

She shook her head. "I should have known better than to ask." She turned to go to her room. "I gave your mom my cell phone number and told her if she needs anything, she should just call me."

He couldn't let her leave thinking he wasn't grateful. He caught her arm. "Gabby, thank you for wanting to help my mother. I do appreciate it."

"You're welcome," she replied politely.

They stood there, his hand on her arm, their gazes locked, vibrations neither of them understood rippling between them.

He knew the instant she decided to pull away. He released her arm and let her go.

After all, wasn't that what he was supposed to do?

* * *

"I love my nails," Rafe's mother said the following afternoon as she grinned at Gabby.

Gabby waved her own just-painted nails in the air to dry them. "It was fun, wasn't it? I like those little flowers painted on yours."

"I enjoyed the facial just as much. How relaxing. The time has gone faster than I expected—thanks to you."

"Well, it would be awful if you were stuck here in bed with nothing to do and no one to talk to."

Rafe entered the room just then and glanced from one woman to the other. "Are we expecting anyone else today?" His eyes were almost brooding, his tone a bit disapproving.

Gabby checked her watch. "I have a phone interview at four, but then I'll make supper."

Rafe's brows arched, "*You'll* make supper?"

Rafe had been cool and distant today. Because of their kiss? Because of her invitation to his mother to stay here? He was backing away from the intensity of what happened when they were together. He didn't see her as the type of woman he wanted to get involved with. So be it.

She tried not to get defensive. She tried to keep her voice light. "You forget I came from Italy. I might have had a nanny and housekeeper, but they were both good cooks. I make a terrific eggplant parmagiana and a mean salad. The ingredients should be arriving within the hour. They include a box of brownie mix. I *do* know how to follow directions. If you'd rather call room service, feel free, but your mom said she'd try my cooking."

So much for not being defensive.

Rafe looked a bit uncomfortable and glanced at his mother. Then he cleared his throat. "I talked to Julie. She'll be returning home early tomorrow morning. She wants you to move in with her until you're up and around again."

Lena frowned. "I want to go home."

"You're not ready to be alone yet, Mom. You definitely can't do the stairs. Julie wants to talk about all of it. I want to be part of that discussion, but I can't leave Gabby alone. I'll have to check her schedule."

"The solution to that is simple," Gabby interjected. "Just ask your sister to come here."

"I don't think that would work. Her husband, Troy, is going in to work tomorrow afternoon so she'd have to bring the baby."

"I don't see the problem," Gabby said.

Lena waved her hand around the room, with the white country French furniture, the fine coverings on the chairs, the polish of the wood. "He's afraid Suzanne might break something. She crawls pretty fast and is almost walking."

"You don't have to worry about the baby. I can watch her," Gabby offered.

"You'll watch her?" Rafe repeated, his astonishment evident. "Gabby, have you had any experience with one-year-olds?"

This time Gabby couldn't help but turn indignant. She propped her hands on her hips, forgetting about the fresh nail polish. "I don't think your mom raised you to be this uncomplimentary toward women, so you must have learned it along the way somewhere. I can cook, I can run a business, I can manage my own life and…I can watch a baby. I don't have brothers and sisters, but my mother does and they have children who have children. I don't live in a vacuum, Rafe, not all the time."

Rafe looked unsettled as if he didn't know what to say.

When Gabby glanced at Lena, she saw a small smile on his mother's lips.

After a few moments, he shook his head. "So you want this meeting to take place tomorrow?"

"I'm free from one until three. At three I have a meeting with the manager of a boutique who would consider carrying my line of purses. If I go that direction." She was becoming more and more sure that's what she wanted to do.

"All right," Rafe gave in. "I'll call Julie and ask her to be here at one." After a long look at his mother and her pretty new nails, and a last glance at Gabby, he left the room to go into the suite.

Gabby didn't realize she was staring after him until Lena asked, "You like him, don't you?"

"He's a good man," Gabby responded automatically.

"Yes, he is, and you're a good woman."

Gabby sent Lena a curious look. "We're very different. And I'm going back to Italy soon."

"Rafe makes trips to the stores in Italy. You make trips here. Would it be so hard to coordinate schedules?"

"It would be hard to coordinate lives."

"Not if doing it means the world to both of you."

Gabby thought about that. She felt as if she were on the verge of her life changing. Yet that change might not include Rafe. "He believes we're very different. He thinks I'm shallow."

"That's not true!" Lena protested. "I think he says the things he does because he doesn't want to get too close."

"Then that doesn't give us much hope, does it?"

"You need to ask him about Connie," Rafe's mother prompted her. "She was his wife and she's been dead for five years. It's time he thinks about making himself happy."

"If he doesn't want to talk—"

"Push him a little, Gabby. He needs a push. I've watched him do nothing but work for years. He uses it to keep a lid on everything he doesn't want to feel. Maybe it's time you popped that lid."

"Maybe I'm not the right one to do it."

"You'll never know unless you try."

* * *

The next afternoon Gabby reached out her arms to the happy baby girl, and the toddler went to her willingly. "I understand your name is Suzanne. That's such a pretty name."

The baby grabbed for one of her gold hoop earrings and Gabby laughed.

Julie reached to take her back. "I don't want her to hurt you." She sounded worried and she'd looked nervous ever since she'd come into the suite.

Gabby quickly unfastened the earring and held it out for the baby to grab. "She won't hurt me."

"If you let her on the floor, she could break something in here, get her fingerprints all over everything."

Gabby again shook her head. "It's okay. She'll be fine. Really. I have some things in the kitchen that should keep her occupied—plastic containers, pots and pans." She turned the child around in her lap and smiled at her. She tickled her tummy and Suzanne giggled.

Julie seemed to relax a bit. "She does love to play with that kind of stuff, rolls of paper towels, too."

"I have one of those." Gabby was trying to ignore Rafe's presence.

Julie looked up at Rafe. "Mom doesn't mind us talking about her?"

"She's watching her favorite soap opera. She says when we decide about her life, we should let her know, then she'll tell us whether she agrees or doesn't agree."

Gabby lifted the baby and rose. "Suzanne will be able to see you from the kitchen, but I'll keep her occupied."

Gabby hadn't really spoken to Rafe all morning. They seemed to be at opposite ends of a great big ocean. She could climb into a boat to cross to him, but she was afraid he wouldn't allow her into his harbor.

Plopping down on the kitchen floor with Suzanne, she heard Julie say, "Mom should move in with me permanently."

"You know she doesn't want to do that."

"She might not want to, but she doesn't have much choice. She can't keep climbing those steps. What if she falls and breaks something more important than her ankle?"

"She's going to say she didn't break anything."

"Are you on her side?"

"I'm just trying to play devil's advocate," Rafe replied calmly. "We can come up with any plan in the world, but if she doesn't agree to it, what good will it do?"

"Maybe we should be talking with *her* about it."

"Not until we come up with a solution, Julie. What do we say—go live with Julie and be happy about it? She likes her privacy. She likes her independence."

Gabby had been thinking something since last evening. She hadn't said anything to Rafe, but maybe it was time to do so. Reaching for Suzanne and lifting her into her arms again, she jiggled her a bit, watched the little girl smile and then returned to the living room.

Both brother and sister gave her their attention. "I know this isn't any of my business, but there might be a solution everyone will be happy with."

"She doesn't want to go to an assisted-living facility and be all by herself," Rafe said adamantly.

"No, I wasn't going to suggest that. Have you ever thought of installing a chairlift?"

The brother and sister looked at each other, puzzled. Julie asked, "A chairlift?"

"Yes, one of my mother's friends has one. If your staircase is wide enough, the chairlift can be installed. That way she could go up and down the stairs on her own without your being worried. I checked online last night and there are several companies in Dallas who sell and install them."

After Rafe and Julie exchanged another look, Rafe said thoughtfully, "I once worked security for a client whose father had one, now that you mention it. He had arthritis in his knees and climbing the stairs was very painful."

"Exactly," Gabby said, rocking Suzanne again to keep her happy.

Rafe addressed his sister. "Why don't you talk to Mom about it? I'll make a couple of phone calls and see if I can get more information."

He sent Gabby an admiring look that she just soaked in. Maybe this time, she'd done something right. Maybe this time, Rafe would believe she didn't just think about herself, but others, too.

Gabby loved playing with Suzanne, she really did. She did finger games with her, peekaboo, hide the spoon under the towel and tear off the paper towels. The baby seemed enthralled with each activity and Gabby felt satisfaction that she could entertain her. She knew being a mother was about so much more, but this could be a start. She'd been thinking about motherhood a lot more the past few days or so. Not as an alternative to what she was doing now, but rather as an addition to her life, a change she would welcome.

About a half hour later, she was still sitting on the kitchen floor with Suzanne, who was lifting spoons from one container to another.

Gabby suddenly felt another presence in the kitchen. Turning slowly, she saw Rafe towering over her. There was such a sad, sad expression on his face and she wanted to know the reason for it.

She patted the floor next to her. "Want to play with us?"

He gave her a crooked half smile and dropped to the floor beside her.

"You looked very sad. What's wrong? Your mom doesn't want the chairlift?"

"Actually, she does. She and Julie are making plans now. I think she'll be very happy with the whole idea."

"And the sadness?"

"Maybe you misread me."

"I don't think so." She knew she couldn't push anymore. She couldn't prompt anymore. He had to want to tell her his secrets. If he didn't, then they really had no place to go.

He didn't respond right away. He watched Suzanne pick up a spoon, transfer it from her right hand to her left. He picked up one of the spoons and handed it to the baby. She grinned at him, shaking both spoons.

That sad expression was there on his face again...in his eyes. "I almost had a child once."

Gabby kept perfectly still, hoping he'd say more.

But Julie came hurrying through the living room, stopped when she saw the three of them in the kitchen and sent Rafe a look that said she understood. Gabby realized that being with his niece was painful for him. It was obvious.

"You're going to have your suite back to yourself," Julie pronounced happily. "Mom's packing her things. She's going to stay with me until her ankle's better and by then, the chairlift will be installed." She dropped to the floor with them and grinned. "We can never repay you for helping us, Gabby. This means a lot. Rafe might have to wait on you hand and foot for the next few days."

Rafe glanced at Gabby. "I might just have to do that."

On Saturday afternoon, Gabby admired the jewelry designs Penny had messengered to her. They were beautiful, intricate, unique.

But they didn't keep her mind off of Rafe. She'd been aware

of him ever since his mother had left with Julie yesterday. She tried to pretend he wasn't there, but that was impossible.

The doorbell rang.

Gabby watched him put his computer aside, rise from the sofa and answer it. He was wearing a T-shirt and jeans again since she hadn't had any outside appointments.

When he came into the kitchen, he had a package in his hands. He looked a bit out of his element when he set it before her.

"What's this?" she asked. The box was wrapped in blue paper with a white bow.

"It's a thank-you gift for helping my mother. It's not much—" He stopped abruptly.

What did he think she expected? "You didn't have to get me anything."

"I know you and Mom made a deal—that she's going to make you an afghan—but I wanted to thank you, too. Go ahead, open it."

Gabby's heart beat fast as she removed the bow and then unfastened the paper. She uncovered a white gift box. Her fingers fumbled because she was both touched and excited.

After she took the lid from the box, she pushed back the paper. What she saw made her smile. She lifted the little glass birdcage out of the box and held it in the palm of her hand. "Thank you. It's beautiful. I can't believe you remembered."

"My job leads me to pay attention." A small smile played on his lips.

Gabby wanted to hug him, wanted to throw her arms around his neck, wanted to kiss him again. Instead, she just looked up at him. "This is very thoughtful. I'll keep it in a special place. You understand how I feel, Rafe, and not many people do."

He nodded.

She took a chance and said, "I'd like to know how you feel about what matters most. Tell me about Connie," she requested.

After he studied her for a few moments, he pulled out the chair around the corner of the table from her and lowered himself into it. "I don't talk about Connie."

She set the birdcage on the table. "Maybe you should. Your mom told me to ask you about her."

His brows arched at that and he looked surprised.

Silence kept stretching between them and she didn't fill it. He shifted uncomfortably in his chair and still she waited.

Finally he explained, "Connie was the daughter of a friend of my mother's." After taking a deep breath, he went on quickly, as if to get the conversation over with. "We met at a Christmas party when I was in college. We got married while I was on the Dallas police force. She understood I wanted to be a Secret Service agent and she always stood by me. After the president's detail, I worked in a field office in Atlanta for a while. Connie got pregnant while we were living there and we couldn't wait until our child was born. I was tied up on a case and we decided it would be a good time for her to come back and visit her family here in Dallas. She had a friend who lived on the south side. I told her to meet her somewhere else to visit, but she wouldn't listen. She was leaving her friend's house, walking to her car, when she was killed by a drive-by shooter aiming for a group of guys on the corner. I lost her and the baby that day."

Gabby clasped his arm. "Rafe, I'm so sorry. I don't know what to say."

"There isn't anything to say. It happened five years ago. I've moved on."

He was motionless under Gabby's hand and she wondered if he was purposefully trying not to react.

"Have you been involved with anyone since then?"

He gave her a look that said it was none of her business. "You need to know when to stop, Gabby."

She bristled and moved her hand from his arm. "That's the type of question anyone would ask when they're getting to know someone."

"Why do you want to know me?"

Should she take a risk? Take a leap? Just how foolish would she look? If she just kept her feelings to herself until she left for Italy, he'd never have to know. But what if something *could* work out between them?

"I'm beginning to feel something for you, Rafe. Maybe I need to know if you feel it, too."

He took her hand. "I'm mightily attracted to you. But if I get involved with you, I put my reputation on the line."

She closed her fingers into his. "Aren't we already involved? Sometimes I think you believe that we grew up so differently that we can't truly relate to each other as adults. But I don't see that. I think we have more in common than we don't."

He shook his head. "Don't delude yourself into thinking our lives are the same. They're not."

She didn't want to fight with him. She didn't want to argue. She wanted him to admit what he felt. "I hop a plane to Los Angeles for a shoot or an interview or a speaking engagement. You hop a plane to Los Angeles to check on the security in a store. After a few days, I hop on a plane to somewhere else. After a few days, you do the same thing. Aren't you tired of hopping? Don't you want to live somewhere? I want to wake up each day knowing where I am. I want a life. I want to be a mother." That had come out and she really hadn't intended it to.

"When did you make *that* decision?"

"I'm twenty-eight and my biological clock is ticking. I don't have to make any rash decisions now. I have a few years if I want to get a business going, stop modeling, stay in San Casciano. I think you'd like it, too. It's about ten miles from Florence. The countryside is full of vineyards and olive groves. In Florence, many of the jewelers are housed on a bridge over the Arno River known as the Ponte Vecchio. It's really unique."

"You'd give up your life in the States altogether? What about your family here?"

"We're not as close as families should be and I'd still like to stay in touch. I'd probably have to come back here to talk to boutique owners and manufacturers. I could get an apartment here for when I visit. I'm sure I could sublet it while I'm gone."

"You're really considering a drastic change."

"It's not so drastic. I've had a good life modeling. I've cut down on assignments over the past year, looking for other opportunities. Some have come my way." She leaned closer and felt him tense. But he didn't pull away.

"You changed the subject," she said gently. "I don't want to talk about *me,* I want to talk about *you.*"

"Why do women think talking will solve something?"

"Because talking *can* solve lots of things. But only if you communicate your thoughts and your feelings. Don't you see that?"

"If you want me to communicate thoughts and feelings about what happened to my wife and my child, that isn't going to happen. After the shooting, I drank for a month, then I put myself on a physical fitness regimen to pull out of it. I still haven't figured out what to do with the pain, but maybe someday I will. People say pain makes you a better person; that it can make you more compassionate, more understanding, more empathetic. Mainly, it still makes me angry. No one wants to hear about that."

"I do."

He pushed away from the table and stood. "You think you do, but you don't. It will just make *you* feel bad, too."

"Do you channel the anger into anything else?"

"Sure. Besides work, I lift weights, run. If I'm in one place long enough, I get back into martial arts. That reestablishes my focus."

"But you don't date."

"I don't date."

"Then why—" She hesitated. "Then why did you kiss me the first time?"

"Because you were so beautiful and I hadn't responded to a woman in five long years."

If she'd wanted bluntness, he'd given it to her. "You wanted to see if I was all my reputation said I might be," she murmured. "The reputation that's exploited in the tabloids."

"That was the only way I knew you, Gabby. Can you blame me?"

"I can blame you for not wanting to look deeper than that girl on the front cover."

"You make an impact. My mind was working slower than my libido."

She was disappointed that he'd seen her the way so many other men did. Yet, she was fairly sure that had changed quickly.

"You want me to talk about my life, yet *you* haven't explained about your involvement with Mikolaus Kutras."

He was right. She hadn't. But she wouldn't go into that unless Rafe really cared. "I stepped into something I shouldn't have. He wasn't the man I thought he was. My pain isn't about losing. It's about Miko making me feel so stupid. I don't have anything to confide, but I think you have a world of feelings buried inside that someday is going to let loose."

"You've read a few self-help books?" he asked sarcastically.

"I've read more than a few. I wanted to know myself better

as well as my family and the people I work with. Having feelings is part of life. Sharing them should be, too."

Rafe rolled his eyes. "That's the end of this conversation. Did I hear you say you're planning to go out tonight?"

No one could cut off a discussion he didn't want to have better than Rafe. She answered his question. "There's a new club opening. My publicist thinks it would be a good idea to go. What do you think?"

"I think we could make it happen if we do it right—a limo to drive you there, a second person for backup. Is the owner used to dealing with celebrities?"

"Yes, or I wouldn't be going."

He thought about it, then nodded. "I don't see a problem. What time will you be ready?"

"Nine o'clock okay?"

"Nine o'clock's fine." He stood, towering over Gabby. "Maybe we *are* getting to know each other, Gabby, but living together like this creates a false intimacy. Don't let it fool you that it's the real thing."

When Rafe left the kitchen, she wondered which of them was deluding themselves.

Chapter Nine

On Monday evening, Gabby sorted the pieces of material, one swatch after another, putting a few aside, the others in a stack. She loved choosing fabric. The sketches Tara had sent from Houston were great. She'd be meeting with her tomorrow.

Rafe was in his own room working on something on the computer. It looked complicated.

She hadn't checked her personal e-mail today, so now she pulled her laptop toward her, opened it and booted it up.

As she did, her cell phone played its recognizable tune.

Ignoring the e-mail for the moment, she picked up her phone from the table. The caller number was her aunt's.

"Aunt Eleanor! How are you?"

There was a pause. "In part, that's why I'm calling. I need to get away and relax, at least for one night. How would you like to join me and Katie at the Yellow Rose Spa on Thursday? We're going to stay overnight. Are you interested?"

Gabby hadn't spent any time with her aunt and she'd like to. Tate's longtime girlfriend, Katie Whitcomb-Salgar, was also someone Gabby enjoyed spending time with. "I'd like to join you. I'm flying to Houston tomorrow. Blake's letting me use his jet. When I return, we can coordinate schedules. It might be better for me to meet you there."

"That's fine. I'll just be thrilled you can come. My children are avoiding me—"

Her aunt's voice broke and Gabby was quick to ask, "Are you all right?"

"Not really. That's why I'd like to spend a little time with you and Katie. I've told her about what I revealed to you and my family. The two of you have some distance from this mess I've made. You have perspective."

Her aunt apparently needed a listening ear. She could certainly provide that. "You'll get it straightened out. I know you will."

"Thank you, honey. I'm looking forward to Thursday. Have a good trip to Houston."

"I will. Take care."

Gabby said goodbye to her aunt and was still thinking about her when she clicked on her e-mail program. When it popped up, she saw she had thirteen messages. Her gaze scanned the list of addresses and she stopped when she came to the ninth one. Miko.

Taking a deep breath she clicked on it and the message appeared. Like magic, she thought, only there was nothing magical about Mikolaus Kutras. She'd found that out the hard way.

His letter to her was short and terse, so like the Miko she'd known in latter days.

Gabby—If you don't answer this I'll get to you in another way. Miko

What was she going to do? Did she have to do *anything?*

She didn't know how long she sat there staring at the message. She was unaware of time. She was unaware of where she was. All she could think of was what Miko had done, and the scene at the club. How had she gotten herself into this mess?

"A dollar for your thoughts." Rafe's deep voice insinuated itself into her reflection.

She tried to joke when she turned to him. "They've really gone up with inflation. But I don't think they're worth a dollar."

"That's not true from the look on your face." He sat down beside her. "What's up, Gabby? Another message from your…friend?"

His tone of voice on the word *friend* annoyed her. "It doesn't matter, Rafe." She pushed back her chair and stood. "It really isn't any of your business."

He spun the laptop toward him.

She childishly slammed down the lid, hoping she didn't break something.

He stood now, too, and grabbed her shoulders. They were close enough to kiss, close enough to relive everything that had gone before and add more erotic sensations to it. But she yanked away and went into the living room.

He called after her. "I don't want to look at it without your permission."

She called back, "Look at it if you want. It's not going to make any difference one way or another."

She hadn't gotten as far as her bedroom when he was right behind her, grabbing her hand, tugging her to the sofa. "Talk to me, Gabby."

Suddenly her cell phone's ring tone sounded from the kitchen table. "That's my phone," she murmured. "I have to get it."

"You can let it go to voice mail," he grumbled. "This is important."

She was already on her feet. "The phone call might be, too. At least let me check the caller ID." Back in the kitchen in seconds, she swiped it from the table, saw the number on the front and opened the phone with a relieved, happy smile. "Dad. How are you?"

"I'm great, honey. How are you?"

"Busy. Working. Shopping."

He laughed—a rich, deep laugh that she'd always loved hearing when she was a child, and just as much now.

"Your mother's making plans for when you come home. I hope you have a clear schedule."

"Just one thing on it."

"Oh?"

"I've been looking at houses on the Internet."

"You have?"

"With you retiring soon, wouldn't it be nice if I had a home base?"

"I don't know. How much are you going to be there?"

"I might be changing some things in my life."

"Jet lag getting to you?"

"You could say that."

"It's more like the photographers are getting to you, right?" he asked, gently rather than teasing.

"Yes."

"You aren't being impulsive, are you?"

"I'm not. I've been thinking about this for the past six months. A place of my own. Maybe a company of my own that creates something new for the marketplace. Do you understand? I can't just stop working."

"I understand. Work has always been important to me, too. Your mother has wanted me to retire for a few years, but I needed to work, to prove something to myself and to her."

"Because she's wealthy?"

"That's part of it. It's not easy marrying a successful actress."

"But Dad, she'd love you whether you worked or not."

"I know that. But a man has his pride, you know. You've got to remember that whenever you date someone."

They both went silent.

"How are you, really? Your mother worries, you know."

She'd never talked with them about the club and what had happened. It wasn't something she was proud of, or something she wanted to bring up.

Despite Miko's e-mails, she thought of the past eight days with Rafe. "I'm good. Really. You tell her not to worry."

"Oh, that'll do it," he said with a chuckle. "So have you picked out houses you want to look at?"

"I have. There are three I'm really interested in."

"Do you want me to take a preliminary look?"

She thought about it. "No, I don't think I do. I really want to take care of things myself, Dad."

"Are you thinking about a time when your mother and I might not be around?"

"Don't say that."

"It's true. But I understand, Gabriella. You have an independent streak just like your mother. But my offer still holds. I intend to be here when you get home. I've found good managers who have to take more responsibility if I'm going to retire, so I can be away more."

"You're actually planning it?"

"I'll still have my hand in from here at home. I might have Vincenzo show me how to make wine."

Vincenzo was their neighbor. He and her father were old friends. "That sounds like a plan. Only, don't expect it to turn out to be an award-winning wine with your first bottle."

"You know me too well. Give me a call the day before you come home. All right?"

"That sounds good. I will. Give Mom my love."

When Gabby closed the phone, she felt happy and misty and wished she was back in Italy *now*. But then she looked at Rafe. He was waiting for her on the sofa.

She slipped her phone into her shorts pocket and joined him there. Maybe it was time she told him the whole story. There was no point keeping it from him. He was going to think about her whatever he wanted to think.

"Your father?" he asked.

She nodded.

"Do you miss him?"

"I do."

Rafe paused a few moments before he said, "That e-mail sounded threatening."

"Miko wants me to call him or write to him. I'm not going to do either."

Rafe thought about her decision. But instead of saying if she was right or wrong, he said, "Tell me what led up to the London tabloid photo."

"Why do you want to know?" His reasons were important to her.

He propped his hands on his knees, looked down at the floor and then raised his head. "Most of the time I've known you, you've been a feisty, independent woman. But whenever you get one of those e-mails, you look lost and lonely. I want to know what causes that."

He wasn't really telling her anything. She hoped he might say he cared about her. But as her bodyguard, maybe he couldn't say that. "I met Miko when I was on a shoot in Greece. There was a party on his yacht. And I have to admit, he swept me off my feet. He was charming and listened to every word I said. I didn't realize then that it was just an act—one he uses with every woman he is interested in."

Rafe's jaw set and his mouth tightened. She instinctively knew he wasn't a womanizer and apparently didn't think much of men who were.

"In between my assignments, I stayed at his villa in Greece. He also had a flat in London. When we were in town we attended shows and parties. When I was back in the States, he showed off his house in the Hamptons. It was all so…romantic. I'd never been involved with anyone before."

Rafe's brows arched and his astonishment was obvious.

"I was waiting for that one perfect man. I wanted a relationship like my mother has with my father. Add to that, I'd been isolated for a long time. Since seventeen I've been focused on my career. I basically worked, saw a few friends and family in between, and that was my life. So I didn't notice at first when Miko started isolating me even more. I mean, I was flattered. He wanted me by his side. He didn't want the outside world to intrude on our time together. But I also didn't realize until later, he wasn't giving me my messages from my family or from my friends."

"It's a pattern," Rafe said in a low voice. "Did he ever physically hurt you?"

There was an intensity in Rafe's eyes she'd never seen there before, as well as a gravelly anger in his voice she didn't want to inspire to erupt. "No. He didn't hurt me. Not physically. But whenever I had a break and stayed at his villa in Greece, he left me alone with the housekeeper more and more. Yet he didn't want me to take on more modeling jobs."

Rafe let out a grunt, as if to say that was a pattern, too.

"When he found out Blake wanted me for this PR campaign in the U.S., he forbade me from doing it. Forbade me!"

At the tone of her voice, Rafe's lips turned up a bit at the corners. "I guess that didn't go over well?"

"I'd grown up always trying to please my parents so they'd

spend more time with me. I thought time equated with love. I tried to please everyone I loved, or who I wanted to love me. But I really wanted to help Blake, to help dig McCord Jewelers out of this mess. We were in London when all of this came down. I was supposed to meet Miko at the club that night. Before he arrived—" Gabby stopped. She really didn't want to go on with this.

"What happened before he arrived?" Rafe prodded gently.

"A woman approached me in the ladies' room. She told me her sister, who was only eighteen, was sleeping with Miko and I should know that. I'm not sure what her reason was for telling me. Maybe frustration because her sister wouldn't listen to her about the type of man Miko was. Maybe it was just kindness in warning me. I don't know. But I… Her words just hurt so bad and I felt so stupid, so naive, so foolish." She said the words before Rafe could.

"And the tabloid photograph?" Rafe prompted.

"I couldn't take the word of a stranger. I couldn't believe I'd been so wrong. I needed to speak with Miko myself. But when he came into the club that night, he brushed me off, saying we'd talk later. Later happened. He snagged me for a dance. I asked him about Tatiana. He stared me straight in the eye and admitted one woman wasn't enough for him. He said he enjoyed the chase too much. When I pulled away from him and turned to leave, he grabbed the back of my dress. The strap ripped and the rest, as they say, is history."

"What did you do afterward?"

"After the paparazzi took their money shot, I ran out of the club, got into a cab and went to Miko's flat. I grabbed everything I thought was necessary and took the first flight for New York. I licked my wounds, made some business contacts then flew to Dallas."

When Rafe took her hand, he held on firmly. "I think you

were courageous to come back here after all that, to start the PR campaign."

"Not courageous. The PR campaign was a diversion for me. During those few weeks in New York, I realized Miko and I never had the emotional intimacy that should be part of a special relationship. We never had shared dreams or goals. I'm not sure we even…shared."

When Rafe ran his thumb over her palm, she forgot everything about Miko—and the tabloid shot. She only thought about Rafe and everything *they'd* shared in the past week. She knew more about him than she'd ever known about Miko. Most of all, she knew exactly the type of man Rafe was—true and strong.

"Had you heard about Mikolaus Kutras's reputation before you dated him?"

"Not really. I saw photographs of him, just as I'd seen photographs of me. I knew better than to believe what I read. And after we met, I thought I was his one true love." She held up the hand Rafe wasn't holding like a stop sign. "Don't even say it. I know how naive I was. Maybe there is no such thing as true love. Yet when I watch my mother and father together, I believe there is."

"I remember my mother and father together. They had it. And I had it with Connie."

Suddenly, Connie's name fell between them in a way Miko's never had. Gabby saw in Rafe's eyes that he was re-thinking this little tête-à-tête they were having and wasn't surprised when he pulled his hand away.

He was still in love with his wife. Gabby guessed he couldn't let himself feel for someone else. He couldn't let himself feel anything for *her*.

She realized with sudden clarity that she felt way too much for Rafe. Falling in love had taken on new meaning. Hearts and roses didn't always have anything to do with it. Connection did. Electricity did. Seeing some of the world in the same ways did.

Yet she knew Rafe believed they were so different. He thought she was someone who needed room service and luxury hotels and trips to parts unknown.

To save them both embarrassment, she stood and motioned to the kitchen. "I think everything in there can wait until tomorrow. I'm going to close down my computer and then turn in."

He didn't argue with her. She wished he'd ask her to stay. She wished…he'd begin to fall in love with her.

As she went to the kitchen she realized how superficial her relationship with Miko had been. With Rafe she felt as if she had a bond of friendship, as well as the extreme attraction to him. Miko had been a fantasy. Rafe was reality.

However, the reality was clear. Rafe still loved Connie. He wasn't ready to move on.

So where did that leave *her?*

The next morning, Rafe opened the manila envelope addressed to him. There was no return address and that made him suspicious.

He studied the photo before he even looked at the note. A multitude of conflicting thoughts fought for dominance in his mind. Gabby didn't need this. His career would be in the tank. There was always a price to pay for something sent anonymously like this. However, if blackmail was involved, someone would have to step forward.

The note read—

Pay me $500,000 and I won't send this to a tabloid. Contact me through P.O. Box 2330, The Mailbox Center, Dallas.

That was it.

Rafe studied the photo once more. He and Gabby were standing on the balcony, kissing. He remembered every sensation from that kiss—the way his body had caught fire, the way Gabby's scent had intoxicated him, the way she'd responded as eager and hungry as he was. Now the question was—should he tell her about the photo? Or should he handle it himself?

This photo would affect him more than her. After all, a lot worse had been printed with her as the subject.

The door to her bedroom opened and he automatically tensed. He was beginning to do that a lot when he was around her for self-preservation's sake. Yet tense wasn't good. When he was tense, he could miss something.

Gabby stopped when she saw him in the foyer, holding the envelope.

"Something from Blake?" she asked. Her cousin often sent information by special messenger.

For a moment, he was distracted by Gabby in white—a white cotton halter top and white shorts that showed off her beautiful legs. His body responded, his pulse rate increasing, adrenaline rushing through him.

"Rafe?" Gabby asked.

What was wrong with him? He never lost focus. But now whenever Gabby was around, he did.

"You need to see this," he said, holding out the photograph with the attached note.

She didn't look down at what was in his hand. First she studied his features. He attempted to let nothing show—not his reaction to her, not his reaction to the photo.

She studied the photo first, and then turned her attention to the note.

"At least we both have our clothes on," she joked.

"Gabby." She was attempting to play this light. She was trying to pretend the photo didn't matter.

She sighed. "This isn't the first time this has happened to me, but it's probably the first time it's happened to you. I'm sorry, Rafe. I'm so sorry. This could affect your reputation, your work, what you want to do next with your life. I never meant to get you involved in all this."

She'd seen the consequences of the photo immediately and she looked as if she meant what she said. If he hadn't realized it before, he realized now that Gabby wasn't a publicity seeker. She wasn't the kind of celebrity who wanted her name in those tabloids or the papers, no matter what the cost.

"It's blackmail," he grumbled.

"Yes, it is. Apparently someone had a long lens. As photos go, it could be a lot worse. For me, anyway. But I know, not for you."

"Oh, it could be worse," he said rubbing his forehead. "What's that old song? A kiss is just a kiss?"

He thought he saw hurt flash in her eyes and he knew he'd once again said the wrong thing. He couldn't seem to do the *right* thing with Gabby. He should have told Blake to find someone else to guard her from the moment he'd met her.

"What do you want to do?" she asked. "Do you want me to pay him?"

"Or her," Rafe murmured. "You'd do that?"

"I would if I thought it would keep the worst from happening."

"You'd have to rely on someone like this to keep their word. That's a huge risk. The photo's probably digital, so it's backed up. This isn't the old days when you could bargain for negatives."

"So you're saying there's no point in paying him?"

"There's no point at all in paying him. But we don't want to let him or her know that. Not just yet, anyway."

"Why not?"

"Several reasons. You'll have to decide if you want to prosecute. If we want to trap whoever this is."

"The P.O. box is probably taken under a false name."

"You have been through this before."

"When I was being stalked…" She shook her head. "Law enforcement set up surveillance, watched the P.O. box that was the return address on those letters. I know the drill."

"And you're not sure it's worth it for this?"

"I won't be hurt by this, Rafe. *You* will. So it's going to be your call."

Had he expected her to fall apart? If he had, he'd been wrong about that, too. Gabby had been through a lot, with the press following her since she was seventeen, with fans who tried to get at her any way they could, the stalkers who had probably terrified her out of her mind. And lately, the Greek tycoon who'd tried to own her and then tossed her away.

When Gabby stepped closer to him, he steeled himself against her stunning fresh face, against her pheromones mingling with his, against needs he didn't even want to admit he had.

"I'll do whatever's best for you."

Whatever was best for him. That was the hell of it. He didn't know what that was. Right now, the best thing for him would be to carry Gabby into her bedroom and join their bodies until neither of them had a coherent thought.

Yet he knew that wouldn't be the best. Not for either of them.

Because he wasn't ready to change his life. He wasn't ready to love again. He wasn't ready to forget Connie and the baby they'd lost.

"We're leaving for Houston," he reminded her. "Let's just forget about this until we get back."

"Forget about it?"

"He's not going to do anything until he hears from us. He wants that money."

"And what do *you* want?" she asked softly.

"I want to stay out of the papers," he returned bluntly, cutting off any chance of personal talk.

Something passed over Gabby's face. Disappointment maybe, because he wouldn't discuss the two of them?

There was nothing to discuss.

Chapter Ten

"I'm glad you agreed to have lunch in the dining room." Gabby glanced at Rafe as they sat at a secluded table, almost completely hidden by potted palms, in the Gallery Hotel in Houston. She liked staying at this hotel for two reasons—the security was great and she enjoyed stopping to gaze at the artists' paintings on the walls. They were all originals.

After talking to the hotel security and seeing the setup, Rafe must have realized this was a low-risk hotel. "With the dining room being almost empty, you're safe."

"My cousin Paige recommended this hotel to me a couple of years ago. The celebrity suites, as she calls them, are comfortable, secluded and quiet. I'd love to go swimming in the rooftop pool. Do you think we can?"

"I'll check into it. Maybe after it closes to the public."

"You're trained as a lifeguard?" she teased.

"Absolutely."

Gabby had tried to keep a light atmosphere between her and Rafe today. It was the only way they'd get through this trip. She didn't want to think about that photograph or Miko's e-mails. She was hoping just to use this overnight excursion as an escape from everything else that was going on.

"Was your object to shop before your meeting this evening?" Rafe asked now.

"I know it's the last thing *you* want to do."

"I've survived worse."

His dry tone made her laugh. "You survived shoe shopping."

"Yes, I did."

There was a flash of awareness in his eyes that told her he remembered putting that shoe on her foot just as well as she did. She felt as if she was playing a game with Rafe. Move forward, then retreat. Move to the side, then retreat again. Come too close— Would they both win? Or lose?

She picked up her menu, knowing she'd decide on some kind of salad.

When they'd walked in, Gabby had been focused on heading to their table. Now she glanced around the rest of the room. Only a few lunchers remained. As she peered into one corner, at first to study the painting on the wall, she recognized the woman at the secluded table. It was her cousin Penny!

Gabby laid down her menu and was ready to push her hair back when she focused on the man sitting with Penny. His back was to her, mostly, but she could catch a bit of his side profile. He looked vaguely familiar. Then she realized why. The man with Penny was Jason Foley!

How could that be possible? The McCords and Foleys were enemies. Penny wouldn't have anything to do with one of them. But there she was, having lunch with Jason.

"What's wrong?" Rafe asked.

Jason suddenly stood, went to Penny and leaned low to her

as he helped her with her chair. Gabby was almost sure his lips grazed her cousin's cheek. Were they having an affair?

Gabby hunched down in her chair a little so Penny wouldn't see her. But she shouldn't have worried. Penny's focus was totally on Jason as she stood and the two of them linked arms to leave the dining room.

Rafe reached across the table and took Gabby's hand. "What's wrong?" he repeated. He looked over his shoulder to stare in the same direction she was staring.

"That was Penny! And Jason Foley."

"One of *the* Foleys?" Rafe inquired with an arched brow.

"How much do you know?" Gabby knew Blake liked Rafe, but were they friends?

"Anyone who works for the McCords, anyone who's ever been around Dallas, knows about the McCord and Foley feud—at least, the fact that the two families can't stand the sight of each other."

"That's not exactly true. Devon, Blake's dad, tried to make things better."

"Why don't you tell me how it started? Something about a card game?"

"It really started way before the card game. The story, not the feud."

"Is this going to get confusing?" Rafe teased.

She liked the sparks of humor in his eyes. She liked...everything about him. Swallowing hard, she admitted, "It's a long story. Are you sure you want to hear it?"

"I'm sure with you telling it, it won't seem long."

Was Rafe saying he actually enjoyed her company? Was he saying he more than enjoyed it? She didn't want to read into it something that wasn't there. She'd done that with Mike.

"All right, we'll try it. If you get bored, let me know." Once again, she glanced in the direction Penny and Jason had exited and shook her head, wondering if she could believe her own eyes.

Then she tried to remember as much as she could about the history of the feud. "There was a treasure ship that sank back in 1898 and Elwin Foley was one of the crew." She went on to tell Rafe about the rumors, the diamond, the mines and the card game.

"But the mine is still on Travis's property?"

"No. Officially, the property still belongs to the McCords."

"If Paige and Blake find it, what would happen to the bad blood between the Foleys and McCords then?"

Gabby sighed. "Blake can't think about that now. He sees that diamond as the end of the problems he's having with the stores. That's what the whole PR campaign is based on."

"Canary diamonds."

"You've got it. And that's why I'm seeing a designer today to design a wardrobe around those gems."

"You look good in yellow. And green. And blue. And red."

She laughed. "Are you trying to flatter me so I don't go shopping?"

"I'm not trying to flatter you, Gabby. I just tell you what I see."

What exactly did he see? A woman who knew her own mind? A woman who'd been fooled? A woman who was beginning to care for him very, very much?

Maybe all protectees fell in love with their protectors.

No. That had never happened to her before, though she had to admit, she'd never had somebody with her twenty-four hours a day before.

"Are you sure that was Penny that you saw? And Jason Foley?"

"I know Penny. I've been around Jason a few times, mostly at clubs in Dallas. He has a reputation for womanizing. She'd better be careful. My guess is he wants something from her."

"It could just be a star-crossed lovers thing," Rafe offered.

When had she last heard a man talk about love in *those* terms? "I really would like to believe that. I might have been naive with Miko, but I'm not naive anymore. If a man comes on too fast, if he's too charming, if he doesn't want to share the things that are important to share, then he wants something other than a relationship."

Gabby and Rafe stared at each other over their menus. She'd thought of the wife and child he'd lost. "Is it too painful to remember your wife?"

He looked down at the table, studied the menu, then set it down on the white linen. "Sometimes, I think it helps to remember. But then when I remember, all I get is sadness. I pull the memory into now and it doesn't belong there."

"Did you have a good marriage?"

"We had a *great* marriage. She didn't seem to mind following wherever work led, though it wasn't easy for her. She was thrilled when she found out she was going to have a baby. With a baby to care for, a child to raise, she'd have company during the times that I was away or had to work long hours. Connie was the greatest. She never complained."

Gabby didn't think she could be that great. If she married someone, she'd want time with him. She didn't want to sit on the edges of his life—she wanted to be smack-dab in the middle of it.

As if echoing her thoughts, he concluded, "You wouldn't make a good Secret Service agent's wife."

Although she knew she wouldn't, her shoulders squared. She could do anything she put her mind to.

"Now don't get all defensive on me, Gabby. You know what I'm talking about. You need to be surrounded by love.

Some professions don't provide an opportunity for that. Secret Service work is one of them."

She felt deflated although she attempted not to show it. "I'm nothing like your wife, am I?"

"Nothing like her," he agreed. But he didn't add that was okay, that Gabby had gifts of her own that she could bring to the table.

Stop it, she told herself. *You don't need anyone's approval. You don't need Rafe's approval. You are who you are, and that's what you have to remember. You need a man who can accept you just the way you are.*

The waitress arrived to take their order.

Gabby concentrated on what she'd eat for lunch rather than Rafe's opinion of her.

For the moment.

Rafe knocked on the door of Gabby's bedroom. "Ready for that swim?" he asked.

After shopping and meeting with the designer, Rafe had watched Gabby as she'd worked with the portfolio of sketches for two hours, making notes on a legal pad. When he'd asked if she'd wanted to go for a swim, she'd assured him she'd change and be out in a few minutes. That was fifteen minutes ago.

Now she opened her door. "Are you sure no one else will be up there?"

The manager had assured him they'd have the rooftop pool all to themselves at midnight. "I have the manager's word."

"Let's hope he's trustworthy. I don't want to be greeted by five camera flashes."

"I'll check it out before you get off the elevator. Don't worry."

She stepped out of her room and Rafe had to admit he was a bit disappointed. She was wearing a turquoise cape thing that covered her body from her neckline to midthigh.

She studied him the same way he was appraising her. Her

gaze drifted down his face to his chest hair, to his gray-and-yellow swim trunks. If she kept examining him like that, she'd soon see something she might not want to see.

He handed her a fluffy white towel and carried one himself. "We might need these."

Their ride up to the roof was silent. Rafe didn't know whether Gabby was tired or just introspective. She'd been enthusiastic about shopping, enthusiastic about those sketches. Yet she was quiet. Was she thinking about that photograph and what they were going to do? What she *should* do? She'd said that it was his call, but that photo affected her, too.

The elevator door slid open. Rafe exited first and checked the area. Not a person in sight. He beckoned to Gabby and she stepped out, too. They both just stood taking in the immense night sky. The breeze was still balmy. Chaise lounges and chairs were placed in a zigzag formation around the pool. A few lights glowed around the edges…a few from within the sea-blue pool.

After she took it all in, Gabby headed for one of the chaise lounges, laid her towel there and slipped off her sandals. She hesitated a moment, then pulled the cape over her head.

As she stood there in the moonlight, Rafe felt an intense longing. She wore a turquoise bikini. He was transfixed by her tall, slim body limned in moonlight. He knew he was staring, but he couldn't help it. Gabriella McCord was perfection in so many ways. Yet underneath, there was a vulnerability and innocence that captivated him. Although she'd been in the public eye for so many years, something about her was still unspoiled. He didn't know how that was possible. At first he thought it was wishful thinking, but since he'd come to know her—

Did he really know her?

There was no point denying his admiration for her. He

crossed to where she stood, tossed his towel down on the lounge chair and studied her.

"Are you comparing me to the models in the swimsuit issue of *Sports Illustrated?*" she asked with a barb in her tone.

He deserved that. "You were among those models, weren't you?"

Now, instead of looking tense, she smiled. "Yes, but that was a few years ago."

"Nothing's changed. You're still as beautiful."

Now *she* studied him. And he read her thoughts. "You know, I don't believe in idle flattery, Gabby."

"I guess…" She seemed unsure. "I guess I don't want you looking at me only on the outside."

"You're a woman with a mind and a heart and a soul. Modeling is what you do, not who you are."

The tilt of her head told him she was trying to decide whether or not to believe him. He supposed too many men had flattered her. Too many men had only looked at the outside. Too many men hadn't really cared about her heart.

He did. And that realization hit like a body blow.

He searched for his voice and found it. "Do you swim or do you wade?"

She smiled. "I actually swim. It's great exercise. I should be doing it in Dallas, but we've just been so…busy."

"Well, now we're not busy." He held his hand out to her. "Come on."

She stared down at his hand for a few moments, as if she were making a commitment if she took it. Finally she slipped hers into his. She felt fragile to him and he realized in some ways, she was.

"The water's warm," she said in delight, as she went down the steps and slid into a float. Without hesitating she did the crawl to the end of the pool, brushed her wet hair back from her face, then did it again.

Rafe needed to work off energy himself, so he followed her, kept pace with her, watched out for her.

She stood, waiting as he finished his third lap. "You're good. Don't feel you have to dawdle next to me. Swim at your own pace."

"I've got more than one pace. Swimming along beside you is fine."

"What do you think about when you're swimming?"

"No one's ever asked me that before."

"Good. Then I'll get a spontaneous answer," she said with a grin.

"I try *not* to think," he admitted. "I get into a rhythm and just let my body work. My mind just hums along. That's why I like swimming, I guess. I find peace there."

"That's another way we're different," she mused. "My mind goes as fast as my strokes. I think about everything from yesterday, today, to what's coming up tomorrow. Swimming is just the backdrop. I relax. The same thing happens when I listen to music or I have a massage or I study beautiful paintings. When *you* relax you empty your mind. When *I* relax I let my feelings take over and they fill me."

"Yet there are times," he said, coming closer to her, "when you don't show emotion, either. You keep it all in."

"That's a secret," she said softly.

"Not to me. I know how to read people pretty well. Your eyes, your hands, the tilt of your chin give away what you're thinking."

"What am I thinking right now?" she asked, a little bit shakily, he thought.

"You're thinking the same thing I'm thinking. That we're on top of the world, there's nobody around and darkness shields us from everything we've left behind. There are absolutely no reporters because we'll be able to hear them sneak up on us in a helicopter."

She laughed, and that was the effect he wanted. He wanted to see her laughing and free in her element, whether that was in a crowd or in the olive groves in Tuscany. He could imagine her, barefoot in a summer dress, running through them.

They were close now, with only the thin layer of water between them. He couldn't stay away from her.

He stroked her wet hair away from her cheek.

With her eyes closed, her lashes were dark and wispy on her cheeks. "Look at me, Gabby," he requested.

When she did, he saw what he wanted to see—a reflection of the hunger he was feeling.

"Can you accept what's happening between us?" she asked in a whisper.

For the moment, he couldn't deny the desire in her eyes or his body's response to her. He knew he should, but he also knew it was time to stop deluding himself. He wanted Gabriella McCord in every primitive way a man wants a woman.

She extended her hand and her fingers traced over a few droplets on his shoulder. His whole body went rigid.

Warning bells clanged and he knew he should dive into that water and swim a few more laps instead of standing here with her. But his racing heart and his aroused body told him differently.

Still, he made a jab at being reasonable for both of them. "We should go back to the suite."

Her body leaned slightly toward his. Her hands slid down his arm to his biceps. She was telling him she didn't want to go back to the suite for the same reason he didn't.

Her bikini was modest—as bikinis went—but it *was* a bikini. His hands encircled her waist, felt her soft skin and slid up to cup her breasts.

Her eyes went wide as she swayed into his hands. His thumbs traced the round upper curve of her breasts. Then he leaned forward and unfastened the top of her bikini. "Is this all right?" he murmured as he did it, not wanting to remind her in any way of that night in the club.

"I want you to touch me, Rafe."

He liked Gabby's decisive clarity, especially now. The bikini top floated away in the water. Rafe barely noticed as he bent his head to her breasts and kissed first one and then the other. Gabby's fingers laced in the hair at the back of his head. When he took her nipple into his mouth and tongued it, she softly moaned.

He did it again.

"I want to hold you," she said, her lips near his neck.

He wasn't sure what she meant, but he raised his head and she moved closer to him, wrapping her arms around him. Her gesture moved him more than anything else could have. He held her, his heart pounding, his body aching for hers.

Slowly he bent his head and sealed his lips to hers. Then his tongue invaded her mouth. She loosened her hold on him, her hands sliding down his back under the waistband of his swim trunks. The contact of her skin on his was electrifying. He hadn't been touched intimately by a woman for so long. He could take her right here in the privacy of the rooftop.

Privacy? What was he thinking?

He wasn't thinking. He was feeling…with a part of his anatomy that had never gotten him into trouble before, but could now.

As her hands moved on his backside, he sucked in a breath. Thoughts from a moment before fled. Arousal clouded his brain like a red haze. He kissed her as if he had never kissed her before and might never kiss her again. While his lips and tongue were busy with that, he pushed down her bikini bottom.

Her hands stilled. Not only stilled, but froze, along with the rest of her body. Where she'd been pushing into him before, pushing toward him, reaching around him, she went stiff. He tried to clear the red haze and could hardly grasp the concept that he wanted to. He hadn't been with a woman in five years and now he was ready to go off like a torpedo.

If he'd learned anything since his college days, he'd learned self-control. It had started in his training as a cop. It had expanded to an art form as a Secret Service agent. He knew he could probably convince her to go further. After all, she'd been as passionate as he'd been. But now something had gotten in the way and he had to find out what. He wanted to let her make the moves, though. Let her tell him. Let her decide what she wanted to do next. It was the only way she wouldn't feel compromised. The only way *he* wouldn't feel as if he'd taken advantage of her.

Her hands slid out of his swim trunks. They hesitated, then folded at his back. When he gazed into her eyes, he saw turmoil there. Before they got into what was going on, he pulled up her bikini bottom. Her cheeks flushed and it was more of a blush than he had ever seen on her.

"I didn't mean we should stop everything," she admitted shakily.

"What part of it did you want to stop?" he asked with the cool reasoning he reached for in sticky situations.

"Rafe, I loved what we were doing. I really did. But I don't want you to think I do this every day, that I'm some kind of tease. Because I'm not. Miko *was* my first. I was telling the truth about that."

"Did you feel we were going too far too fast?"

"I think fast would have taken us exactly where we wanted to go. But that's why I stopped. Because I thought about afterward."

"You flying to Italy? Me going to New York?"

"No. I just had a question."

If he answered the question right, could they get back to what they were doing? Probably not. The mood had been fatally broken.

"What question?" This was probably going to be a hum dinger.

"You said you didn't date after your wife died."

"That's right."

"Did you...did you have sex with anyone?"

He kept silent for a long time, still holding Gabby, still gazing into her eyes. Suddenly, any anger or defensiveness or annoy ance at her question fell away. He needed to tell her the truth.

"About a month after Connie died, I had a one-night stand with someone from work. But that night was a complete con tradiction to everything Connie and I had. I never did it again."

Her arms tightened again a little, maybe in comfort, maybe in sympathy.

A giant "no" built up inside of him. He didn't want comfor or sympathy from her. What he wanted, he couldn't even name

"What are you getting at, Gabby?"

"This is hard for me to ask, so it will probably be hard fo you to answer. But I need to know. Do you still love Connie?"

That wasn't what he expected, though with Gabby he neve knew *what* to expect. He released his arms from her and too a step back. The water was less forgiving than real space. I seemed to keep him closer to her.

She let go of him, too, but the look in her eyes said sh didn't want to.

The pain he'd held inside for five long years spurted ou "Thinking about Connie and remembering her hurts. Don' you understand that, Gabby? It's not the kind of hurt from stubbing your toe or slicing your finger. It *never* goes away It never heals. What makes it worse is that you think you'r forgetting all the things you loved most. I wake up and can' quite remember the timbre of Connie's laugh, the mussy way her hair fell around her face in the morning. Do you know what it's like to lose the memories of the one you love?"

"I can't even imagine," she almost whispered. Then her voice grew stronger. "The reason I stopped, the reason I had to ask was— If you still love her, I don't want to feel like a substitute."

"You're *not* a substitute," he erupted, all calm gone now.

"What am I, Rafe? A pretty girl you'd like to have sex with?"

That question stumped him. If he said she was, he'd be in trouble. If he said she wasn't, he'd be in trouble. If he kept silent, he'd be in trouble. He was in so deep, he might never make it out.

So he fell back on being reasonable. "This attraction between us happened fast. We both wanted to explore it. I didn't think further than that."

She stood perfectly still, gazing into his eyes and searching for truth. "You're not answering my question. Don't spin this for the best effect. Just honestly tell me. What was going to happen here, Rafe? More importantly, what was going to happen afterward?"

"I wasn't thinking about afterward! I didn't think you were, either. What's wrong with just living for now? For getting some enjoyment out of now? For feeling pleasure now?"

When she shook her head, tendrils of wet hair slipped over her shoulder. "Nothing's wrong with it if that's what you want. I'm just not sure that's what *I* want."

Frustrated beyond sense, he couldn't imagine where she was going with this. "Gabby. You're famous. You jet-set all over the world. You have women who design dresses for you. You have an artist in Rome who's going to make you a line of purses. You can buy as many pairs of shoes as you want and wear them as many places as you'd like. You like talking to people, being in the limelight, even being in front of the cameras when it's your choice."

"And because of all that you don't think I want a serious relationship?"

He'd never thought about it. After all, the last thing he'd wanted was to be involved in a relationship, wasn't it? "I don't know. Do you?"

"Only with someone who has no ties to the past. Someone who wants a serious relationship, too. Someone who wouldn't be afraid to look further than the next year and glimpse what the future might hold."

He couldn't believe what he was hearing. She'd recently jumped out of a relationship that had hurt her. "Oh, Gabby. You might think you want that now. But you're on the rebound. You want to know you're beautiful. You want to know you're desirable and that a man wants to be only with you."

She tilted her head and narrowed her eyes. "You think I'm attracted to you on the rebound?"

"Can you say you're not?"

"I'm *not* on the rebound, Rafe. I might not be completely over the situation with Miko because it was a troubling one. But I *am* over him. I'm over what I thought we had because we didn't have it. I'm not a sixteen-year-old who moves from crush to crush not understanding how one relationship can be different from another."

"You said you haven't had much experience. How do you know if you're jumping into a situation that's right for you or wrong for you?"

"I just know. But I'm not the one who's shackled by a past relationship. *You're* the one who isn't free."

Did he even desire to be free? Or did he want to be tied to Connie for the rest of his life? Did he want to think about the child they might have had?

Quickly, Gabby caught her bikini top and put it on. Then she headed for the steps. "I've had enough swimming for tonight. I'm going back to the room. If you want to stay, feel free."

"You know I can't stay," he said to her back, feeling as if he'd lost the bond that had developed between them.

"You can just see me to my suite and then come back up. I promise I won't go anywhere."

Maybe tonight that was a good idea. Maybe if he returned up here and swam enough laps to push his demons off his heels, he could be with Gabby tomorrow without remembering how close they'd come to making this assignment of his a disaster.

Yes, he'd return and work off all the adrenaline. He'd work off all the desire. He'd work off all the longing.

And then he could go back to the suite and guard Gabby as if she were any other client.

Chapter Eleven

"What's in the folder?" Rafe asked Gabby as they climbed the steps to his mom's screened-in porch.

To say the atmosphere between them had been awkward ever since their episode in the pool last night would be a gross understatement. Today they'd taken polite conversation to an art form.

"I have the listings for three houses I chose in the Tuscany area. When I talked to your mom about the idea, she sounded as if she might be interested. I thought she'd like to see them."

"Is that what you were doing on the plane?" She hadn't spoken to him on their trip back to Dallas. But what had really gotten to him was the way she'd avoided direct eye contact, too.

Now, however, her gaze met his and held for the first time all day. "Yes. If you had spoken to me on the plane, I would have shown them to you."

"You weren't a chatterbox, either," he grumbled.

"I didn't think you wanted to talk."

"Okay, I didn't," he admitted, knowing this wasn't the time to have the discussion, but jumping into it anyway. "Our little interlude in the pool was embarrassing for both of us. I never should have let it happen."

"I was there, too. And the truth is, Rafe, a lot more might have happened."

She was right. It might have. "Until you started Twenty Questions."

"Are you upset because I stopped what was happening or because you don't want to think about Connie—you don't want to think about moving on?"

Rafe was actually surprised that thunder didn't rumble and lightning didn't strike. There was that much electricity in the air.

The door to Lena's house opened and his mother stood there, smiling at them. "Well, are you going to come in? You've been standing out here a good five minutes." She looked from one to the other. "Or do you want me to shut the door and go inside and wait until you're finished?"

"Of course not," Rafe replied, not even checking with Gabby. "We came to see *you.*"

"How was your trip to Houston?" Lena asked sweetly.

"Fine," they said in unison, and his mom laughed.

"Oh, I can see it was *very* fine. Come on in. I made one of Rafe's favorite suppers—barbecued baby back ribs, baked potatoes, corn on the cob and salad. For dessert, his favorite chocolate cream pie."

Rafe gave his mother a hug. "It sounds wonderful."

Inside the house, the kitchen air conditioner was running, but Lena motioned Gabby to follow her. "Let me show you my chairlift. It's absolutely wonderful. Rafe tells me it was your idea."

Gabby glanced over her shoulder at him. "It was his, too."

Lena sank down in the seat, pressed the button and she was

on her way up the stairs. "I just swivel and get off," she demonstrated easily at the top. Then she sat down again and pressed the button to descend.

When she was once more at the bottom, Gabby asked, "And how are you feeling?"

"I use my cane when I go out, but I'm fine around here. I just can't do anything stupid again." She motioned to the folder in Gabby's hand. "What's that?"

"Pictures of houses. I'm thinking of choosing one of them."

"I can look at them while we're having dessert. Come on. Everything's ready." After Lena sat down at the kitchen table she asked, "So, what's going on with the two of you?"

"Going on?" Gabby looked startled.

"We're just tired, Mom," Rafe replied, trying to keep his tone casual. "Gabby had a meeting this morning before we flew back. You know the toll traveling takes."

"Not on *you*. And I suspect not on Gabby, either. Both of you are used to it."

"Let's drop it, Mom, okay?" His voice lost its casual quality.

"I suppose you want to drop it, too?" she asked Gabby.

"That would probably be best."

Lena shook her head. "No. Talking is better than silence. But the two of you haven't learned that yet. You will, if you spend enough time together."

Rafe didn't think talking would be what happened if he spent much more time with Gabby. Talking was definitely low on the priority list.

Supper was delicious, as always, and Rafe complimented his mother more than once. Over chocolate cream pie, Gabby showed her the printouts of the three houses. It turned out Lena liked Gabby's favorite, too. It was more of a cottage than a villa and closer to her parents' home than the other two.

"Will you have enough room there?" Rafe asked, trying to ignore the way his heart jumped when her gaze met his.

"It has one bedroom downstairs, and two bedrooms upstairs. I think that's plenty. It's not as if I have parties with lots of guests. Most of all, I like the hand-painted tiles in the bathroom and kitchen, the little stone-walled courtyard with its gate, the trellises in the back beside the patio."

"The price seems fair."

"It's off the beaten path, and I like that. I'd have my privacy. And the road beyond the olive groves behind the house would lead directly to my parents' villa."

"I think you've already made up your mind," Lena said with a twinkle in her eye.

"I think so, too, unless something's drastically wrong with the place. Unless the pictures were taken in such a way that they hide all its quirks and problems. I'll have to inspect it myself." She pushed away her dessert dish. "If you'll excuse me, I'm going to freshen up in the powder room."

"Down the hall to your left," Lena told her.

Gabby followed his mother's directions and Rafe could hear the door shut and lock.

"Earth to Rafe," Lena said, amusement in her voice.

He hadn't even been aware he was watching Gabby leave. "I'm right here, Mom."

"No, I don't think you are. I think you're lost somewhere between the past and now. Did you tell Gabby about Connie?"

"Yes, I did. But that was a mistake."

"Why? Surely she understood how painful that was?"

"Oh, I think she understood that."

"Then what *didn't* she understand?" his mother asked perceptively, not letting him off the hook.

"She doesn't understand that I can't pretend that Connie never existed."

"That can't be what Gabby wants."

"She might not even know what she wants. A month ago, she was involved with someone else."

"Has she talked about that?"

"Yes, she has. It wasn't pleasant. She made a bad choice."

"So, maybe now she's trying to make a good choice. But you have to open a door for her, Rafe. If you keep yourself closed off, you'll never find love again."

"We're different, Mom. We came from different upbringings. She's always had everything she ever wanted."

Lena clucked her tongue. "Don't underestimate her. She's had material possessions. But you know they don't always make a person happy."

"Gabby's happy. She just feels restricted sometimes by her lifestyle. But I don't think it's a lifestyle she'd want to give up."

"How do you know that, Rafe? Really know? Maybe you *don't* know it at all. Maybe you just want to believe it. That way, you don't have to make a decision of your own."

His mother couldn't be right, could she?

"I thought your bodyguard might stay and come in here, too," Eleanor teased Gabby with a soft smile. The sauna at the Yellow Rose Spa gave the women privacy.

Gabby wasn't sure how to respond. She'd had to convince Rafe the hotel security was good and she'd be fine, even safe, with her aunt and Katie. Gabby and her aunt had always been close, but they hadn't had much time together lately and Gabby felt a bit out of touch. She was glad Katie had joined them. She felt comfortable with her. She'd been Tate's girlfriend for a long time.

"You don't have to comment, if you don't want to," Gabby's aunt said.

"He's very protective, but I'm sure he'll be glad for a day off

so he doesn't have to watch over me. He has family in the city.
He can spend time with them," Gabby remarked offhandedly.

"I see."

After an awkward pause, Katie asked, "Why is talking
about men-women relationships so difficult?" Her brown eyes
were a bit sad. She had fastened her dark hair on top of her
head with a clip, just as Gabby had.

The three of them sat wrapped in white, fluffy towels on
benches in the sauna, Gabby on the top level, Katie and her
aunt on the lower level.

"Maybe it's hard because we make fools of ourselves,"
Gabby offered.

"Fools of ourselves. Isn't *that* the truth!" Eleanor agreed.
"And it doesn't even matter which generation we're talking
about." Her aunt's voice was filled with sadness. Gabby had
been able to hear the pain there, and she suspected what that
was from—her aunt's torn relationships with her children.

Gabby thought about spotting Penny with Jason. Should
she say anything to her aunt? No, better to keep quiet for now.
"How are you doing with Blake, Tate, Paige, Penny and
Charlie? Or would you rather I didn't ask?"

"Blake's so angry and bitter," Katie murmured. "I wish he
could get over it, for his sake, as well as yours," she empa-
thized, turning toward Eleanor.

"How is Tate doing?" Gabby asked Katie.

"I absolutely don't know these days. He's shut me out.
He's a different man now than he was before he left for Baghdad and I don't know if I can…be with him anymore. I've
always wished he could be a little bit more like Blake. Blake's
so confident in what he wants. And he actually listens when
I talk to him."

Katie was staring at the wall and didn't seem to want to be
pressed any further.

Eleanor took the hint, too. "My children are all complicated, but Paige and Blake do seem to be having a terrible time with this. And Charlie, bless him, who should be having the worst time of any of them, spoke to me yesterday about the possibility of meeting Rex, finding out what his biological father is truly like."

"Why did you decide to say something now, Aunt Eleanor?" Gabby asked.

"With Devon gone, the time had come."

The heat of the sauna, the scent of eucalyptus and redwood, the privacy of their enclosed cubicle led to sharing. "Do you feel like talking about it, or do you want to keep it to yourself?" Gabby asked.

Eleanor looked from Gabby to Katie. "I would tell any of my children if they wanted to know. Charlie hasn't even asked what the whole story was. Maybe he's afraid to hear." Eleanor sighed. "I fell in love with Rex when I was sixteen. We saw each other almost every day for three years! Then one night we argued. I wanted to get married and start having children. But he insisted we should wait. He wanted to be financially secure. I was hurt and questioned his commitment to me, so I walked out. When he didn't call, I accepted a date with Devon. He'd been phoning for months, trying to convince me I should be with *him*. That night with Devon, I was still angry with Rex. I let things get out of hand and they went too far. I should never have gone out with Devon, let alone allowed anything to happen."

Gabby placed her hand on her aunt's shoulder. "Aunt Eleanor, I'm so sorry."

"The infidelity would have been bad enough, and yes, I considered it that. But I found myself pregnant...with Blake. That sealed the deal. Devon asked me to marry him, and I accepted. What else could I do? At least that's the way I felt back then. Now I know I should have gone out on my own, raised the child by myself until I made a good decision. But I didn't. I had a terrible time bonding with Blake, maybe because I thought he took me away from my one true love. Our relationship was never what it should have been. But then the others came along. I tried to convince myself I had the life I wanted. But Devon and I were never close—not like Rex and I once were."

Katie asked, "How did Rex come back into your life?"

Eleanor looked down at her hands in her lap. "As the years passed, Devon was away more and more. I suspected he wasn't faithful and I was so lonely. I often thought about those years with Rex. So I separated from Devon for a while and called Rex. I found out he still had feelings for me, too. We had an affair. But for the sake of the children, I ended it."

"But you were pregnant with Charlie?" Gabby asked.

"Yes. And to keep my family intact, I told Devon the baby was his. Love makes us do such foolish things."

Eleanor had opened her heart and Gabby respected her for that. She also felt she should be honest about that tabloid photo that had probably embarrassed everyone in the family. "I know all about doing foolish things. I guess you were wondering if that tabloid photo was the real thing."

"Only if you want to tell us," Katie offered with empathy.

"It was real, all right." Gabby told the women what had led up to that picture. "Afterward, I knew I never really loved Miko. Not the kind of love my parents had. I left London without looking back. The whole situation was my fault because I didn't see the signs. I didn't want to see the signs. And now that I've met Rafe—" She stopped, not knowing how much she wanted to say.

"And now that you've met Rafe?" Eleanor prodded.

"Rafe is a man like my father—true and loyal. He cares about his family. It's so obvious he's a good man. There's no pretense, no dishonesty. And the feelings I have for him…they scare me. In such a short time, they're so strong. So I have to wonder if I'm being foolish all over again."

Katie swiveled around, her feet up on the bench, her arms wrapped around her knees. "It sounds to me as if you've learned the difference between a man of pretense and a man with integrity. That's a good thing, Gabby. Don't be afraid of those feelings. See where they'll lead you."

"I guess I really have nothing to lose, do I?" Gabby asked.

"Only your heart," Eleanor replied.

Only her heart. That was the bottom line. Was she willing to risk it all over again?

Gabby gave Rafe a bright smile when she saw him sitting in the lobby of the Yellow Rose Spa. She'd missed him. The seaweed wraps, the apricot scrubs and her time in the sauna with Eleanor and Katie had been terrific. But she'd really missed Rafe.

He stood when he saw her coming toward him. He was dressed in a suit because he was taking her to the TV station for an interview. In the Western-cut jacket, bolo tie, black slim trousers and black boots he couldn't have looked sexier.

"Have you been waiting long?" she asked.

"Nope. I got up, had breakfast and here I am."

She looked at him suspiciously. "What time did you drive in from the city?"

"I was in the room next to yours last night."

"Rafe. Why? I told you I'd be fine here with Eleanor and Katie."

"I just made sure."

She didn't know whether to be exasperated with him or to

hug him. "I'm glad Katie and Eleanor didn't know you were there. They would have felt spied on."

"Mrs. McCord knew. We happened to go for ice at the same time last night. She just winked and put her finger to her lips."

Gabby shook her head. "You might as well have told me. I mean, after all, you could have joined us for a pedicure."

He rolled his eyes. "Too cute. I thought it was better if you didn't know, so you'd feel freer."

"I guess freedom is all in perception, isn't it? I thought I was on my own and the whole time, I was being watched."

"Not watched, protected. There's a difference. After all, I did stay out of the sauna."

She imagined Rafe with her in the sauna, the steamy heat, the towels that could have so easily slipped, the cocoonlike feel of the room that could have led to emotional intimacy, as well as physical intimacy.

His thoughts must have gone the same place as hers. "You were in there a long while."

"We were having a profound discussion."

"Private?"

"Very. Women have a tendency to bare their souls when they're being pampered."

"I'll have to remember that."

Their gazes locked and held.

"When do men bare their souls?" she asked, really curious.

"Maybe never. I think our layers of protection are thicker. I have a feeling men in saunas discuss sports scores."

"Don't you have a good friend you really let your hair down with?"

"I once did."

Now she was afraid to press him further. Maybe he'd had a good friend when he was in college. Maybe when he was in the Secret Service. Maybe it had been his wife. For the past twenty-four hours she hadn't thought about Rafe's revelations. She'd only thought about whether or not they might have a future beyond these few weeks. But his past, just like hers, was always with him.

"Did you take advantage of any of the amenities while you were here?" she asked flippantly.

"Room service. I really could get used to that. When I get back to New York picking up takeout won't be nearly as convenient."

Was he looking forward to that? To being done with her?

"Are you involved in the New York scene?" she asked, curious about his life there. "The shows, the clubs, the restaurants?" He couldn't work *all* the time.

"A show when my mom or Julie come to visit. But as for the rest—I belong to a gym. I can walk for hours, appreciating the idiosyncrasies of New York, the variety of people who live there. It's a city like no other. I really have a boring life, Gabby. Not at all like yours."

"Until you have an assignment. Until you fly to L.A. to update security or to Atlanta to test a new security system. I imagine you have meetings with the top people in the industry so you can provide the McCords with the most up-to-date systems. I don't think your life is as boring as you want me to believe it is. You're always pointing out the differences between us, Rafe. I guess I should just take the hint."

His brows drew together. "What hint is that?"

"The hint that you don't really want to be involved with me. That this is really just an assignment. That I'm no more important to you than one of the billionaires you used to cover on a business trip."

She so wanted him to deny her conclusions. She so wanted him to pull her into his arms in the middle of the lobby. But Rafe wouldn't do that even if he *did* care. He was a private man, always cool, calm and collected. Public displays would never be comfortable for him. She imagined that picture of the two of them kissing. It was a lot more upsetting to him than he wanted to admit. If that went public—

"All my clients are important to me." His voice had an even-tempered calm that annoyed her.

"Once in a while, Rafe, I just wish you'd stop being diplomatic and let the lid come off."

His lips twitched up in amusement. "That would entertain you?"

"That would enlighten me. If it happened, then I'd know what you were really feeling."

"What I'm feeling doesn't matter, Gabby."

"It does to anyone who cares about you."

Her heart pounded three times before he asked, "Do you care?"

"Yes, I do."

They were two people in the middle of a sumptuous lobby with ceramic tile floor, leather furniture, copper chandeliers. Yet she felt as if they were alone in the center of a huge ocean.

He dispelled her fanciful imaginings. "Where's your luggage?"

She looked around, trying to get her bearings. She pointed to a bellman standing beside a weekender case on wheels. "Right there. How about yours?"

"My duffel bag's already in the car. It's parked in the front row. Do you want to walk to it or do you want me to drive under the portico?"

He was asking her if she wanted to be an ordinary person or if she wanted to have the star treatment. She wished they were beyond this. She wished—

She wished Rafe would let his lid blow with her. She wished he'd tell her if he cared or if he didn't. "I'll walk," she said, then headed for the door. She knew Rafe would follow her.

After all, that was his job.

* * *

Was she being a fool?

Gabby went straight to her bedroom when she and Rafe returned to the suite after her interview. He went to his.

They hadn't had much to say to each other since their conversation in the spa lobby. The winds of conflict had blown them back and forth from the very personal to the impersonal. All the while, Rafe had been stoic and she couldn't catch a hint of what he was feeling.

She quickly changed from her jacketed sundress and high heels to her favorite kaftan, a swirl of color that always made her feel happy.

Well, almost always. She and Eleanor and Katie had had such a good time, such a relaxed time. Even when they'd spoken about the men in their lives, they'd done it with some perspective.

But Gabby didn't have any perspective now. Barefoot, ready to just flop on her bed and listen to music, she knew she had to talk to Rafe about her schedule tomorrow.

She exited her bedroom and saw he wasn't in the living room, nor in the kitchen. Going to the adjoining room door, she slipped through. The door on his side was open. She tapped lightly and then went in. After all, the door *was* open.

At first, she just stood very still and stared. She'd seen Rafe's chest bare before, but she hadn't seen—the rest of him. He was standing by the dresser absolutely naked, fishing in one of the drawers for something. He might not have heard her, but now he sensed her presence. He drew himself up straight. All of his wonderful physical qualities seemed to register at once—the sharp line of his jaw, the black hair arrowing down the middle of his chest, trailing lower and lower. His hips were slim, his legs were long, his thighs muscled. And he was—magnificent. Absolutely magnificent.

"I'm sure there's some kind of line to cover a situation like this, but I'm not sure what it is at the moment," he said wryly.

She knew she really should leave. Instead, she walked toward him and didn't stop until she was standing in front of him.

"Why aren't you running in the other direction?" he asked her.

"Why aren't you?"

"That answer's obvious. I'm not dressed." He smiled, but it was forced.

"You could easily grab something."

"Gabby, you should leave." His smile dropped away.

His voice had grown a little huskier and she could see why. He was becoming aroused. The seriousness of her being in Rafe's room like this hit her. This wasn't a game. She didn't just want an affair. She didn't want Rafe thinking she did. Suddenly, she didn't feel like the confident woman she pretended to be. Her insecurities came bubbling up.

She backed away from him. "I'm sorry I barged in," she murmured and turned to go.

As Gabby left Rafe's room, she heard a drawer open and shut. She heard Rafe swear. She'd just stepped into the little hall between their rooms when he caught up to her. He was wearing boxer shorts, a drawstring at the waist. But that really didn't change the way her body was tingling, the way her awareness of him invaded every particle of her being.

"I don't know what to do about you." The look in his eyes was as conflicted as his voice.

She didn't know what to say. She didn't know if his remark was good or bad. She didn't know if it meant he felt something or he didn't. Turmoil must have shown in her eyes.

His voice turned very gentle as he took her face between his hands. "What's wrong?"

"I don't want you to think I react this way to all my bodyguards."

"You told me there was no one serious before Kutras."

"I'd never slept with a man before Miko."

Rafe swore, ran his thumbs slowly over her lips and then confessed, "I'm not sure I should resist this anymore."

This chemistry? This attraction? This feeling? Before she could ask, Rafe brought her closer to him and bent his head. Their kiss started slow and tender. Rafe nibbled at the corners of her mouth, then sealed his lips to hers. But the almost chaste pressure gave way as the heat of their bodies escalated…as she pressed closer to him and he pressed closer to her. She opened her lips and invited him into her mouth. He accepted her invitation and took the opportunity to explore everything he hadn't before. This kiss was different from the others. It was the portal to more than a kiss. It was the portal to a physical adventure with Rafe.

He broke away, braced a hand on either side of her on the wall and took in a deep breath. "Is this what you want, Gabby? Is this what you really want?"

"I do," she whispered, feeling as if she were making more of an emotional commitment than a physical one.

He leaned into her, kissed her again as if to make sure, then he tore away once more to ask, "Your bedroom or mine?"

"Yours is closer."

He led her to his bed and kept his arm around her while he swiped back the covers. It was as if he thought she'd run away. She wasn't running anywhere but toward him.

As he kissed her this time, he scrunched her kaftan in his hands until he lifted it up to her knees, then her thighs, then her waist. His lips clung to hers before he pulled away and shifted the kaftan over her head.

Her hair was mussed and she raised her hand to smooth it, but he shook his head. "Don't. I like it that way."

She stood there, in violet lacy panties and bra, feeling more

self-conscious than she'd ever felt at any shoot. Heat was
creeping into her cheeks.

Rafe enveloped her in his arms. "You're almost too beautiful to touch."

She braced her hands on his chest. "I won't break, Rafe.
Honest. But I am worried that…that I can't please you."

His gaze was searching and he realized that she was being
sincere. "This isn't about pleasing me, Gabby. This is about
both of us giving pleasure and taking it. If you're scared
about anything—"

"I'm never scared when I'm with you."

Her words seemed to release all the desire he'd been locking
away. He unhooked her bra and tossed it onto the nightstand.
Then he skimmed her panties down her legs. But he didn't stop
there. He knelt before her, placed his hands on her hips and
kissed her navel. She'd never experienced anything like the sensations that rushed through her. Especially when he kissed lower.

"Rafe. What are you doing?"

"Getting you ready."

He got her ready, all right. By the time he was done kissing
and teasing and touching, she could hardly catch her breath.
Then something happened she never expected. His tongue
tantalized just the right spot. Sparklers ignited all through her
body. She tingled and shook and held on to Rafe's shoulders
so she wouldn't fall.

He swept her into his arms while her body was still trembling and laid her on the bed. Then he climbed in beside her,
held her close and murmured against her cheek, "Just let me
know when you're ready for more."

"That must have been an orgasm," she finally said in awe.

He leaned slightly away. "You never had one of those
before?"

She shook her head. "Never."

Rafe smiled at her. There was satisfaction in his smile that said he was glad he was the one who had given her the gift. Now she wanted to give *him* a gift.

For a few moments her fingers played in his chest hair. But then she moved her hand down his body. She tugged at the drawstring at his waist and he skimmed his boxers down his legs. When she touched him he closed his eyes.

She bent her cheek to him, and he sucked in a breath. "Gabby, you don't have to."

"I want to." She wanted to love him in every way there was to love a man. She'd never known this kind of intimacy before, and she wanted it with Rafe.

Suddenly, Rafe moved like lightning and she lay on her back. "Are you on birth control?" he murmured.

She nodded.

He levered himself on his arms above her. "I want to be inside you."

She wanted him inside of her and to show him that, she raised her knees. He probed her entrance without pushing in.

"Don't treat me like I'm going to break, Rafe. I want to feel your passion."

His first thrust was smooth and measured, but then hunger and need took over. She held on to him, clawed his shoulders, welcomed the building excitement like a woman who had never been loved in this way before. She felt her connection to Rafe grow, their bond become stronger. Each thrill that ran through her body pushed her to a new sensual height. Her first orgasm had been unexpected and pleasurable. But now, when Rafe reached between them, she felt as if he'd found the essence of who she was. She spun, collecting colors like a diamond. Reflections of happiness and joy, awe and pleasure rainbowed around her. She cried Rafe's name, letting herself go, letting her spirit fly to meet his. Rafe answered her call, groaned his release, shuddered and collapsed on top of her. She held him, shaken by what had just happened between them.

A few minutes later he rolled to his side, one arm around her.

"That was wonderful," she breathed. As she said the words, reality settled in and hit her hard.

She knew Rafe had fought against his attraction to her. And now he might regret what had happened. "I just want you to know, I don't expect anything from you. I mean, I'll be leaving soon. You'll be going back to your regular routine. So...I don't want you to worry about what I'm feeling or anything like that. I'm cool with this. It happened and it was wonderful, but I know we have separate lives."

Rafe put his finger over her lips. "Gabby, stop. Don't dissect what happened. You're rebounding from a relationship. I never expected to be attracted to someone the way I'm attracted to you." He propped up on an elbow. "But we probably shouldn't let this happen again. If we do, it will be that much harder to say goodbye."

And she knew they had to say goodbye. She had her life, he had his.

"I should go back to my room," she murmured, tears burning in the back of her eyes.

"You don't have to hurry."

Yes, she did. The longer she stayed, the harder it would be to leave.

As Rafe had said, the harder it would be to say goodbye.

Chapter Twelve

One moment Gabby thought she was in heaven, the next… She looked at Rafe and saw his regrets.

Unfortunately she didn't have appointments this morning. Wouldn't you know it? So she and Rafe were cooped up in the suite.

At least he was staying in his room, working, though part of her missed him so much she wanted to cry. It was an emotional missing, something she'd never felt before—like a part of her was somewhere else.

She focused on her e-mails, answering one to her mother and another to a friend in London.

When the phone in the room buzzed, she absently picked it up. It was the front desk. "Ms. McCord, we have a package for you."

"Is it large or small?" she asked automatically.

"Small. Would you like someone to bring it up?"

"Yes, that would be great. Thank you."

She wasn't going to bother Rafe with this. Maybe he hadn't even heard the phone. His room had a separate line.

Someone rapped on the door and Gabby went to it, checking the peephole. She recognized the bellman who had been handling most of her packages and mail. She'd grabbed a bill from her purse and now, when he handed her a small gift bag, she tipped him. "Thanks, Roger. I really appreciate this."

"No problem, Ms. McCord. If you need anything else just let me know."

She'd already given Roger an autograph on one of the hotel brochures and he'd been deeply appreciative.

"My wife said she saw your interview on TV. She said to tell you you were great, as usual."

"Thank you. I had a friendly interviewer, so it was easy."

"You have a good day, now, Ms. McCord."

"I will." She shut the door and returned with the gift bag to the living room. This reminded her of when Rafe had given her the little birdcage. Could this be from him, too?

She recognized the shiny black bag with the gold "L." Larsen's Jewelers, one of McCord's rivals. Rafe wouldn't have gone to a rival jewelry store. She suddenly wondered if she should open it, not knowing who had sent it. But the small box was wrapped in silver, with a silver ribbon. It looked harmless enough. There was no card on the outside. Maybe she'd find one inside.

She undid the ribbon and took off the lid. On the black velvet lining inside the box she found a tanzanite and diamond tennis bracelet. She blinked. There had to be at least five or six carats of stones on the bracelet. The card was tucked into one corner of the velvet. She took it from its miniature envelope and froze.

Gabby, I want you back. M.K.

Gabby heard Rafe's footsteps in the hallway that led into the living room. Briefly she thought of hiding the present and bag under the sofa cushion. But what was the point? She was going to send the bracelet back. She supposed she could have Roger do it. Then Rafe wouldn't have to know.

But then there Rafe was, towering over her, looking down at the present in her lap. "*I'm* supposed to answer the door," he said gruffly.

"It was Roger. I knew it would be okay."

"Gabby, sometimes the most natural-looking circumstances seem okay but aren't."

"I don't want to fight."

He was silent for a few moments, then he rubbed his hand across his forehead. "Neither do I. Do I have to ask who it's from?" He could see the bracelet on the black velvet, the absolute beauty of it. It didn't take a jeweler to know it was an expensive piece.

"Probably not." She handed Rafe the card that had come with it.

The lines around his eyes grew deeper as he frowned. "He thinks he can buy you back. Can he?"

A pain pierced her heart. "Did you mean that as an insult? Didn't you learn anything about me last night?"

"I think we'd better leave last night out of this."

"You want to forget about it?" Hadn't making love meant anything to him? Was she the only one with her heart on the line?

"I can't forget about it any more than you can. But we have to. And I wasn't insulting you. I just meant that some women can be wooed with gifts. It's obviously meant as an apology. He thinks you might be willing to forgive him. Do you want to resume your relationship?"

She was in love with Rafe. She didn't want to be with anyone else. Yet how could she tell him that when he so obviously wanted to just get his time with her over with and move on? "I don't want to be with Miko. I want to be with a man who wants one woman for the rest of his life."

Their gazes locked and held and she wouldn't look away. She wanted him to pull her into his arms and kiss her and make love to her again, telling her he wanted her, too, and somehow they'd work something out. But he wasn't reaching for her and he wasn't saying anything.

Rafe's cell phone suddenly buzzed. They both jumped. With a scowl he took it from his belt and checked the number. Then he put it to his ear, listened for a few moments and said, "I'll tell her," and closed the phone.

"What will you tell me? Was it Blake?"

"Yes, it was. He wants you to come to the mansion this evening. The family is gathering again."

"Did he say why?"

"You know Blake. He can be a man of few words."

"Like you."

He ignored the jab. "It's a family meeting. He said Eleanor wanted it. He didn't sound too happy. I guess you'll find out what it's all about when you get there."

"Are you supposed to come, too?"

"I'll be waiting for you to bring you home. It's not until seven."

"I guess it might take that long to get hold of everybody."

"What would you like to do today? And don't say shopping," he warned her.

She had to smile. "What are my choices?" She would like to see his mom again, but he might not want her getting involved that way, either.

"We could take a ride out of town and sneak you into a Saturday afternoon rodeo, if we do you up right."

"You really think I could go to a rodeo without anybody recognizing me?"

"Sure. There are lots of pretty blondes at rodeos."

She saw the amusement in his eyes and knew he was kidding.

"How about a wig?" he asked. "Do you have one? That can really make a difference. A different color, a different style, short maybe, with some big sunglasses, jeans with holes in the knees, boots, one of those girlie blouses that ties at the waist. You'd look just like any other Texas gal out for a day at the rodeo."

His scenario sounded fun. They both could use a little fun. "I'd like to try it. Thanks for thinking of it. I haven't seen a good rodeo since I was here last year. Did you ever try a bucking bronc?"

"I tried one of those electronic bulls in a honky-tonk a couple of times."

"And?"

"And I learned to stay on pretty well. I even won a few bets. My fellow Secret Service agents didn't think a geek could do it."

"*You're* not a geek," she protested, certainly never thinking of him in that way.

"I know my way around computers. One of my specialties is Internet security. That makes me a geek. But it's good to be a geek *and* your bodyguard. That fills in my résumé a bit."

"As if you need it filled in," she muttered.

He laughed. "I do have work to do for the next hour or so. Will you be okay?"

"I'll be fine."

He picked up the bracelet and ran his thumb over it, letting it shimmer in the daylight. "It would look pretty on your wrist."

"I'm not keeping it. I'm going to package it up, call down for Roger and ask him to send it back to Miko for me."

"He's escalating his attempts to woo you back."

"They're not going to work."

For a moment she thought she saw turmoil in Rafe's eyes. Then it was gone so fast she might have imagined it. She stood and went to the kitchen. He turned toward his room. They went their separate ways.

She'd have to get used to that.

"I thought we should have this meeting," Eleanor said, looking nervous but regal that evening, "so everyone could air what they're feeling. I want to keep my family together. You've all gone your separate ways and been silent. None of you have called me to discuss this. I spoke with Gabby and Katie when we went away for our spa day. But my own children, who I want to talk to, *won't* talk to me."

All of Eleanor's children were gathered in one of the mansion's sitting rooms, none looking too happy. Gabby almost felt as if she shouldn't be there. She wasn't one of the children and she could understand what had happened to Eleanor. But then, Devon hadn't been her father and she didn't have to absorb the fact that her mother had been unfaithful to her father.

Blake sat, blond head bowed, hands between his legs. He looked as if he were restraining every thought, every motion and every emotion in his body. He didn't look up and he didn't say a word.

Penny began, "This is hard for us to deal with, Mom. You've got to realize, we all thought we knew who you were. And now we have to rearrange our thinking."

"You all knew that I was in love with Rex when I was a teenager. You heard the stories. We were committed to each other—we just couldn't agree on when we would marry and we had a fight. I was young and I was foolish, and Devon had been trying to…to get my attention for a long time. We had dinner, we had wine and I gave in, thinking I had lost Rex."

Blake's body tensed even more and he finally turned his head toward his mother. But his voice was completely even, devoid of any emotion. "We all know what happened next. You got pregnant. You couldn't be an unwed mother in those days, so you married our father."

"I did. I tried to be happy with my life. But years later, Devon and I both knew something was missing. I suspected he'd been having an affair."

Now all of her children were looking at her.

"Suspected," Paige asked bitterly, "or knew?"

"I never had proof, if that's what you mean. But a woman knows."

Paige just rolled her eyes and it was easy to see she hadn't forgiven her mother, either.

Tate looked deep in thought and seemed as if he didn't want to venture into the subject. Not here, maybe not ever.

Charlie, however, had been restless ever since he'd come in. Now he said, "I've been close to all of you and I don't want anything to change that."

Penny moved next to him and took his hand. "You're my brother, Charlie. You'll always be my brother, whether your name is McCord or Foley."

The name Foley brought silence to the room. After several awkward minutes, no one had broken it.

Eleanor sighed and looked as if she had tears in her eyes. "I know you think you have a lot to forgive me for. I'm not perfect, just as you aren't perfect. We all want our lives to go along an easy road, but that rarely happens. But I can see trying to talk to all of you like this was wrong. I thought I could answer your questions, but you don't even want to ask them. So I guess it will be up to each of you to talk to me about this on your own. Until then, just know that I love all of you very much. I always have." She looked at Blake and then glanced away.

Gabby thought Eleanor was acting guilty. Maybe because she couldn't bond to Blake as she'd wanted to after he was born. She must have resented him for putting her into this marriage with a man she didn't love. What an awful situation for all of them to be in.

And Charlie? Had he been more loved because he was Rex Foley's son? The son of the man Eleanor truly loved?

The questions weren't Gabby's to ask, or to know the answers to.

Eleanor stood. "I believe Blake and Paige have information to share with you about some plans they're making. I don't need to be part of this. I'll be upstairs if anybody would like to talk afterward."

Eleanor left the living room, looking hurt, frustrated and dejected. Gabby hoped her children could come to see her as a person, not just their mother, and maybe give her the understanding she needed.

Blake waited until his mother left and he could hear her footfalls on the hardwood floor.

Penny looked up at her brother. "Blake, you were awfully hard on her."

"If you want to forgive her, that's fine. But don't tell me I should. I have a lot more to forgive her for."

"Just think about her living with our father all those years and not loving him," Paige said, shaking her head. "How could she do that?"

"She probably did it for us," Tate reminded them.

Blake stood and paced to the mantel. "Enough about all that. I want to tell you what Paige and I have planned. As I told you before, from the clues on the deed to the mines, we believe the Santa Magdalena diamond is in the Eagle mine on Travis Foley's ranch. Paige is going to…nose around…get the lay of the land…and then steal it."

"Steal it?" Gabby asked in spite of herself.

"Those mines are still ours, Gabby. Travis just has a lease to the land. So we have every right to look in that mine. We just don't want Foley to know what we're doing."

"So you're going to sneak in?" Penny asked her twin.

"Yes, that's exactly what I'm going to do. And then I'm going to find that diamond and put the McCords on the upswing again."

At one time Gabby might have gone along with a plan like this. It seemed dangerous and adventurous and exciting. But what if Paige got caught? Wouldn't this only make the feud worse? And what about the diamond? Would the McCords try to break the lease and put Travis off the property? It was all so complicated and she wasn't sure Blake and Paige knew exactly what they were getting themselves into. Especially Paige. Sure, she was the gemologist. But still…

"Gabby, don't look so worried," Paige entreated her. "I'll be fine. I'm a big girl, and very inventive. Believe me, before you all know it, this will be over. We'll have the Santa Magdalena diamond and a PR campaign that really cooks."

Gabby thought Paige was being naive. Or maybe her cousin just wanted this so much she was rationalizing her way into it, just as Gabby had rationalized her relationship with Miko.

The brothers and sisters began talking among themselves. Gabby stared into space for a few moments, thinking about Rex and Eleanor and how they'd been in love as teenagers. And how that love had never died. Would Charlie want to speak to his father? Just how would he feel about him?

She didn't hear her name until Blake asked, "Gabby, are you here with me?"

He was standing over her and she smiled up at him. "I'm here."

"I just want to tell you, you're doing a great job. I've had positive feedback from my customers and we're getting a good response to the print and TV ads."

"I'm glad this is working."

He glanced over his shoulder at his family. "What spa did you and Katie and Mother go to?"

"The Yellow Rose Spa. It was a real women's getaway."

"So, Katie enjoyed it?"

"I believe so. She's serious much of the time, but she smiled a lot and liked the treatments."

Blake paused and seemed to hesitate. Then he dug his hands into his trouser pockets and met her gaze again. "Did Katie ask about me?"

Gabby remembered what Katie had said about Blake, the admiring note in her voice. Was she rethinking her relationship with Tate? Were there sparks between her and Blake that had never been fanned into flame? Gabby supposed that was possible. But what would happen between the brothers if Katie severed her involvement with Tate and began a relationship with Blake? Would Tate be able to accept Blake in Katie's life?

Another triangle! Maybe if this did happen, Blake could see how his mother might have gotten caught up in a triangle just as easily.

Gabby answered Blake's question. "Our conversations were in confidence and I don't really feel I can share them. But Katie did say you're a good listener." Gabby thought it was best to leave Tate out of this.

Blake looked as if he'd found another batch of canary diamonds. "Thanks for telling me," he said with a genuine smile. "I know you'll be leaving for Italy soon. Give me a call when you get home and we'll plan what's next."

After taking another glance at Paige, Penny and Tate, who were involved in a discussion, Gabby said, "I'll do that. Do you think there's any reason for me to stay now?"

"Do you have something going on tonight?"

She wanted to spend as much time as possible with Rafe. They didn't have that many days left. Maybe they could take out the golf cart again or something fun like that. She just wanted to be with him.

Even if he doesn't want to be with you?

She didn't know if he did or not. Maybe tonight she'd have to ask him.

After the meeting at the McCord mansion, Gabby sat with Rafe at the suite's dining-room table, picking at her room service meal. So much of everything was filling her head...not only what had gone on at the McCords'—Eleanor's sadness, her children's bitterness and resentment—but all of Gabby's feelings for Rafe. They hadn't spoken on the way home and Gabby had realized Rafe looked almost as preoccupied as she felt.

Now here they were, pushing their food around, not exchanging much more than, "Can you pass a packet of salt?" She tried to search for a topic, a safe one, and finally she simply asked, "What do you think of the McCord family crisis?" He'd been standing outside the parlor where the family had met. He'd certainly heard Eleanor's plea to her children for understanding.

"I don't get involved."

She knew what he meant. When he was a bodyguard, he simply stood like a statue. He didn't listen or have an opinion. Hogwash!

"Don't act as if this is simply another assignment." That brought his gaze to hers.

"What do you want to know? What I think doesn't matter in all this."

If he was talking about the McCords, that was one thing. If he was talking about the two of them, that was another. Still, she kept her exasperation tamped down, trying to put out of her head the image of his hands on her body, the feel of his kisses, the way his beard stubble had grazed her cheek. "Blake's pretty upset, although he's trying not to show it."

"I wouldn't want to be Charlie," Rafe mumbled.

"I guess *he* is the one smack-dab in the middle of two feuding families. And now he might have allegiance to both of them."

Silence drove a wedge between Gabby and Rafe once more. She put down her fork. It was silly to pretend she was eating. "What are we going to do about the photo?" She guessed she didn't have to explain *which* photo.

"I'm still tracing the person who sent it."

"I thought we weren't going to go ahead with that."

"It won't hurt to have the information, no matter what we decide to do."

No matter what they decided to do. If that picture was published, it could ruin Rafe's reputation and career. "Would the publication of it be as damaging if it came out after I go back to Italy? Would people wonder if it was a fake?"

Rafe shrugged, as if it didn't matter. But he said, "The people who count would still wonder if I had had a personal relationship with a client. It would affect who would sign on with me."

"You could just work for the McCords forever," she tried to joke, knowing it was a feeble attempt.

Rafe didn't even try to smile. Instead, he tossed his napkin down, stood, crossed the room and went out to the balcony.

Should she follow or not? Did he want her to? Or did he want to be alone? She'd never seen him show even a bit of temper. She'd never seen him show much emotion—until they'd made love. Since then he'd been so much more introspective, quiet in a different way than his stoic Secret Service persona.

The balcony was the hot spot, the place where it had happened. But she couldn't keep herself from going to him. She loved him.

They stood in the silent night, looking out into the darkness. "Do you think anyone is watching now?" he asked.

This time she didn't think about "should" or "shouldn't." She laid her hand on his shoulder. "I'm sorry."

He turned toward her so fast her hand dropped from him. "Don't say that, Gabby. You have nothing to be sorry for. This is just the situation we're in. And when you touch me, even like that—"

The hunger in his eyes amazed her. It was all wrapped up with desire and longing and the knowledge they only had a few days together. She wanted and needed intimacy with Rafe. So she went for it. "What happens when I touch you?"

He grabbed her hand, pulled her back inside the suite, then pressed her against the wall inside the door. His lips came down on hers hard, until he was her world. He couldn't get enough, and neither could she. They could have been anywhere—on a desert island, in the middle of Times Square, atop a ruin in Cozumel. It simply didn't matter. Only their passion mattered. Only the fact they would soon be separated mattered.

Only the fact that she loved him mattered.

He laced his fingers into her hair, held her head, angled his lips and searched her mouth with his tongue, chasing the desire that would match his. Gabby's blood was running so hot, so fast, she didn't need to breathe. She just needed to follow wherever Rafe led.

When he leaned his body into hers, she could feel how badly he wanted her. She was already ready. The slightest pressure at the right place and she'd unwind before she even had her clothes off.

Rafe must have felt the same way because his hands left

er hair, moved down her body to the hem of her shirt and
yanked it up and over her head. His gaze was penetrating and
inquiring. Did she want to do this here and now? Did she want
him in this way?

"Yes," she said without hesitation.

With her assent, he ridded her of her shorts and her panties.
She helped him undress until they were both panting, eager,
more than ready.

She took him in her hands.

"Gabby, I can't take much foreplay."

"Only a little," she promised, stroking him with a sensu-
ality that had him gritting his teeth.

"You can be a vixen," he whispered.

"Only around you."

"Turn around," he whispered.

She did as he said, trusting him.

She braced her hands on the wall while he held on to her hips.
And then he was inside her, fast and furious, pushing and with-
drawing, until she thought she'd go crazy with needing him.

"Rafe," she called.

"I'm here." Her world as she knew it exploded, and she
wished the moment could last forever. Seconds later he
found *his* release, then he wrapped his arms around her and
held her tight.

After they caught their breath, she turned to face him, not
at all embarrassed, proud she'd matched his desire, pleased
that they could ignite such passion in each other.

"Are you okay?" he asked, searching her face.

"I'm great," she replied with a wide smile.

Laughing, he lifted her into his arms and carried her
through the living room and the hallway into his bedroom. She
held on tight, wondering if she could ever tell him she loved
him…wondering what would happen if she did.

Chapter Thirteen

Gabby exited the car Marjorie had sent for her and slipped through the back door of McCord Jewelers. It was midnight and Rafe was back at the hotel sleeping. She hoped to heaven he wouldn't wake up until she was back in her room.

The past twenty-four hours had felt gloriously like a honeymoon. She and Rafe had explored each other's bodies, shared meals, spoken of their childhoods and made love in every room. At least *she* was making love. Rafe cared for her, that was obvious in the way he touched her and kissed her and held her. But he hadn't said the words, and she didn't know what he was feeling. Maybe she was just an escape for him—from his past, from his work, from everything outside the hotel window.

The past two weeks had flown by. She didn't have any more personal appearances and she was relieved. The reality was, she'd be gone in a few days. She wanted to give Rafe something special to remember her by. When she left it for him, she couldn't have regrets.

They'd made love all evening, but she had a shoot early tomorrow morning, so she'd teasingly told him tonight she needed to get her beauty rest and it might be better if they slept in their separate rooms. He'd seemed to understand. She didn't like deceiving him, but she certainly didn't want him with her when she picked out his present.

Sometimes a girl had to do what she had to do on her own.

A few phone calls had arranged it. Joe and Roger from the hotel staff were eager to help. She'd be back in her room before Rafe even knew she was gone.

Marjorie was sitting on one of the stools at the diamond case, going over inventory sheets.

As Gabby approached, she said, "I'm sorry to bring you out so late, but I didn't know how else to do this."

"I'm a night owl. Don't worry, there's always plenty of work here for me to do. What can I show you?"

"Is it all right if I just look around on my own awhile? I'm not sure what I want. Rafe's not a diamond cuff link kind of guy."

"More rough-and-tumble?" Marjorie asked with a wink.

"You could say that," Gabby returned with a smile, remembering their last tumble in bed. If she left and never saw him again… She couldn't think about that. She just couldn't.

She knew he wouldn't accept an over-the-top gift, so she had to keep this simple. Peeking in one case after another, peering at watches, keyrings, diamond rings and other masculine jewelry items, her attention was focused on choosing a gift. She was looking so hard, wanting to get back so quickly, she was barely aware of the glare of headlights outside. When she saw the flash of beams in the window, she didn't think much of it. This was a busy street, even at night.

She'd looked over most of the inventory when Marjorie came over to her.

"Can't find what you're looking for?"

"It seems ridiculous with everything that's here, but nothing seems just perfect."

"I have something in the back that just came in. Let me get it for you."

"I can come with you," Gabby said, and followed Marjorie around the back of the desk down the hall to her office. When Marjorie opened the door, Gabby saw a few boxes sitting on her desk.

"Each piece is unique and handcrafted." She picked up a gray box lined with black velvet and handed it to Gabby. At once, she was excited. "Now this I like." She was holding a fourteen-karat gold tie bar inlaid with turquoise and onyx.

"Here's the second one," Marjorie said, giving it to her. The second tie bar was more of a mosaic in lapis, carnelian, onyx and green turquoise.

Gabby ran her hand over the robin's-egg-blue turquoise on the first one. "Is this from the Kingman mine?"

"Yes, it is."

She didn't hesitate. "This is the one I want, no doubt about it. I think he'll like it. Do you have any of those little black gift bags left? The shiny ones with the lavender straw?"

"I might. Let me check my closet." Marjorie looked and found the bag in question. Gabby put the box inside, tied the bag with a black satin ribbon and then gave Marjorie her credit card.

"I'll take this out to the desk."

As they came down the hall to the main part of the store, they heard noise outside.

Gabby stared out the front window. She was horrified at what she saw. There were people there looking in—women and men—and she saw some were talking on cell phones. That was the last thing she needed. People meant press…photographers. She felt like throwing a tantrum, but knew that wouldn't do any good. She had to think practically. Maybe she could still get out the back where the chauffeur waited.

"I'm going to try to sneak out the back."

"Wait. I still have your credit card."

"Don't worry. I'll pick it up another time. I've got to get going."

When Gabby reached the back exit, there were two photographers waiting, standing outside their cars blocking in her car and driver. She was trapped. There was nowhere to go. She *could* do something stupid. She could try to get out of this without Rafe. But she knew she shouldn't. She knew he would know the best thing to do.

She took out her phone and dialed his cell.

"Gabby?" he asked when he answered, in a sleepy, almost languorous voice that caused a tremble up her spine.

"Hi, Rafe. I need your help."

"Can't get to sleep? Need a massage?"

There was humor in his voice. Before he left his room and figured out she wasn't there, she'd better tell him. "Rafe, I had something I had to do tonight and I'm not in the suite."

Silence. She imagined he was getting up and going to check. In a matter of moments he asked in a tense voice, "Gabby, where are you?"

"I'm at McCord Jewelers, and there's a crowd growing outside. Somebody must have caught sight of me in here and called someone else and they called the press."

He swore. "What in the hell are you doing at McCord's?"

"I told you, there was something I needed to do on my own."

"Yeah, well, you can see where that got you. Don't move. I'll be there as soon as I can. I suppose the back isn't clear, either?"

"No. Some photographers have our car blocked."

"Whose car?"

"Marjorie sent one for me."

He digested that.

"If I tell her to send him home, maybe the photographers will leave."

"Don't be naive. You know better than that. Don't stick your head outside the door. Tell Marjorie not to, either. I'll be there as fast as I can."

He clicked off without even saying goodbye.

Rafe hadn't spoken to her since he'd arrived at the store. Gabby knew he was mad. He didn't yell or throw things, he just set his jaw, scowled and spoke in a low, controlled voice—not to her, but to the two men he brought with him, to the officers in the two patrol cars who had driven up behind him.

In the back of the store he put his arm around her, moved her close to him and bodyguards walked on either side of them. The patrol cars sent a warning to everyone else not to make a move. Once Rafe had Gabby inside the car, they sat in the backseat a good two feet apart. He didn't touch her. He didn't look at her.

Because he was afraid he would say something he shouldn't? She was sure that was going to come. Determined not to let him see it, she'd put the little black bag in her purse.

Back at the suite he opened the door, checked the place as he usually did and gave her a nod. He went to the living room. She went to her bedroom and left her purse on the dresser.

He called to her. "Gabby, are you coming out?"

"It's late."

"We need to talk."

"Not if you're going to yell at me."

He peered in her bedroom door. "This isn't funny."

"I didn't say it was. But you're acting as if I committed a crime."

He raked his hand through his hair. "Why would you do something so stupid?"

"Rafe, I told you before. I feel trapped here sometimes."

"Have you felt trapped since last night?"

He meant when they were making love. "No, of course not. But once in a while, I just have to do something on my own. I needed a present for someone."

"So why didn't you take me with you?"

"You really don't understand, do you? You've had this assignment for two weeks, but this is my life, day and night, all the time. Once in a while I have to do something out of the ordinary. Once in a while I have to take a risk or I'll go crazy. I don't always have a bodyguard—it depends on the town and what I'm going to do, if I'll be recognized or not. As I said, back in Italy I don't have to worry. That's why I can't wait to get back there. I won't have a bodyguard, and I'll feel normal."

"For you, normal could be dangerous. Don't you realize that?"

"I realize I have to take precautions. I thought I did tonight. Who would expect me to be at the store after midnight? But I didn't wear a disguise, and I should have. I'm sorry, Rafe. I'm sorry I interrupted your sleep. I'm sorry I snuck out. I'm sorry our lives are so different."

His gaze locked on to hers and for a moment, just for a moment, she thought he might tell her they weren't that different. She thought he might kiss her and lead her to bed. She thought he might hold her through the night.

But he didn't. Instead, he just said, "I'll see you in the morning. You've got to get some sleep for that shoot tomorrow."

And then he was gone.

Gabby sank down on her bed, wishing she could postpone the shoot tomorrow. She was afraid she was going to look as if she had lost her best friend.

The following afternoon, Rafe went to his room in the suite with a heavy heart. He'd done a great job of damaging everything he and Gabby had shared, and he wasn't even sure why.

Yes, he *was* sure why. He was distancing himself from her and had taken the first opportunity to do it. Her little escapade at the jewelry store had been the perfect jumping-off point. He *had* to distance himself, didn't he? She was leaving. He wasn't ready to commit to anything or anybody.

He'd avoided answering the question running in his mind. Why had he acted so strongly when Gabby had called for help?

He knew why. He hadn't been able to protect his wife because she'd gone somewhere on her own. Gabby had brought it all back. Thank goodness Gabby's recklessness hadn't led to disaster.

He'd wanted to gather her up and make love to her all night. But he'd known if he had done that, it would be even harder to let her go.

They'd come back from the shoot a little while ago. He'd ordered room service, but she said she didn't want anything. So he'd eaten a burger in the kitchen by himself. Now she was still in her bedroom.

As soon as he walked into his room, he stopped. There was a shiny black bag on his bed. He went over to it and stared at it as if it might bite him. There was a note with it, written on hotel stationery. He took the letter from the envelope.

Rafe,
I want to thank you for all you've done while I've been
in Dallas. I so enjoyed meeting your family, but most of

*all, spending time with you. I'll never forget what we
shared. Thanks again for everything you did for me.*
  Gabby

He didn't want to open the gift…he really didn't. But another
part of him was too curious to let it be. He untied the black satin
bow and stuck his hand into the lavender straw. When he pulled
out the gray velvet box, he just stared at it. Finally, he opened
it. The tie bar was exquisite. Gabby had wonderful taste. But
he didn't know what to think. Had she risked being followed
by photographers to buy him a gift? Why would that mean so
much to her? Simply because of good manners? Gabby always
confused him and this wasn't an exception. But he had to know
what she was thinking. That was all-important to him.

As he was coming out of the room, there was a knock on
the door. He was surprised. Usually the doorman or the con-
cierge called on his cell phone to tell him if someone was
coming up. Maybe Roger was just delivering another package.

Rafe went to the door, peered out the peephole and froze.
He knew who the man was. Mikolaus Kutras.

A visceral reaction to the man gripped Rafe. His stomach
clenched and he felt adrenaline rushing to his fingertips. One
main thought pummeled him—this was the man who had
taken Gabby's virginity and squandered it. This was the man
she'd run from. This was the man she hadn't finished with yet.
Every instinct told him not to open that door.

But his reason told him he had to. He just wished— What?
That he hadn't blown up at Gabby?

He never blew up. He always remained calm. But since
she'd been here, she'd encouraged him to act in ways he never
had before.

He tamped down every feeling that had rushed to the fore-
front, forced calm onto his features and opened the door.

"Is Gabriella McCord in?" Kutras asked, with a quick, dismissive appraisal of Rafe.

Rafe stared back at the tall, lean, dark-haired man in a penetrating way. "Who's calling?" he asked in a voice that sent the message no one would get by him without a good reason.

"Just tell her Miko's here. She'll want to see me."

Rafe hoped from the bottom of his soul that that wasn't true, yet he had to give Gabby the choice. She was a free agent. And he suddenly didn't like that idea any more than he liked her meeting with Kutras.

Rafe stepped back and let the man in. Without another word he went to Gabby's bedroom and knocked on the door. When she opened it, he forced himself not to notice that she looked beautiful in her tan linen slacks and cream silk blouse. He forced himself to deny his response to her, as well as everything else that had happened since he'd begun this assignment. This man could be sorry for everything that happened and persuade Gabby to accompany him in his private jet back to the Greek Islands.

Rafe found himself saying stiffly, "Mikolaus Kutras is here to see you."

Gabby went a shade paler and he didn't know if it was a good sign or not. He offered, "I can tell him to leave."

To Rafe's chagrin she hesitated, then said, "I'll see him. But I need to see him alone."

Rafe didn't like that idea any more than letting the man in. "You want me to leave?"

She studied Rafe's face for a long time. Then she squared her shoulders. "Yes. There's no need for you to stay. I'll be fine."

He so wanted to step into that room with her and lock the door behind him. He found there were a few things he'd like to say before he left, but they were all muddled in his head and he couldn't quite clear them or make sense of them. So instead, he stepped aside when she exited her bedroom and went into the living room to meet with her former lover.

Rafe did not want to leave, but the way Gabby and Kutras were staring at each other, he knew he had to. He left the suite, letting the door lock behind him.

Gabby's hands trembled a little as she gazed at the man who had changed her life. He'd changed it because, after their disastrous relationship, she'd known exactly what she did want and didn't want in a partner. She'd learned what infatuation was. She'd learned what a man said and what a man did were often two very different things, at least in Miko's case, though not in Rafe's.

"Hello, Miko." She was proud of herself that her voice didn't shake, that she could stand coolly facing him, knowing he had to finish this.

He came toward her then, and would have enveloped her in a huge hug, but she stepped back.

He studied her quizzically. "What's the matter? How did you like the bracelet I sent? I see you're not wearing it. Does it need some adjustment?"

"I returned the bracelet to your London flat."

"I haven't been back there. But I don't understand why you returned it. Don't you realize I'm trying to make up to you for what happened?"

"There's no way to make up for what happened."

"Now, Gabby, don't be immature about this. Men and women's relationships are always in a state of flux."

"Flux? Don't take me for a fool, Miko. Or maybe you just don't understand the difference in our points of view."

His handsome features pretended puzzlement. "What point of view is that? We had fun together. You know we did. And we can again."

"No, we can't. You only want me back until you have me. Then you'll run off to someone else again. I don't want to be in that kind of relationship. I'm not interested in that type of relationship. If I ever decide to commit to a man, he and I will be life partners. We'll share our dreams and our ideas. We'll cooperate to make a life together, never lie to each other, never cheat. Fidelity, loyalty and friendship are the basis of any good relationship. I didn't know that when I met you. You did sweep me off my feet, but I had a hard landing and it taught me what I needed to know."

Miko laughed. "I think you've been in Dallas too long."

"The place doesn't matter. It's my outlook that's changed."

"Outlook?" he scoffed. "Maybe you've been spending too much time with provincial relatives."

"The McCords aren't provincial. And even if they were—'

Miko looked angry as he approached her again and reached out. "You don't understand what you're giving up."

She quickly sidestepped him. "I know what I want."

After a tense moment, he asked with less temper. "Something has changed, hasn't it?"

"A lot has changed. I'm figuring out what I want to do with my life."

"You have everything you could want."

"Maybe I once did, but now I want something different. I'm figuring out what will fulfill me. I'm figuring out what love is."

The quiet between them in the suite was palpable.

"Does this have something to do with the man who let me in? Do you think you love *him?*"

She could deny it, but what was the point? The truth really could set her free. "It does."

"You're making a mistake. Do you know what I could give you? Caviar on my yacht every morning, sunsets in the Alps at night."

Gabby could now see clearly what she wanted, and it wasn't any of the things Miko was suggesting. "I want children and a loving husband who puts us first."

He dismissed her yearning sarcastically. "You want a dream."

"Maybe. But I hope it's a dream I can make a reality someday."

One thing Gabby knew about Miko, whether he was gambling, investing in global markets or running a new business venture, he knew when to cut his losses and leave. That's what he did now.

He actually gave her a sad smile and said, "If anyone can find what you're looking for, it's you."

Then he left the suite and didn't look back.

Gabby collapsed on the sofa, glad Miko had come, glad he'd said the things that she had. Now she realized she had to finish packing. Maybe she'd see if she could get a flight out tonight. Staying here with Rafe, when she loved him, knowing he didn't love her, hurt too much. If she returned to Italy, maybe she'd start to heal. Maybe she could figure out the course of the rest of her life.

Rafe hadn't gone far. He'd positioned himself just outside the suite door and waited. Yes, it could be a long wait, especially if Gabby and Kutras reconciled. But she might need him. She might open that door and yell for his help. He couldn't just leave her unprotected.

Only about twenty minutes had passed when the door to the suite opened. Rafe felt so relieved when he saw Kutras. The green haze of jealousy he'd denied since Kutras had come to the door evaporated. If the Greek and Gabby had reconciled, they'd be locked in each other's arms in her bed. In spite of himself, Rafe looked for lipstick on Kutras's pristine white shirt collar. He found none.

Mikolaus Kutras didn't just leave. He saw Rafe, stoppe
and looked him in the eye. "You are a very lucky man."

After that enigmatic statement, the Greek tycoon walke
down the hall, stepped inside the elevator and disappeare
from sight.

"Gabby?" Rafe called her name as he came back into th
suite.

A half hour after Miko had left, Gabby took the turquois
sandals from the floor of the closet, fitted them in the suitcas
around her other items and knew she was finished. Th
packing was done and it was time to leave. All she had to d
was say goodbye to Rafe. Thank goodness, as a celebrity, sh
could get a seat on the last flight out.

She'd left her bedroom door open a few inches. Raf
rapped on it.

"Come in," she called, not sure exactly what she was goin
to say to him.

Rafe looked different somehow and she couldn't quite put he
finger on the difference. His hair was too short to be dishevele
yet she had the feeling he'd run his hand through it lately man
times. Maybe it was his expression. He looked…unsettled.

"I reserved a seat on a flight to New York tonight," sh
explained as she moved clothes in the suitcase to keep he
hands busy.

"I thought you weren't leaving until the day after tomorrow

"I changed my mind. I thought it would be better for bo
of us if I leave today."

He approached her slowly, as if he was afraid she'd run awa
if he moved too fast. "You didn't spend much time with Kutras

"No, I didn't."

Now Rafe did run his hand through his hair. "I waite
outside in case you needed me."

How was she supposed to take that? As if he'd done his job? Or as if he really cared? She closed the lid of her suitcase and ran the zipper around it. "I didn't need you, Rafe. Some things a woman has to do on her own."

"Kutras said something when he left."

She brought her gaze to Rafe's. "What did he say?"

"He said I'm a very lucky man. Can you tell me why?"

She wasn't foolish. She wasn't naïve. But she did believe in dreams. And she wanted her dream to come true. So she threw caution to the wind and risked her heart. "Miko picked up on what's happened, I guess. I love you, Rafe. I can't leave without saying it. I know you don't want to hear it, but I can't deny the truth. That's why I'm leaving now. It hurts to be around you when I want you to be more than a bodyguard."

Her hand was still on the zipper of the suitcase. Rafe came to her and took both of her hands in his. When he ran his thumbs over her palms, she could have melted at his feet.

"I found the present," he said in a low voice. "But I don't want a thank-you present. I want *you*...forever. Before you came into my life, I was stuck in the past. I considered myself tough and ready for anything, but I wasn't ready for you. *You* pulled me from the past into now, and I fought it. I fought it hard. I fought you. But when Kutras came to that door today, I realized part of me would die if you reconciled with him. At first I thought it was jealousy. But it wasn't. It was love for you. After Kutras left, I called Joe and asked him to watch the suite while I took a walk. I had to get perspective. I only made it outside the back entrance when I realized perspective meant nothing. My feelings for you meant everything."

He squeezed her hands. "I love you. I want you to be my wife. I want to have children with you. I want to spend the rest of my life with you."

She was crying now and couldn't seem to find her voice. Rafe loved her. He *really* loved her.

He pulled her into his arms. "*Am* I a lucky man, Gabby? Will you marry me?"

"Yes, yes, I'll marry you!" she responded happily, throwing her arms around his neck. They'd shared many kisses, but this one was full of promise. This one was full of love, yearning, tenderness and the passion that she knew they'd share for a lifetime.

His lips clung to hers and then he lifted his head, breaking the kiss. "We're going to have to figure out what kind of future we want."

"I want to have your babies."

He grinned. "We might need a bit of time together first. But we can practice a lot."

She laughed and laid her head against his chest. Then she realized they had some unfinished business. "What are we going to do about the photograph?"

"I really don't think that's a problem anymore. I don't care if that picture of us kissing is published everywhere. I want the whole world to know I love you."

"Show me how much," she suggested.

He lifted her into his arms and carried her to the bed. "Gladly. And then we'll go get a marriage license."

Gabby lovingly laid her hand against his face and ran her thumb across his lips. "Will you, Rafael Balthazar, be my bodyguard for a lifetime?"

He kissed her thumb and assured her, "I'll watch over and love you forever."

When Rafe laid her down on the bed and came down beside her, Gabby reached for him, believing the dreams they shared would come true.

Epilogue

Gabby and Rafe sat on a blanket on the rise of a gentle hill under a cypress tree, looking over the vista of plowed fields and olive groves. Rafe poured wine into the wineglasses she'd brought along in the picnic basket. Their small villa, with its stone walls, wooden doors and hand-painted tile accents was nestled in the valley below.

"So, do you really love our house?" Gabby asked. It was the one she'd found on the Internet and the first that they'd looked at when they'd flown to Italy.

"I do. And it will be a home soon, rather than a house."

Their furniture was being delivered tomorrow. They'd done everything in such a short amount of time. They'd married in Dallas, with Rafe's mother and sister and the McCord family present. Eleanor had graciously let them use her estate for the wedding. Then they'd flown to Italy for their honeymoon, mixing lovemaking with house buying and visiting her parents.

For the most part they'd stayed at a bed-and-breakfast, but last night they'd brought bedrolls and air mattresses and made love in their new house.

"What do you really think of my parents?" Gabby asked.

"I think they love you very much, and if your mother could, she'd have our wedding here all over again."

"She's throwing the reception. I don't know how she put it together so fast." The following evening relatives and friends in the area would be invited to celebrate Gabby and Rafe's marriage in the villa where she grew up.

"Am I going to meet royalty?" he joked.

"Do you want to meet royalty?" Gabby asked, amused.

He reached out and stroked her hair. "You're royalty enough for me."

After a quick but sound kiss, Rafe produced a newspaper from under the picnic basket. "What's that?" Gabby asked.

"Look and see." He held it up for her and she saw the front page of the tabloid. It was the picture of the two of them kissing.

"You said you wanted the whole world to see." She studied him closely to see his reaction.

"Yes, I did. And I don't mind a bit. How about you?"

"I'm proud to be your wife. But what if you decide to leave McCord's and go out on your own again? Will this affect what you do?"

"No. I fell in love with the woman I was guarding. What could be wrong with that?"

"Absolutely nothing," she murmured, as he leaned close for a kiss. She tasted wine on his lips. She also tasted the desire that always took them both away to another place where the two of them found paradise.

After the kiss slowly ended, Rafe tilted his forehead against hers. "When we have children, I'll specialize in online security for the McCords and Blake can find someone else to travel. We can make this our home base, maybe stay here most of the year and find a place in Dallas for the rest. What do you think?"

"I know we talked about waiting to have children. But Rafe, I think I'm ready now. Are you?"

"More than ready." He took her wineglass from her hand, set his along with hers in the picnic basket and kissed her again.

As the Tuscan sun rippled over the hills, Gabby knew she'd found the life she'd wanted—a life with Rafe.

* * * * *

Cherish

TEXAS CINDERELLA *by Victoria Pade*

A hidden diamond and a dramatic feud! Will Tate be able to keep his family secrets from sassy journalist Tanya, even as he falls in love?

THE TEXAS CEO'S SECRET *by Nicole Foster*

Katerina and Blake were meant to be friends, linked by marriage – but not to each other. But a passionate kiss changes everything.

STAR-CROSSED SWEETHEARTS *by Jackie Braun*

Hiding from the press in Italy, actress Atlanta wants to be alone. Will former bad boy Angelo show her that the limelight is fleeting and it's family and love that count?

SECRET PRINCE, INSTANT DADDY! *by Raye Morgan*

When pretty Ayme tracks him down, deposed royal Darius, sure he is th● father of her late sister's baby, must decide how he can fulfil his destiny and find his own happiness.

AT HOME IN STONE CREEK *by Linda Lael Miller*

Everyone in Ashley 's life is marrying and starting families. Now Jack, the man who broke her heart years ago, is back. But is he who she thinks he is?

On sale from 17th September 2010
Don't miss out!

Available at WHSmith, Tesco, ASDA, Eason and all good bookshops

www.millsandboon.co.uk

A MIRACLE FOR HIS SECRET SON
by Barbara Hannay

Freya never intended Gus to find out about their son. But when young Nick needs a kidney transplant she tracks him down. Could this be their chance to be a family?

PROUD RANCHER, PRECIOUS BUNDLE
by Donna Alwood

Wyatt and Elli have already had a run-in. But when a baby is left on his doorstep, Wyatt needs help. Will romance between them flare as they care for baby Darcy?

ACCIDENTALLY PREGNANT!
by Rebecca Winters

Left pregnant and alone, Irena is determined to keep her baby a secret. Can Vincenzo, the man she had a passionate affair with, give her the love she needs?

10/023b

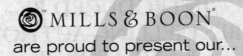

All the magic you'll need this Christmas...

Do fairy lights and family make the perfect Christmas?

Angels in the Snow

Sarah Morgan

When **Daniel** is left with his brother's kids, only one person can help. But it'll take more than mistletoe before **Stella** helps him...

Patrick hadn't advertised for a housekeeper. But when **Hayley** appears, she's the gift he didn't even realise he needed.

Alfie and his little sister know a lot about the magic of Christmas – and they're about to teach the grown-ups a much-needed lesson!

Available 1st October 2010

Mystery, magic and... marriage

Sorcery and seduction…
A dark and spooky night…
Trick, treat…or a Halloween temptation?

*Things are not quite as they seem on
All Hallows' Eve…*

Available 1st October 2010

THE

Balfour LEGACY

EIGHT SISTERS, EIGHT SCANDALS

VOLUME 5 – OCTOBER 2010
Zoe's Lesson
by Kate Hewitt

VOLUME 6 – NOVEMBER 2010
Annie's Secret
by Carole Mortimer

VOLUME 7 – DECEMBER 2010
Bella's Disgrace
by Sarah Morgan

VOLUME 8 – JANUARY 2011
Olivia's Awakening
by Margaret Way

8 VOLUMES IN ALL TO COLLECT!

2 FREE BOOKS
AND A SURPRISE GIFT

We would like to take this opportunity to thank you for reading this Mills & Boon® book by offering you the chance to take TWO more specially selected books from the Special Moments™ series absolutely FREE! We're also making this offer to introduce you to the benefits of the Mills & Boon® Book Club™—

- **FREE home delivery**
- **FREE gifts and competitions**
- **FREE monthly Newsletter**
- **Exclusive Mills & Boon Book Club offers**
- **Books available before they're in the shops**

Accepting these FREE books and gift places you under no obligation to buy, you may cancel at any time, even after receiving your free books. Simply complete your details below and return the entire page to the address below. You don't even need a stamp!

YES Please send me 2 free Special Moments books and a surprise gift. I understand that unless you hear from me, I will receive 5 superb new stories every month, including a 2-in-1 book priced at £4.99 and three single books priced at £3.19 each, postage and packing free. I am under no obligation to purchase any books and may cancel my subscription at any time. The free books and gift will be mine to keep in any case.

Ms/Mrs/Miss/Mr _____ Initials _____

_____

Surname _____

Address _____

_____

_____ Postcode _____

E-mail _____

Send this whole page to: Mills & Boon Book Club, Free Book Offer, FREEPOST NAT 10298, Richmond, TW9 1BR